ANDONG AGIMAT
THE MYSTERY OF THE TALISMAN

A graphic novel by
ARNOLD ARRE

TUTTLE Publishing
Tokyo | Rutland, Vermont | Singapore

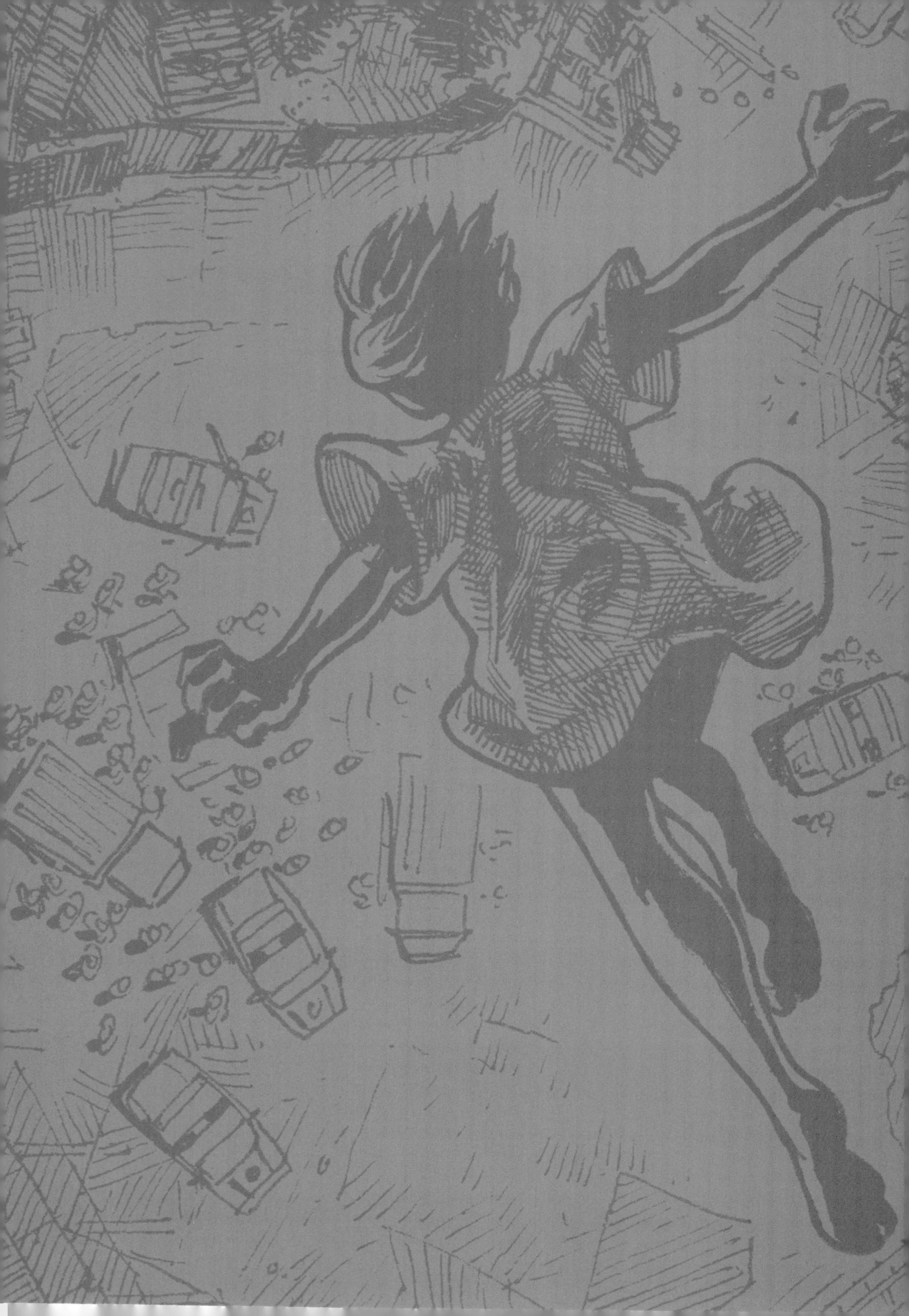

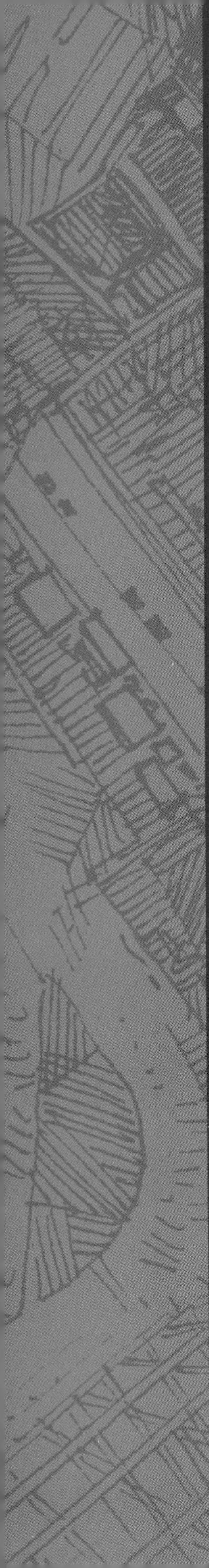

"What would you like you see in a superhero comic?"

That was the question Arnold asked us in the wake of the resurgence of interest in Darna perpetuated by the new comic book and talk of a movie and TV series.

Of course, Arnold already had something in mind when he asked our opinion about this distinctly American invention: a being gifted with powers and abilities greater than that of an ordinary person who fights injustice in a colorful circus costume.

Coming from depression-era immigrant creators in New York, the superhero is the most identifiable symbol of American comics. I stress the term American because the superhero is not the most popular image in comics from other cultures. And even when the superhero is transplanted to other cultures, the concept takes on different permutations such as the bug-headed riders and crayon colored rangers in Japan, kung fu fighters in China, amoral thieves in Italy and masked luchadores in Mexico.

In the Philippines, while Mars Ravelo borrowed heavily from American iconic figures such as Superman, Captain Marvel and Wonder Woman, other super heroic figures without the colorful costumes have been popular. The herioc "agimat" stories and movies have been popular to Filipinos and can be traced to our myths and legends.

With Mythology Class, Arnold went back to these myths and legends. With his interest in FPJ and Ramon Revilla action movies, he now brings these legends to the streets. So what kind of superheroes did Arnold have in mind? Superheroes without the cultural trappings of American comics. Superheroes steeped in mythology but sharpened by the dirty grey tabloid world. Superheroes that are different and yet familiar. New and yet remembered.

The world of Andong Agimat.

Emil Flores
Quezon City
January 2006

I think storytellers tend to be unsatisfied people. After all, why else would we go around creating our own worlds, reshaping reality, analyzing people's thinking processes and behaviors to put actions and words into characters we control? I think a lot of storytellers are not content with simply recounting and recording the reality we see around us. We feel that the universe can be better, or if not necessarily better, can have more meaning to it.

And we storytellers aren't only unsatisfied with reality. We are often unsatisfied even with the fictional realities crafted by other storytellers. Heck, we are often unsatisfied with the stories we ourselves have written in the past. So we constantly create new stories, and we deconstruct and pick apart the world around us and the stories we consume and then try to reconstruct new stories in our never ending quest to find a satisfaction that deep inside we know will never come.

Arnold Arre is definitely one storyteller who is constantly unsatisfied. I've read (and published) most of his works and it's clear Arnold is always trying to imagine a better world and better stories. The Mythology Class showed how unsatisfied he is with the mundane real world and with the Westernized escapist fantasies meant to take readers away from it. *Trip to Tagaytay* showed his dissatisfaction with the present Philippines and the existing takes on what the future of the Philippines would be. *Martial Law Babies*, *After Eden*, and *Halina Filipina* all showed many examples of his distaste for how low a lot of local pop culture has fallen, how superficial love stories have become, and how the mindset of Filipinos has devolved. All his graphic novels have taken the various tropes of past stories and used them to reconstruct new realities, characters, and experiences that make readers believe in a better and/or more meaningful world.

With *Ang Mundo ni Andong Agimat*, Arnold takes on genres whose main purpose is to allow readers to escape reality: superheroes and Filipino fantasy/action movies. These are stories that grew popular precisely because of both the readers and storytellers need to escape reality. But as the popularity of these genres have grown, the tropes that make up their structure have become worn out. So Arnold again works his magic and embraces the elements that allows these stories to do what they do best, but reconstructs and combines them in new ways that create a whole new story that does more than allow for escapism. With each scene, with each character's line, it made me imagine Arnold reading old superhero comics or watching old Filipino films and telling himself, "This could be so much better. This could do so much more. Audiences deserve better. The world deserves better." And as I turn the final page of this graphic novel, I feel he has shown us that indeed, something better was possible. And that's what the main character of Andong (and all the other characters in this Filipino epic) face in this story: a constant desire to be better, to

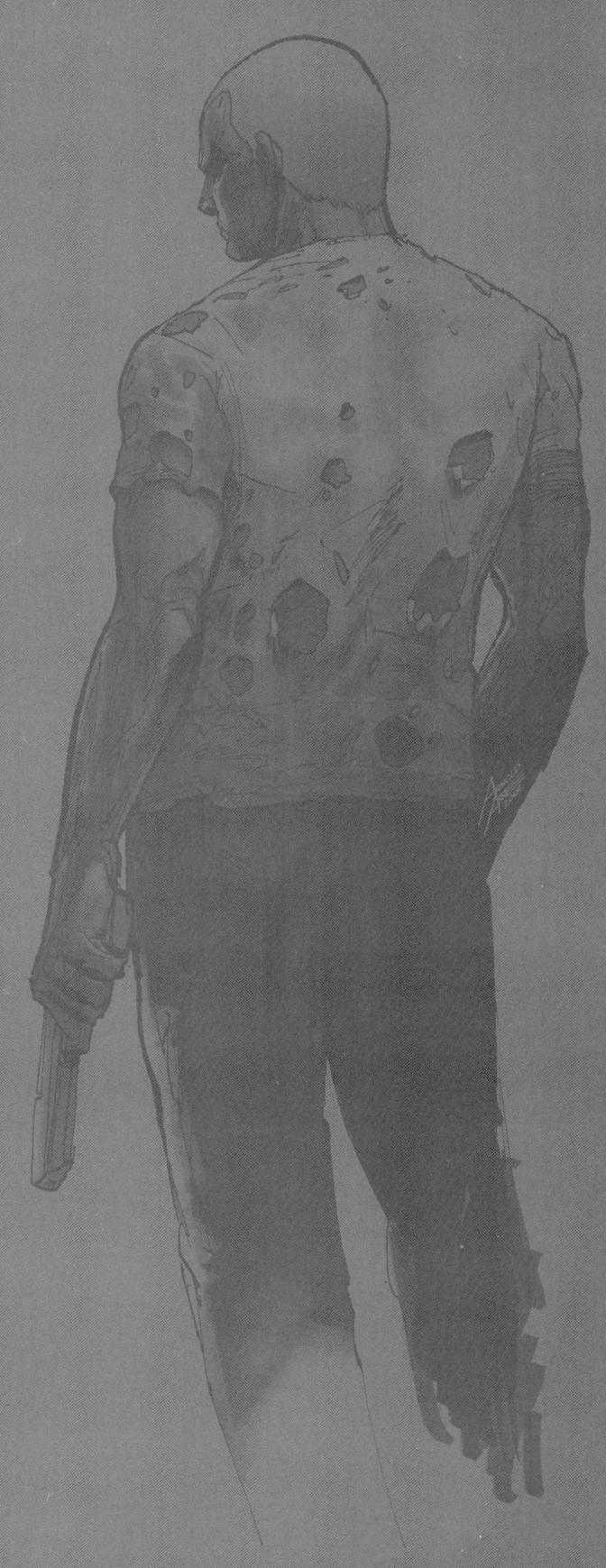

make the world better, because they aren't satisfied with who they are or the world around them.

I can't wait to see what type of stories Arnold will come up with next, what brilliant new realities he will create for us. It may be mean of me to say so, but I hope the world continues to irritate and dissatisfy him, like grains of sand irritating a clam and forcing it to turn them into beautiful pearls to find relief. I hope the man is never satisfied, because as a reader I will never be satisfied no matter how many amazing stories he produces.

JAMIE BAUTISTA
Alabang
September 2017

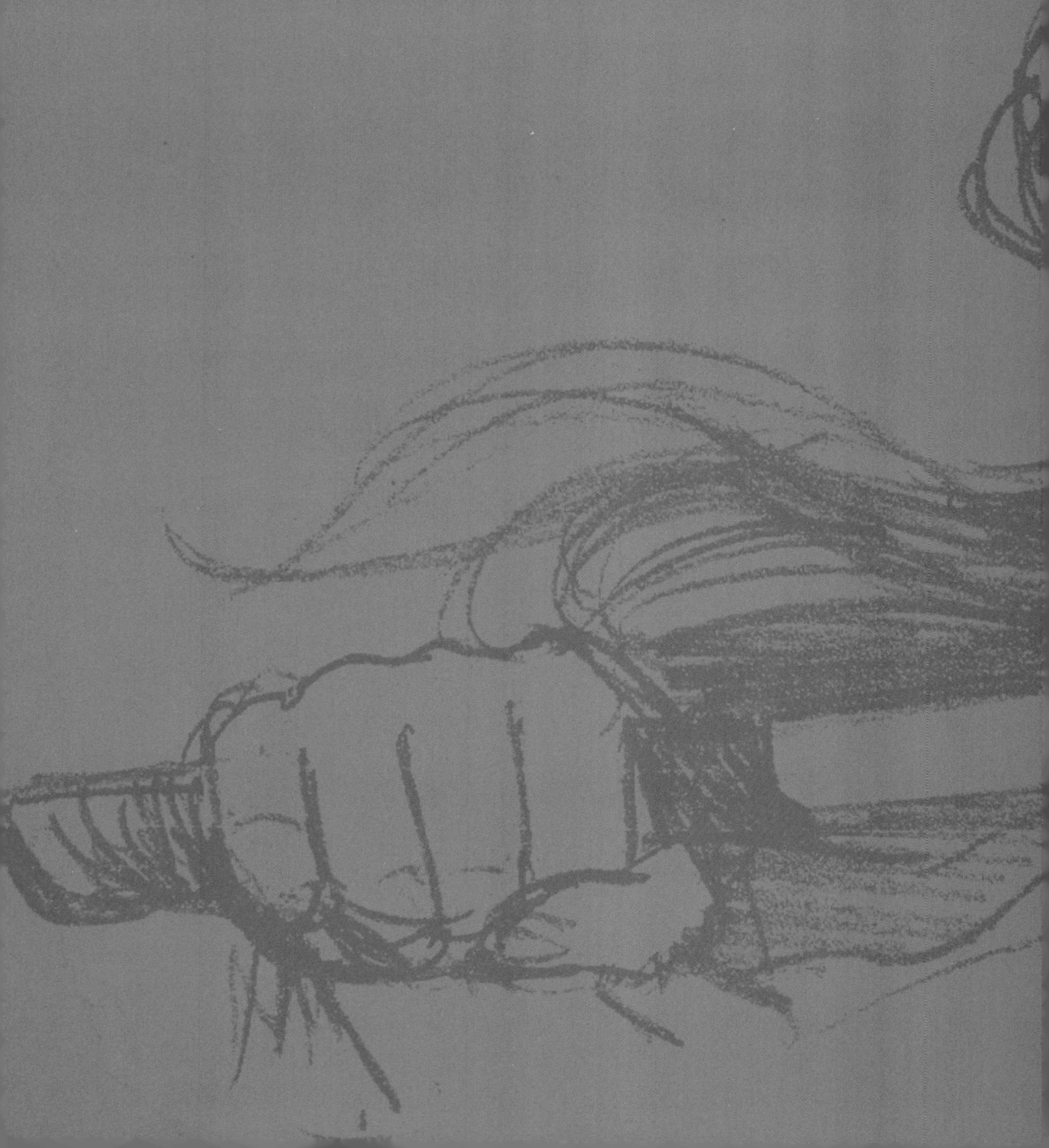

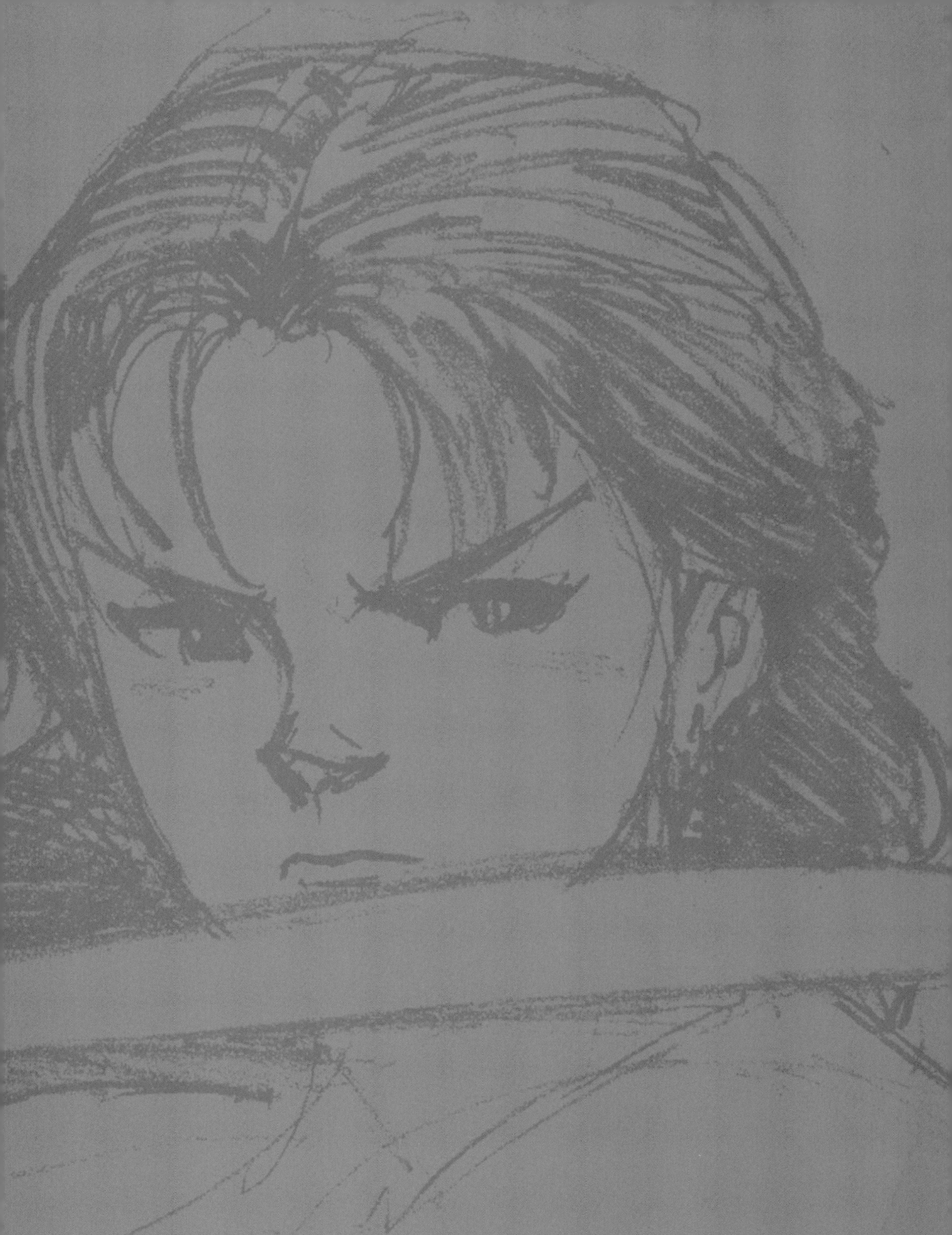

Para kay Cynthia… ang liwanag sa aking mundo.

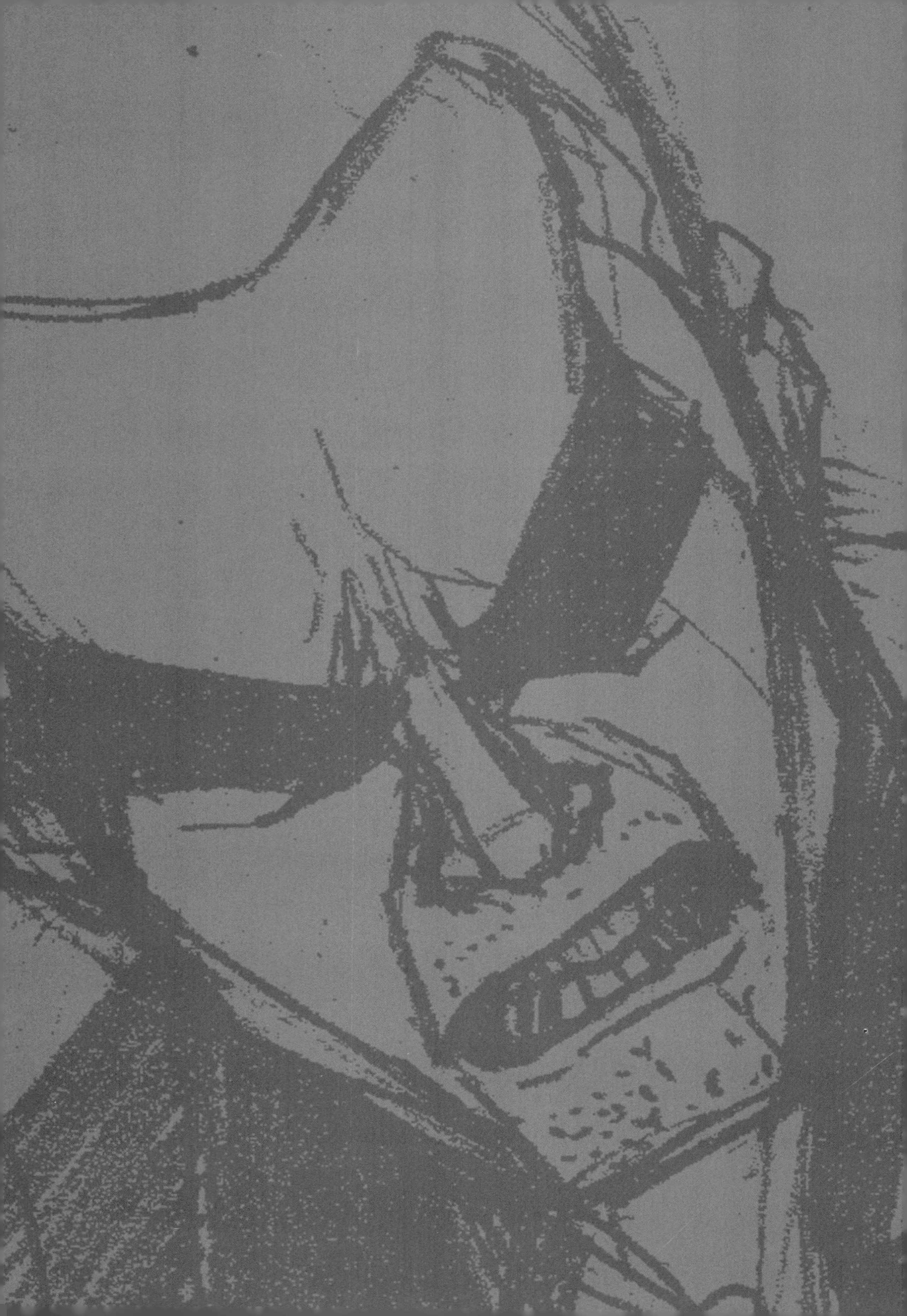

Whether you believe it or not, my grandfather says, there was a time in our world when it was ruled by the strongest and most powerful beings on the face of the earth.

Some of them became guardians of justice… Defending the oppressed.

Others, however, became servants of darkness… Arriving to spread a gruesome plague among the population.

And from the century of conflict between these two forces were born the colorful stories of courage and bravery that shaped their world.

This is a world covered in miracles and wonders.

This is the world of Andong Agimat.

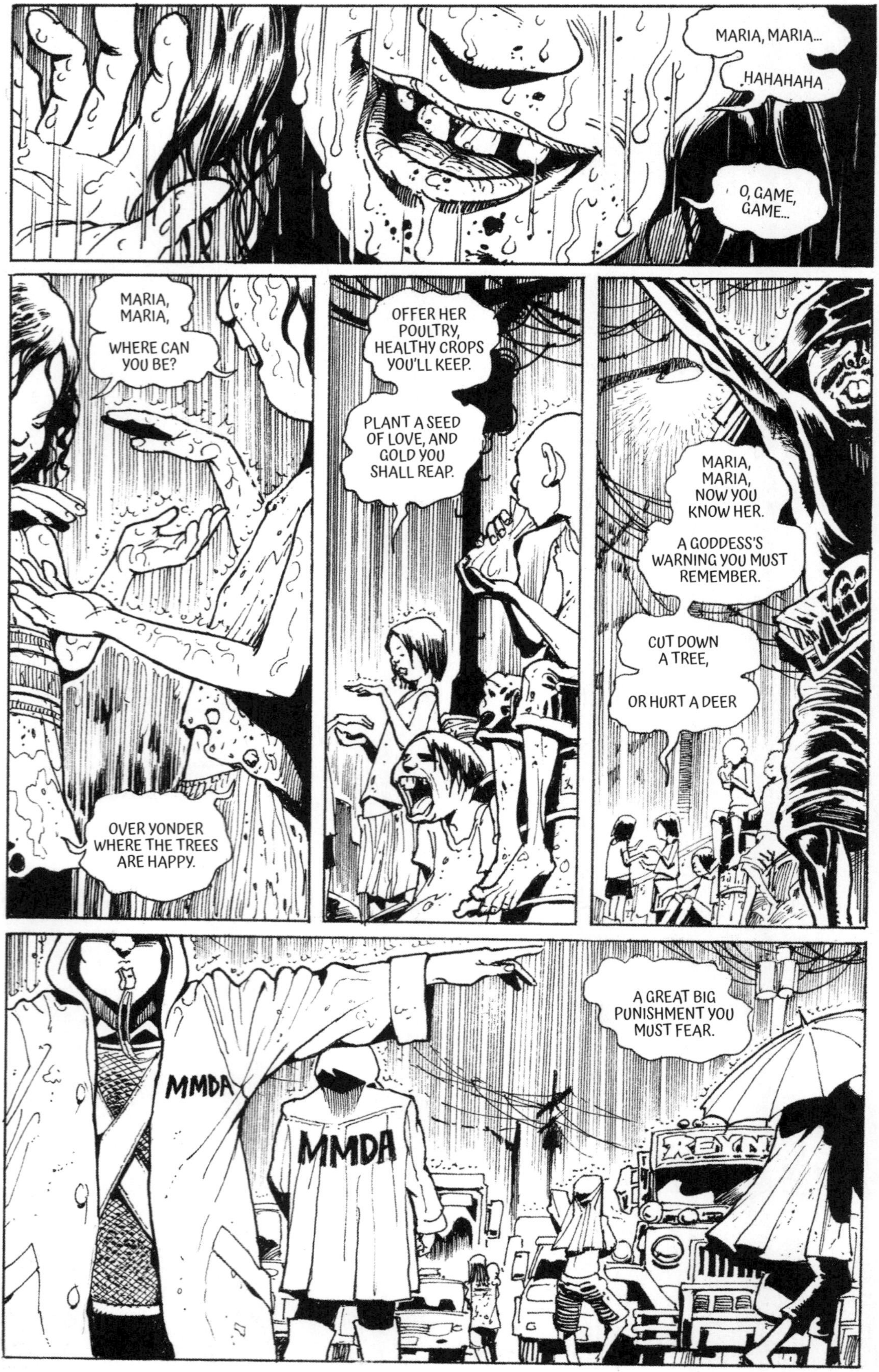
MARIA, MARIA...
HAHAHAHA
O, GAME, GAME...
MARIA, MARIA,
WHERE CAN YOU BE?
OVER YONDER WHERE THE TREES ARE HAPPY.
OFFER HER POULTRY, HEALTHY CROPS YOU'LL KEEP.
PLANT A SEED OF LOVE, AND GOLD YOU SHALL REAP.
MARIA, MARIA, NOW YOU KNOW HER.
A GODDESS'S WARNING YOU MUST REMEMBER.
CUT DOWN A TREE,
OR HURT A DEER
A GREAT BIG PUNISHMENT YOU MUST FEAR.
MMDA
MMDA

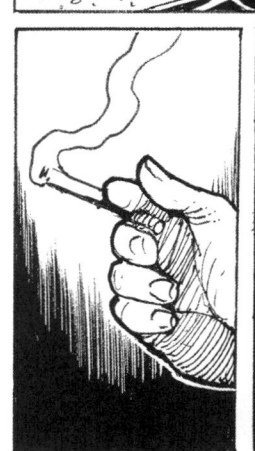

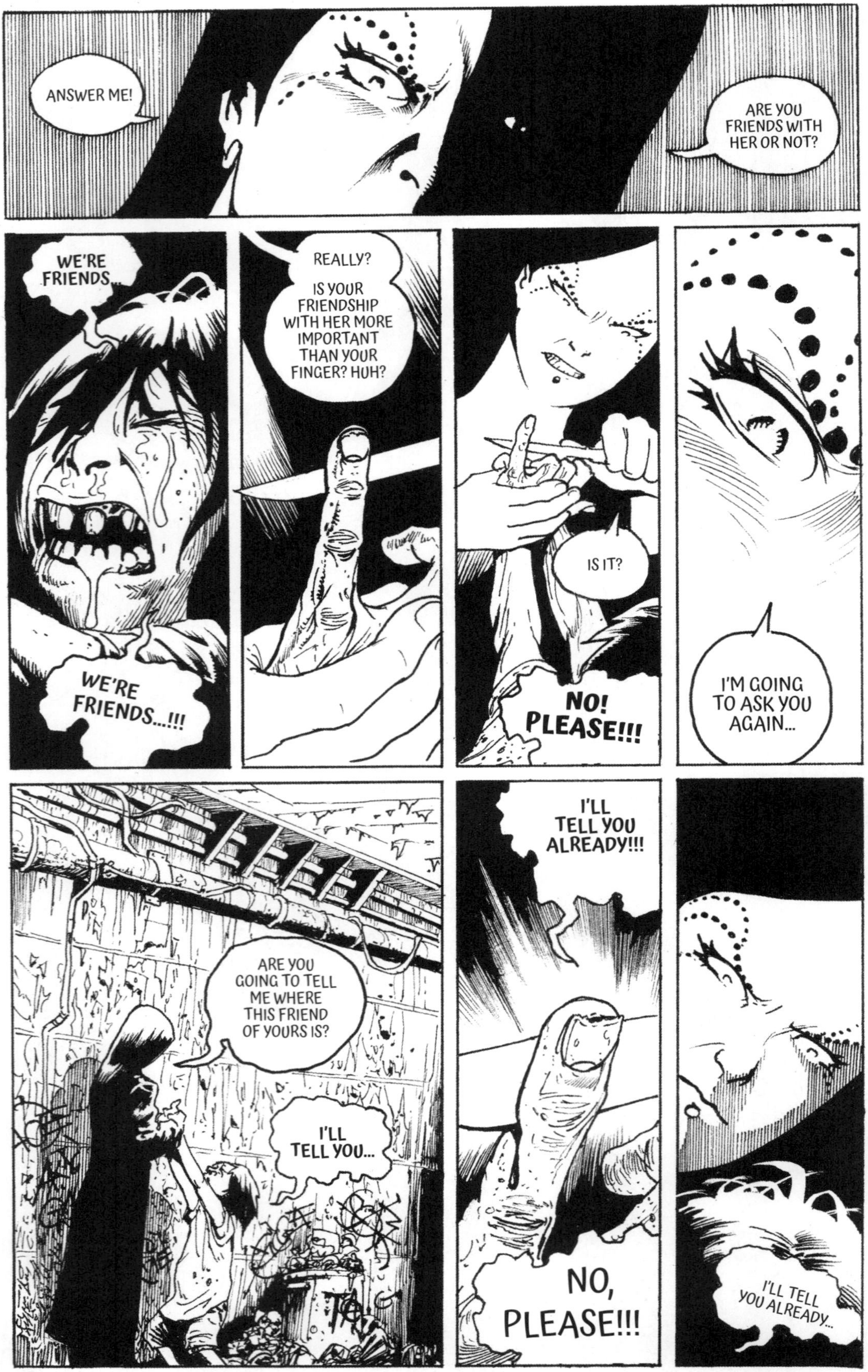
ANSWER ME!
ARE YOU FRIENDS WITH HER OR NOT?
WE'RE FRIENDS...
WE'RE FRIENDS...!!!
REALLY?
IS YOUR FRIENDSHIP WITH HER MORE IMPORTANT THAN YOUR FINGER? HUH?
IS IT?
NO! PLEASE!!!
I'M GOING TO ASK YOU AGAIN...
ARE YOU GOING TO TELL ME WHERE THIS FRIEND OF YOURS IS?
I'LL TELL YOU...
I'LL TELL YOU ALREADY!!!
NO, PLEASE!!!
I'LL TELL YOU ALREADY...

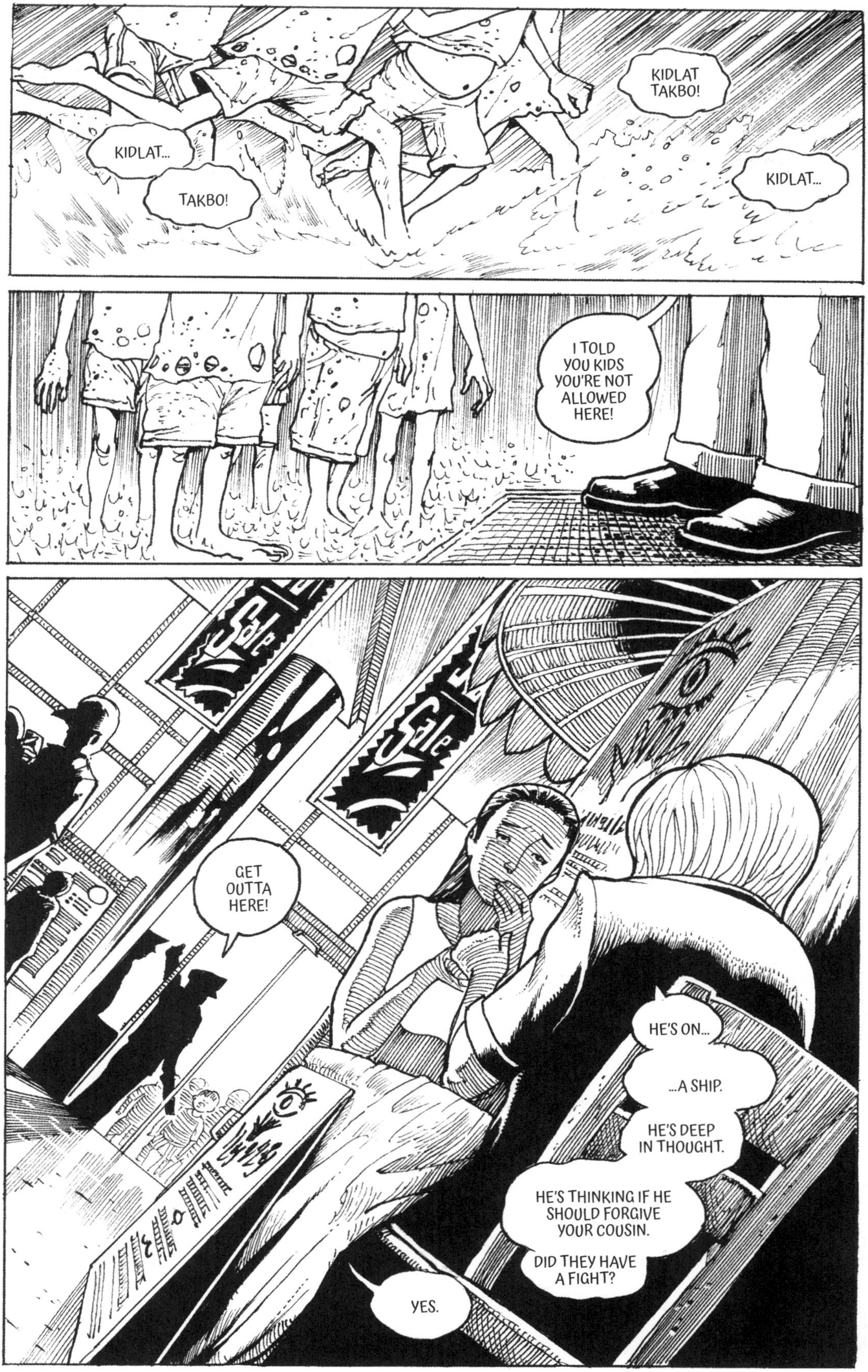
KIDLAT...
TAKBO!
KIDLAT TAKBO!
KIDLAT...
I TOLD YOU KIDS YOU'RE NOT ALLOWED HERE!
GET OUTTA HERE!
HE'S ON...
...A SHIP.
HE'S DEEP IN THOUGHT.
HE'S THINKING IF HE SHOULD FORGIVE YOUR COUSIN.
DID THEY HAVE A FIGHT?
YES.

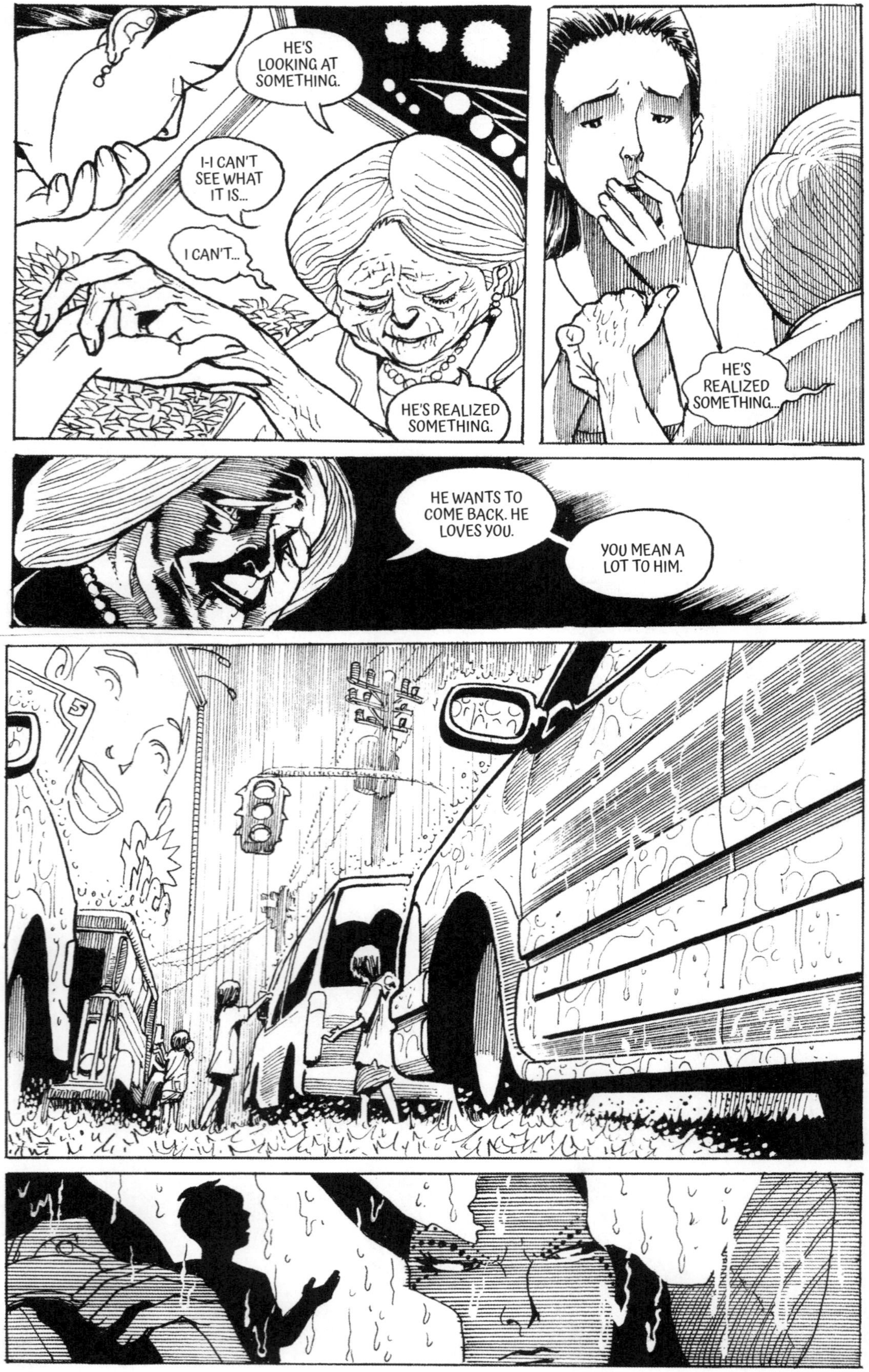
HE'S LOOKING AT SOMETHING.
I-I CAN'T SEE WHAT IT IS...
I CAN'T...
HE'S REALIZED SOMETHING.
HE'S REALIZED SOMETHING...
HE WANTS TO COME BACK. HE LOVES YOU.
YOU MEAN A LOT TO HIM.

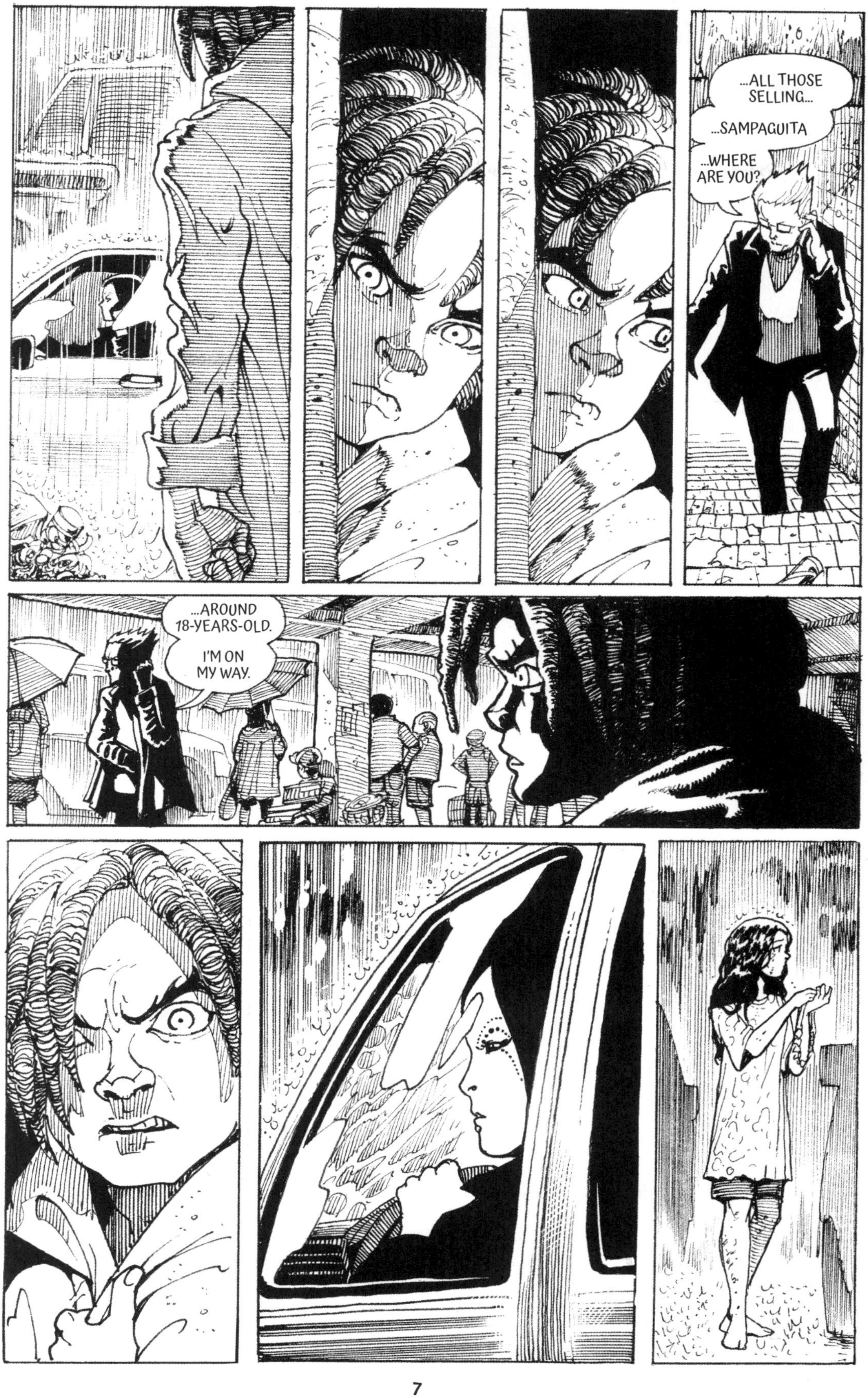
...ALL THOSE SELLING...
...SAMPAGUITA
...WHERE ARE YOU?
...AROUND 18-YEARS-OLD.
I'M ON MY WAY.

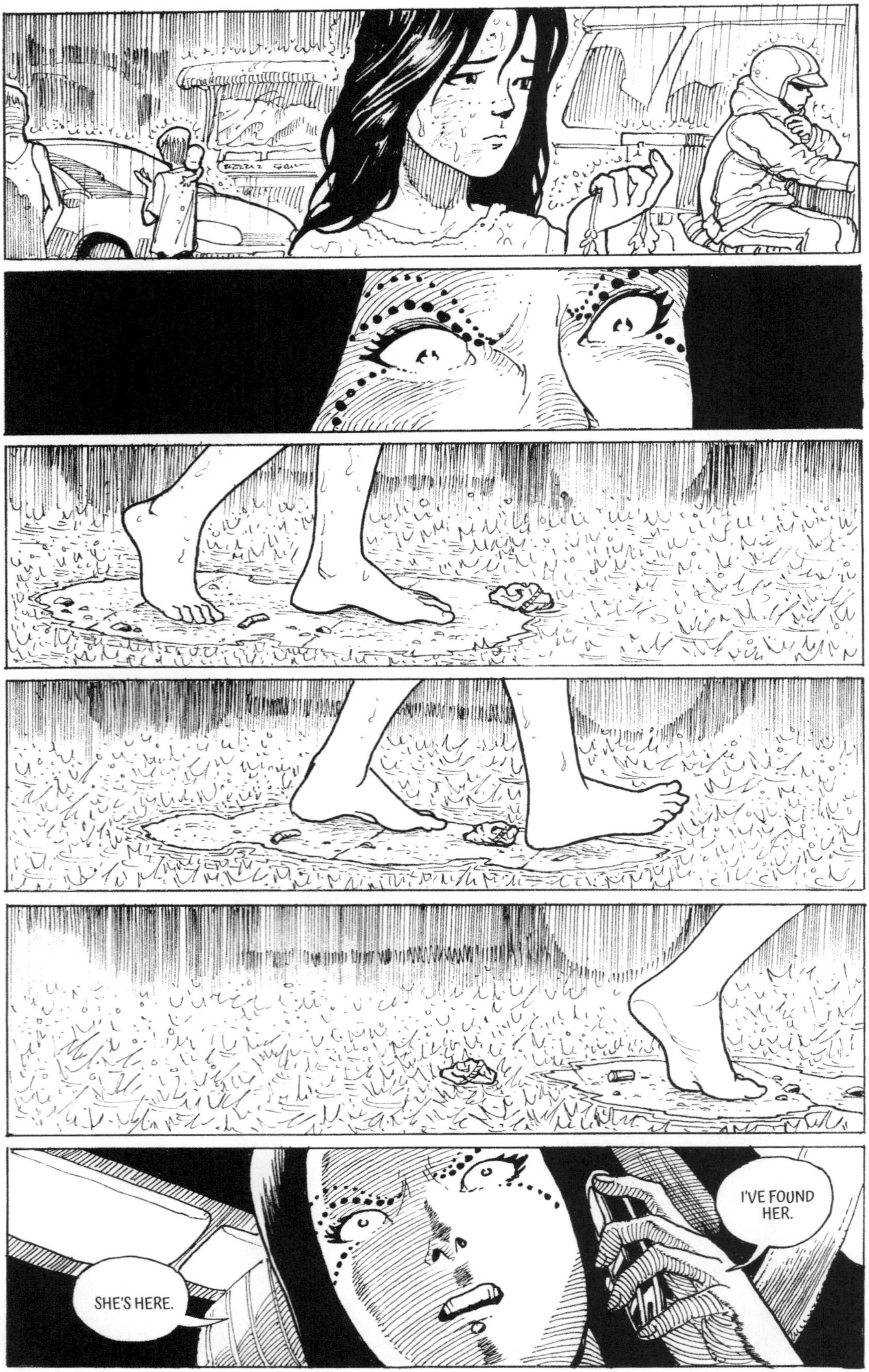
I'VE FOUND HER.
SHE'S HERE.

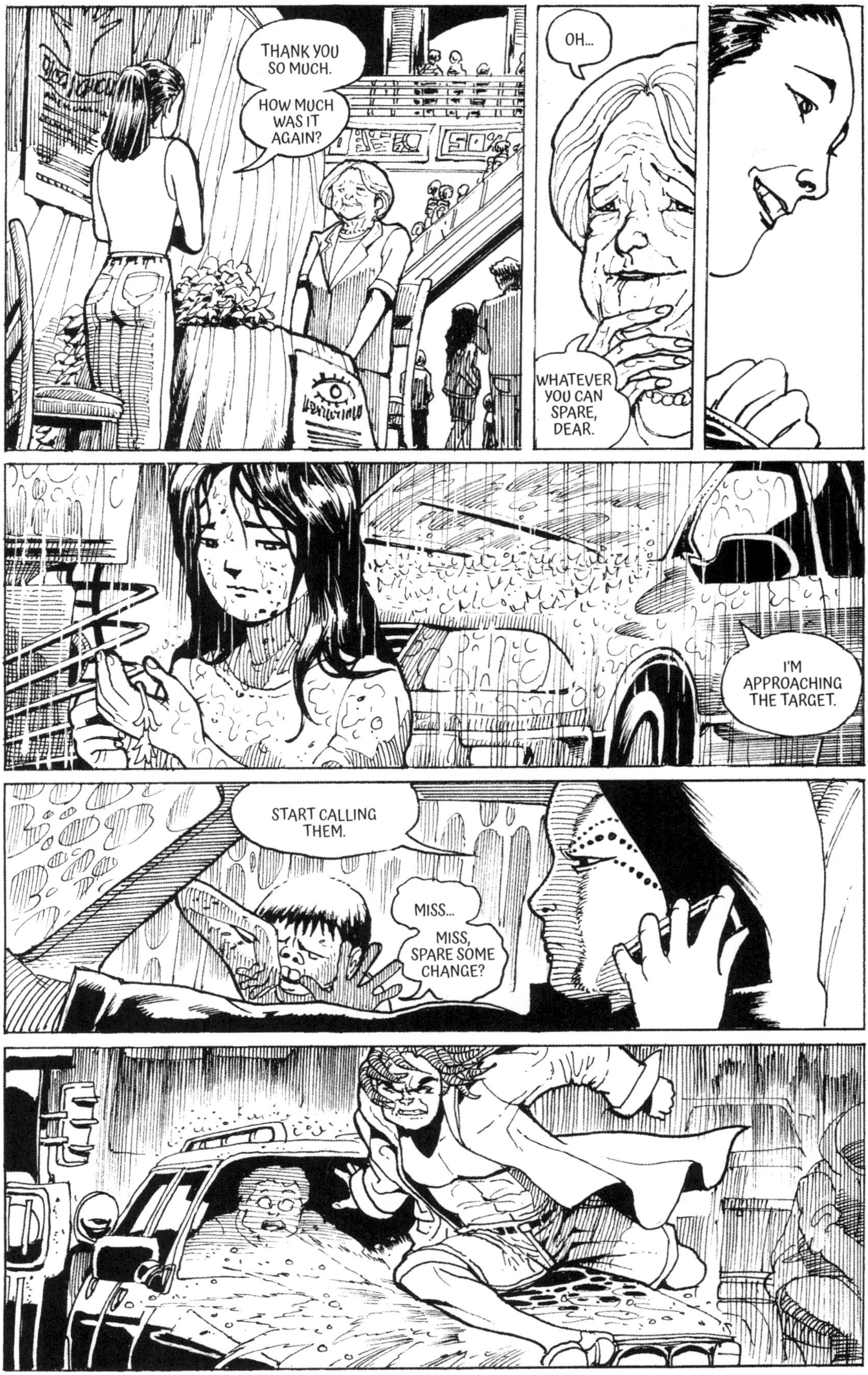
THANK YOU SO MUCH.
HOW MUCH WAS IT AGAIN?
OH...
WHATEVER YOU CAN SPARE, DEAR.
I'M APPROACHING THE TARGET.
START CALLING THEM.
MISS...
MISS, SPARE SOME CHANGE?

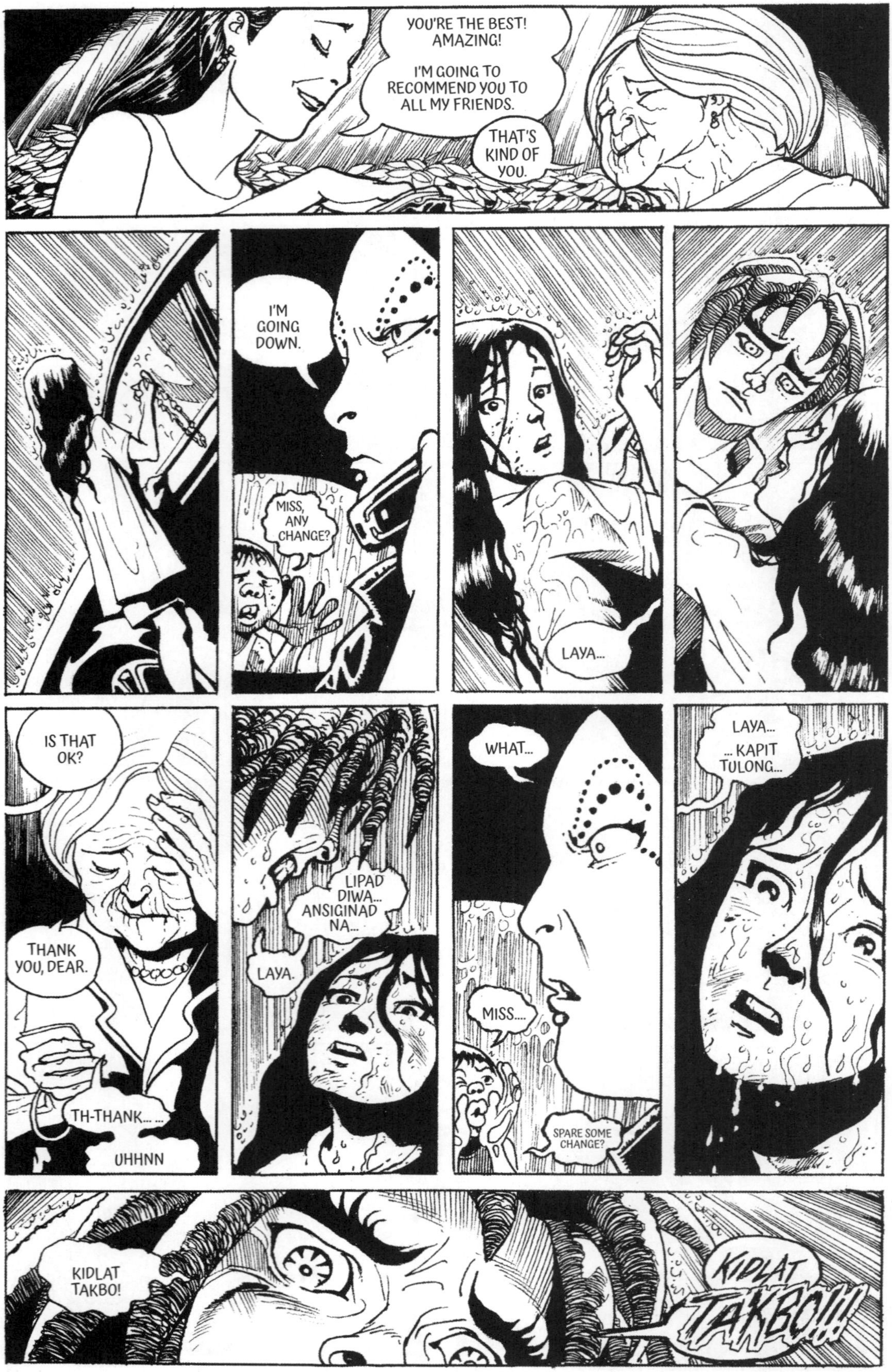

YOU'RE THE BEST! AMAZING!
I'M GOING TO RECOMMEND YOU TO ALL MY FRIENDS.
THAT'S KIND OF YOU.
I'M GOING DOWN.
MISS, ANY CHANGE?
LAYA...
IS THAT OK?
THANK YOU, DEAR.
TH-THANK.... ...
UHHNN
LIPAD DIWA... ANSIGINAD NA...
LAYA.
WHAT...
MISS....
SPARE SOME CHANGE?
LAYA...
... KAPIT TULONG...
KIDLAT TAKBO!
KIDLAT TAKBO!!!

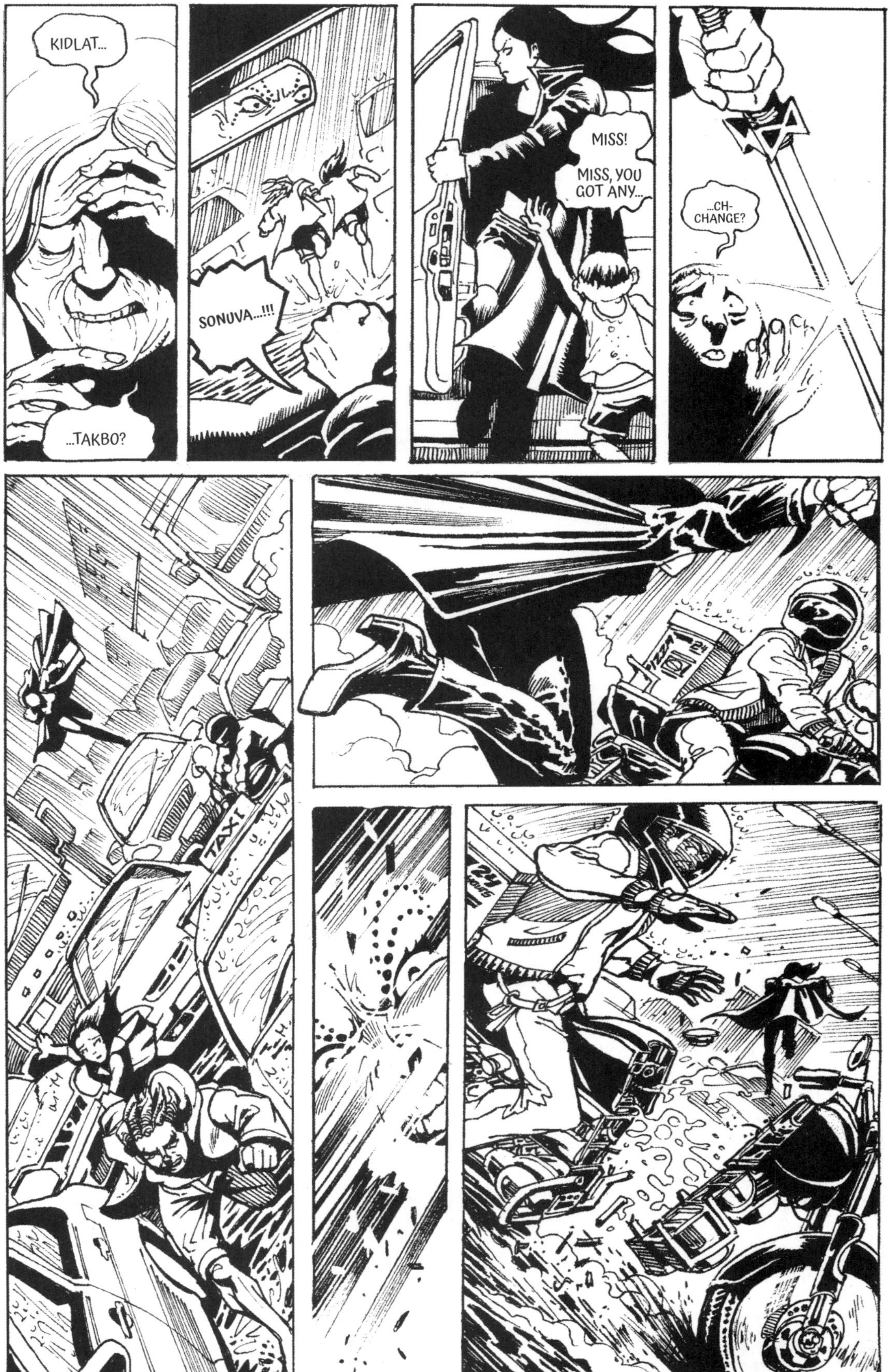
KIDLAT...
...TAKBO?
SONUVA...!!!
MISS!
MISS, YOU GOT ANY...
...CH-CHANGE?
TAXI

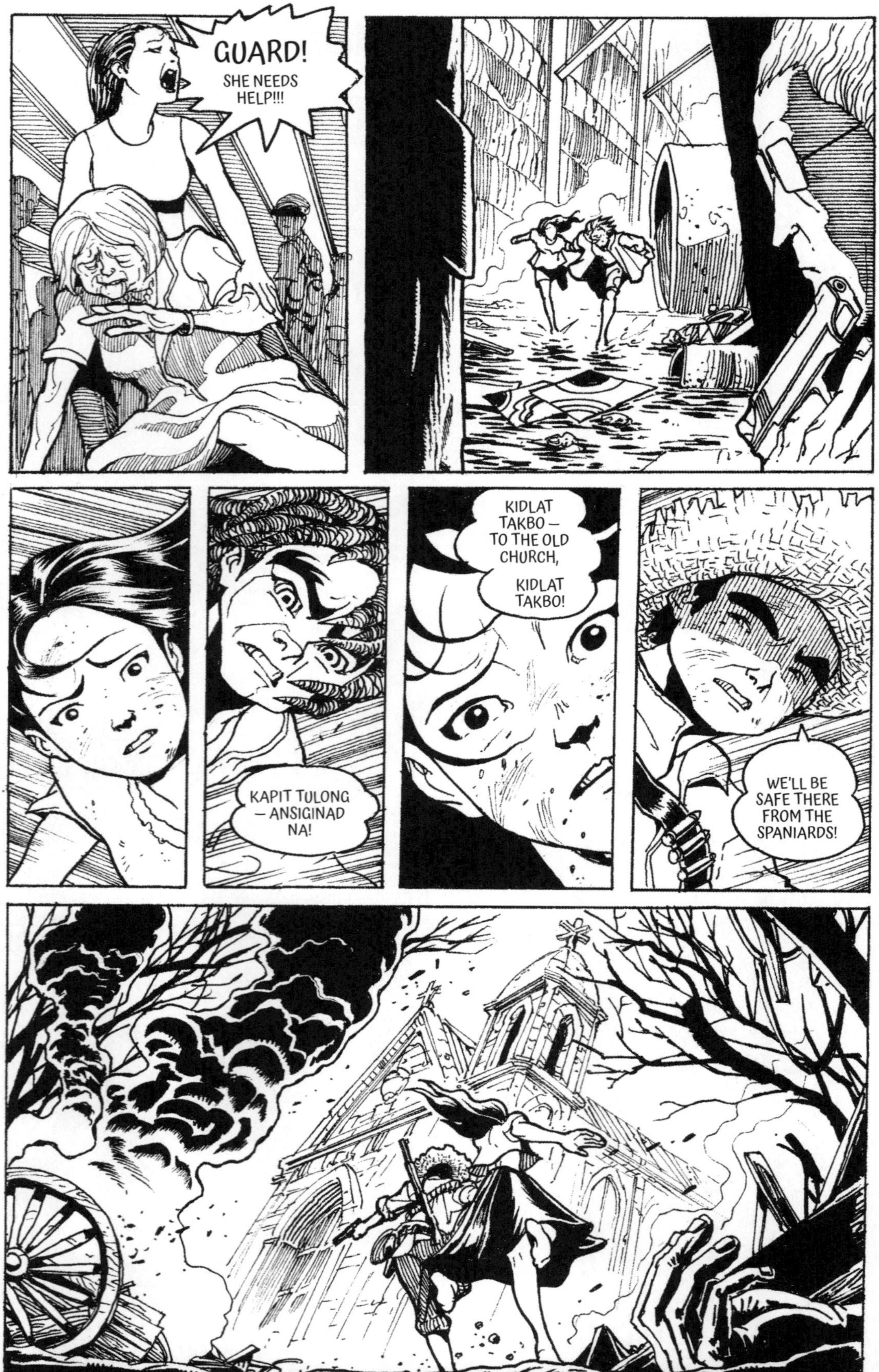
GUARD! SHE NEEDS HELP!!!
KAPIT TULONG — ANSIGINAD NA!
KIDLAT TAKBO — TO THE OLD CHURCH, KIDLAT TAKBO!
WE'LL BE SAFE THERE FROM THE SPANIARDS!

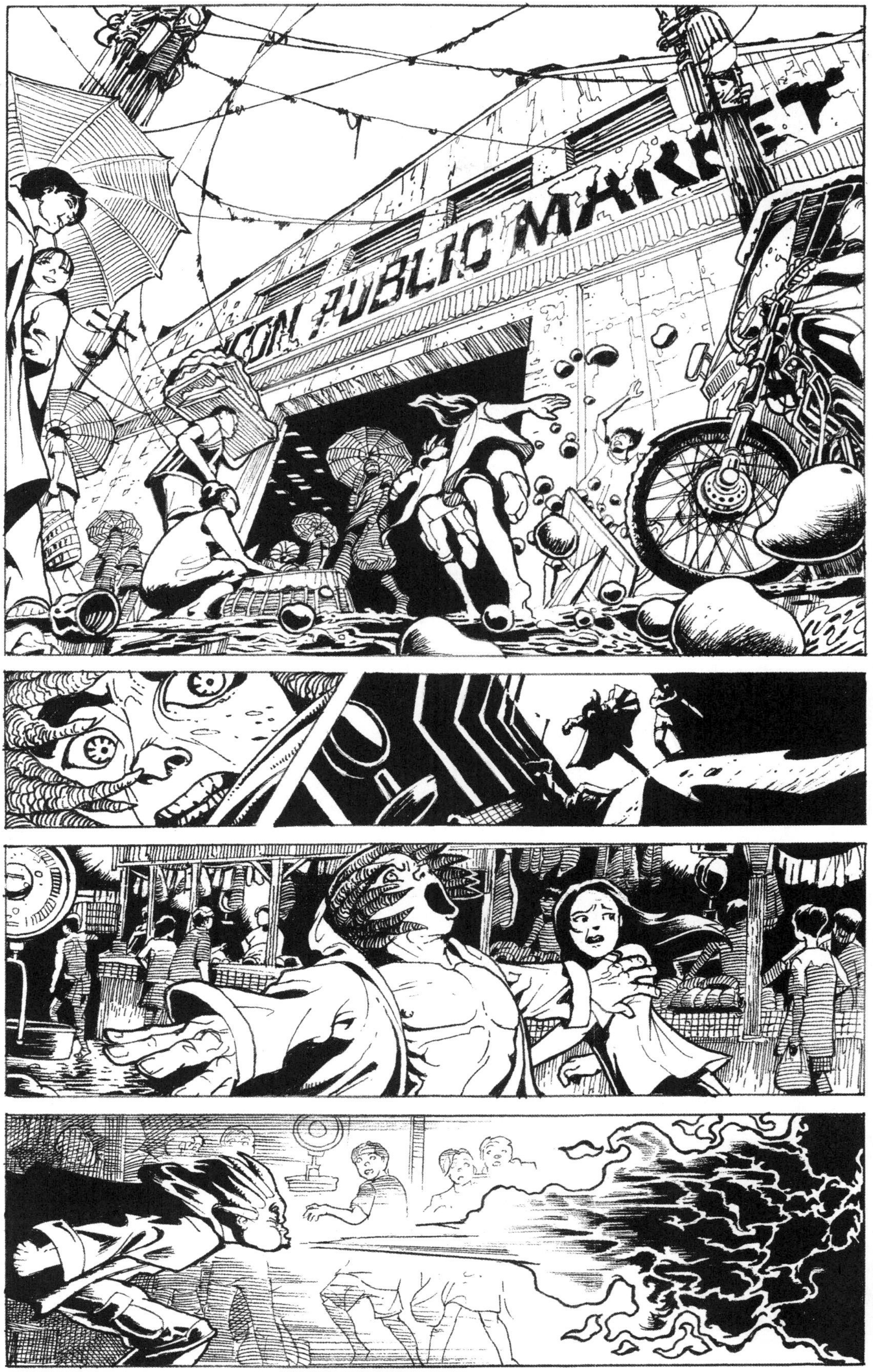
CON PUBLIC MARKET

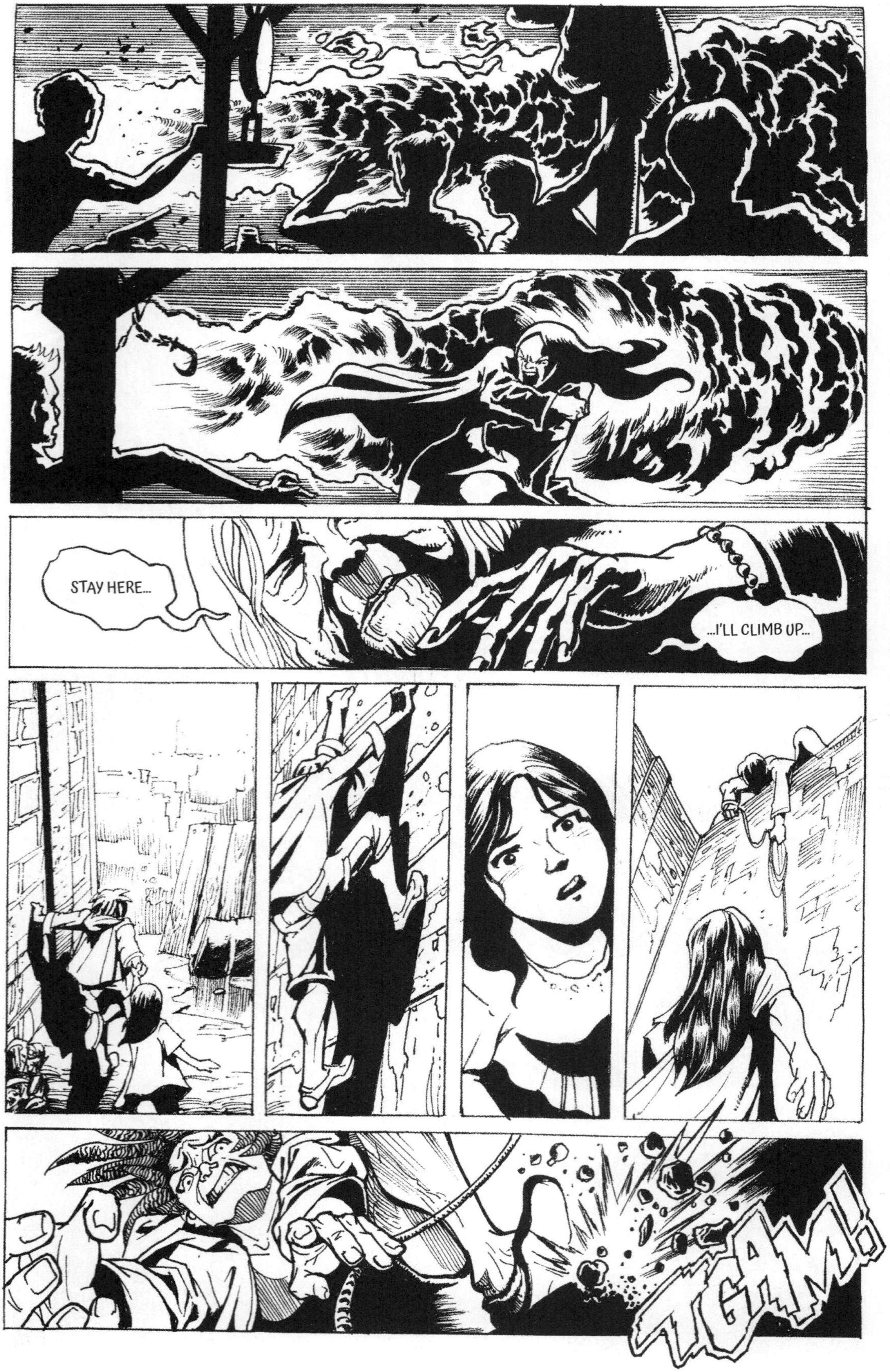
STAY HERE...
...I'LL CLIMB UP...
TGAM!

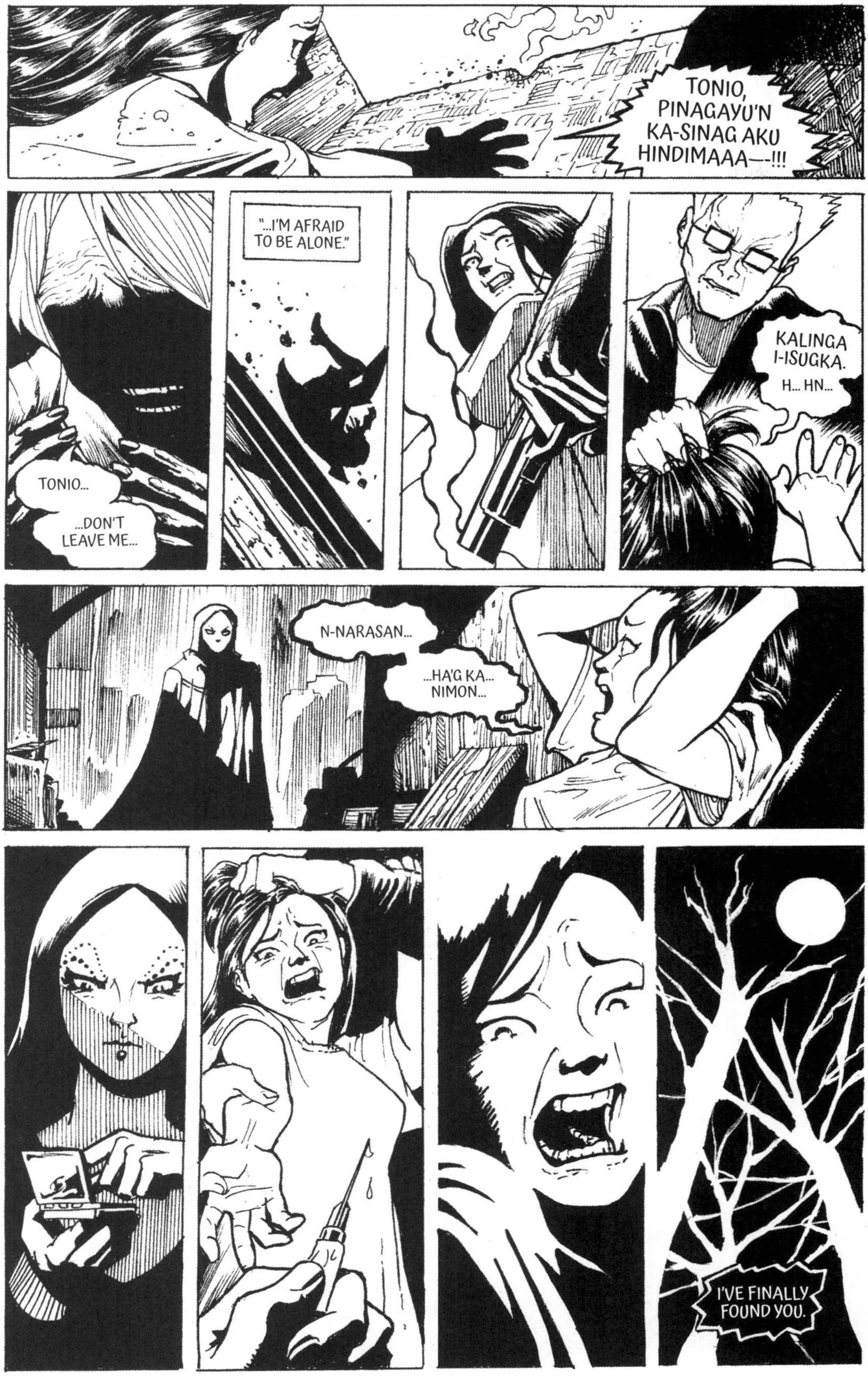
TONIO, PINAGAYU'N KA-SINAG AKU HINDIMAAA---!!!
TONIO...
...DON'T LEAVE ME...
"...I'M AFRAID TO BE ALONE."
KALINGA I-ISUGKA.
H... HN...
N-NARASAN...
...HA'G KA... NIMON...
I'VE FINALLY FOUND YOU.

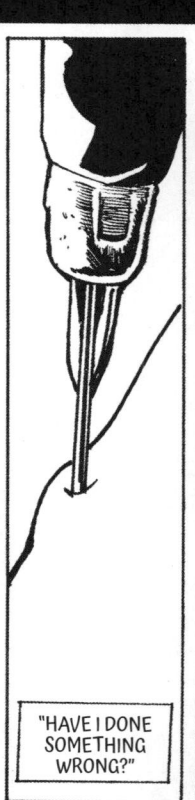

"WHY ARE YOU DOING THIS?"

"HAVE I DONE SOMETHING WRONG?"

"PLEASE DON'T HURT ME."

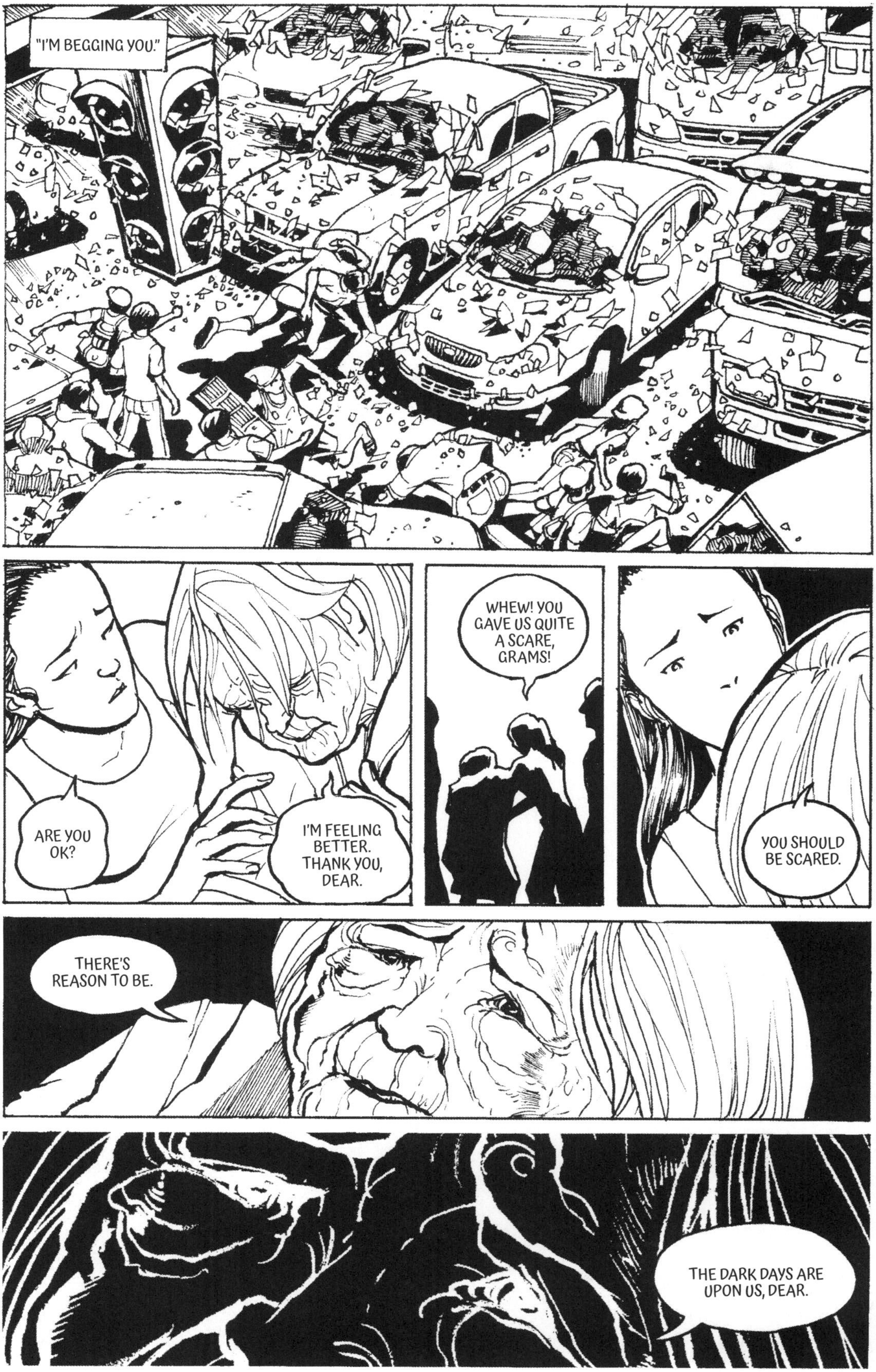
"I'M BEGGING YOU."
ARE YOU OK?
I'M FEELING BETTER. THANK YOU, DEAR.
WHEW! YOU GAVE US QUITE A SCARE, GRAMS!
YOU SHOULD BE SCARED.
THERE'S REASON TO BE.
THE DARK DAYS ARE UPON US, DEAR.

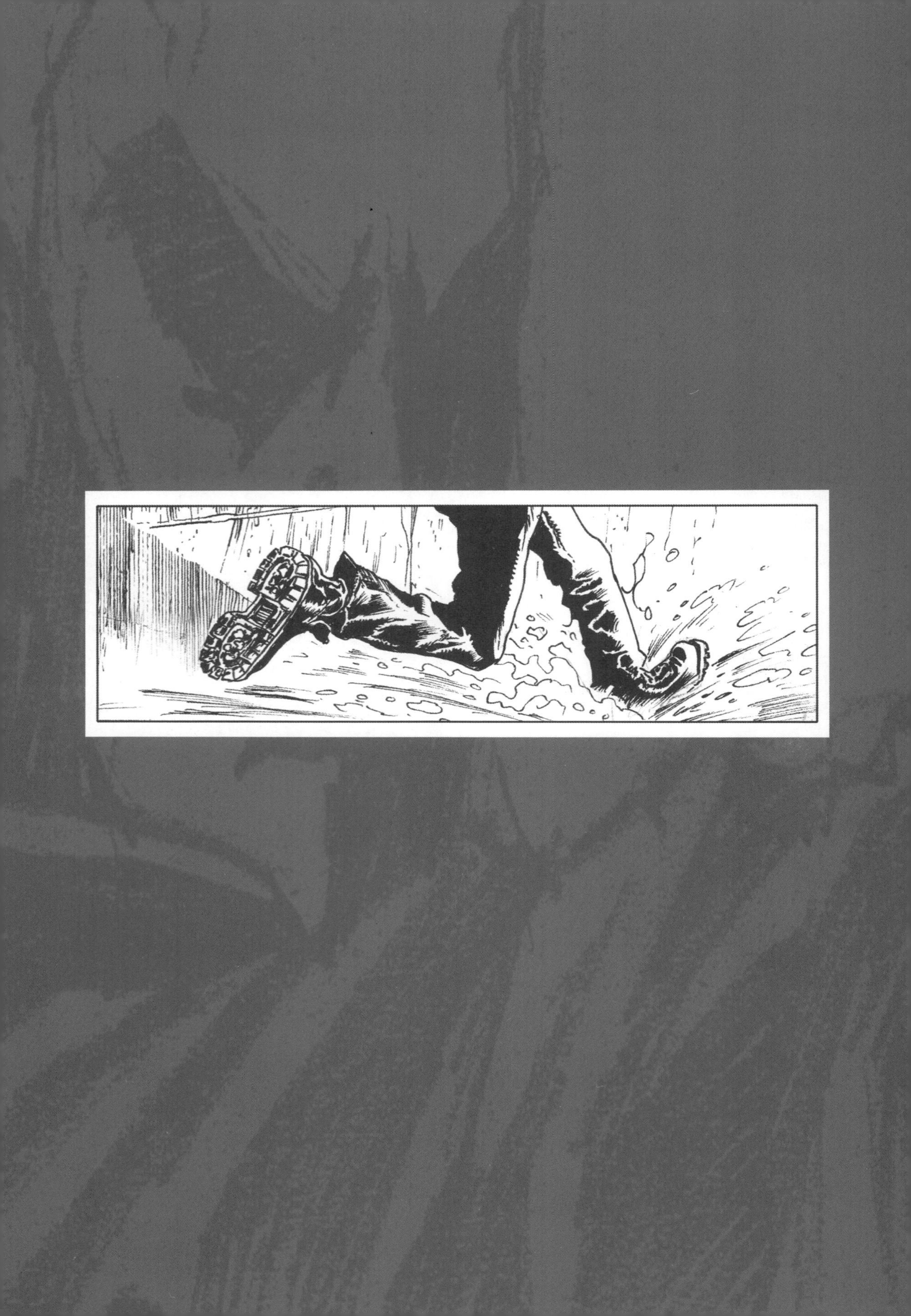

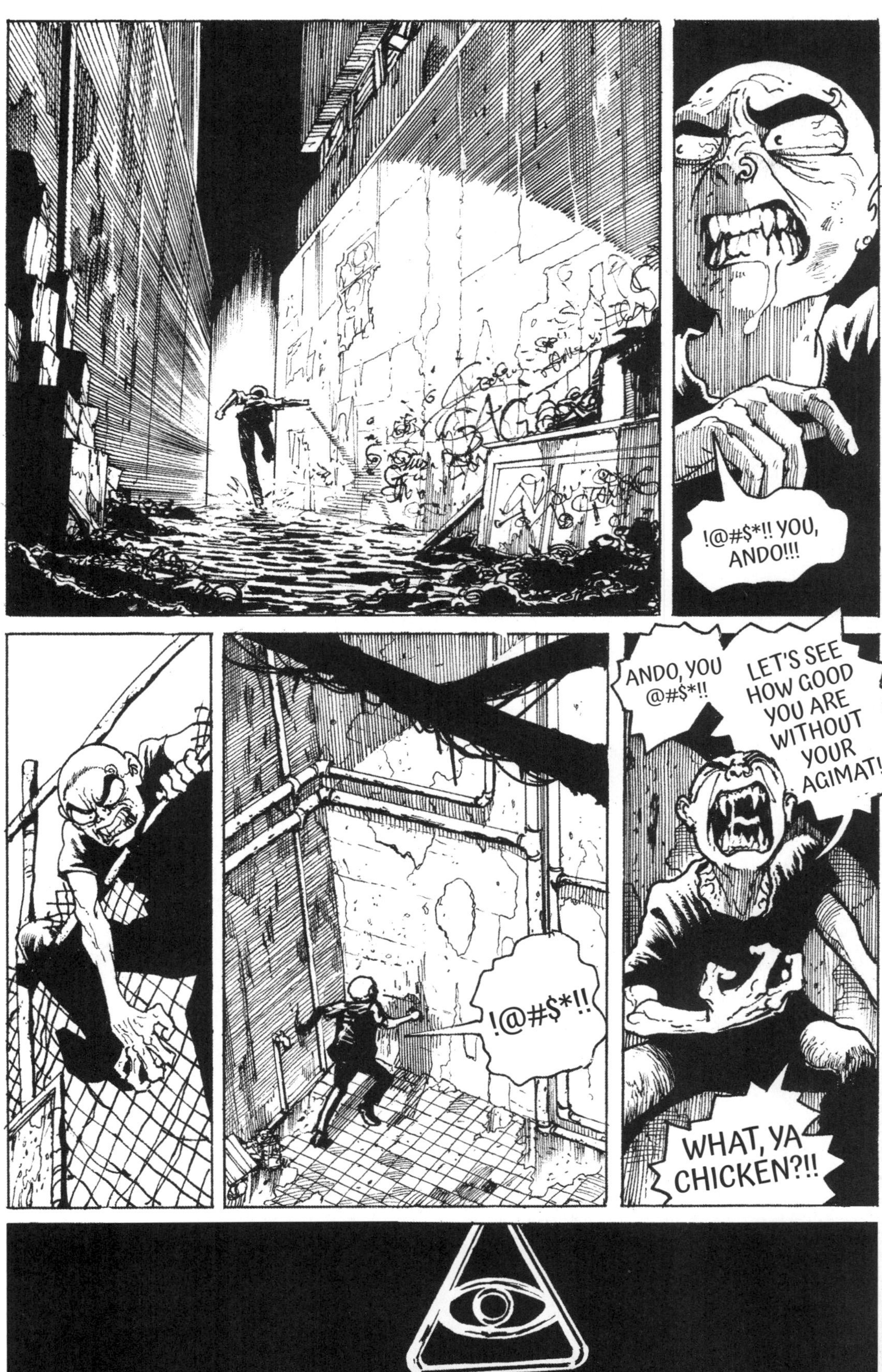
!@#$*!! YOU, ANDO!!!
!@#$*!!
ANDO, YOU @#$*!!
LET'S SEE HOW GOOD YOU ARE WITHOUT YOUR AGIMAT!
WHAT, YA CHICKEN?!!

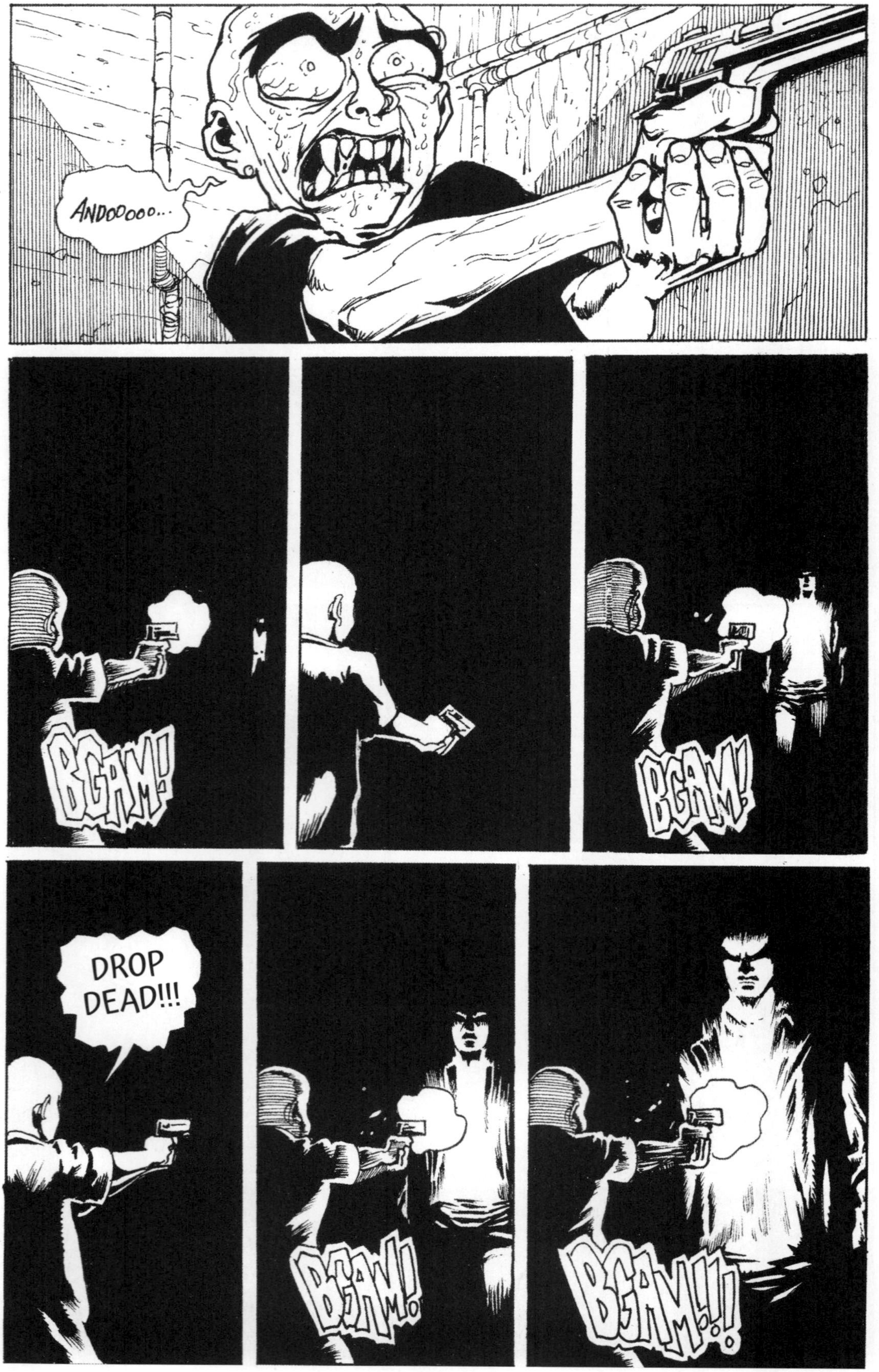
ANDOOOOO...
BGAM!
BGAM!
DROP DEAD!!!
BGAM!
BGAM!!!

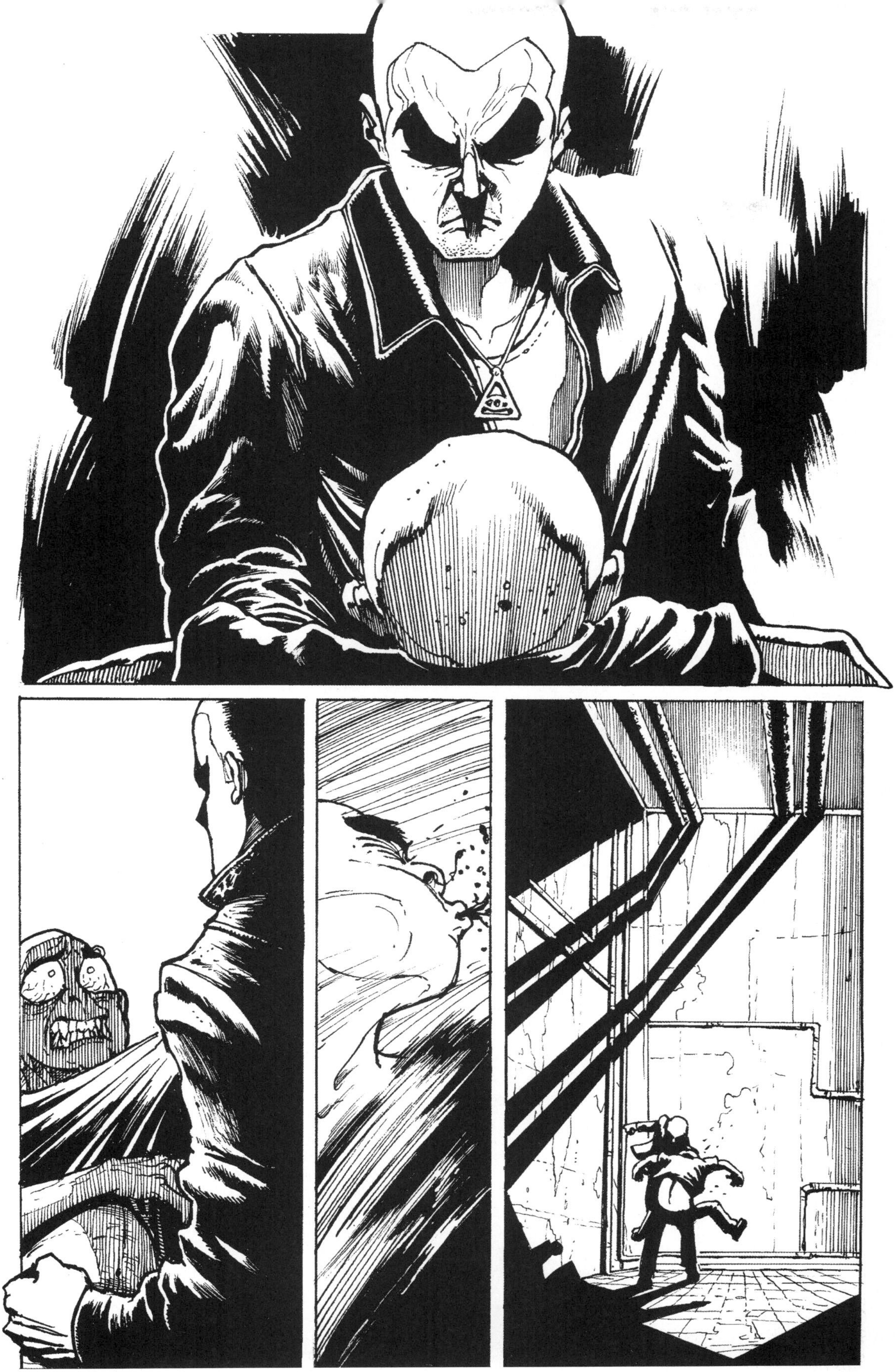

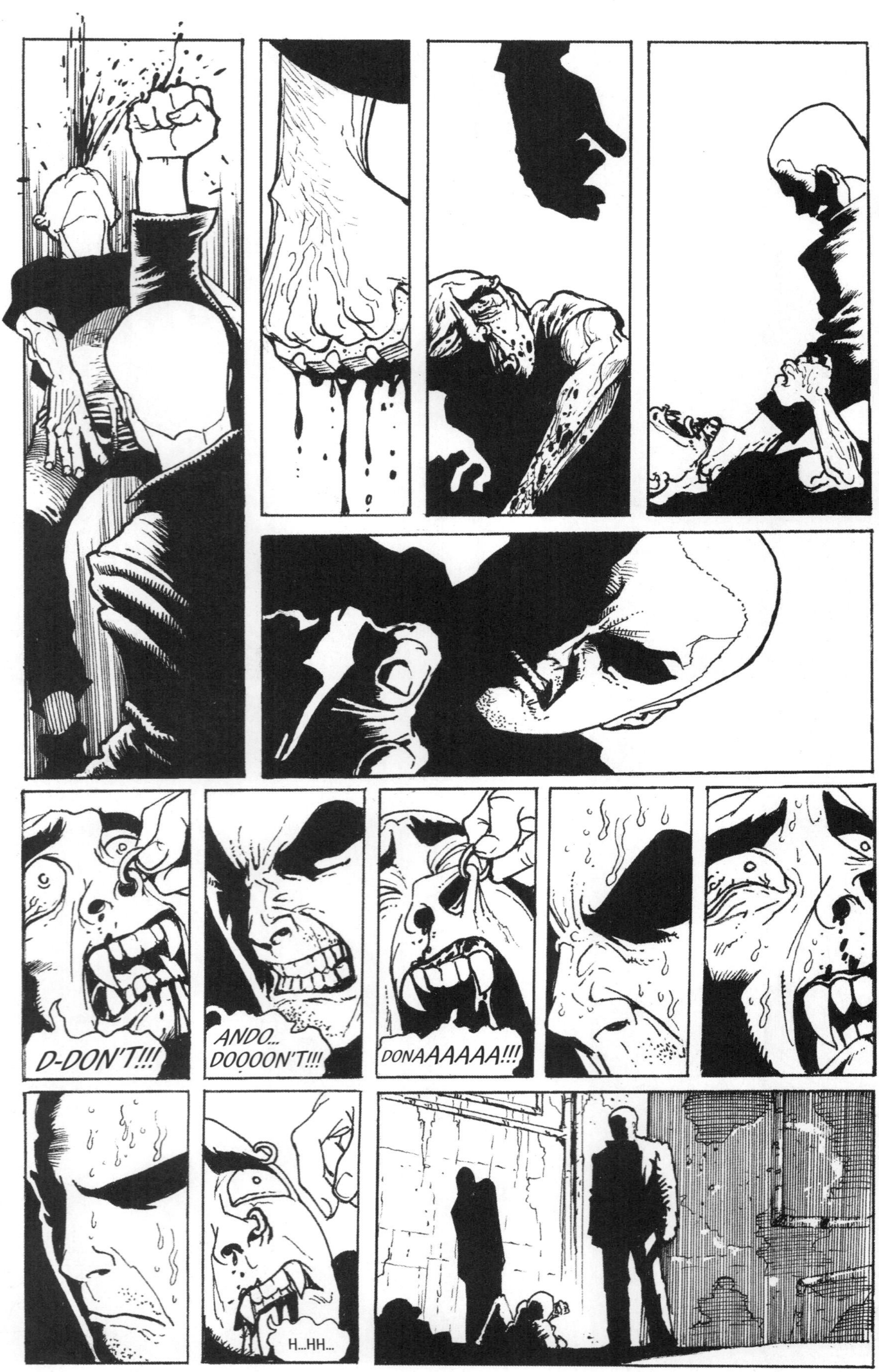
D-DON'T!!!
ANDO... DOOOON'T!!!
DONAAAAAA!!!
H...HH...

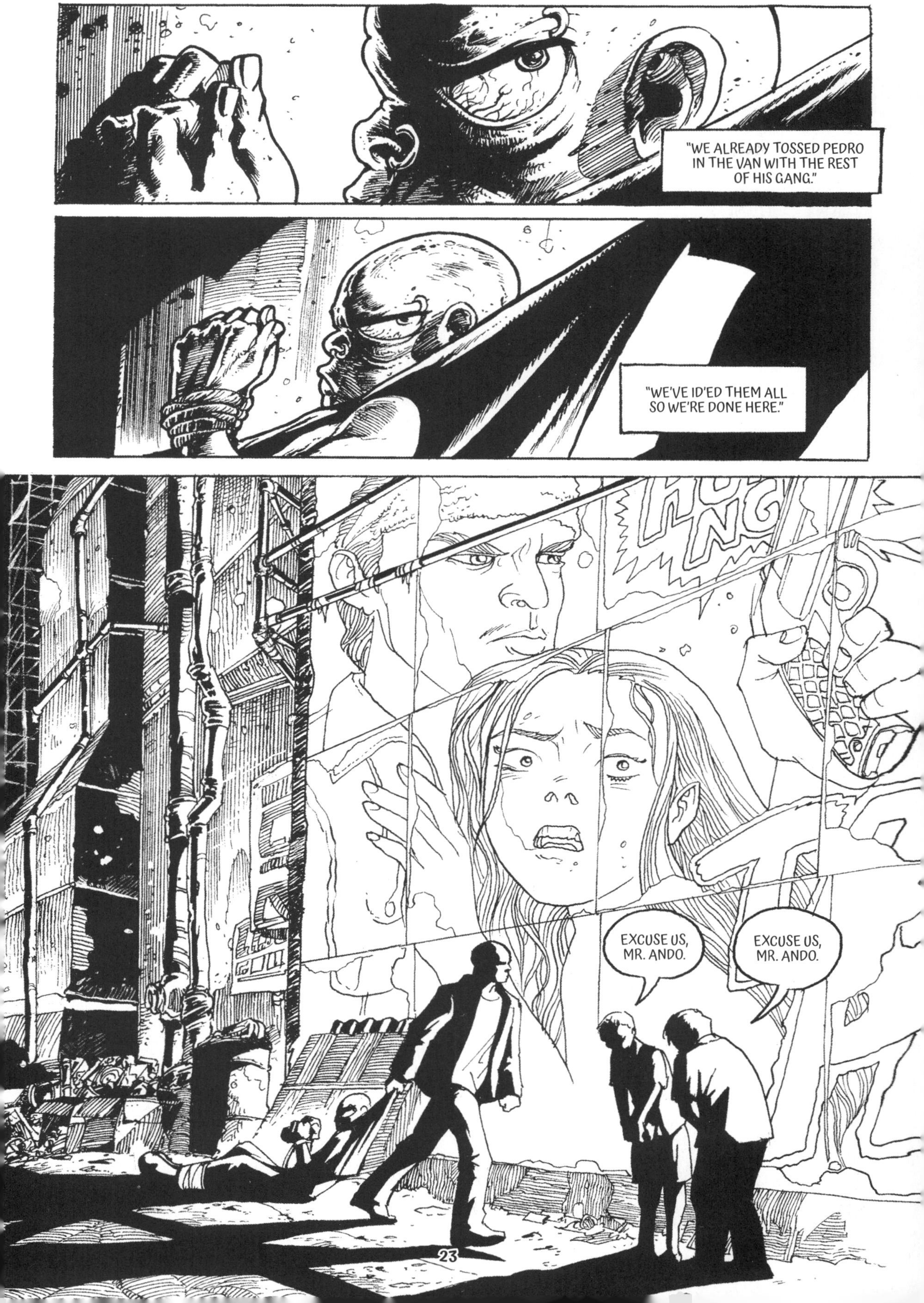
"WE ALREADY TOSSED PEDRO IN THE VAN WITH THE REST OF HIS GANG."
"WE'VE ID'ED THEM ALL SO WE'RE DONE HERE."
EXCUSE US, MR. ANDO.
EXCUSE US, MR. ANDO.

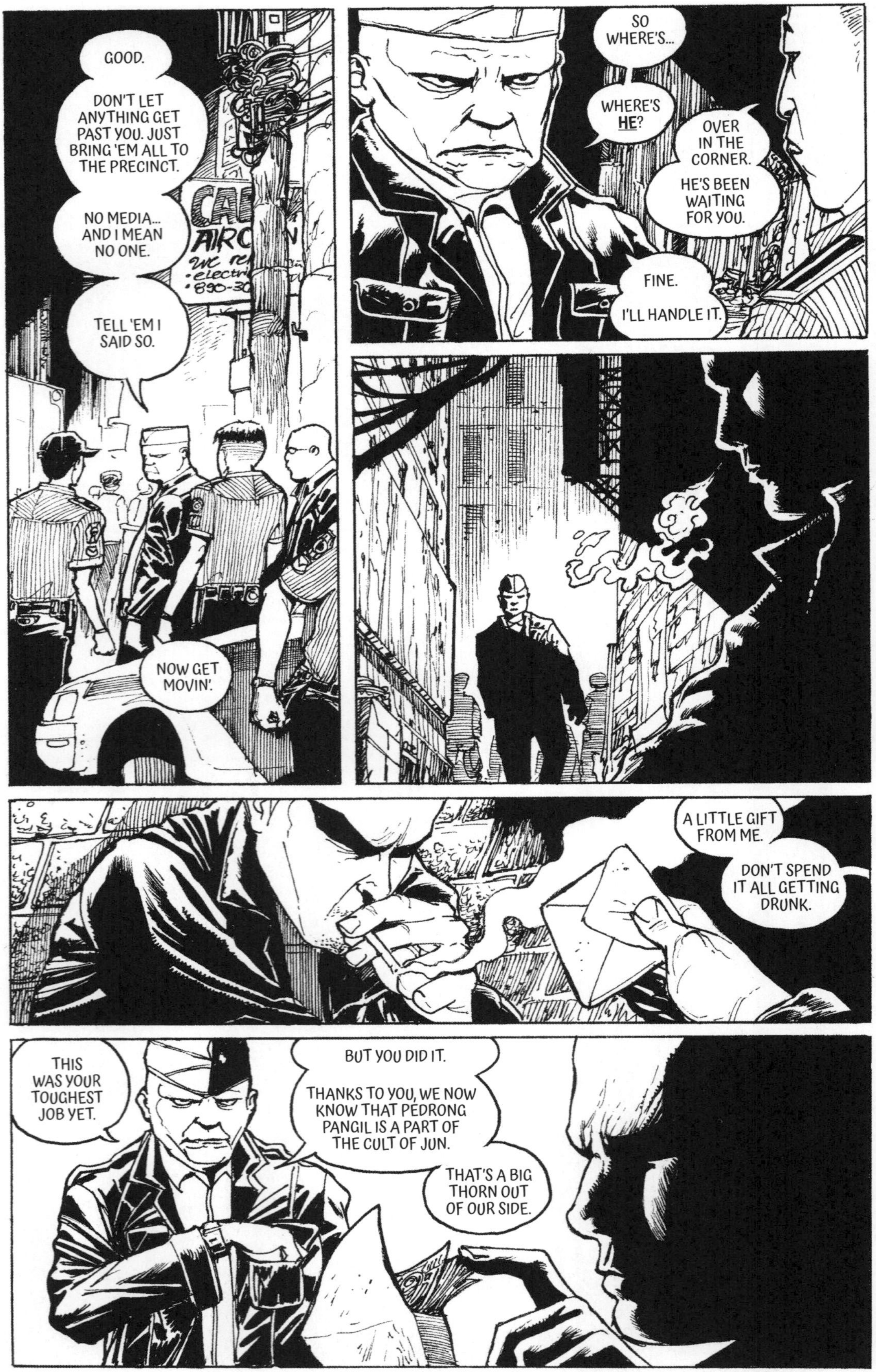

GOOD.
DON'T LET ANYTHING GET PAST YOU. JUST BRING 'EM ALL TO THE PRECINCT.
NO MEDIA... AND I MEAN NO ONE.
TELL 'EM I SAID SO.
NOW GET MOVIN'.
SO WHERE'S...
WHERE'S HE?
OVER IN THE CORNER.
HE'S BEEN WAITING FOR YOU.
FINE.
I'LL HANDLE IT.
A LITTLE GIFT FROM ME.
DON'T SPEND IT ALL GETTING DRUNK.
THIS WAS YOUR TOUGHEST JOB YET.
BUT YOU DID IT.
THANKS TO YOU, WE NOW KNOW THAT PEDRONG PANGIL IS A PART OF THE CULT OF JUN.
THAT'S A BIG THORN OUT OF OUR SIDE.

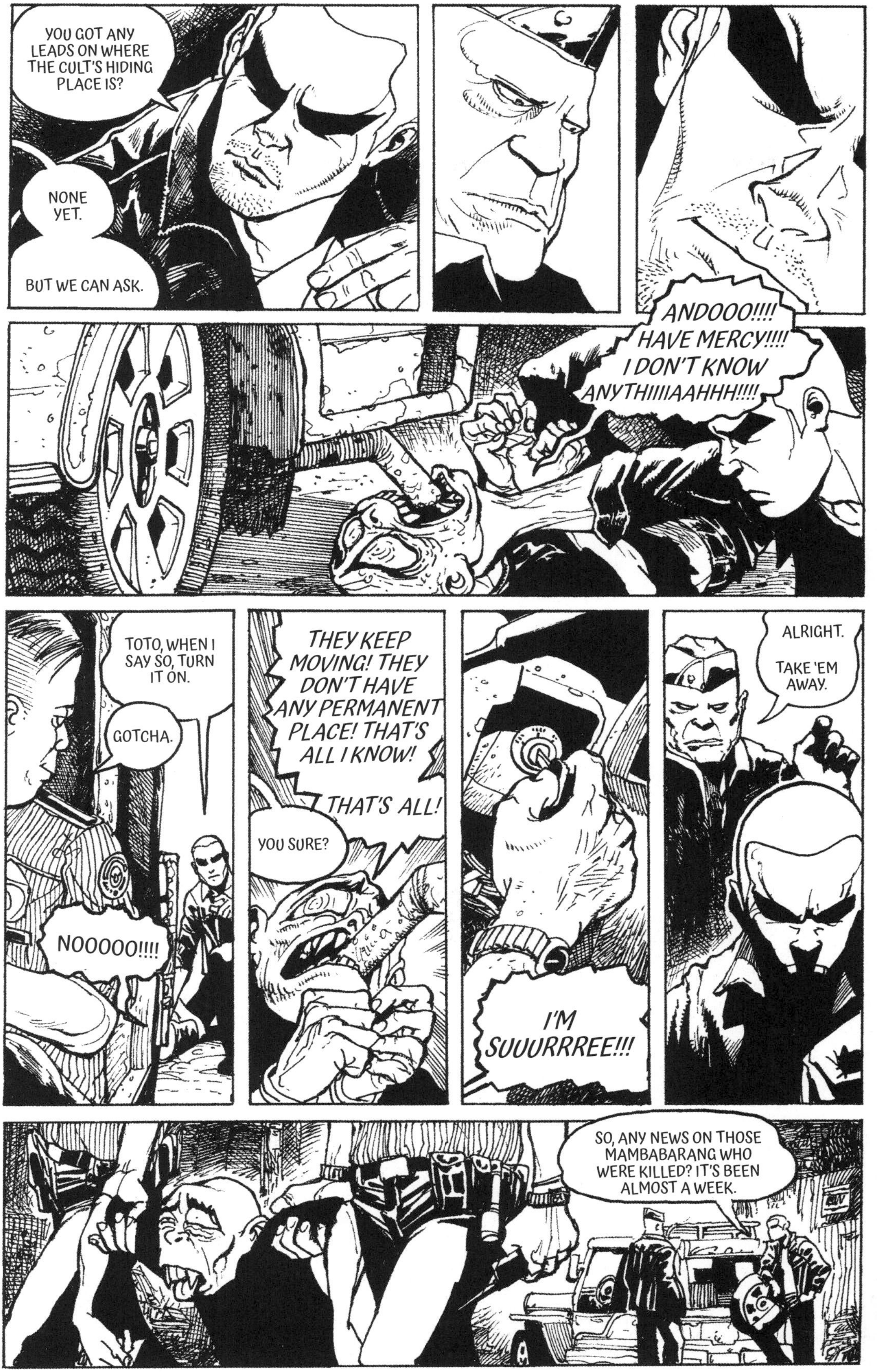
YOU GOT ANY LEADS ON WHERE THE CULT'S HIDING PLACE IS?
NONE YET.
BUT WE CAN ASK.
ANDOOO!!!! HAVE MERCY!!!! I DON'T KNOW ANYTHIIIIAAHHH!!!!
TOTO, WHEN I SAY SO, TURN IT ON.
GOTCHA.
NOOOOO!!!!
THEY KEEP MOVING! THEY DON'T HAVE ANY PERMANENT PLACE! THAT'S ALL I KNOW!
THAT'S ALL!
YOU SURE?
I'M SUUURRREE!!!
ALRIGHT.
TAKE 'EM AWAY.
SO, ANY NEWS ON THOSE MAMBABARANG WHO WERE KILLED? IT'S BEEN ALMOST A WEEK.

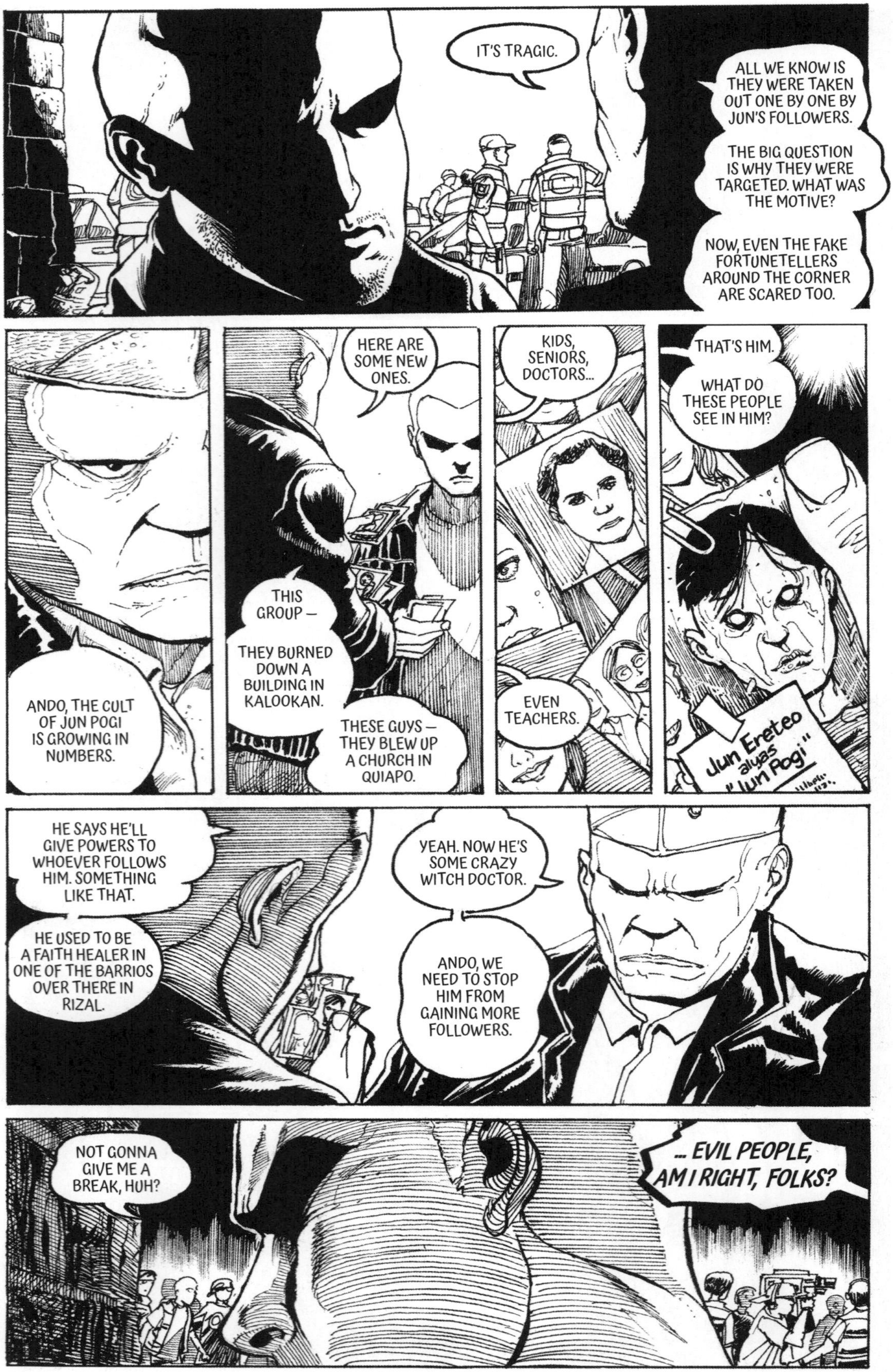
IT'S TRAGIC.
ALL WE KNOW IS THEY WERE TAKEN OUT ONE BY ONE BY JUN'S FOLLOWERS.
THE BIG QUESTION IS WHY THEY WERE TARGETED. WHAT WAS THE MOTIVE?
NOW, EVEN THE FAKE FORTUNETELLERS AROUND THE CORNER ARE SCARED TOO.
ANDO, THE CULT OF JUN POGI IS GROWING IN NUMBERS.
HERE ARE SOME NEW ONES.
THIS GROUP —
THEY BURNED DOWN A BUILDING IN KALOOKAN.
THESE GUYS — THEY BLEW UP A CHURCH IN QUIAPO.
KIDS, SENIORS, DOCTORS...
EVEN TEACHERS.
THAT'S HIM.
WHAT DO THESE PEOPLE SEE IN HIM?
Jun Ereteo alyas "Jun Pogi"
HE SAYS HE'LL GIVE POWERS TO WHOEVER FOLLOWS HIM. SOMETHING LIKE THAT.
HE USED TO BE A FAITH HEALER IN ONE OF THE BARRIOS OVER THERE IN RIZAL.
YEAH. NOW HE'S SOME CRAZY WITCH DOCTOR.
ANDO, WE NEED TO STOP HIM FROM GAINING MORE FOLLOWERS.
NOT GONNA GIVE ME A BREAK, HUH?
... EVIL PEOPLE, AM I RIGHT, FOLKS?

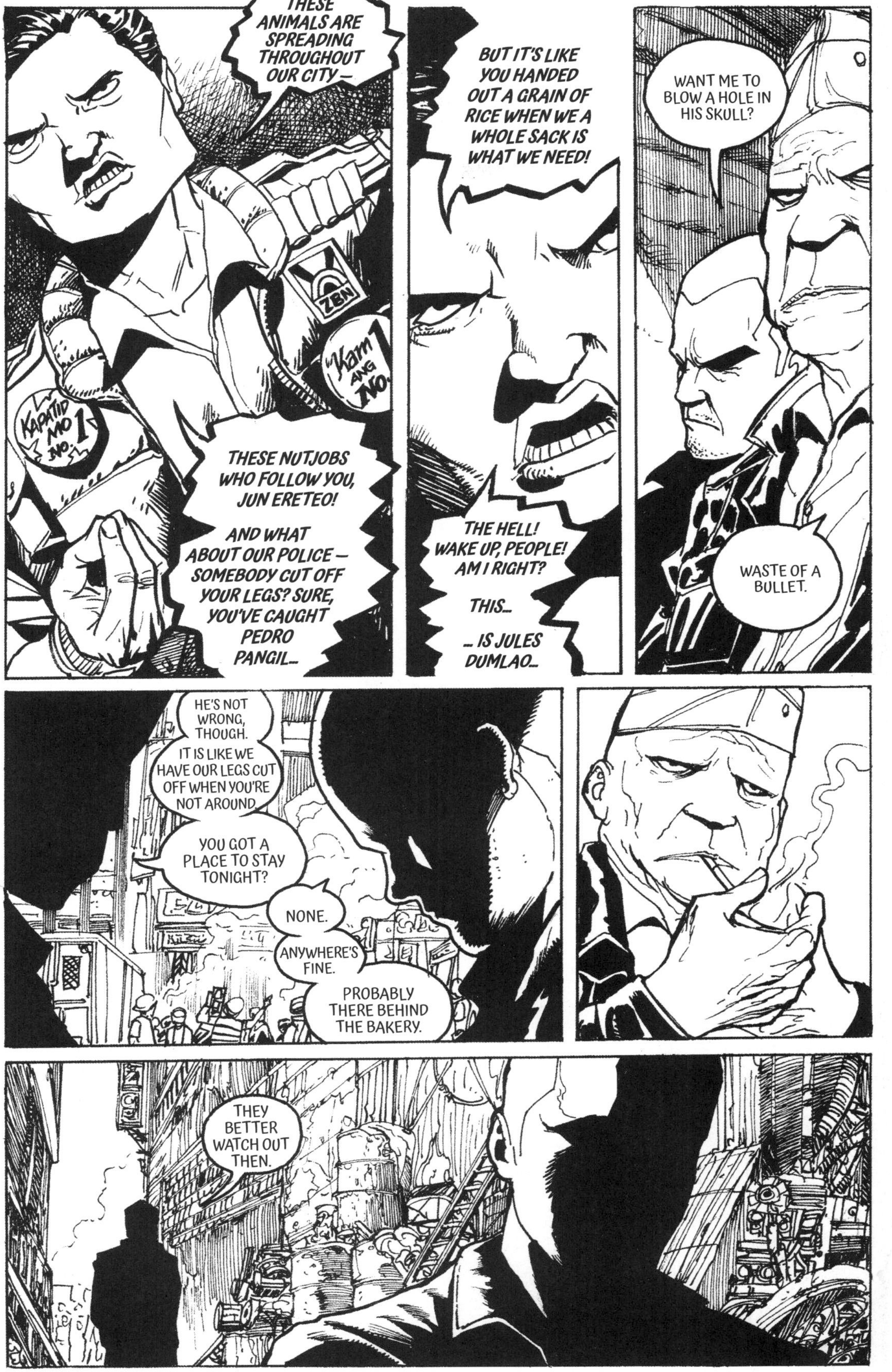
THESE ANIMALS ARE SPREADING THROUGHOUT OUR CITY —
ZBN
KAPATID MO 1 No. 1
"Kam 1 ANG No.
THESE NUTJOBS WHO FOLLOW YOU, JUN ERETEO!
AND WHAT ABOUT OUR POLICE — SOMEBODY CUT OFF YOUR LEGS? SURE, YOU'VE CAUGHT PEDRO PANGIL...
BUT IT'S LIKE YOU HANDED OUT A GRAIN OF RICE WHEN WE A WHOLE SACK IS WHAT WE NEED!
THE HELL! WAKE UP, PEOPLE! AM I RIGHT?
THIS...
... IS JULES DUMLAO...
WANT ME TO BLOW A HOLE IN HIS SKULL?
WASTE OF A BULLET.
HE'S NOT WRONG, THOUGH.
IT IS LIKE WE HAVE OUR LEGS CUT OFF WHEN YOU'RE NOT AROUND.
YOU GOT A PLACE TO STAY TONIGHT?
NONE.
ANYWHERE'S FINE.
PROBABLY THERE BEHIND THE BAKERY.
THEY BETTER WATCH OUT THEN.

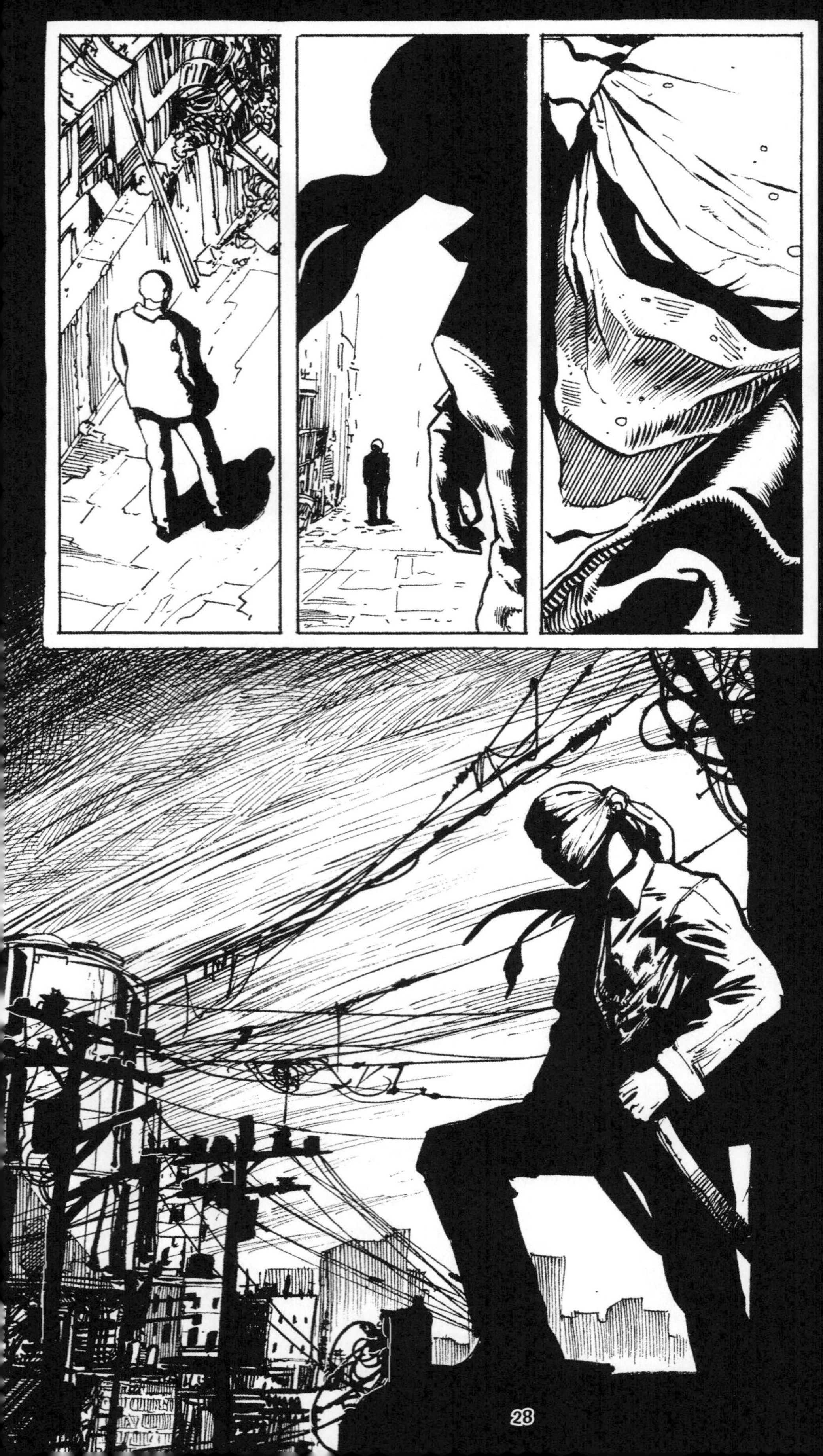

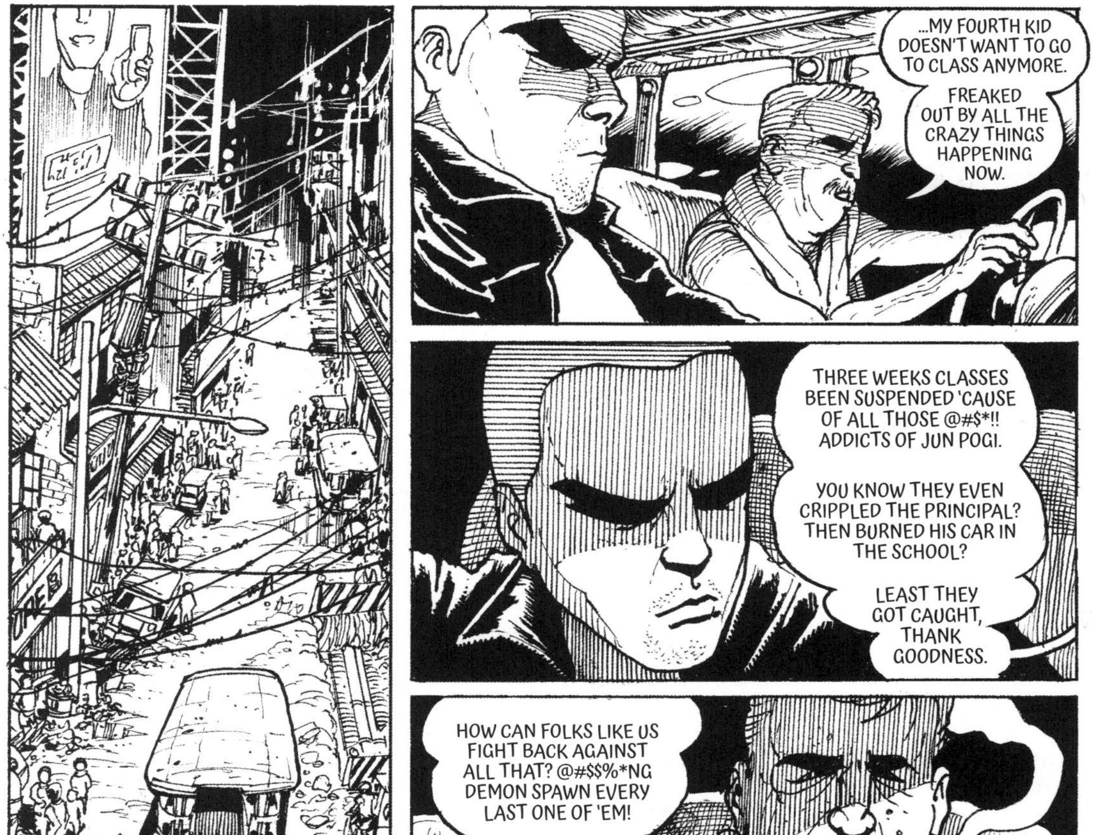
...MY FOURTH KID DOESN'T WANT TO GO TO CLASS ANYMORE.
FREAKED OUT BY ALL THE CRAZY THINGS HAPPENING NOW.
THREE WEEKS CLASSES BEEN SUSPENDED 'CAUSE OF ALL THOSE @#$*!! ADDICTS OF JUN POGI.
YOU KNOW THEY EVEN CRIPPLED THE PRINCIPAL? THEN BURNED HIS CAR IN THE SCHOOL?
LEAST THEY GOT CAUGHT, THANK GOODNESS.
HOW CAN FOLKS LIKE US FIGHT BACK AGAINST ALL THAT? @#$$%*NG DEMON SPAWN EVERY LAST ONE OF 'EM!
ANDO...
...IF THERE'S ANYTHING YOU CAN DO...
I'LL CHECK OUT THE PLACE TOMORROW.
CALL IF THERE'S TROUBLE.
WILL DO.
HAVE A BITE, MANG ANDO?
FRESHLY COOKED.

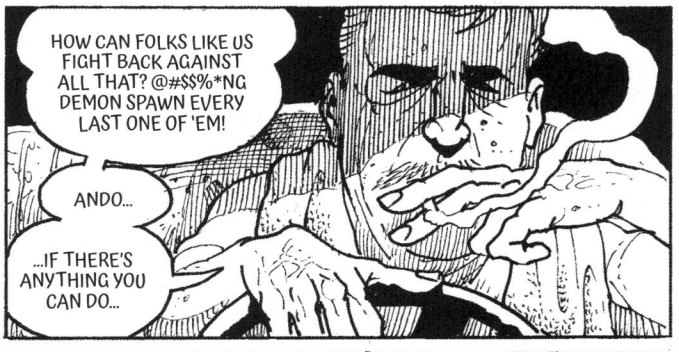

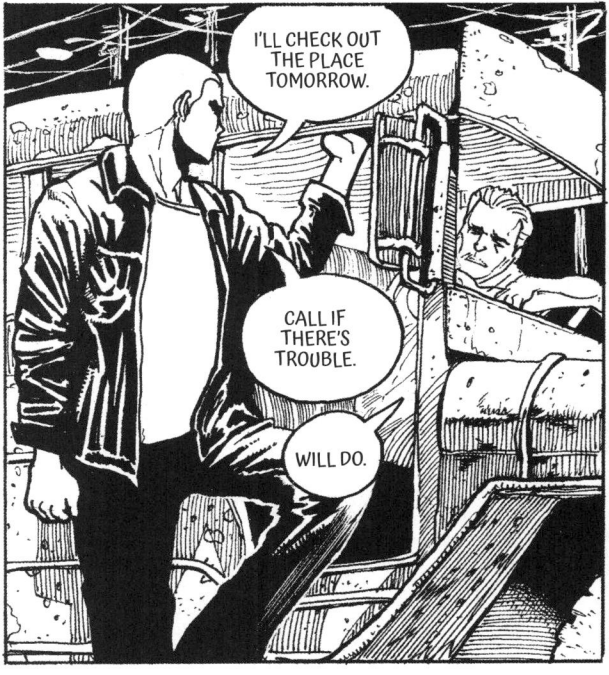

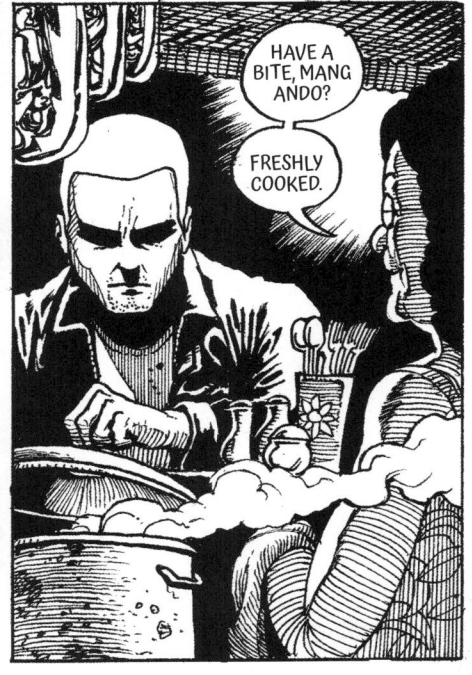

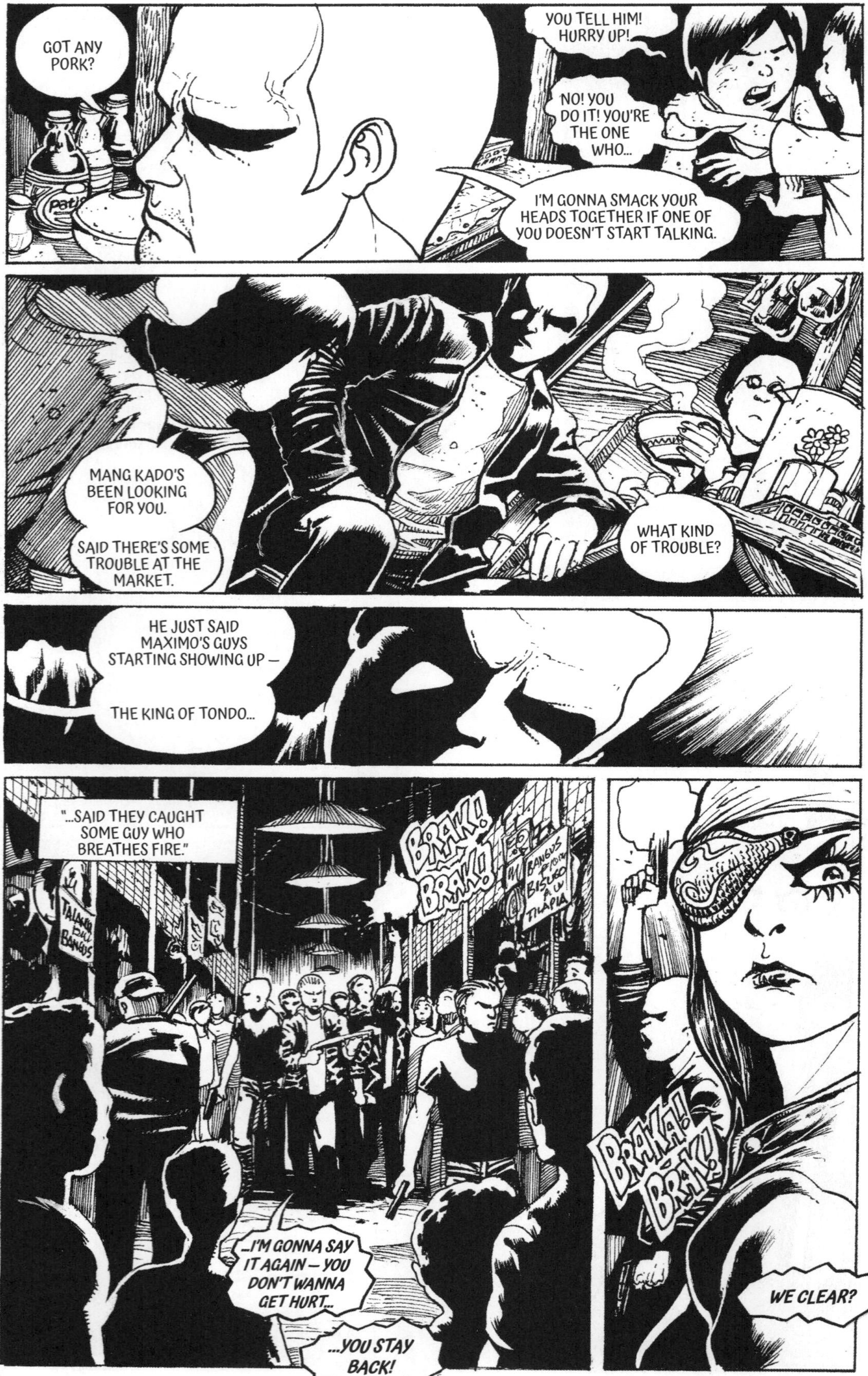
GOT ANY PORK?
YOU TELL HIM! HURRY UP!
NO! YOU DO IT! YOU'RE THE ONE WHO...
I'M GONNA SMACK YOUR HEADS TOGETHER IF ONE OF YOU DOESN'T START TALKING.
MANG KADO'S BEEN LOOKING FOR YOU.
SAID THERE'S SOME TROUBLE AT THE MARKET.
WHAT KIND OF TROUBLE?
HE JUST SAID MAXIMO'S GUYS STARTING SHOWING UP —
THE KING OF TONDO...
"...SAID THEY CAUGHT SOME GUY WHO BREATHES FIRE."
BRAK! BRAK!
...I'M GONNA SAY IT AGAIN — YOU DON'T WANNA GET HURT...
...YOU STAY BACK!
BRAKA! BRAK!
WE CLEAR?

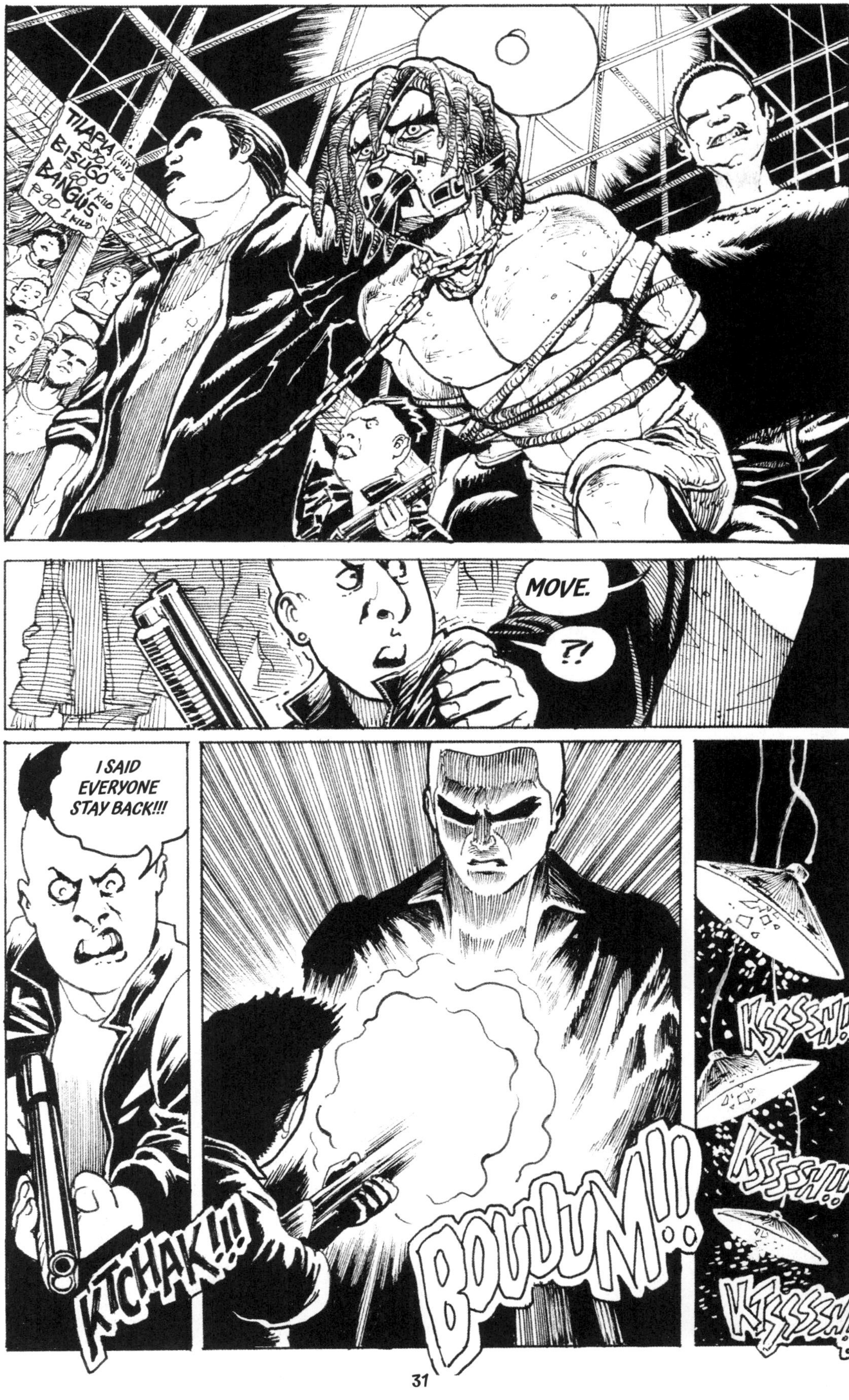
TILAPIA (lit) P50 1 kilo
BISUGO P60 1 kilo
BANGUS P90 1 kilo
MOVE.
?!
I SAID EVERYONE STAY BACK!!!
KTCHAK!!!
BOUUUM!!
KSSSSH!!
KSSSSH!!
KTSSSSH!!

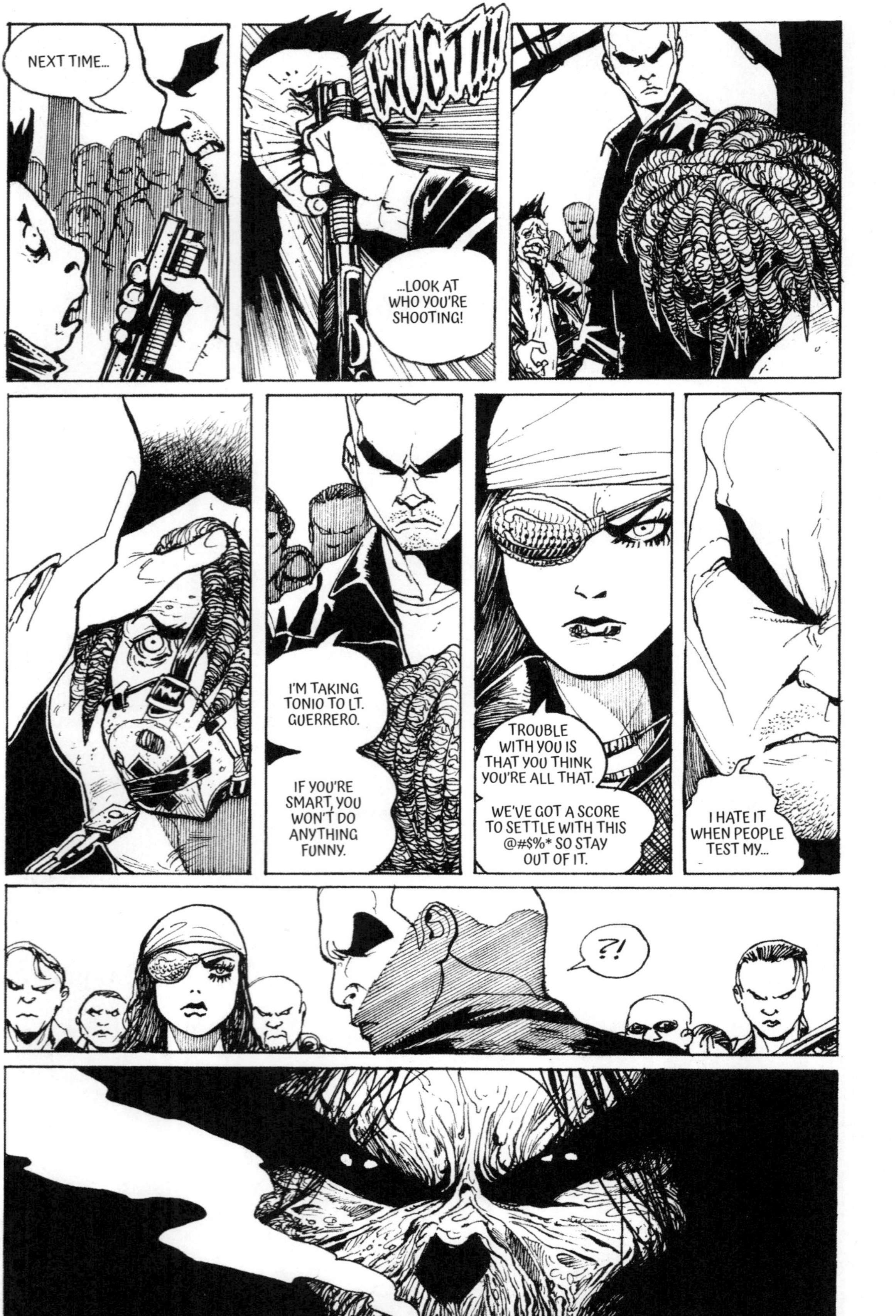
NEXT TIME...
WUGT!!!
...LOOK AT WHO YOU'RE SHOOTING!
I'M TAKING TONIO TO LT. GUERRERO.
IF YOU'RE SMART, YOU WON'T DO ANYTHING FUNNY.
TROUBLE WITH YOU IS THAT YOU THINK YOU'RE ALL THAT.
WE'VE GOT A SCORE TO SETTLE WITH THIS @#$%* SO STAY OUT OF IT.
I HATE IT WHEN PEOPLE TEST MY...
?!

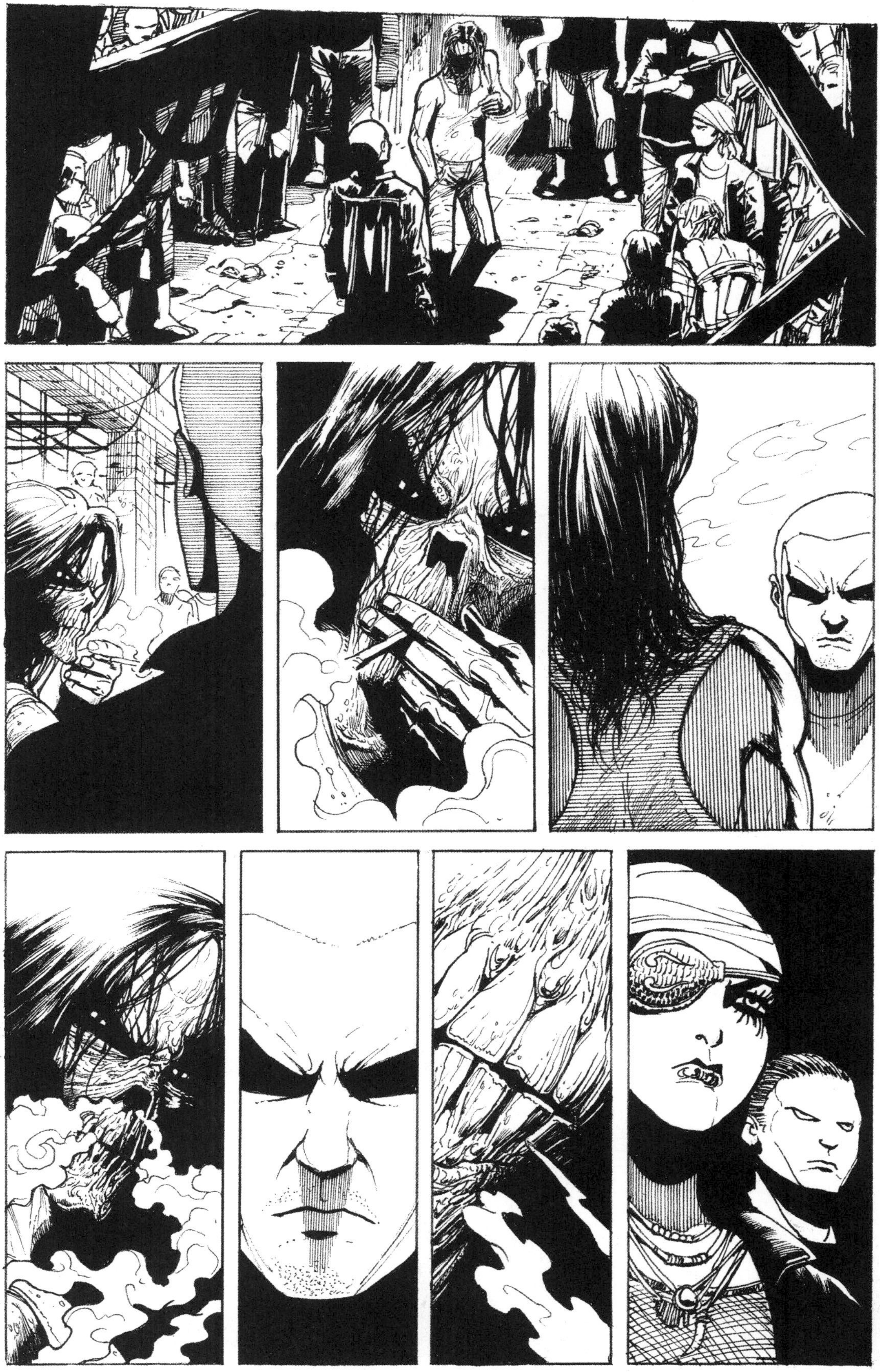

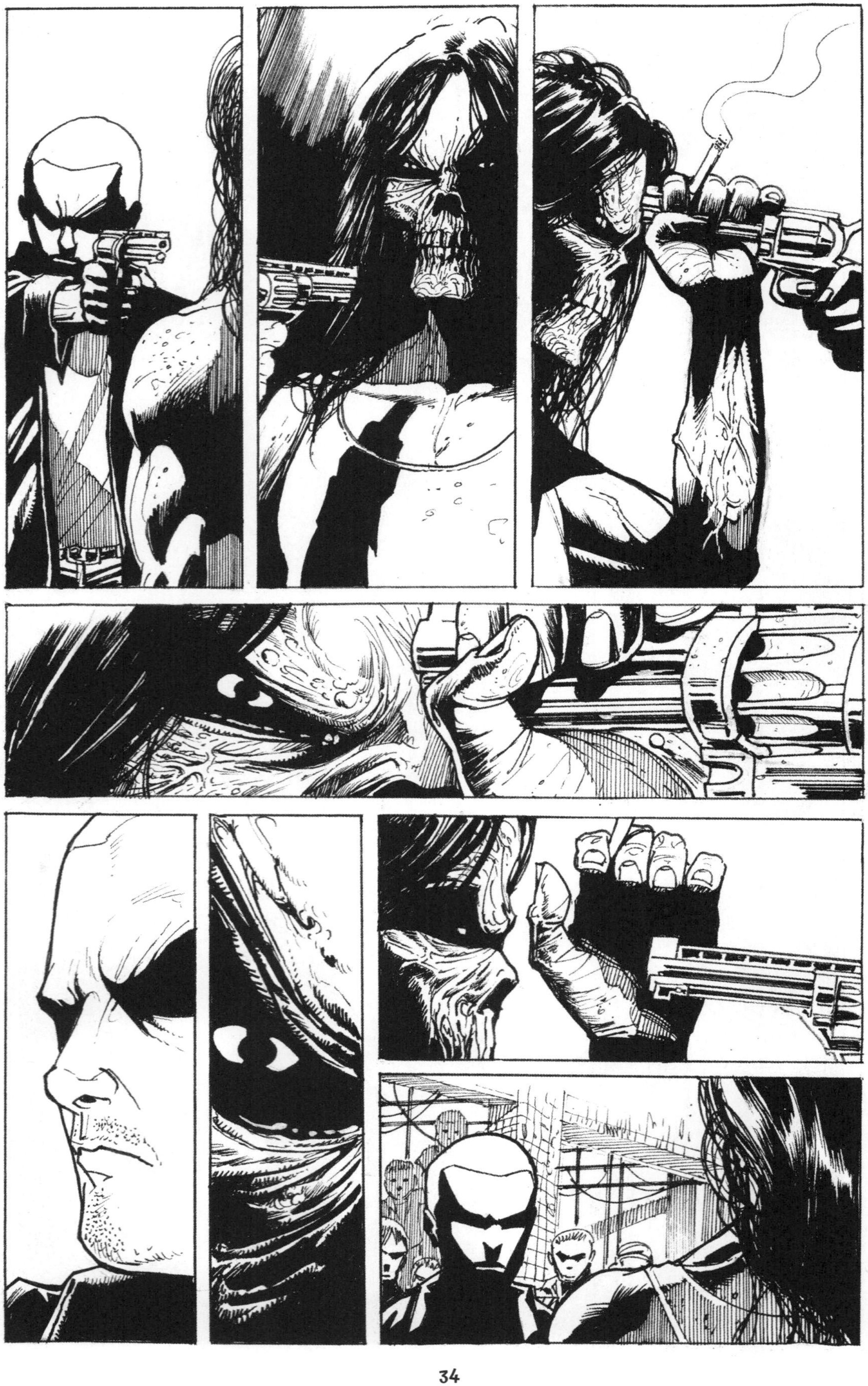

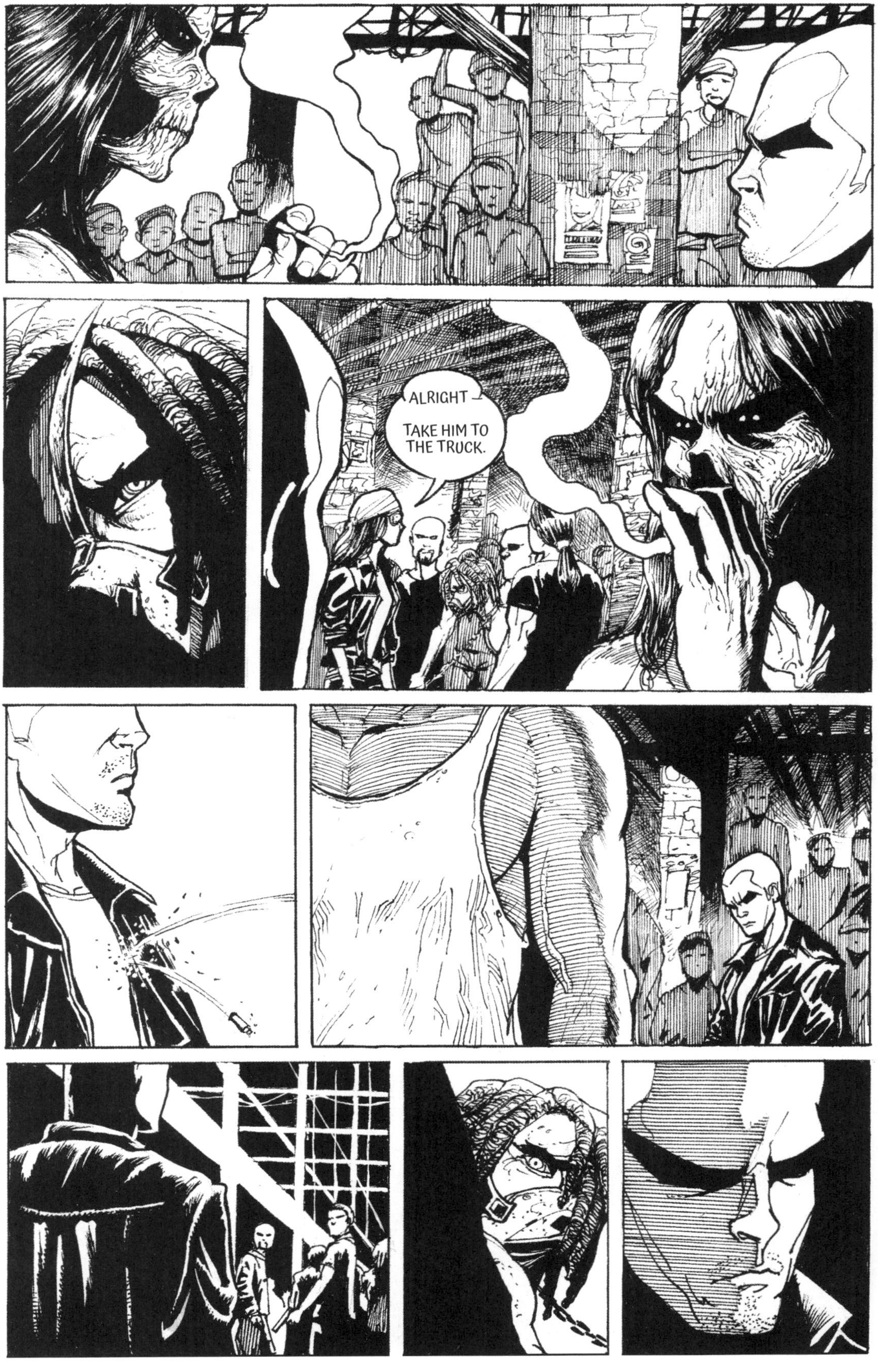
ALRIGHT –
TAKE HIM TO THE TRUCK.

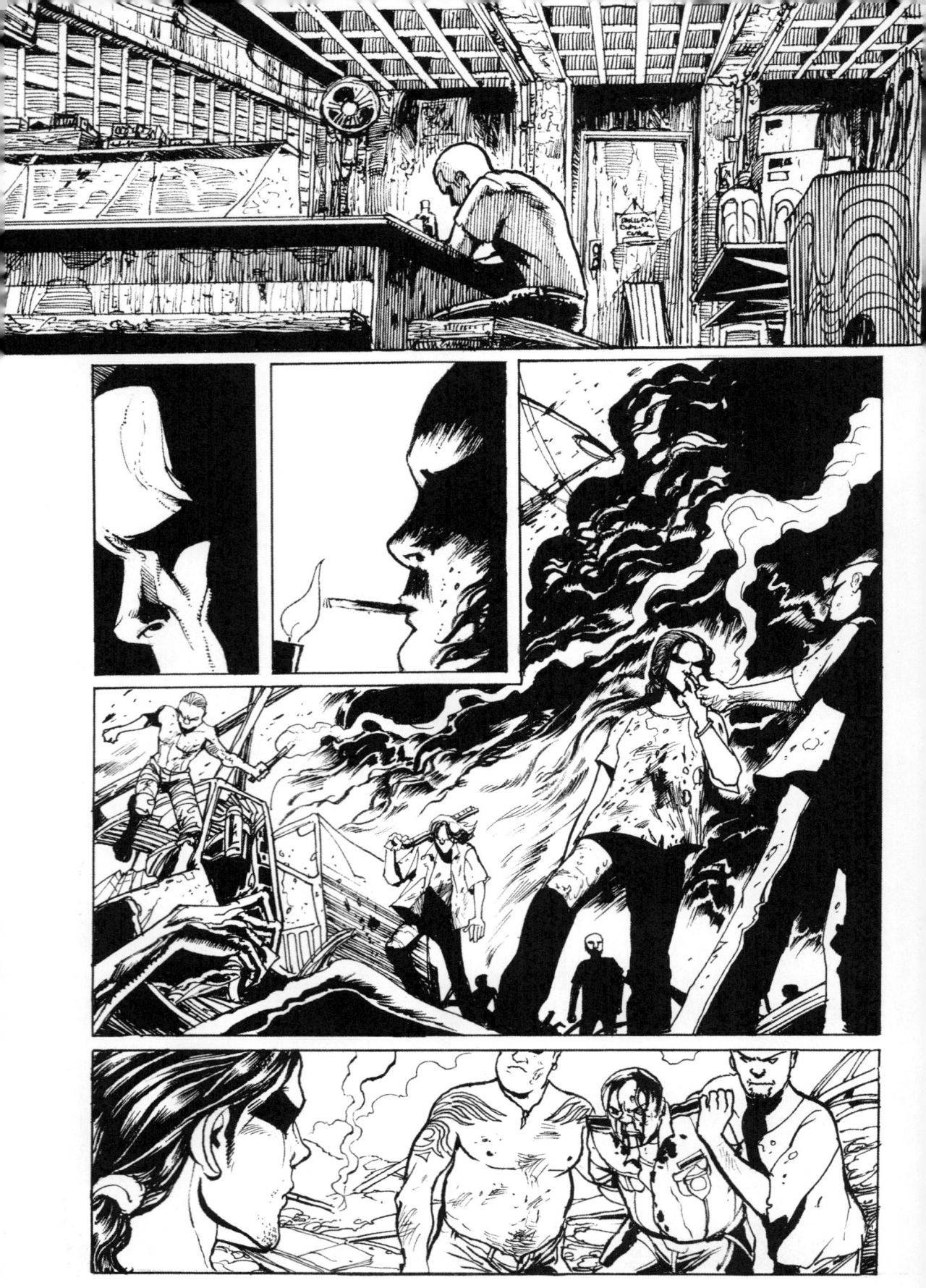

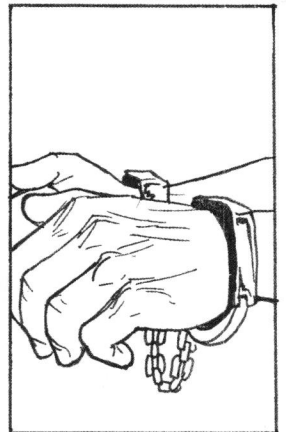

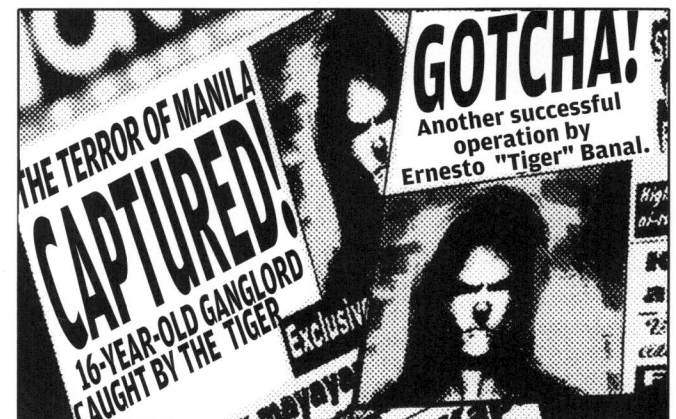

THE TERROR OF MANILA
CAPTURED!
16-YEAR-OLD GANGLORD CAUGHT BY THE TIGER

GOTCHA!
Another successful operation by Ernesto "Tiger" Banal.

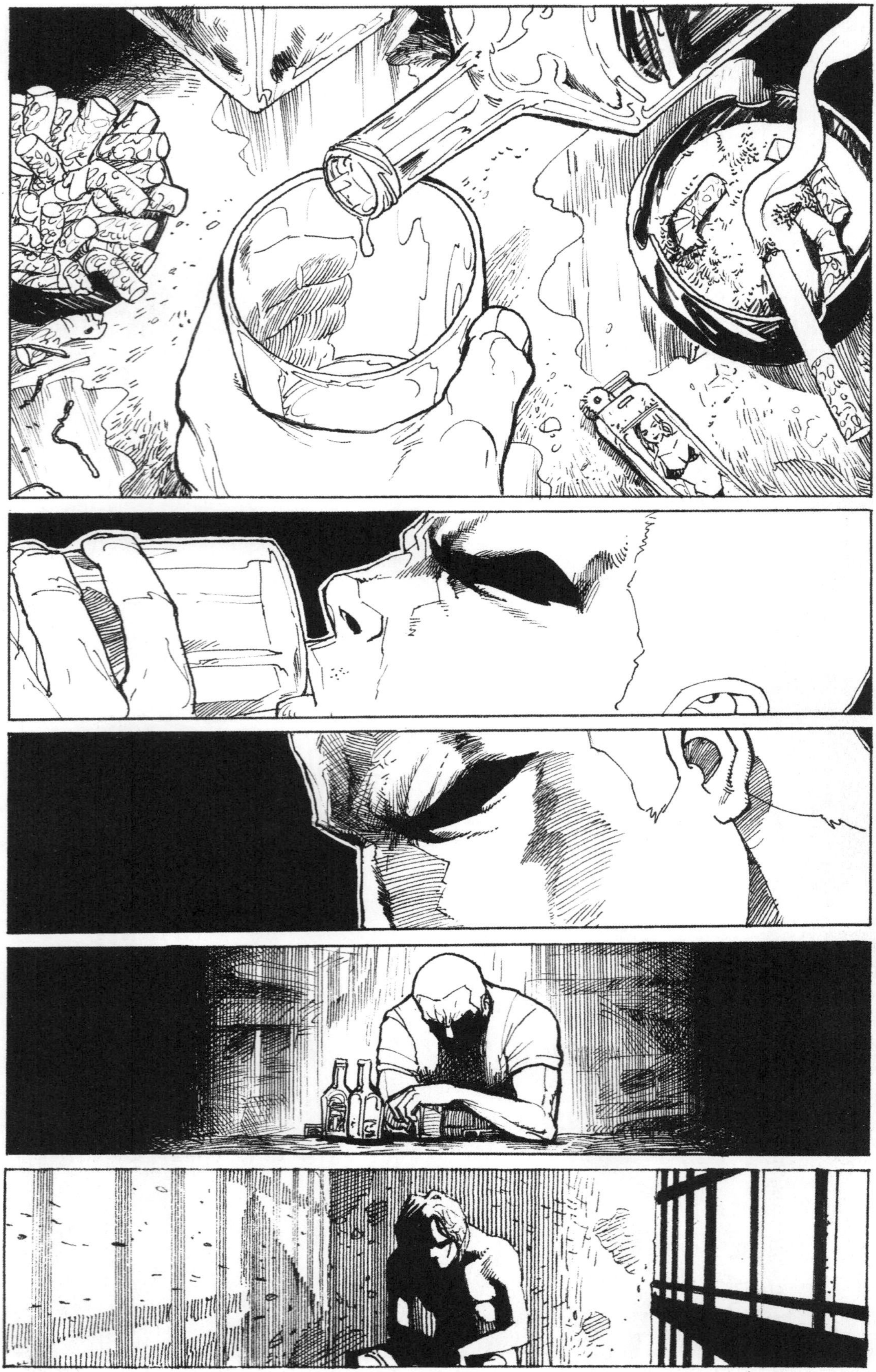

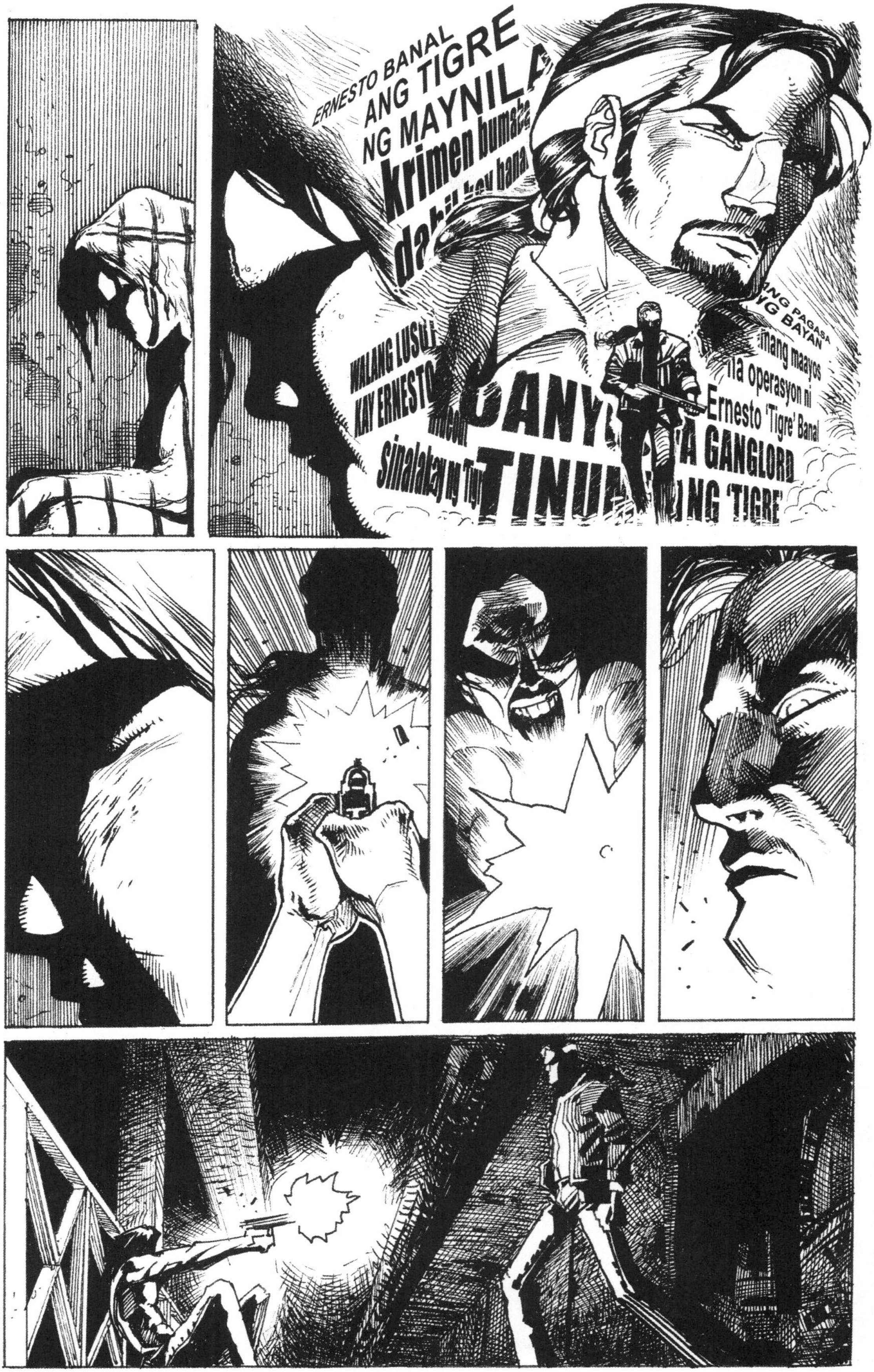
ERNESTO BANAL
ANG TIGRE
NG MAYNILA
krimen
WALANG LUSU
KAY ERNESTO
mang maayos
operasyon ni
Ernesto 'Tigre' Banal
GANGLORD
TINU
NG 'TIGRE'

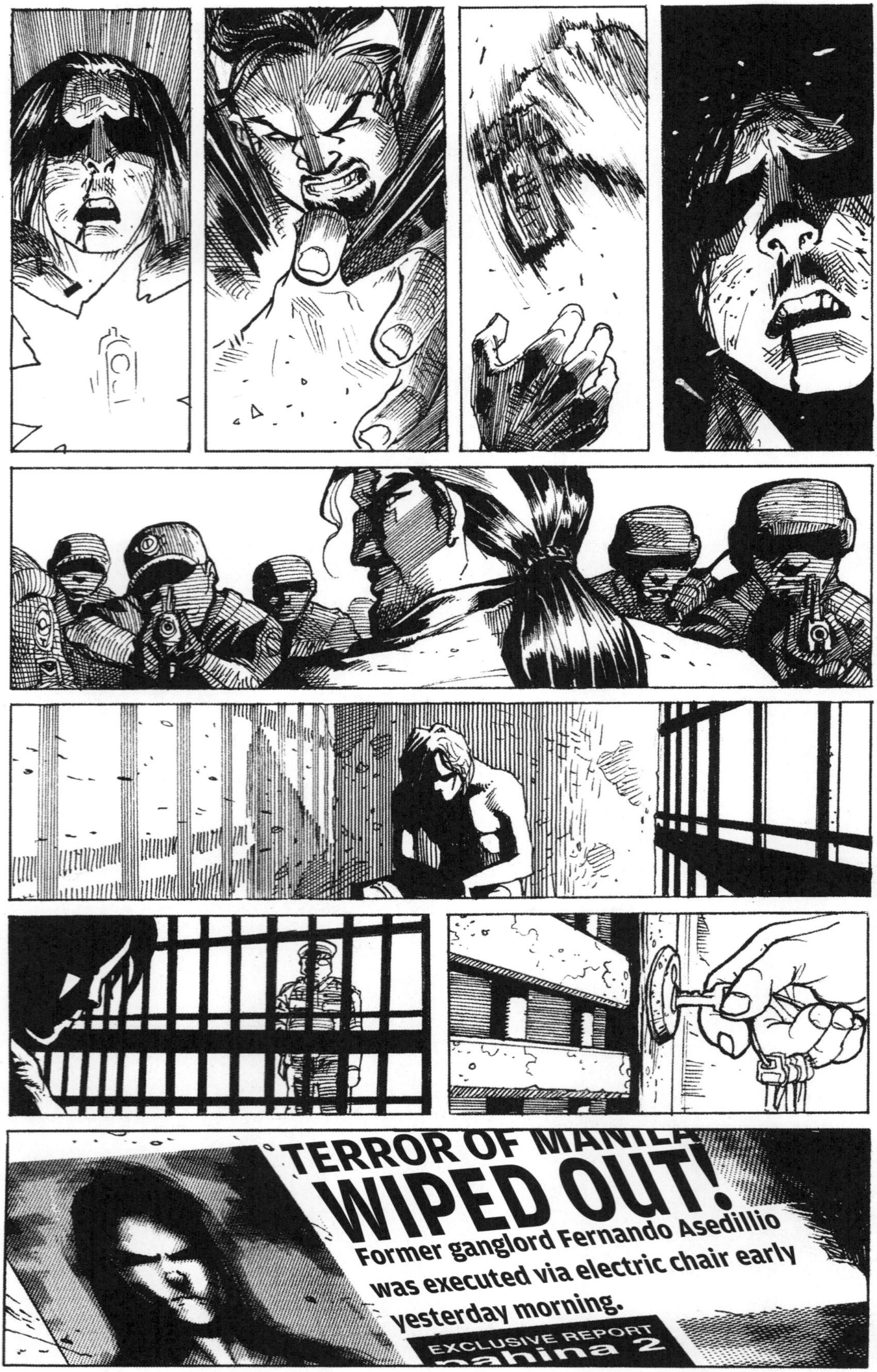
TERROR OF MANILA
WIPED OUT!
Former ganglord Fernando Asedillio was executed via electric chair early yesterday morning.
EXCLUSIVE REPORT
pahina 2

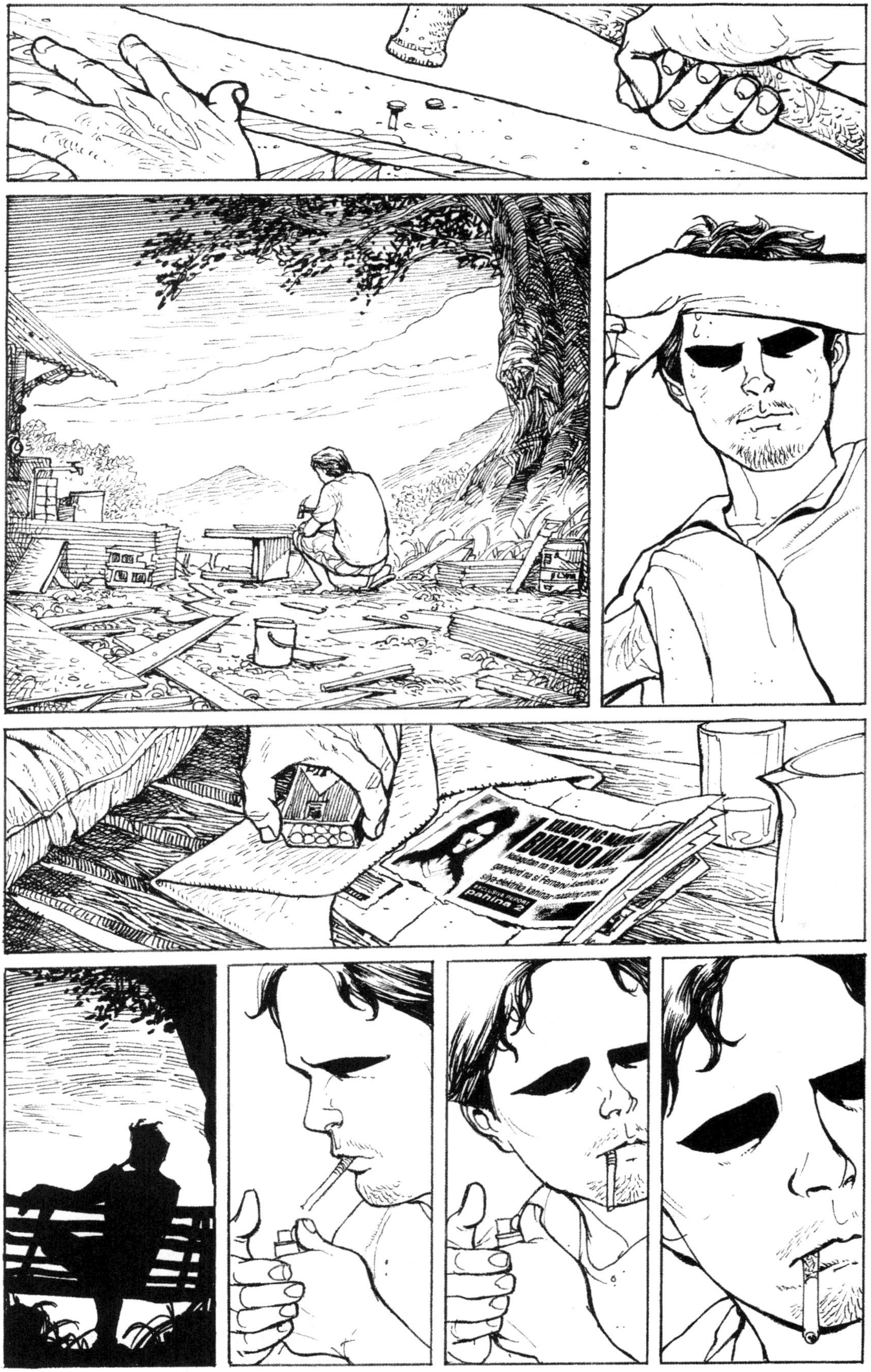
KILABOT NG
BURADO
EXCLUSIVE REPORT
pahina 2

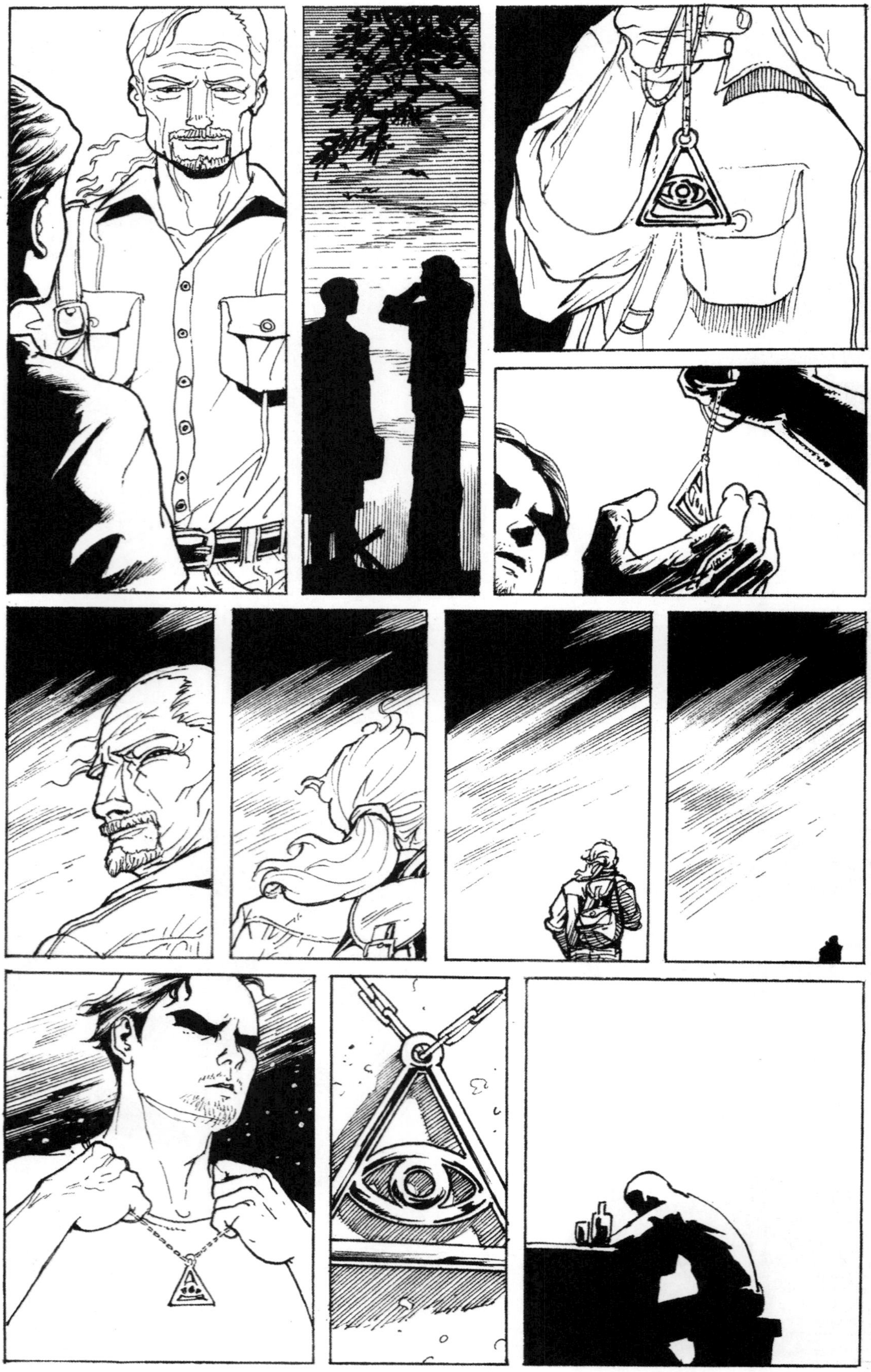

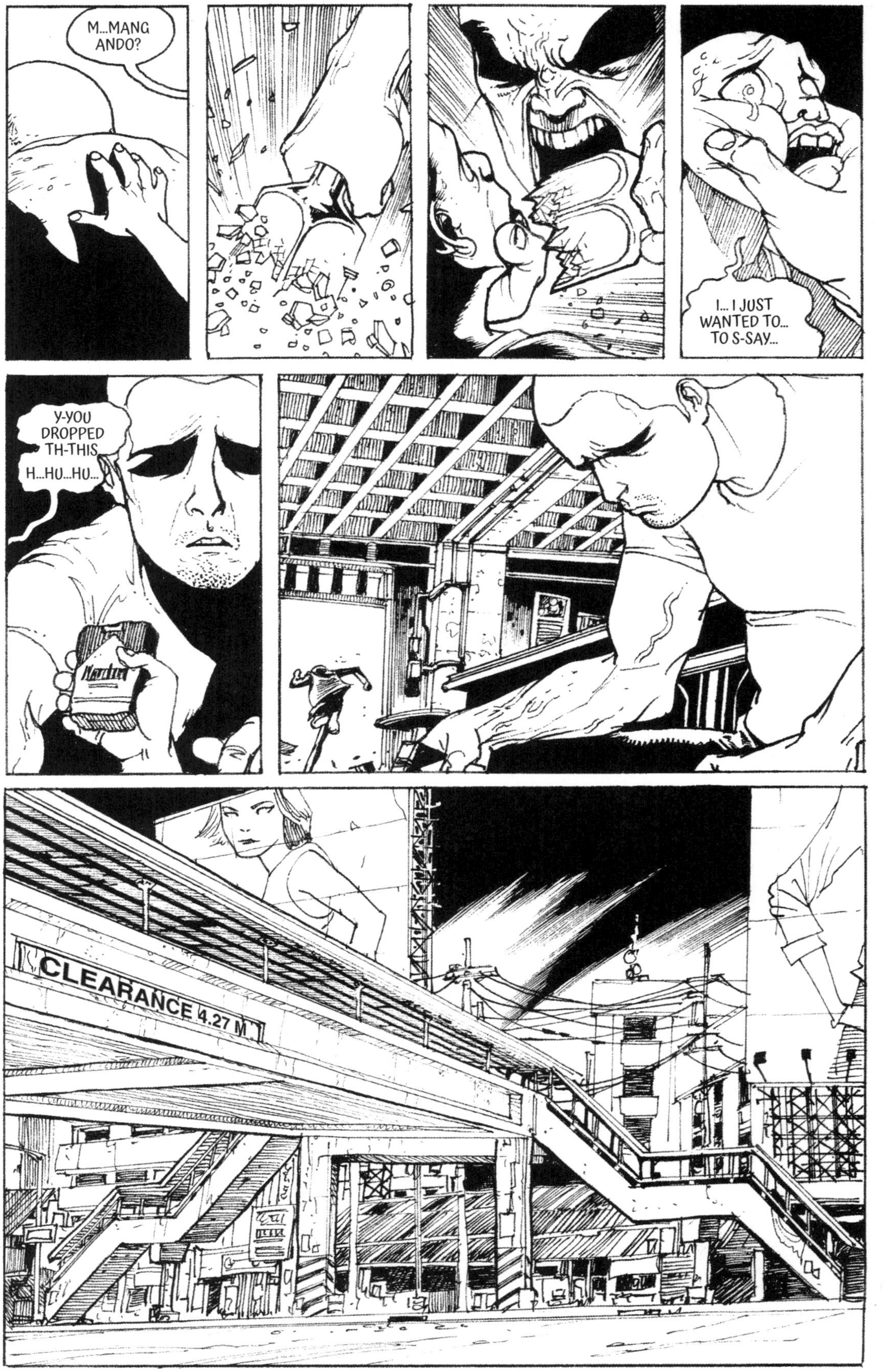
M...MANG ANDO?
I... I JUST WANTED TO... TO S-SAY...
Y-YOU DROPPED TH-THIS
H...HU...HU...
CLEARANCE 4.27 M

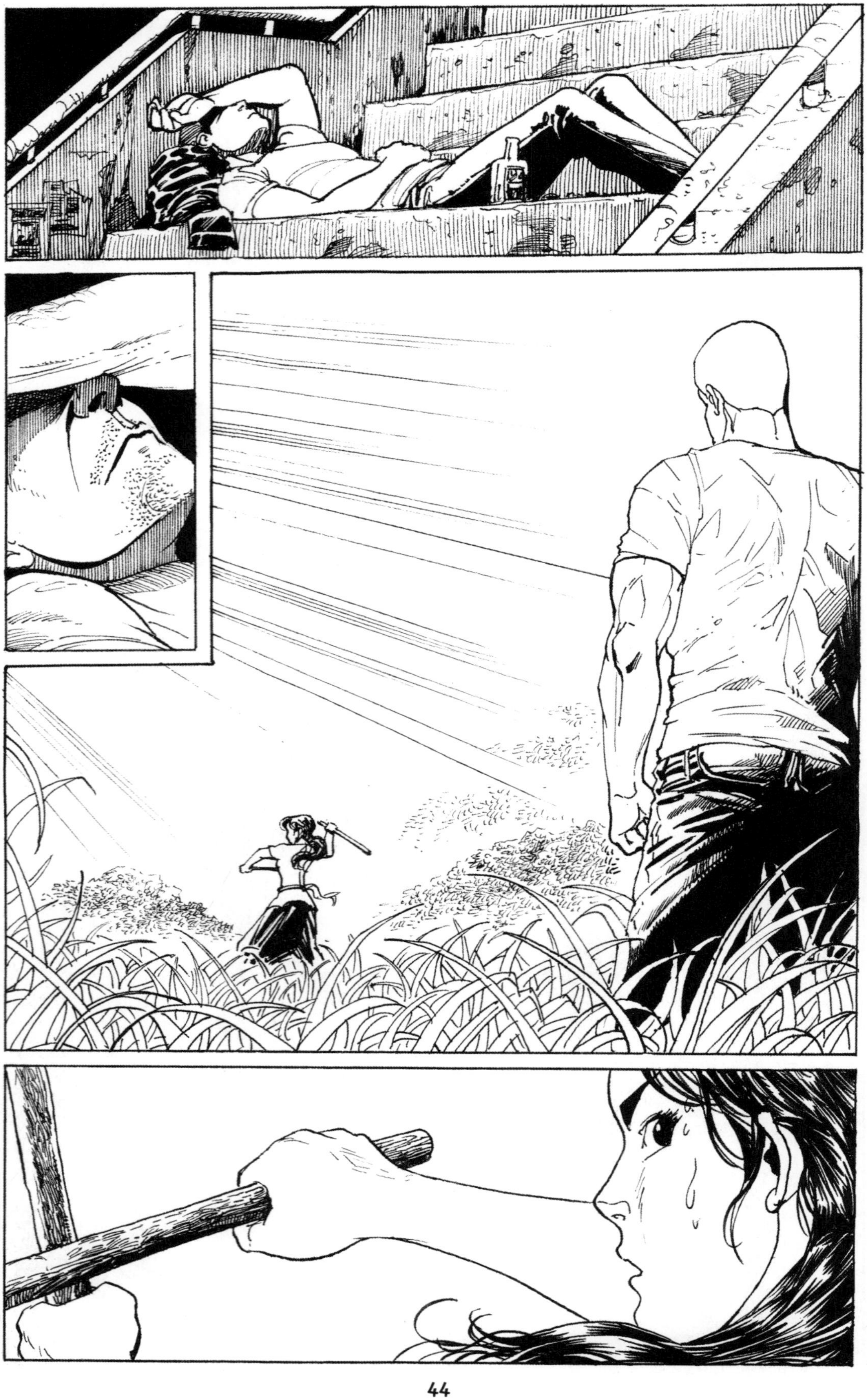

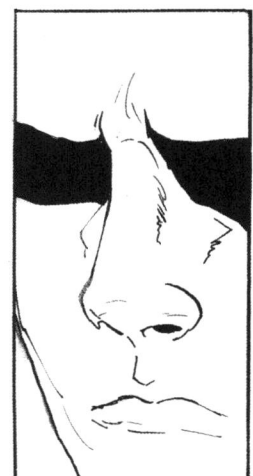

ANDOOO... UP TO NOW?

SILANG STILL FILLS YOUR DREAMS?

THIS IS GETTING TIRESOME.

WAKE UP! SLEEP AT OUR PLACE! IT'LL BE CHRISTMAS SOON!

IT'S COLD!

L...LAWIN. WHAT... TIME IS IT?

AH... I DUNNO.

HMMM... LOOKS LIKE WE GOT PAID TODAY, HUH?

URHUEKK!! URRAK!!

I DON'T HAVE A WATCH.

FINE. THANKS.

"PANGIL" DIDN'T GIVE YOU ANY TROUBLE?

HE PUT HOLES IN MY JACKET.

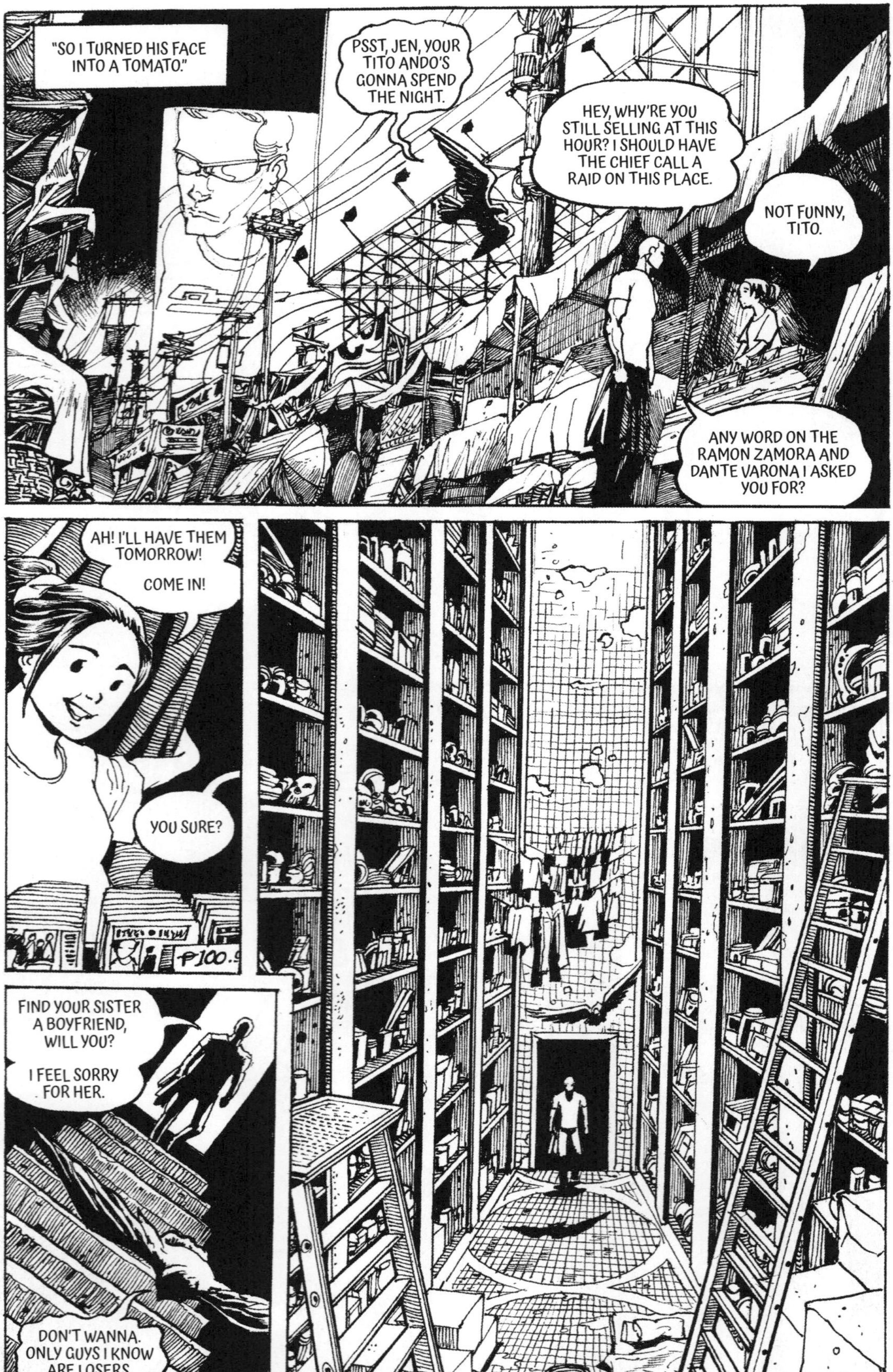
"SO I TURNED HIS FACE INTO A TOMATO."
PSST, JEN, YOUR TITO ANDO'S GONNA SPEND THE NIGHT.
HEY, WHY'RE YOU STILL SELLING AT THIS HOUR? I SHOULD HAVE THE CHIEF CALL A RAID ON THIS PLACE.
NOT FUNNY, TITO.
ANY WORD ON THE RAMON ZAMORA AND DANTE VARONA I ASKED YOU FOR?
AH! I'LL HAVE THEM TOMORROW!
COME IN!
YOU SURE?
FIND YOUR SISTER A BOYFRIEND, WILL YOU?
I FEEL SORRY FOR HER.
DON'T WANNA. ONLY GUYS I KNOW ARE LOSERS.

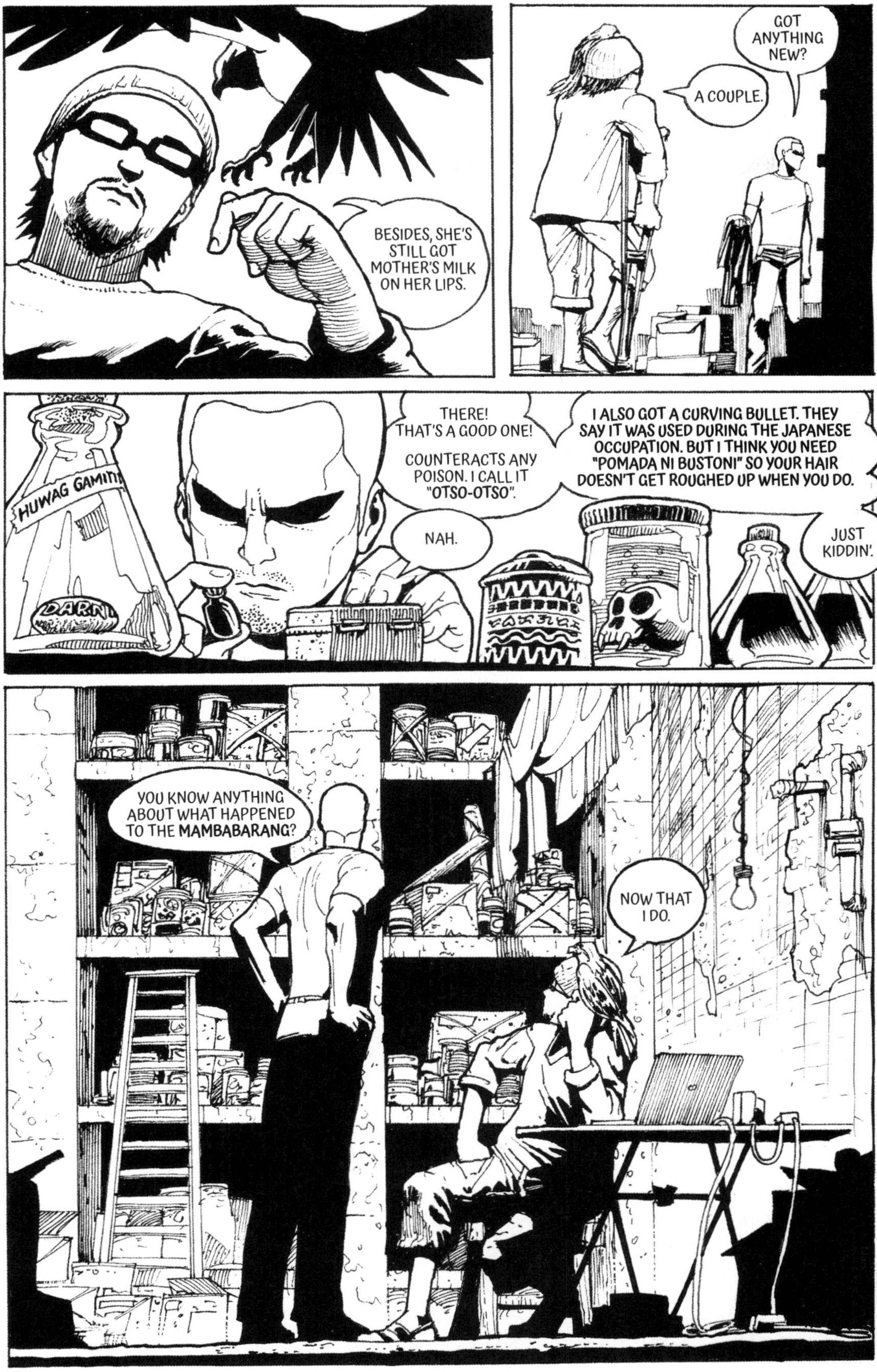
BESIDES, SHE'S STILL GOT MOTHER'S MILK ON HER LIPS.
GOT ANYTHING NEW?
A COUPLE.
HUWAG GAMITIN
DARNA
THERE! THAT'S A GOOD ONE!
COUNTERACTS ANY POISON. I CALL IT "OTSO-OTSO".
NAH.
I ALSO GOT A CURVING BULLET. THEY SAY IT WAS USED DURING THE JAPANESE OCCUPATION. BUT I THINK YOU NEED "POMADA NI BUSTONI" SO YOUR HAIR DOESN'T GET ROUGHED UP WHEN YOU DO.
JUST KIDDIN'.
YOU KNOW ANYTHING ABOUT WHAT HAPPENED TO THE MAMBABARANG?
NOW THAT I DO.

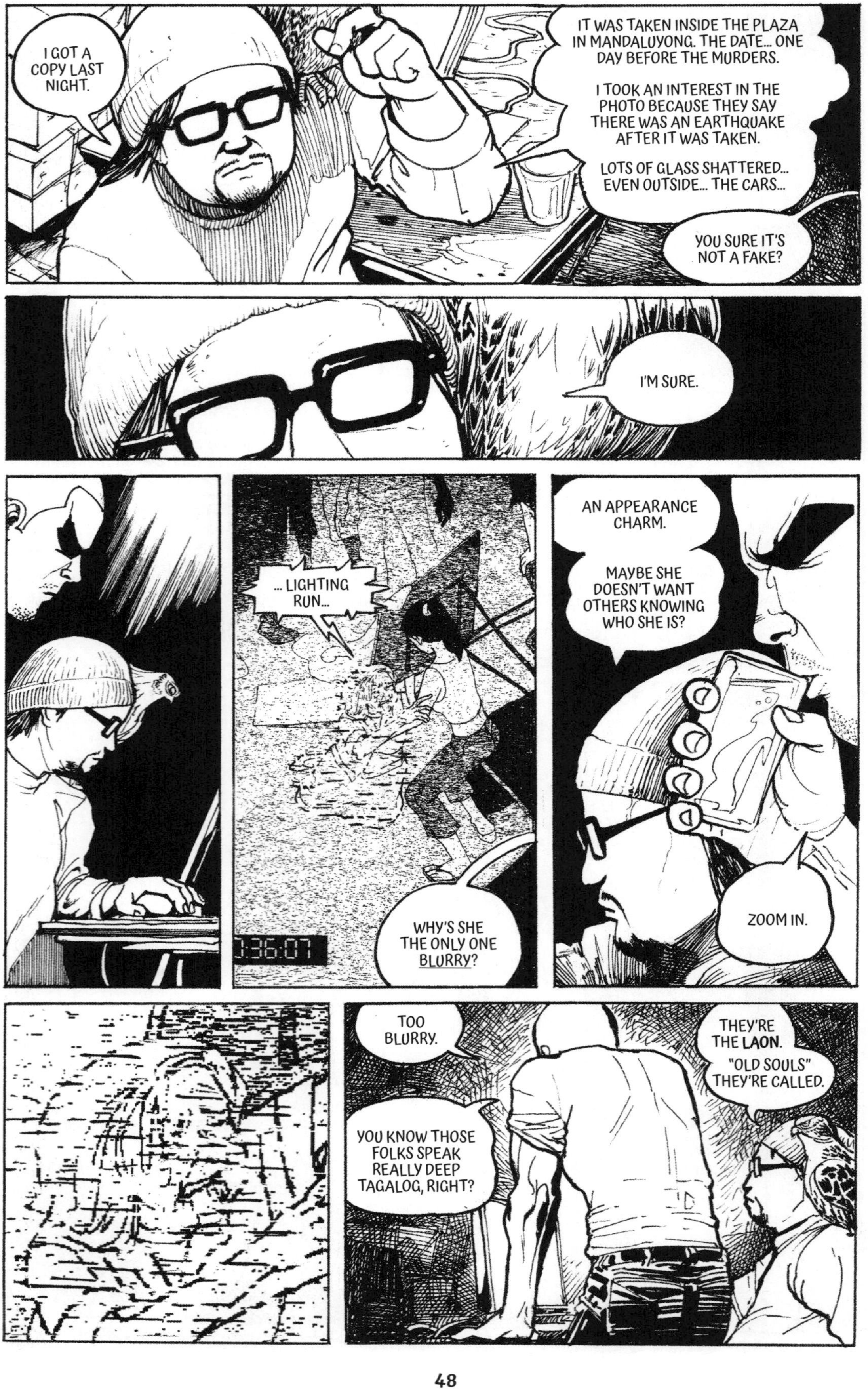
I GOT A COPY LAST NIGHT.
IT WAS TAKEN INSIDE THE PLAZA IN MANDALUYONG. THE DATE... ONE DAY BEFORE THE MURDERS.
I TOOK AN INTEREST IN THE PHOTO BECAUSE THEY SAY THERE WAS AN EARTHQUAKE AFTER IT WAS TAKEN.
LOTS OF GLASS SHATTERED... EVEN OUTSIDE... THE CARS...
YOU SURE IT'S NOT A FAKE?
I'M SURE.
... LIGHTING RUN...
0:36:07
WHY'S SHE THE ONLY ONE BLURRY?
AN APPEARANCE CHARM.
MAYBE SHE DOESN'T WANT OTHERS KNOWING WHO SHE IS?
ZOOM IN.
TOO BLURRY.
THEY'RE THE **LAON**.
"OLD SOULS" THEY'RE CALLED.
YOU KNOW THOSE FOLKS SPEAK REALLY DEEP TAGALOG, RIGHT?

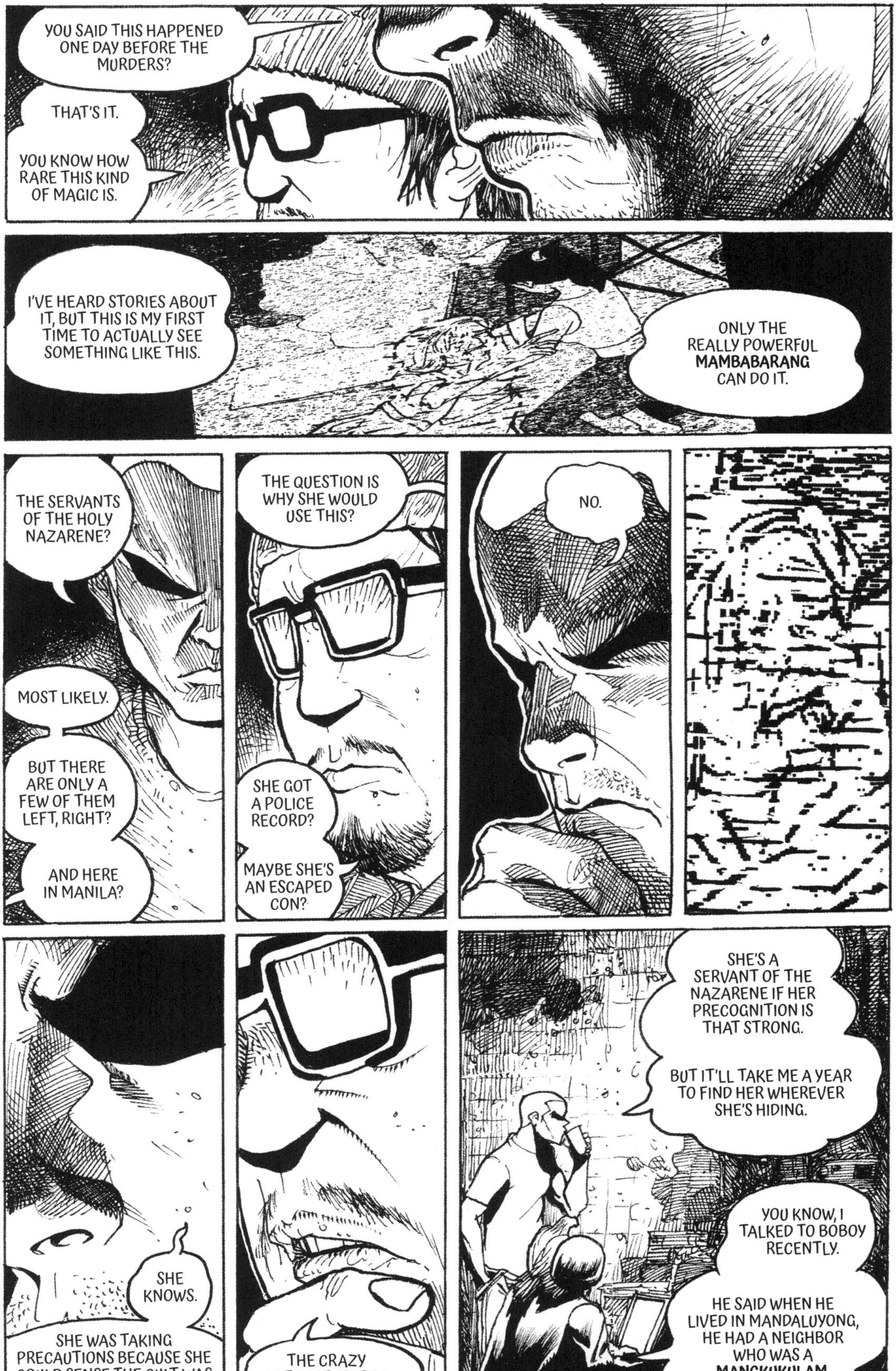
YOU SAID THIS HAPPENED ONE DAY BEFORE THE MURDERS?
THAT'S IT.
YOU KNOW HOW RARE THIS KIND OF MAGIC IS.
I'VE HEARD STORIES ABOUT IT, BUT THIS IS MY FIRST TIME TO ACTUALLY SEE SOMETHING LIKE THIS.
ONLY THE REALLY POWERFUL **MAMBABARANG** CAN DO IT.
THE SERVANTS OF THE HOLY NAZARENE?
MOST LIKELY.
BUT THERE ARE ONLY A FEW OF THEM LEFT, RIGHT?
AND HERE IN MANILA?
THE QUESTION IS WHY SHE WOULD USE THIS?
SHE GOT A POLICE RECORD?
MAYBE SHE'S AN ESCAPED CON?
NO.
SHE KNOWS.
SHE WAS TAKING PRECAUTIONS BECAUSE SHE COULD SENSE THE CULT WAS GOING TO CAUSE TROUBLE.
THE CRAZY WITCH PREPARED FOR IT.
SHE'S A SERVANT OF THE NAZARENE IF HER PRECOGNITION IS THAT STRONG.
BUT IT'LL TAKE ME A YEAR TO FIND HER WHEREVER SHE'S HIDING.
YOU KNOW, I TALKED TO BOBOY RECENTLY.
HE SAID WHEN HE LIVED IN MANDALUYONG, HE HAD A NEIGHBOR WHO WAS A **MANGKUKULAM**.

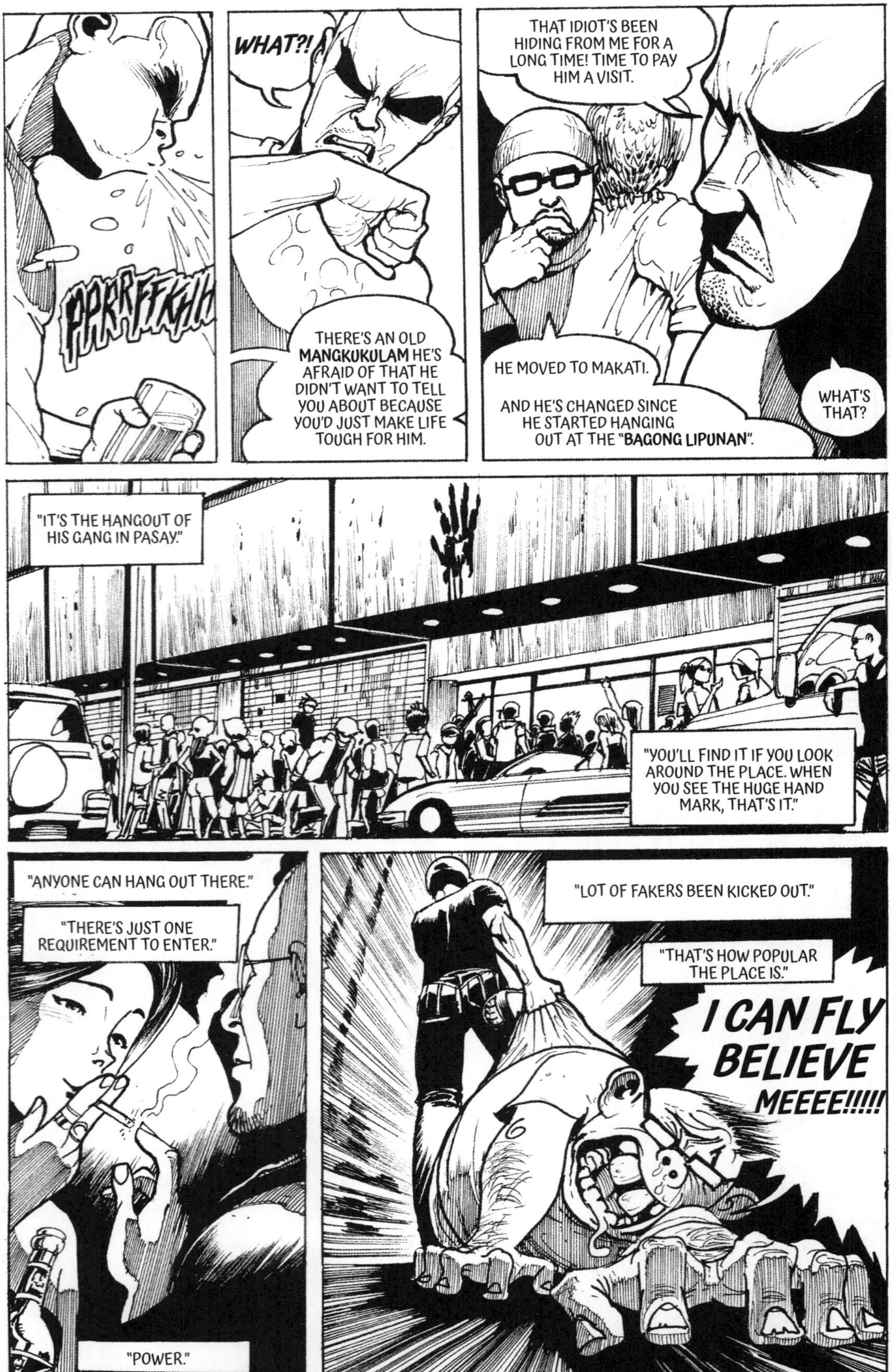
PPRRFFKHH
WHAT?!
THERE'S AN OLD MANGKUKULAM HE'S AFRAID OF THAT HE DIDN'T WANT TO TELL YOU ABOUT BECAUSE YOU'D JUST MAKE LIFE TOUGH FOR HIM.
THAT IDIOT'S BEEN HIDING FROM ME FOR A LONG TIME! TIME TO PAY HIM A VISIT.
HE MOVED TO MAKATI.
AND HE'S CHANGED SINCE HE STARTED HANGING OUT AT THE "BAGONG LIPUNAN".
WHAT'S THAT?
"IT'S THE HANGOUT OF HIS GANG IN PASAY."
"YOU'LL FIND IT IF YOU LOOK AROUND THE PLACE. WHEN YOU SEE THE HUGE HAND MARK, THAT'S IT."
"ANYONE CAN HANG OUT THERE."
"THERE'S JUST ONE REQUIREMENT TO ENTER."
"POWER."
"LOT OF FAKERS BEEN KICKED OUT."
"THAT'S HOW POPULAR THE PLACE IS."
I CAN FLY BELIEVE MEEEE!!!!!

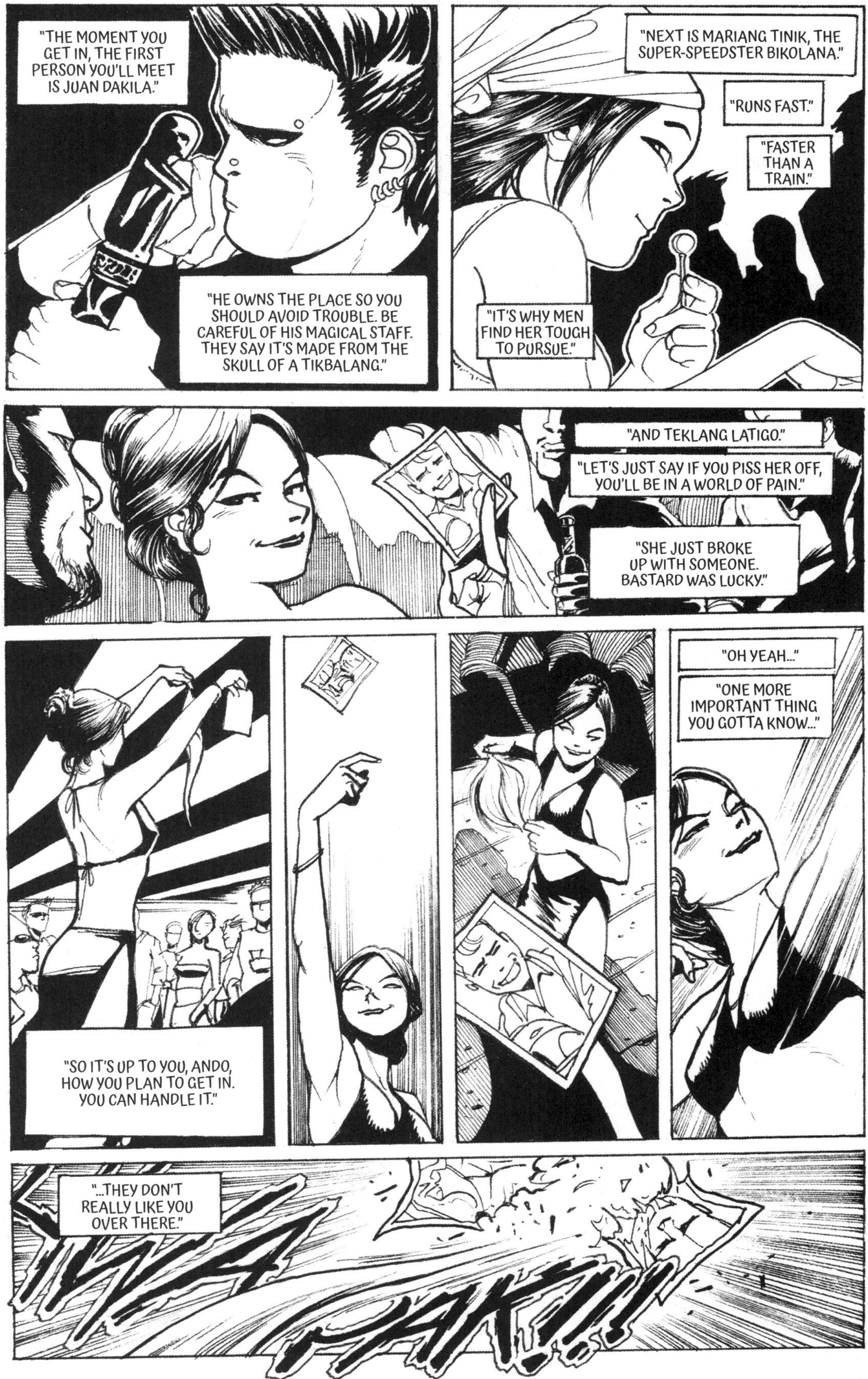

"THE MOMENT YOU GET IN, THE FIRST PERSON YOU'LL MEET IS JUAN DAKILA."
"HE OWNS THE PLACE SO YOU SHOULD AVOID TROUBLE. BE CAREFUL OF HIS MAGICAL STAFF. THEY SAY IT'S MADE FROM THE SKULL OF A TIKBALANG."
"NEXT IS MARIANG TINIK, THE SUPER-SPEEDSTER BIKOLANA."
"RUNS FAST."
"FASTER THAN A TRAIN."
"IT'S WHY MEN FIND HER TOUGH TO PURSUE."
"AND TEKLANG LATIGO."
"LET'S JUST SAY IF YOU PISS HER OFF, YOU'LL BE IN A WORLD OF PAIN."
"SHE JUST BROKE UP WITH SOMEONE. BASTARD WAS LUCKY."
"SO IT'S UP TO YOU, ANDO, HOW YOU PLAN TO GET IN. YOU CAN HANDLE IT."
"OH YEAH..."
"ONE MORE IMPORTANT THING YOU GOTTA KNOW..."
"...THEY DON'T REALLY LIKE YOU OVER THERE."
WA PAK!!

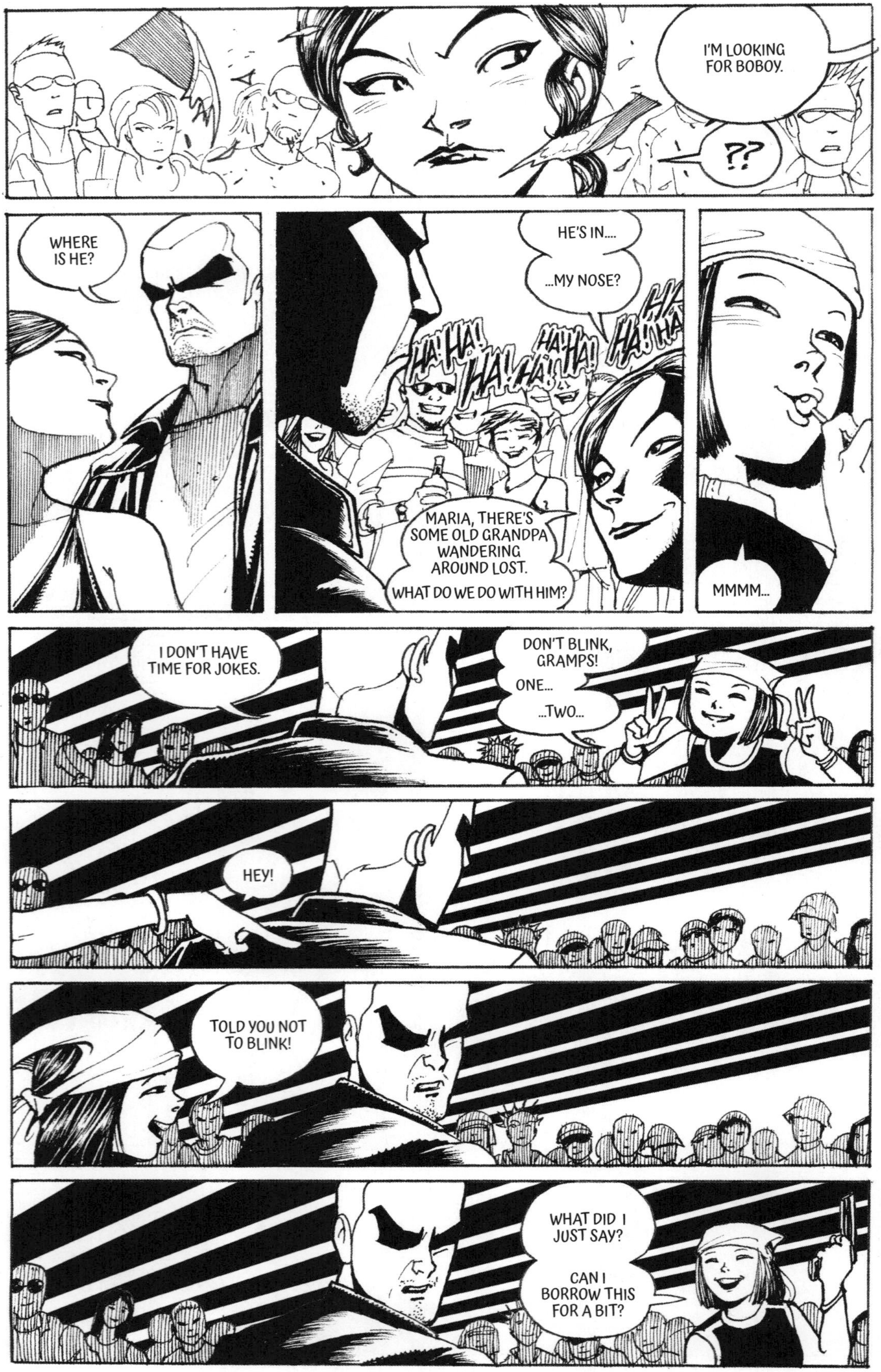
I'M LOOKING FOR BOBOY.
??
WHERE IS HE?
HE'S IN....
...MY NOSE?
HA! HA! HA! HA! HA! HA! HA! HA! HA! HA!
MARIA, THERE'S SOME OLD GRANDPA WANDERING AROUND LOST.
WHAT DO WE DO WITH HIM?
MMMM...
I DON'T HAVE TIME FOR JOKES.
DON'T BLINK, GRAMPS!
ONE...
...TWO...
HEY!
TOLD YOU NOT TO BLINK!
WHAT DID I JUST SAY?
CAN I BORROW THIS FOR A BIT?

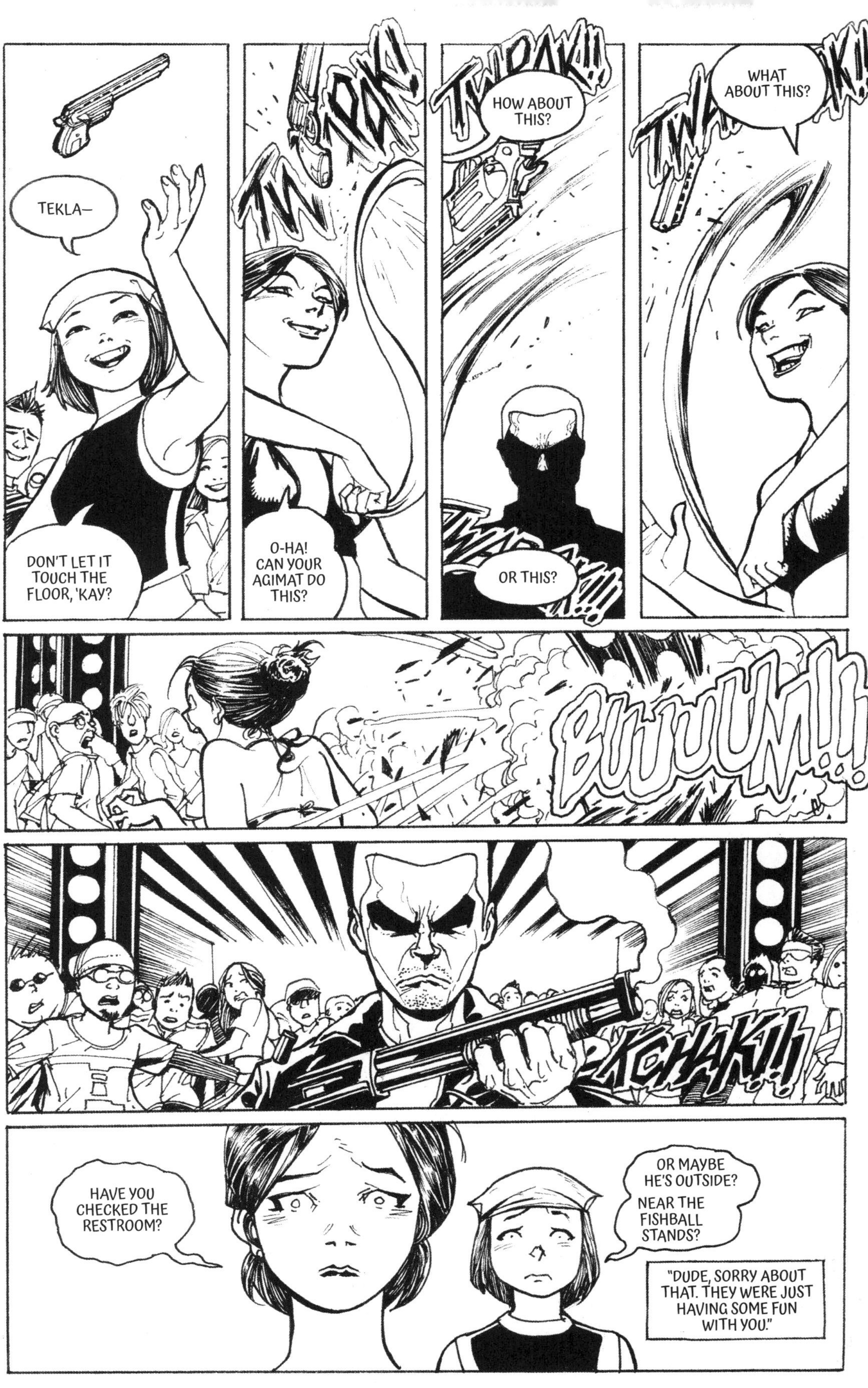
TEKLA—
DON'T LET IT TOUCH THE FLOOR, 'KAY?
O-HA! CAN YOUR AGIMAT DO THIS?
HOW ABOUT THIS?
OR THIS?
WHAT ABOUT THIS?
HAVE YOU CHECKED THE RESTROOM?
OR MAYBE HE'S OUTSIDE?
NEAR THE FISHBALL STANDS?
"DUDE, SORRY ABOUT THAT. THEY WERE JUST HAVING SOME FUN WITH YOU."

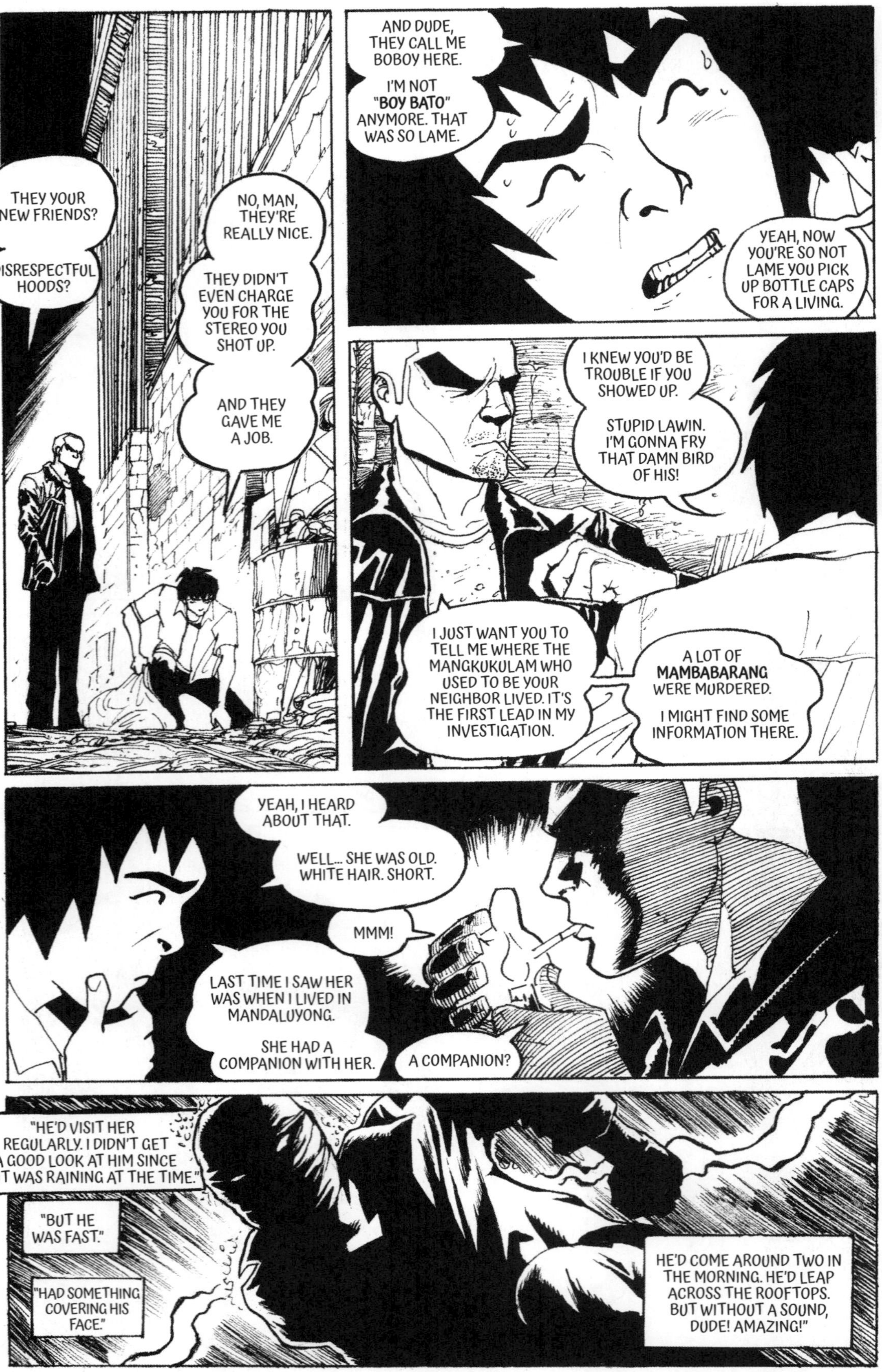
THEY YOUR NEW FRIENDS?
DISRESPECTFUL HOODS?
NO, MAN, THEY'RE REALLY NICE.
THEY DIDN'T EVEN CHARGE YOU FOR THE STEREO YOU SHOT UP.
AND THEY GAVE ME A JOB.
AND DUDE, THEY CALL ME BOBOY HERE.
I'M NOT "BOY BATO" ANYMORE. THAT WAS SO LAME.
YEAH, NOW YOU'RE SO NOT LAME YOU PICK UP BOTTLE CAPS FOR A LIVING.
I KNEW YOU'D BE TROUBLE IF YOU SHOWED UP.
STUPID LAWIN. I'M GONNA FRY THAT DAMN BIRD OF HIS!
I JUST WANT YOU TO TELL ME WHERE THE MANGKUKULAM WHO USED TO BE YOUR NEIGHBOR LIVED. IT'S THE FIRST LEAD IN MY INVESTIGATION.
A LOT OF MAMBABARANG WERE MURDERED.
I MIGHT FIND SOME INFORMATION THERE.
YEAH, I HEARD ABOUT THAT.
WELL... SHE WAS OLD. WHITE HAIR. SHORT.
MMM!
LAST TIME I SAW HER WAS WHEN I LIVED IN MANDALUYONG.
SHE HAD A COMPANION WITH HER.
A COMPANION?
"HE'D VISIT HER REGULARLY. I DIDN'T GET A GOOD LOOK AT HIM SINCE IT WAS RAINING AT THE TIME."
"BUT HE WAS FAST."
"HAD SOMETHING COVERING HIS FACE."
HE'D COME AROUND TWO IN THE MORNING. HE'D LEAP ACROSS THE ROOFTOPS. BUT WITHOUT A SOUND, DUDE! AMAZING!"

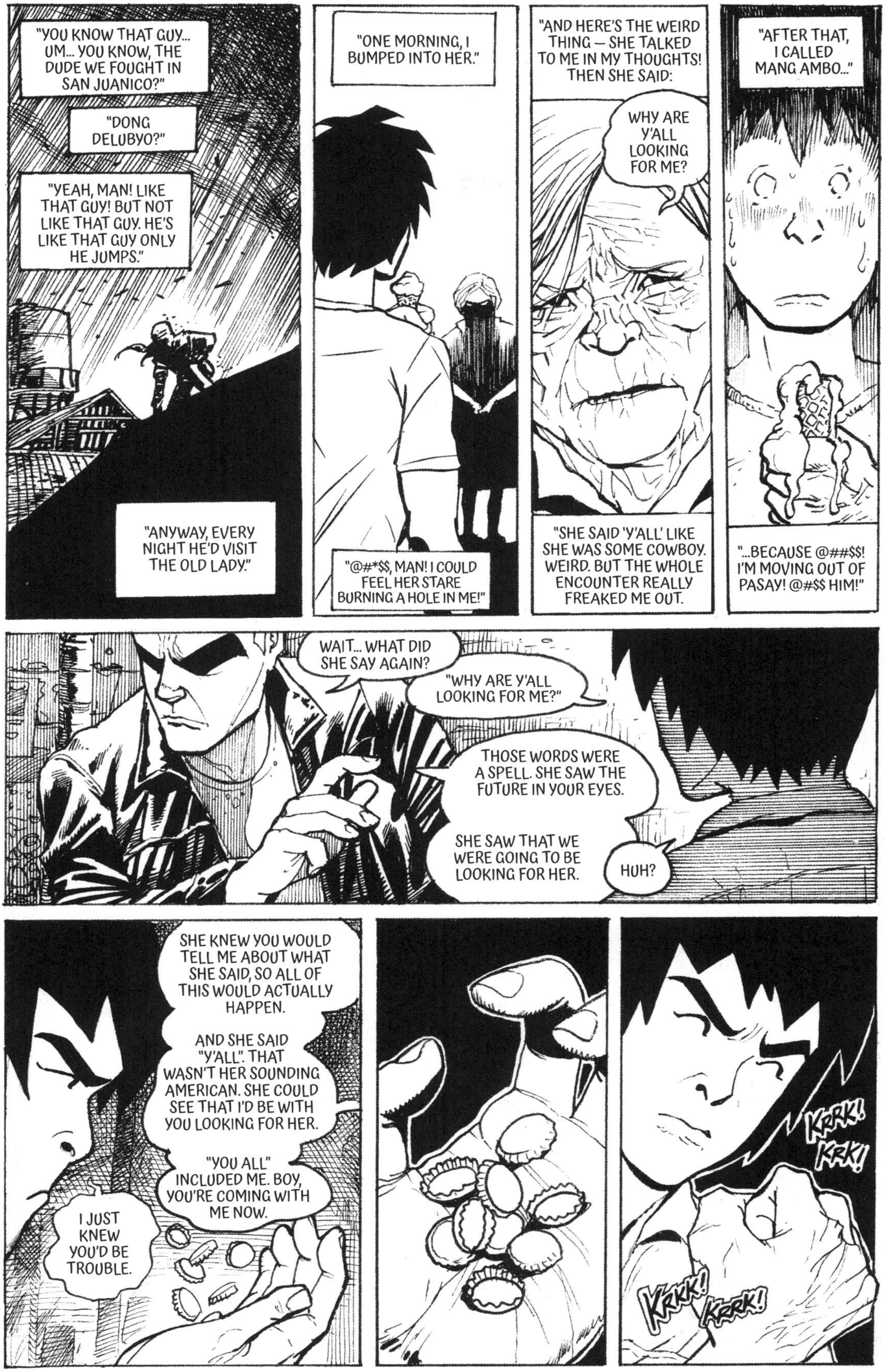
"YOU KNOW THAT GUY... UM... YOU KNOW, THE DUDE WE FOUGHT IN SAN JUANICO?"
"DONG DELUBYO?"
"YEAH, MAN! LIKE THAT GUY! BUT NOT LIKE THAT GUY. HE'S LIKE THAT GUY ONLY HE JUMPS."
"ANYWAY, EVERY NIGHT HE'D VISIT THE OLD LADY."
"ONE MORNING, I BUMPED INTO HER."
"@#*$$, MAN! I COULD FEEL HER STARE BURNING A HOLE IN ME!"
"AND HERE'S THE WEIRD THING — SHE TALKED TO ME IN MY THOUGHTS! THEN SHE SAID:
WHY ARE Y'ALL LOOKING FOR ME?
"SHE SAID 'Y'ALL' LIKE SHE WAS SOME COWBOY. WEIRD. BUT THE WHOLE ENCOUNTER REALLY FREAKED ME OUT.
"AFTER THAT, I CALLED MANG AMBO..."
"...BECAUSE @##$$! I'M MOVING OUT OF PASAY! @#$$ HIM!"
WAIT... WHAT DID SHE SAY AGAIN?
"WHY ARE Y'ALL LOOKING FOR ME?"
THOSE WORDS WERE A SPELL. SHE SAW THE FUTURE IN YOUR EYES.
SHE SAW THAT WE WERE GOING TO BE LOOKING FOR HER.
HUH?
SHE KNEW YOU WOULD TELL ME ABOUT WHAT SHE SAID, SO ALL OF THIS WOULD ACTUALLY HAPPEN.
AND SHE SAID "Y'ALL". THAT WASN'T HER SOUNDING AMERICAN. SHE COULD SEE THAT I'D BE WITH YOU LOOKING FOR HER.
"YOU ALL" INCLUDED ME. BOY, YOU'RE COMING WITH ME NOW.
I JUST KNEW YOU'D BE TROUBLE.
KRRK! KRK!
KRRK! KRRK!

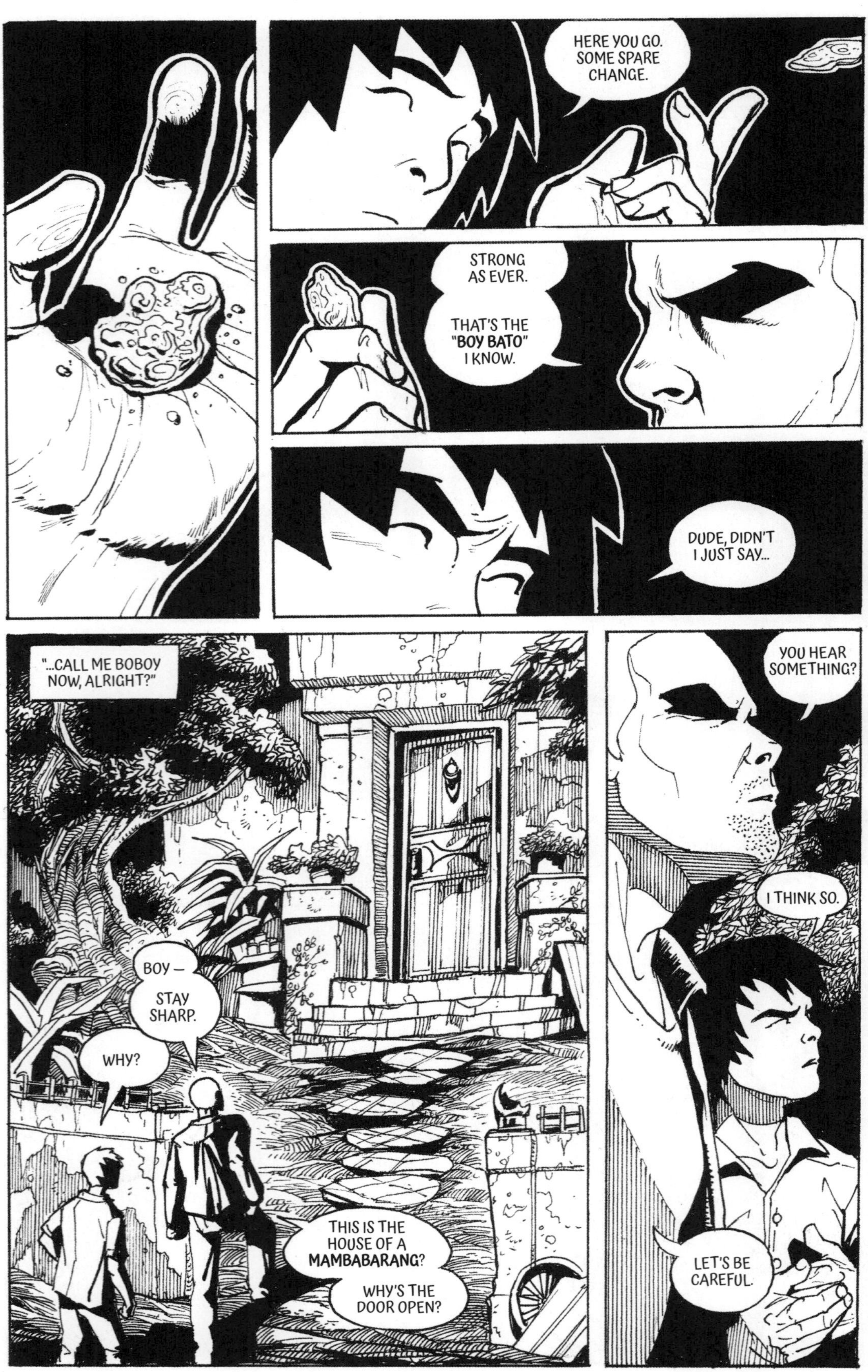

HERE YOU GO. SOME SPARE CHANGE.
STRONG AS EVER.
THAT'S THE **"BOY BATO"** I KNOW.
DUDE, DIDN'T I JUST SAY...
"...CALL ME BOBOY NOW, ALRIGHT?"
BOY —
STAY SHARP.
WHY?
THIS IS THE HOUSE OF A **MAMBABARANG**?
WHY'S THE DOOR OPEN?
YOU HEAR SOMETHING?
I THINK SO.
LET'S BE CAREFUL.

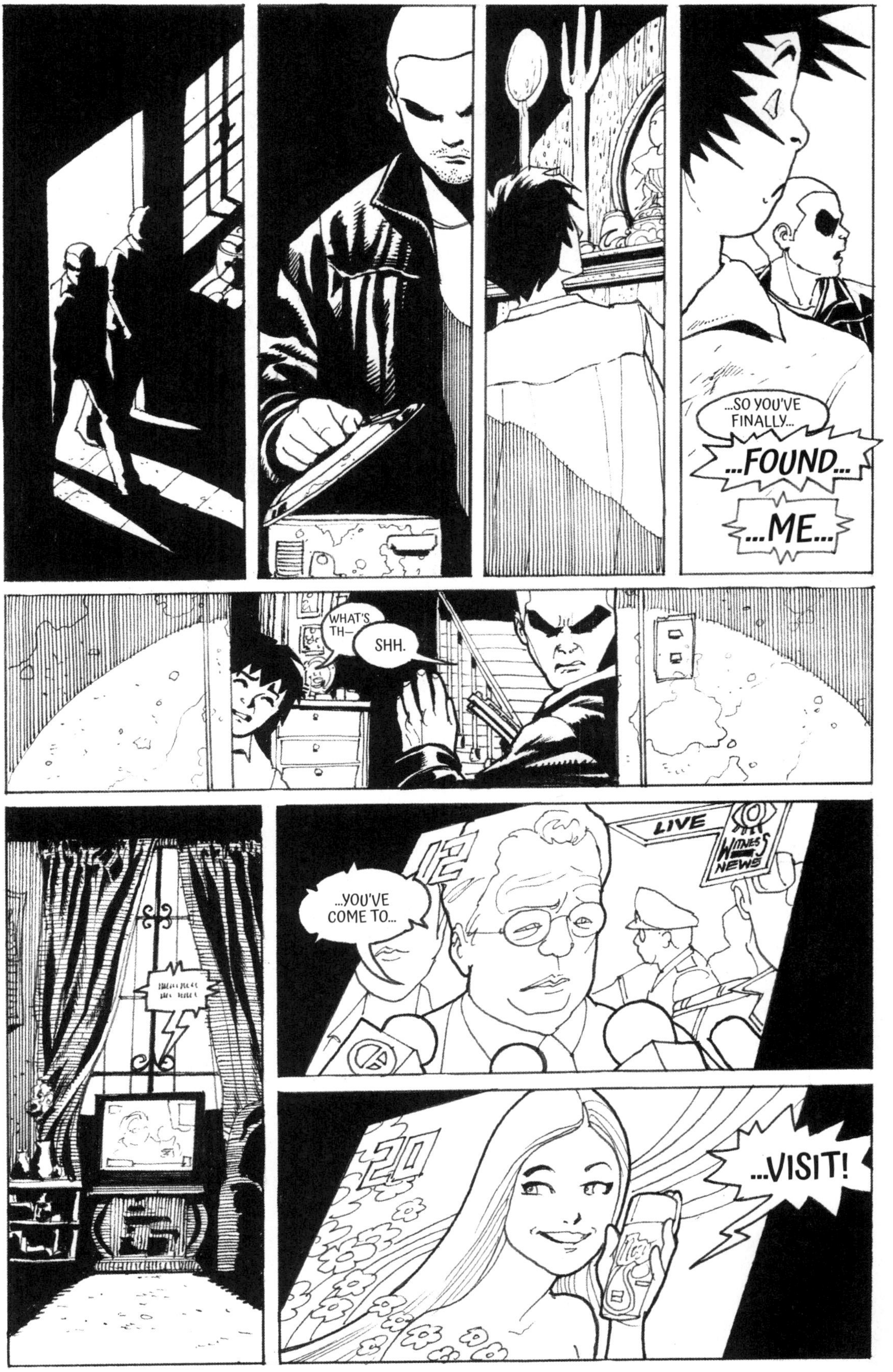
...SO YOU'VE FINALLY...
...FOUND...
...ME...
WHAT'S TH—
SHH.
LIVE
WITNESS NEWS
...YOU'VE COME TO...
...VISIT!

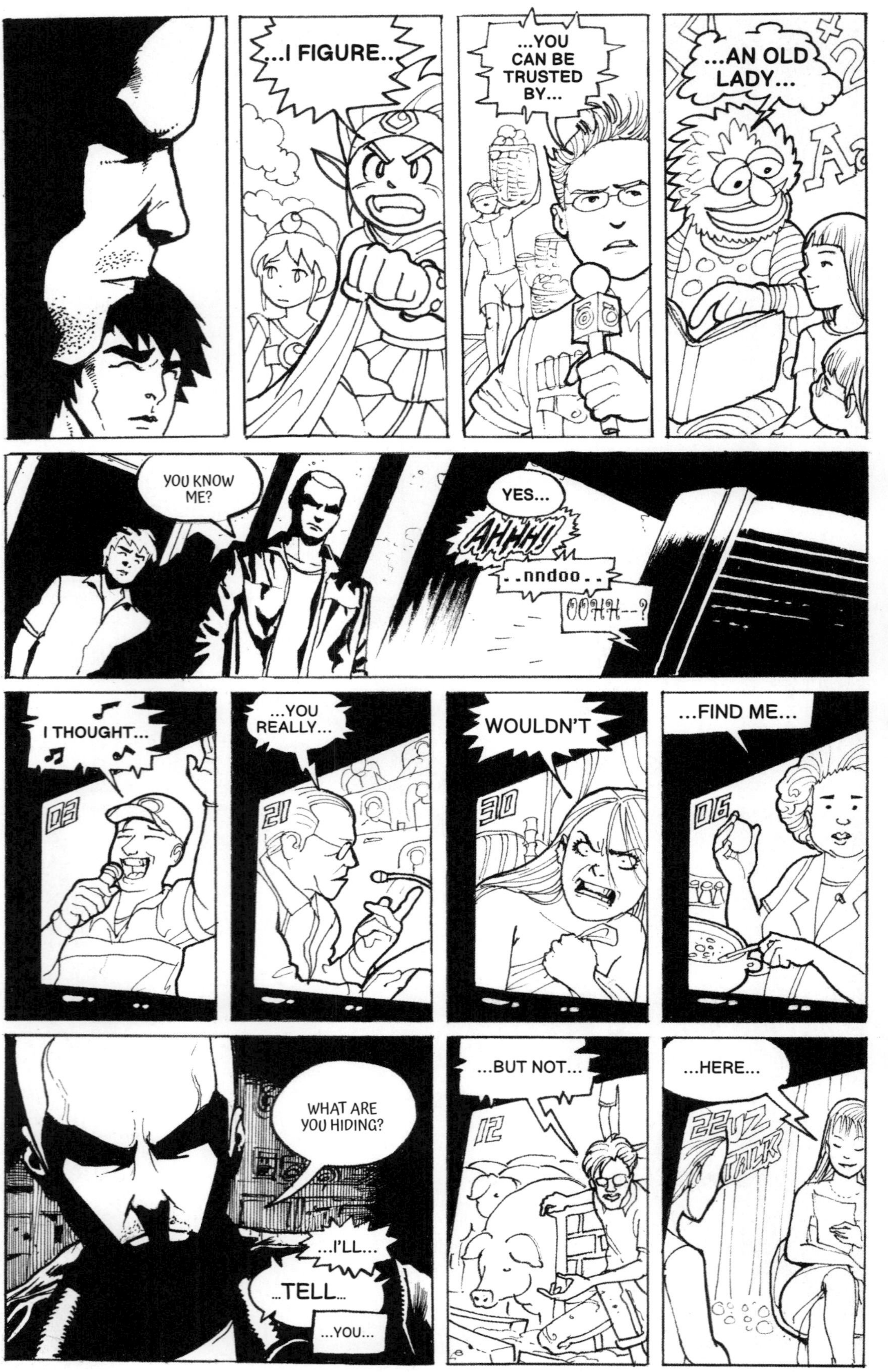
...I FIGURE...
...YOU CAN BE TRUSTED BY...
...AN OLD LADY...
YOU KNOW ME?
YES...
AHHH!
..nndoo..
OOHH--?
I THOUGHT...
...YOU REALLY...
WOULDN'T
...FIND ME...
WHAT ARE YOU HIDING?
...I'LL...
...TELL...
...YOU...
...BUT NOT...
...HERE...

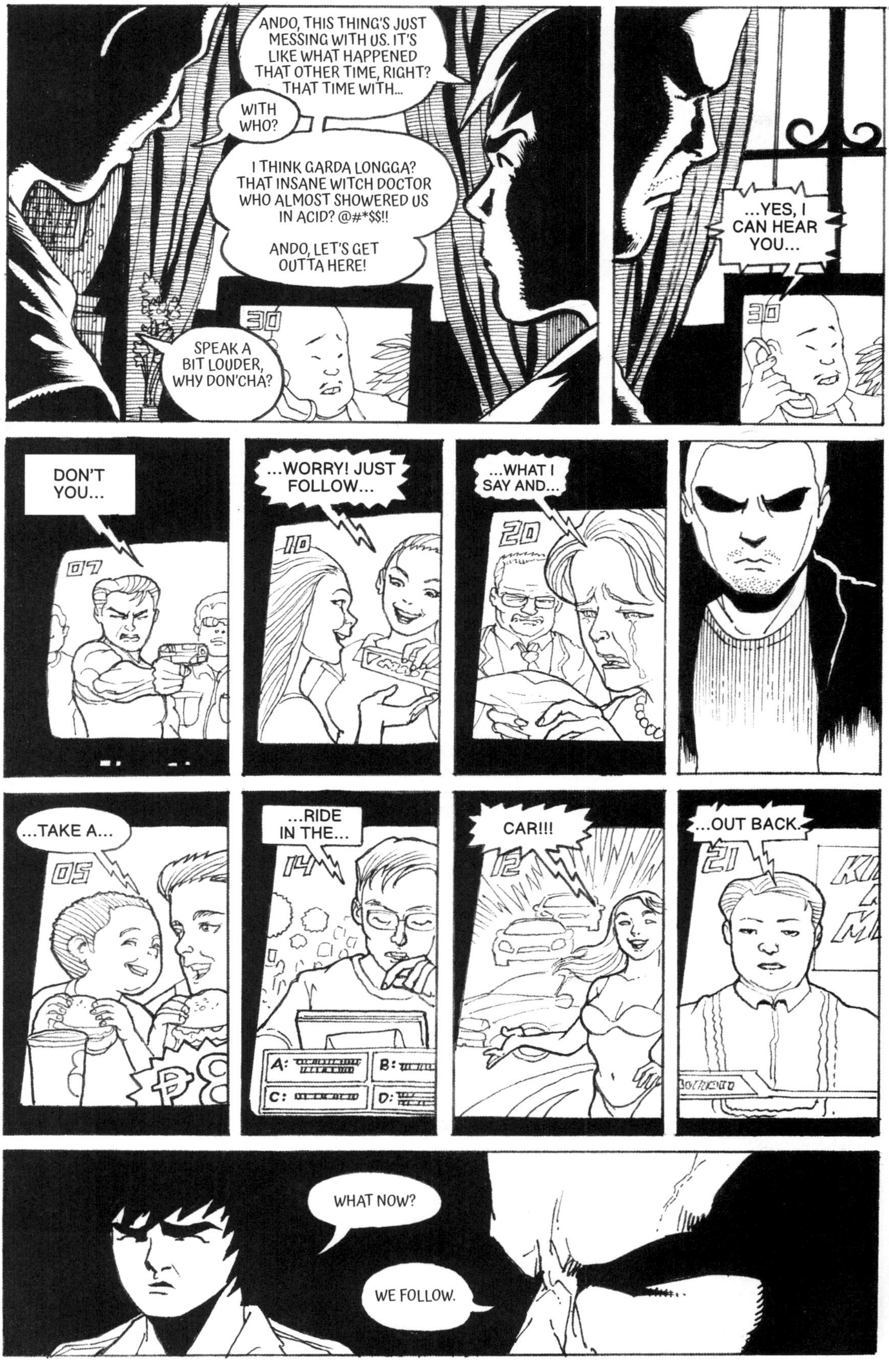
ANDO, THIS THING'S JUST MESSING WITH US. IT'S LIKE WHAT HAPPENED THAT OTHER TIME, RIGHT? THAT TIME WITH...
WITH WHO?
I THINK GARDA LONGGA? THAT INSANE WITCH DOCTOR WHO ALMOST SHOWERED US IN ACID? @#*$$!!
ANDO, LET'S GET OUTTA HERE!
SPEAK A BIT LOUDER, WHY DON'CHA?
...YES, I CAN HEAR YOU...
DON'T YOU...
...WORRY! JUST FOLLOW...
...WHAT I SAY AND...
...TAKE A...
...RIDE IN THE...
CAR!!!
...OUT BACK.
WHAT NOW?
WE FOLLOW.

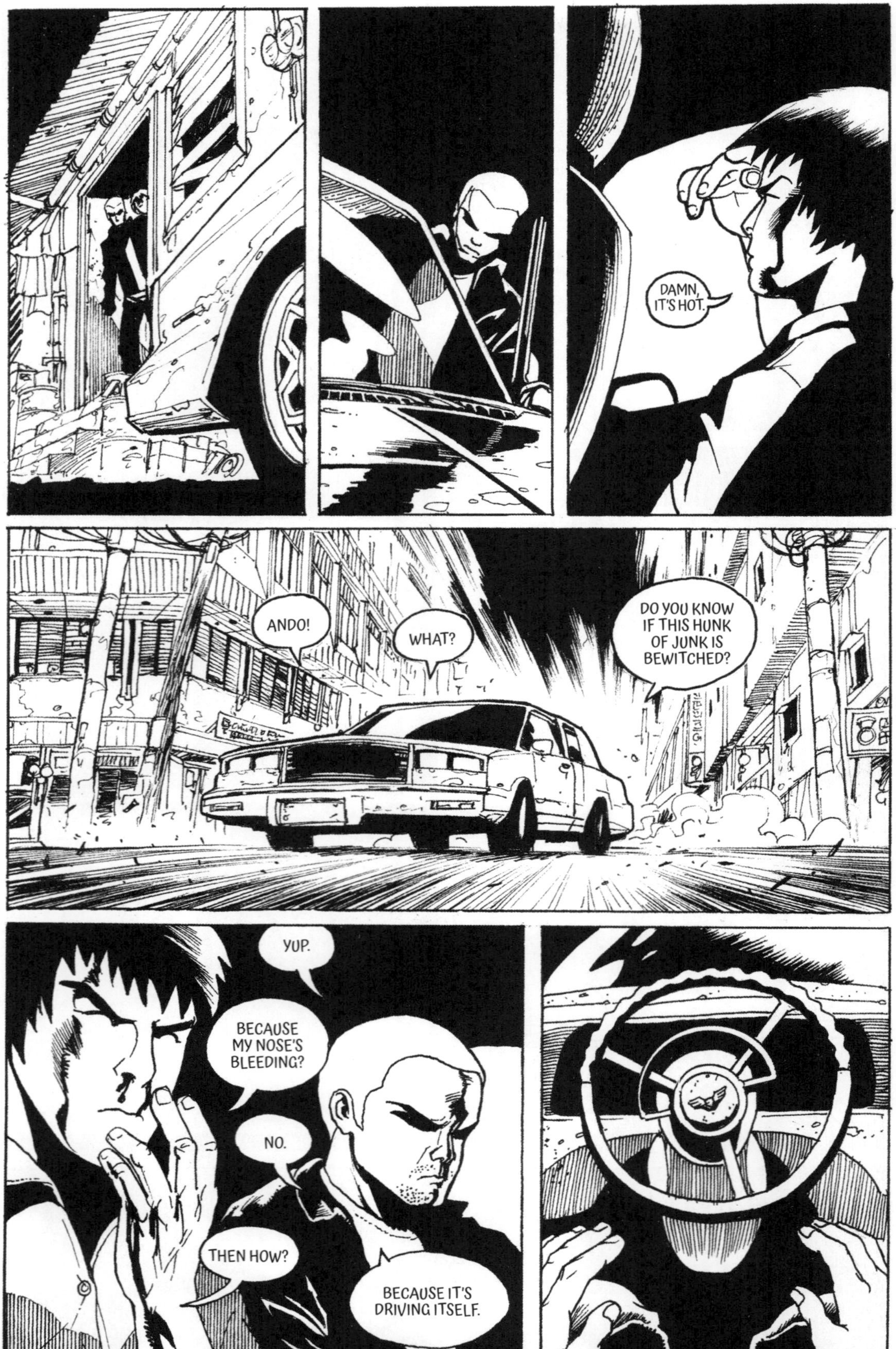
DAMN, IT'S HOT.
ANDO!
WHAT?
DO YOU KNOW IF THIS HUNK OF JUNK IS BEWITCHED?
YUP.
BECAUSE MY NOSE'S BLEEDING?
NO.
THEN HOW?
BECAUSE IT'S DRIVING ITSELF.

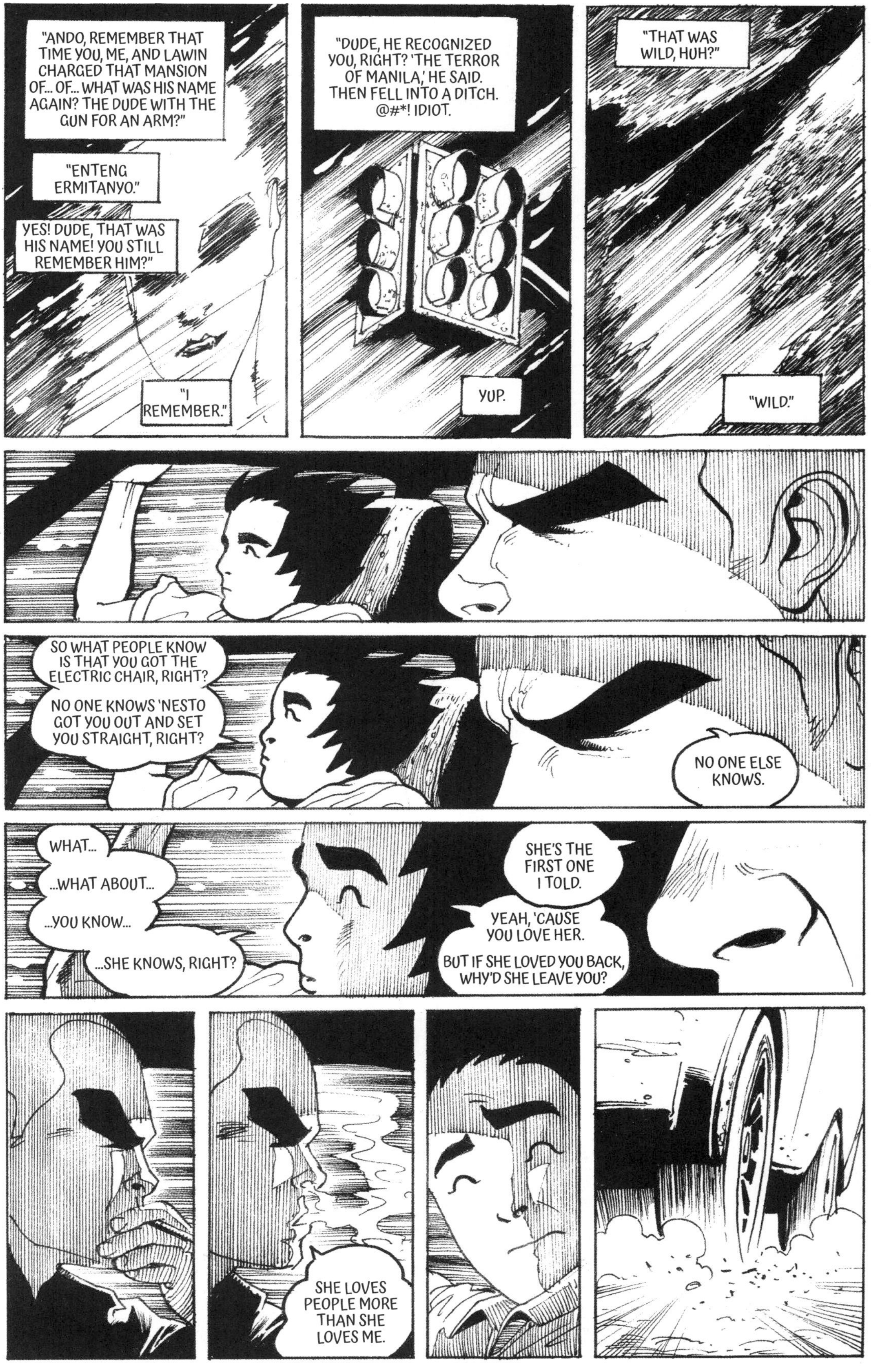
"ANDO, REMEMBER THAT TIME YOU, ME, AND LAWIN CHARGED THAT MANSION OF... OF... WHAT WAS HIS NAME AGAIN? THE DUDE WITH THE GUN FOR AN ARM?"
"ENTENG ERMITANYO."
YES! DUDE, THAT WAS HIS NAME! YOU STILL REMEMBER HIM?"
"I REMEMBER."
"DUDE, HE RECOGNIZED YOU, RIGHT? 'THE TERROR OF MANILA,' HE SAID. THEN FELL INTO A DITCH. @#*! IDIOT.
YUP.
"THAT WAS WILD, HUH?"
"WILD."
SO WHAT PEOPLE KNOW IS THAT YOU GOT THE ELECTRIC CHAIR, RIGHT?
NO ONE KNOWS 'NESTO GOT YOU OUT AND SET YOU STRAIGHT, RIGHT?
NO ONE ELSE KNOWS.
WHAT...
...WHAT ABOUT...
...YOU KNOW...
...SHE KNOWS, RIGHT?
SHE'S THE FIRST ONE I TOLD.
YEAH, 'CAUSE YOU LOVE HER.
BUT IF SHE LOVED YOU BACK, WHY'D SHE LEAVE YOU?
SHE LOVES PEOPLE MORE THAN SHE LOVES ME.

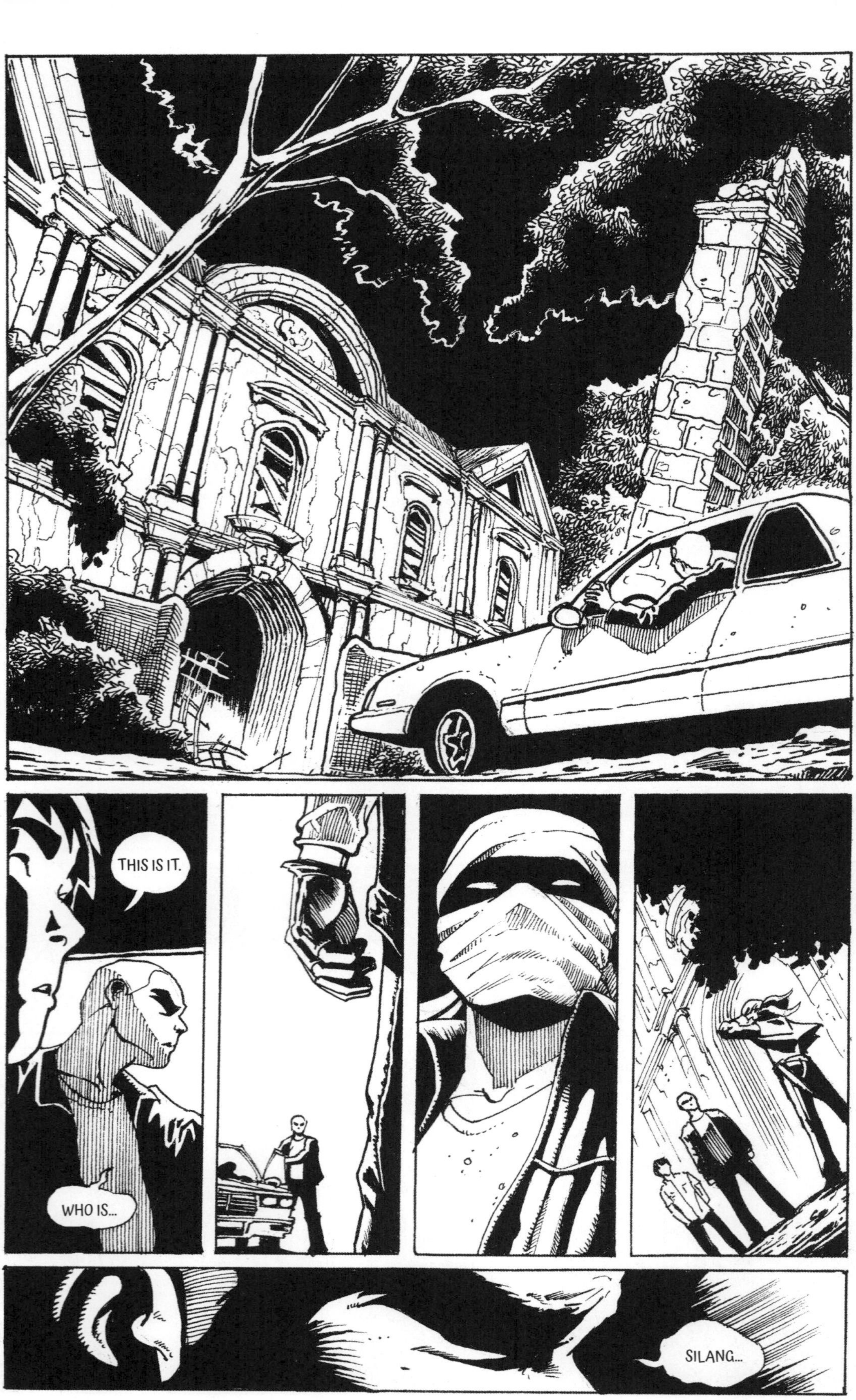
THIS IS IT.
WHO IS...
SILANG...

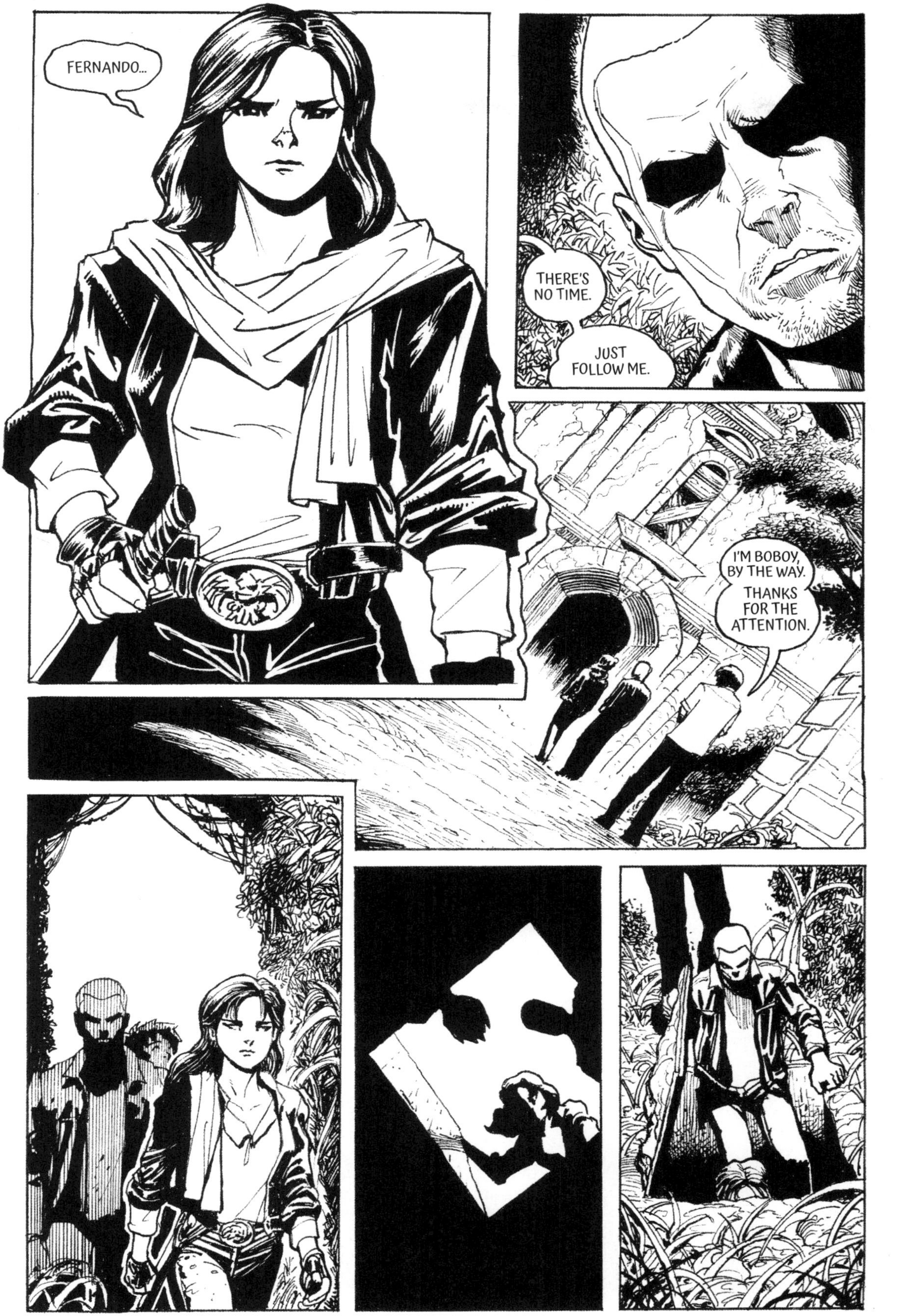
FERNANDO...
THERE'S NO TIME.
JUST FOLLOW ME.
I'M BOBOY, BY THE WAY.
THANKS FOR THE ATTENTION.

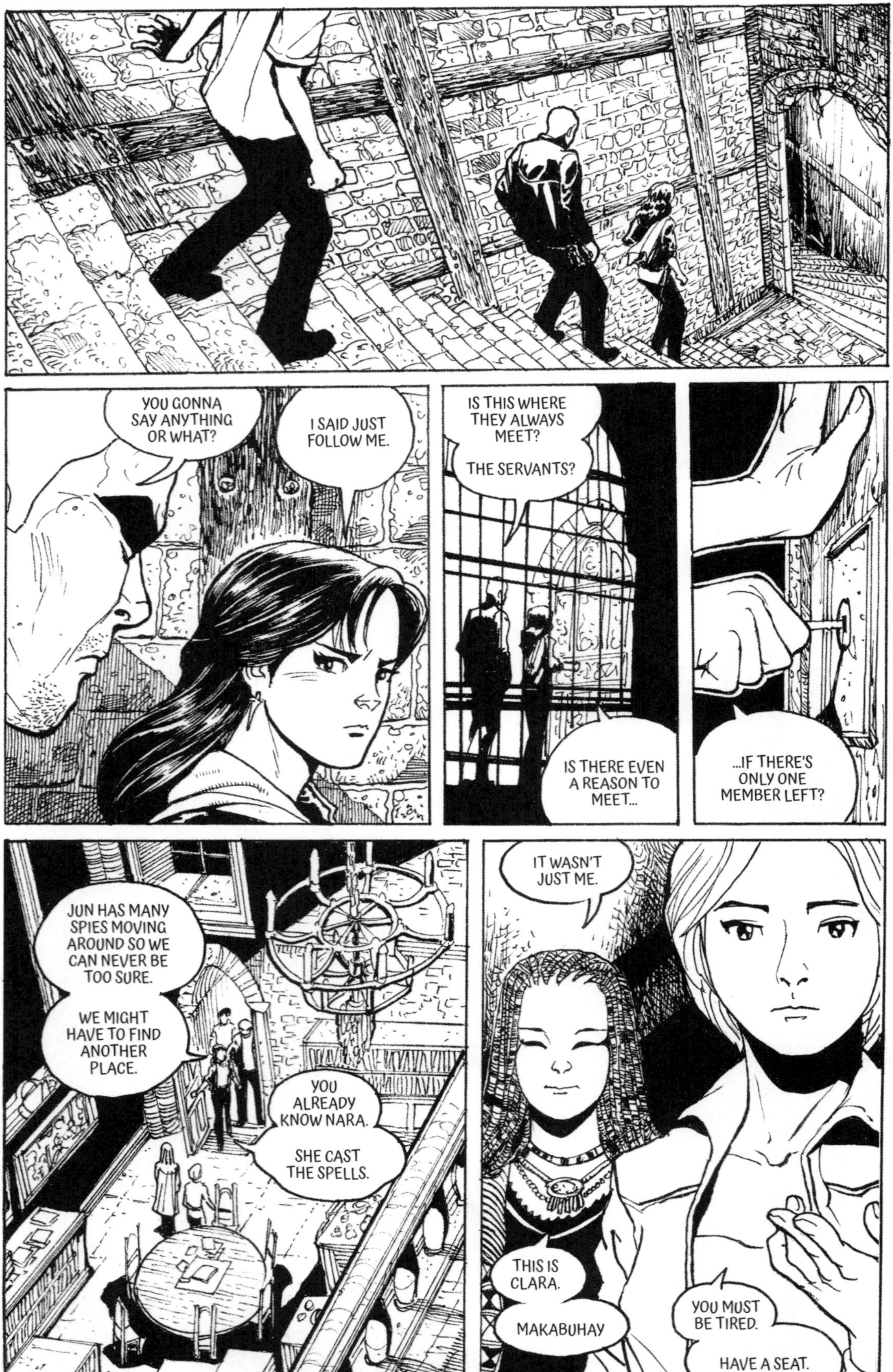
YOU GONNA SAY ANYTHING OR WHAT?
I SAID JUST FOLLOW ME.
IS THIS WHERE THEY ALWAYS MEET?
THE SERVANTS?
IS THERE EVEN A REASON TO MEET...
...IF THERE'S ONLY ONE MEMBER LEFT?
JUN HAS MANY SPIES MOVING AROUND SO WE CAN NEVER BE TOO SURE.
WE MIGHT HAVE TO FIND ANOTHER PLACE.
YOU ALREADY KNOW NARA.
SHE CAST THE SPELLS.
IT WASN'T JUST ME.
THIS IS CLARA.
MAKABUHAY
YOU MUST BE TIRED.
HAVE A SEAT.

YOU... WHY WEREN'T YOU IN ILOCOS?

WHAT'S THIS REALLY ABOUT?

"IF FOR A HOLY AND HIGHER PURPOSE YOU ARE NEEDED BY OTHERS..."

"...YOU WILL LEARN HOW TO BE TAKEN BY THE LORD IN THE WOMB OF THE WAVES."

...NARA USED TO BE MY STUDENT IN SPELLCASTING.

SILANG HAS BEEN A DEAR FRIEND...

...EVEN BEFORE YOU TWO MET.

THEY HELPED ME ESCAPE AND HID ME AWAY.

EVEN BACK THEN I ALREADY SENSED IN A DREAM THE DARK DAYS THAT ARE COMING.

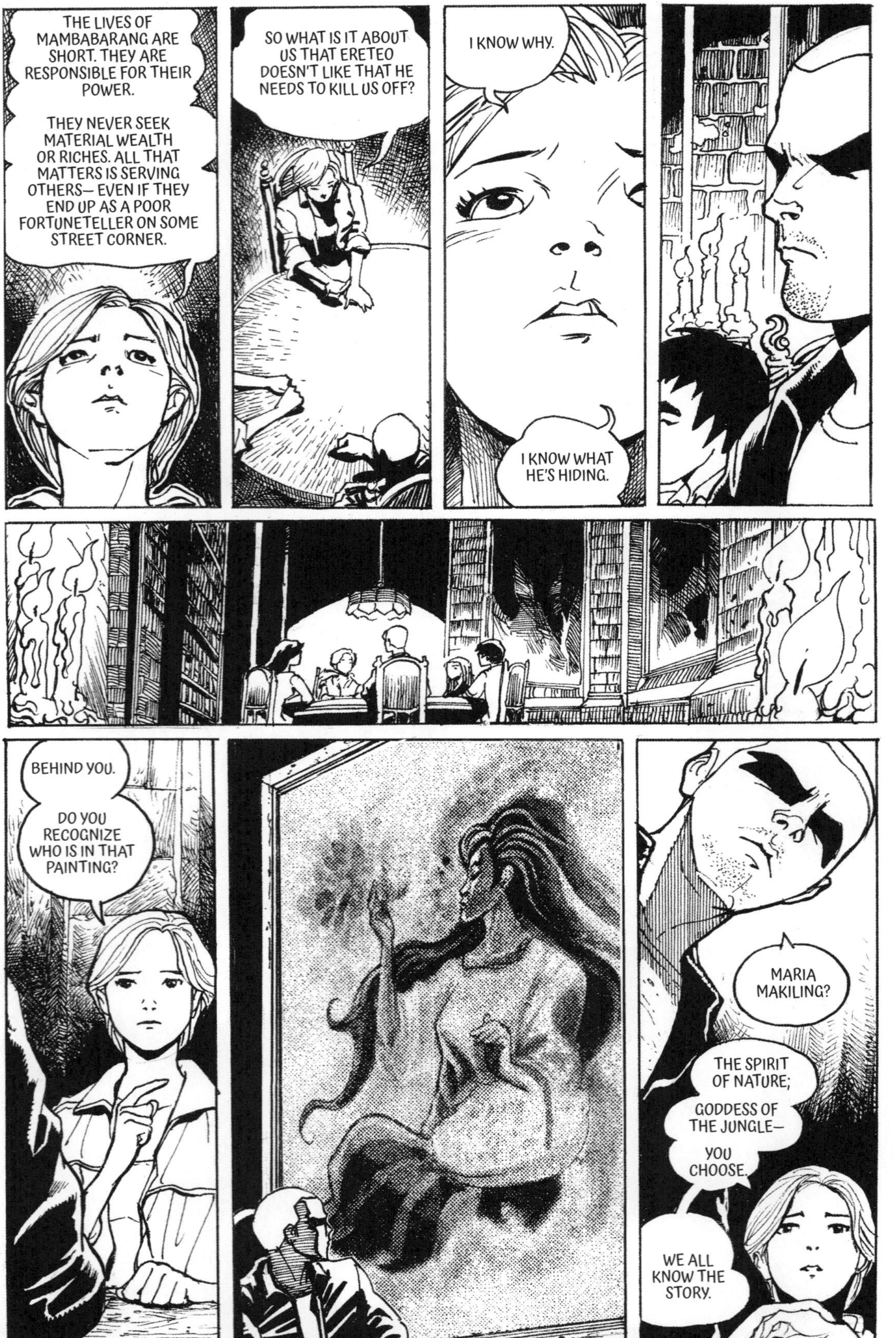

THE LIVES OF MAMBABARANG ARE SHORT. THEY ARE RESPONSIBLE FOR THEIR POWER.
THEY NEVER SEEK MATERIAL WEALTH OR RICHES. ALL THAT MATTERS IS SERVING OTHERS— EVEN IF THEY END UP AS A POOR FORTUNETELLER ON SOME STREET CORNER.
SO WHAT IS IT ABOUT US THAT ERETEO DOESN'T LIKE THAT HE NEEDS TO KILL US OFF?
I KNOW WHY.
I KNOW WHAT HE'S HIDING.
BEHIND YOU.
DO YOU RECOGNIZE WHO IS IN THAT PAINTING?
MARIA MAKILING?
THE SPIRIT OF NATURE;
GODDESS OF THE JUNGLE—
YOU CHOOSE.
WE ALL KNOW THE STORY.

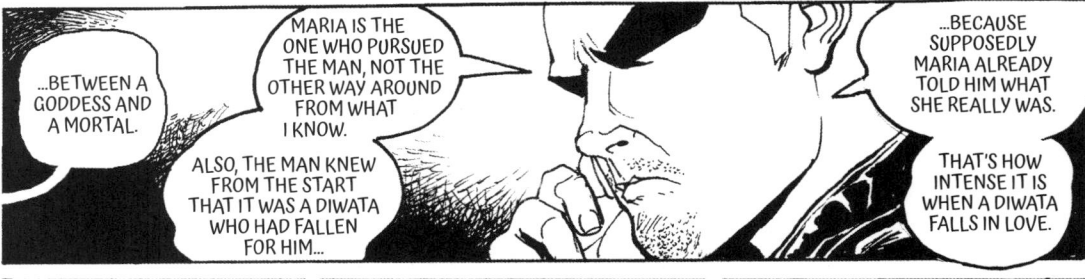

"THE GODDESS MARIA WAS JUST AN OBSERVER FROM THE WORLD ABOVE."

BUT THE HEART CANNOT BE DENIED ONCE SOMETHING IN IT STIRS.

IT BEAT FOR A MORTAL, A KATIPUNERO WHO SACRIFICED IN HER WOODS...

...WHO DEFENDED MARIA'S HOME FROM THE INVADING SPANIARDS WHO WERE DESECRATING IT IN THE NAME OF WEAPONS AND WAR.

THAT IS WHEN MARIA FELT FOR THE FIRST TIME TRUE LOVE.

SHE TOOK HUMAN FORM AND REVEALED HERSELF TO HIM.

SHE THANKED HIM.

AND SO STARTED AN AFFECTION THAT WOULD GROW INTO A LOVE FOR THE AGES...

...BETWEEN A GODDESS AND A MORTAL.

MARIA IS THE ONE WHO PURSUED THE MAN, NOT THE OTHER WAY AROUND FROM WHAT I KNOW.

ALSO, THE MAN KNEW FROM THE START THAT IT WAS A DIWATA WHO HAD FALLEN FOR HIM...

...BECAUSE SUPPOSEDLY MARIA ALREADY TOLD HIM WHAT SHE REALLY WAS.

THAT'S HOW INTENSE IT IS WHEN A DIWATA FALLS IN LOVE.

PERHAPS... FROM WHAT IS WRITTEN, THIS IS THE ONLY INCIDENT WHERE SHE TRUSTED A MORTAL.

BUT THEY DIDN'T LAST, RIGHT?

BECAUSE THAT WAS A FORBIDDEN LOVE, RIGHT?

ONE WAS MORTAL...

AND THE OTHER...

ALL WE KNOW IS THAT MARIA WAS CURSED BECAUSE OF THEIR LOVE.

THE CURSE OF FORGETFULNESS.

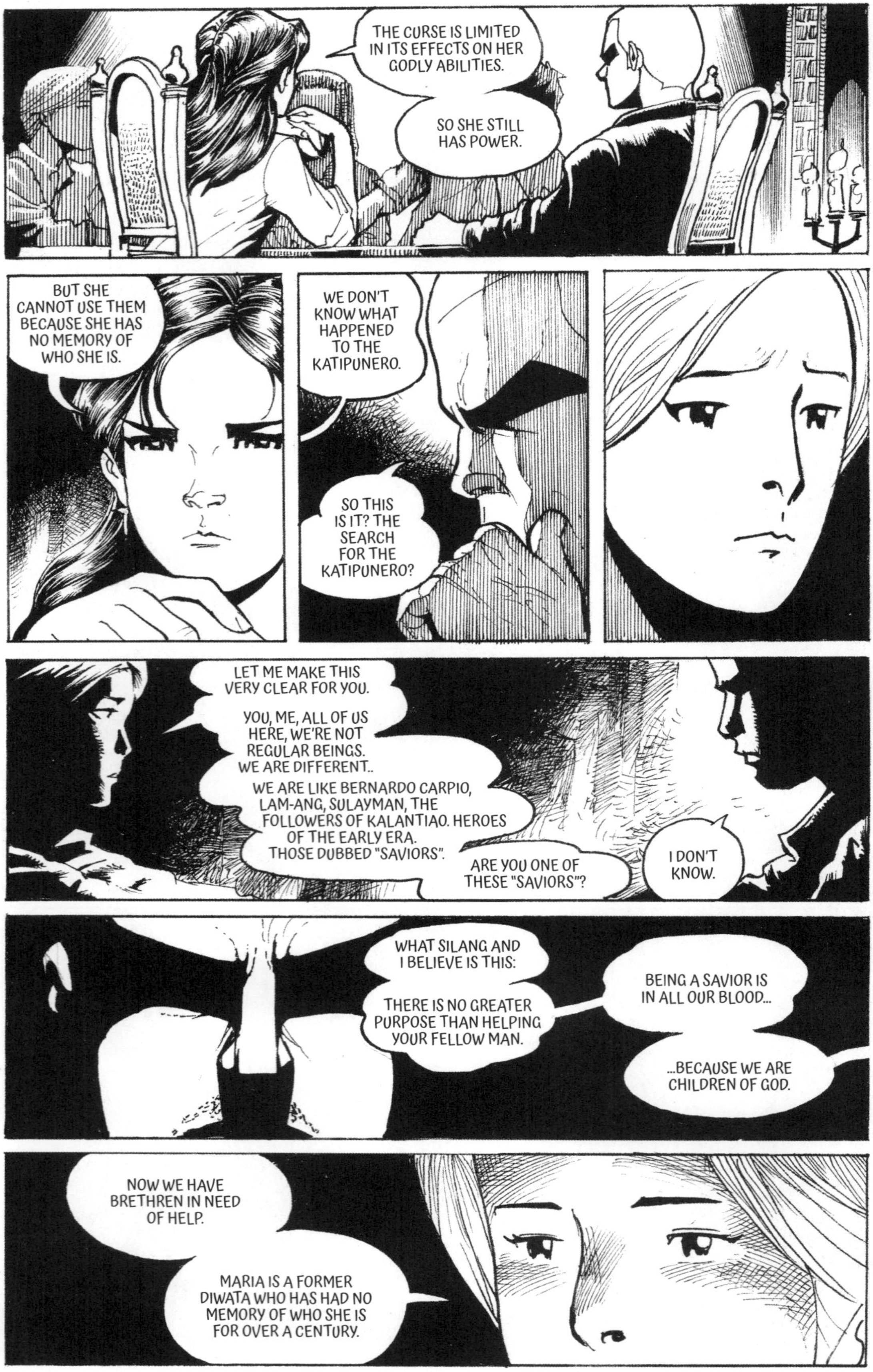
THE CURSE IS LIMITED IN ITS EFFECTS ON HER GODLY ABILITIES.
SO SHE STILL HAS POWER.
BUT SHE CANNOT USE THEM BECAUSE SHE HAS NO MEMORY OF WHO SHE IS.
WE DON'T KNOW WHAT HAPPENED TO THE KATIPUNERO.
SO THIS IS IT? THE SEARCH FOR THE KATIPUNERO?
LET ME MAKE THIS VERY CLEAR FOR YOU.
YOU, ME, ALL OF US HERE, WE'RE NOT REGULAR BEINGS. WE ARE DIFFERENT..
WE ARE LIKE BERNARDO CARPIO, LAM-ANG, SULAYMAN, THE FOLLOWERS OF KALANTIAO. HEROES OF THE EARLY ERA. THOSE DUBBED "SAVIORS".
ARE YOU ONE OF THESE "SAVIORS"?
I DON'T KNOW.
WHAT SILANG AND I BELIEVE IS THIS:
THERE IS NO GREATER PURPOSE THAN HELPING YOUR FELLOW MAN.
BEING A SAVIOR IS IN ALL OUR BLOOD...
...BECAUSE WE ARE CHILDREN OF GOD.
NOW WE HAVE BRETHREN IN NEED OF HELP.
MARIA IS A FORMER DIWATA WHO HAS HAD NO MEMORY OF WHO SHE IS FOR OVER A CENTURY.

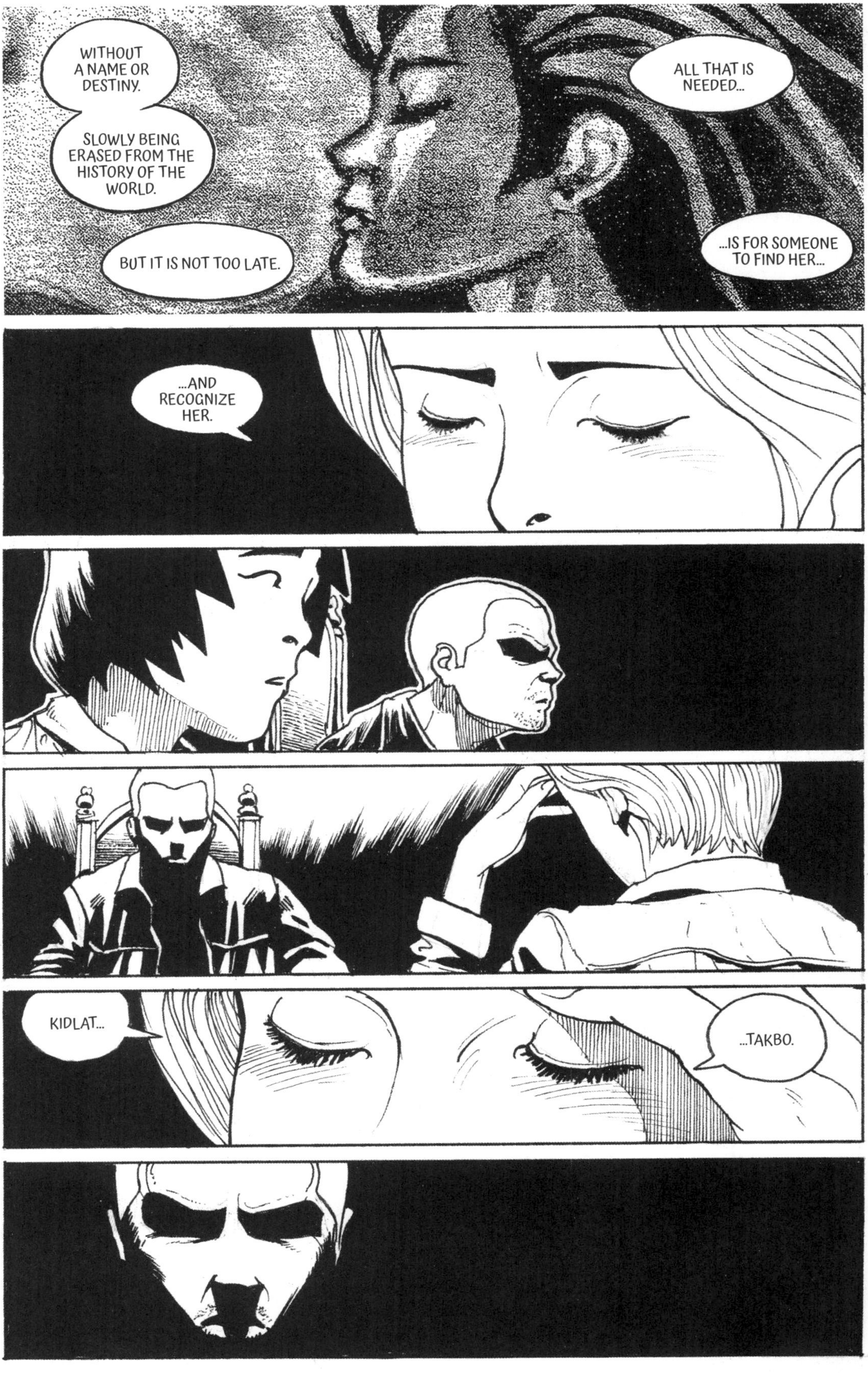
WITHOUT A NAME OR DESTINY.
SLOWLY BEING ERASED FROM THE HISTORY OF THE WORLD.
BUT IT IS NOT TOO LATE.
ALL THAT IS NEEDED...
...IS FOR SOMEONE TO FIND HER...
...AND RECOGNIZE HER.
KIDLAT...
...TAKBO.

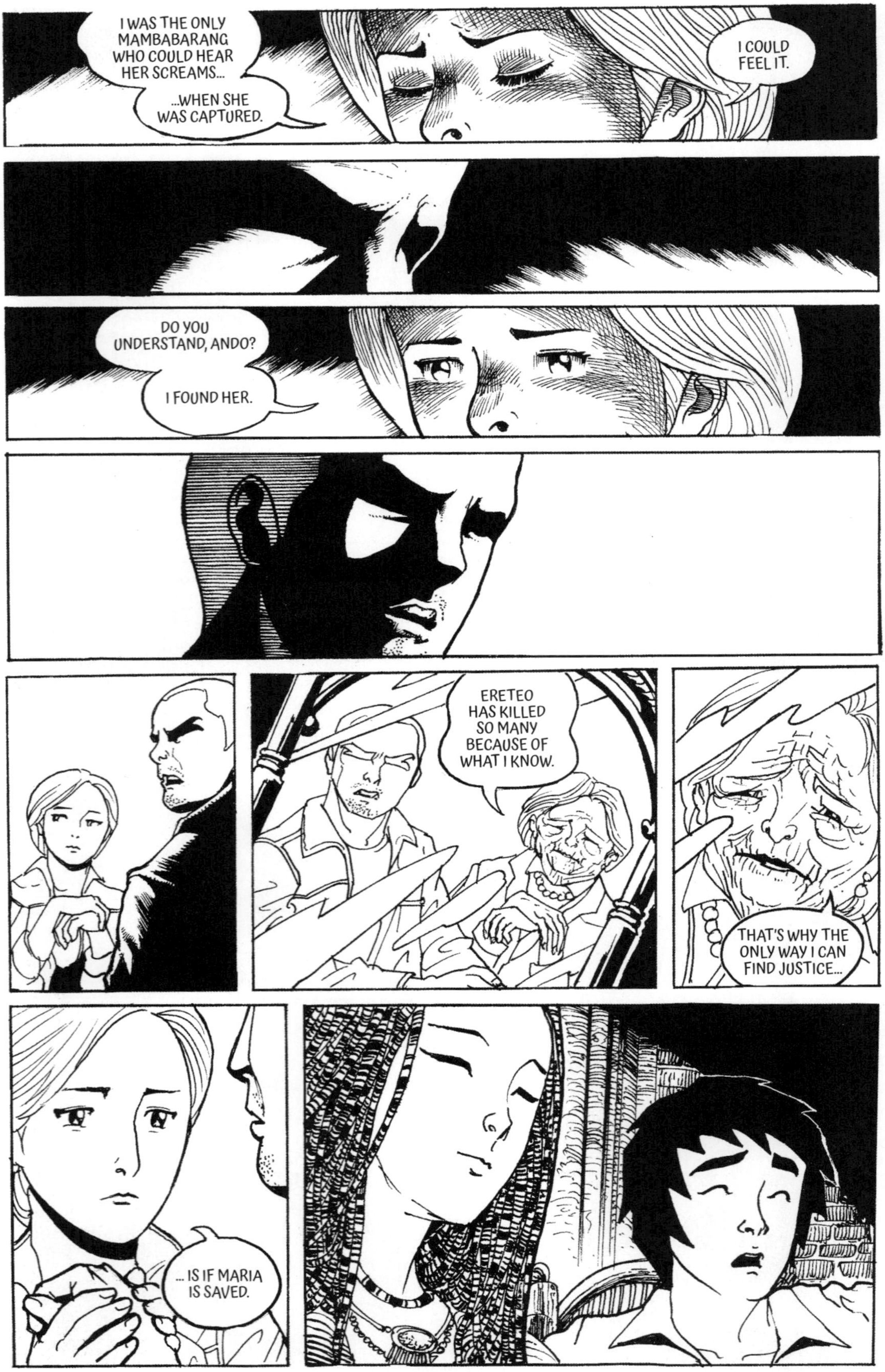
I WAS THE ONLY MAMBABARANG WHO COULD HEAR HER SCREAMS...
...WHEN SHE WAS CAPTURED.
I COULD FEEL IT.
DO YOU UNDERSTAND, ANDO?
I FOUND HER.
ERETEO HAS KILLED SO MANY BECAUSE OF WHAT I KNOW.
THAT'S WHY THE ONLY WAY I CAN FIND JUSTICE...
...IS IF MARIA IS SAVED.

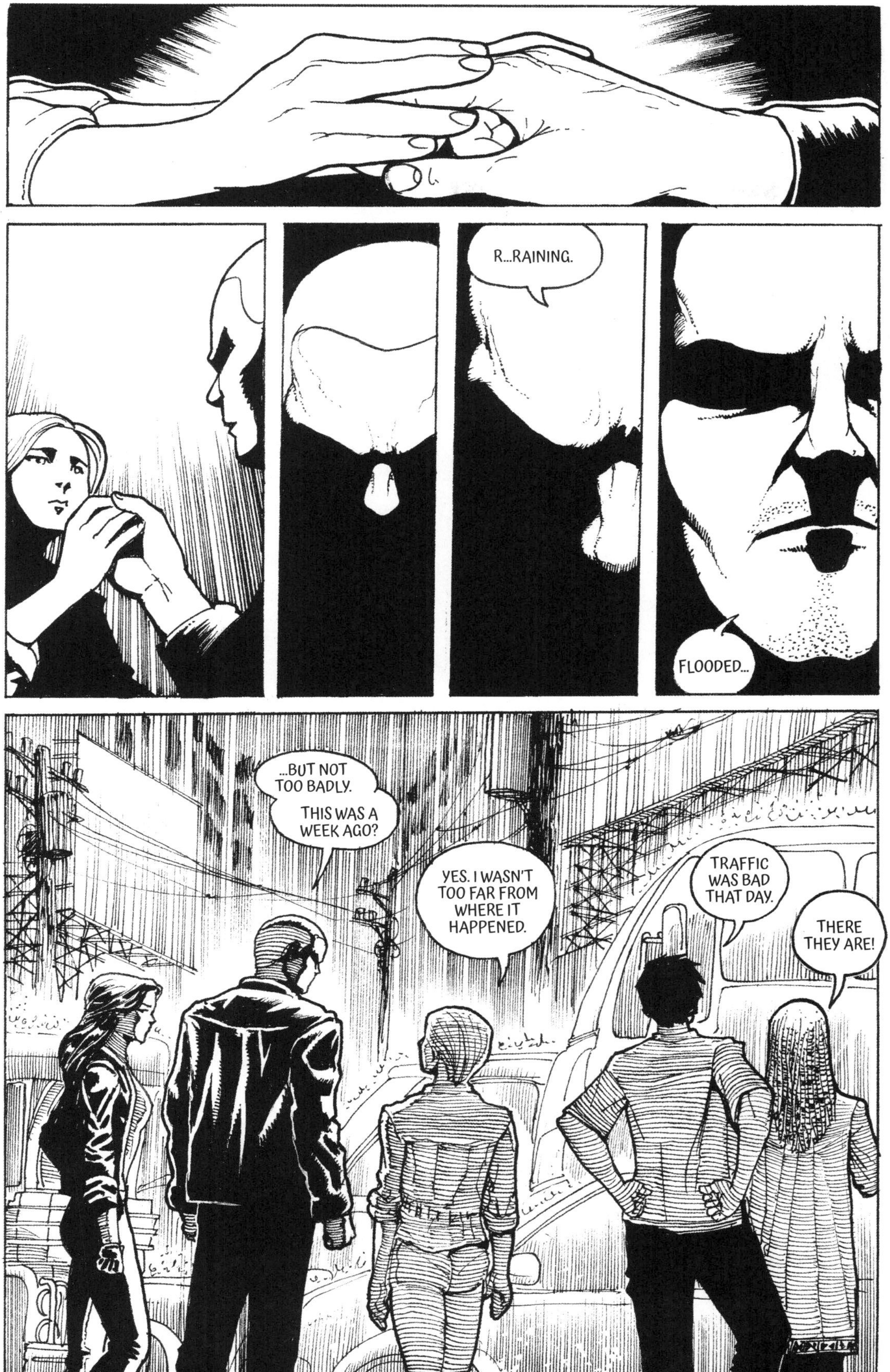
R...RAINING.
FLOODED...
...BUT NOT TOO BADLY.
THIS WAS A WEEK AGO?
YES. I WASN'T TOO FAR FROM WHERE IT HAPPENED.
TRAFFIC WAS BAD THAT DAY.
THERE THEY ARE!

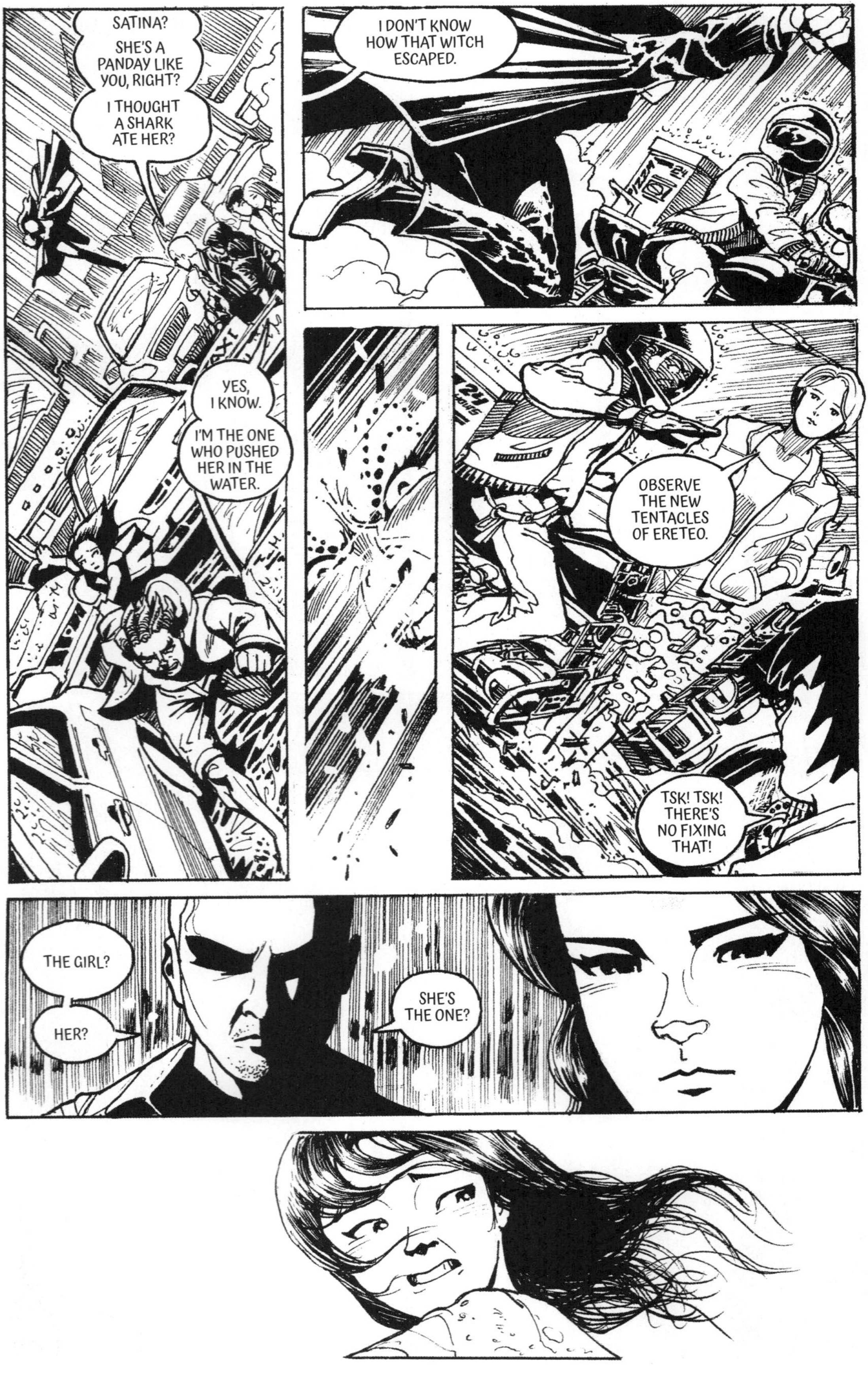
SATINA?
SHE'S A PANDAY LIKE YOU, RIGHT?
I THOUGHT A SHARK ATE HER?
YES, I KNOW.
I'M THE ONE WHO PUSHED HER IN THE WATER.
I DON'T KNOW HOW THAT WITCH ESCAPED.
OBSERVE THE NEW TENTACLES OF ERETEO.
TSK! TSK! THERE'S NO FIXING THAT!
THE GIRL?
HER?
SHE'S THE ONE?

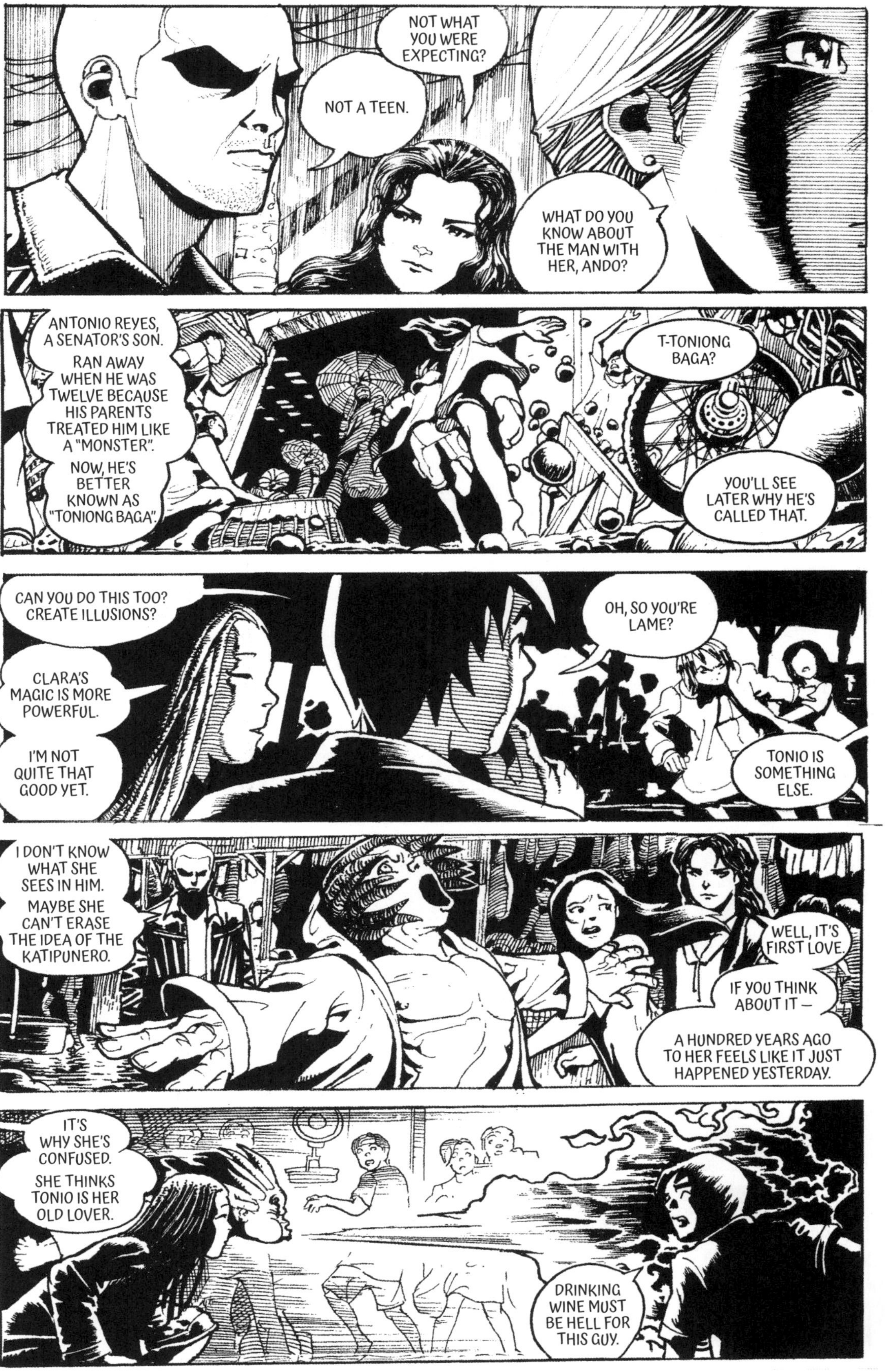
NOT WHAT YOU WERE EXPECTING?
NOT A TEEN.
WHAT DO YOU KNOW ABOUT THE MAN WITH HER, ANDO?
ANTONIO REYES, A SENATOR'S SON.
RAN AWAY WHEN HE WAS TWELVE BECAUSE HIS PARENTS TREATED HIM LIKE A "MONSTER".
NOW, HE'S BETTER KNOWN AS "TONIONG BAGA".
T-TONIONG BAGA?
YOU'LL SEE LATER WHY HE'S CALLED THAT.
CAN YOU DO THIS TOO? CREATE ILLUSIONS?
CLARA'S MAGIC IS MORE POWERFUL.
I'M NOT QUITE THAT GOOD YET.
OH, SO YOU'RE LAME?
TONIO IS SOMETHING ELSE.
I DON'T KNOW WHAT SHE SEES IN HIM.
MAYBE SHE CAN'T ERASE THE IDEA OF THE KATIPUNERO.
WELL, IT'S FIRST LOVE.
IF YOU THINK ABOUT IT —
A HUNDRED YEARS AGO TO HER FEELS LIKE IT JUST HAPPENED YESTERDAY.
IT'S WHY SHE'S CONFUSED.
SHE THINKS TONIO IS HER OLD LOVER.
DRINKING WINE MUST BE HELL FOR THIS GUY.

IT COULD BE THAT TONIO IS LIKE THE KATIPUNERO BECAUSE THEY BOTH HAVE SOMETHING TO FIGHT FOR.

MARIA SEES SOULS, NOT PHYSICAL APPEARANCES.

NOW...

...OBSERVE.

HE GOT AWAY.

THERE'S STILL A CHANCE FOR US TO FIND HIM.

IF WE FIND HIM, WE CAN FIND MARIA.

IT'S NOT THAT EASY.

HE WAS CAPTURED BY MAXIMO — THE KING OF TONDO. HE'S HOLDING A PRETTY BIG GRUDGE.

WHAT HE PLANS TO DO WITH TONIO, I DON'T KNOW.

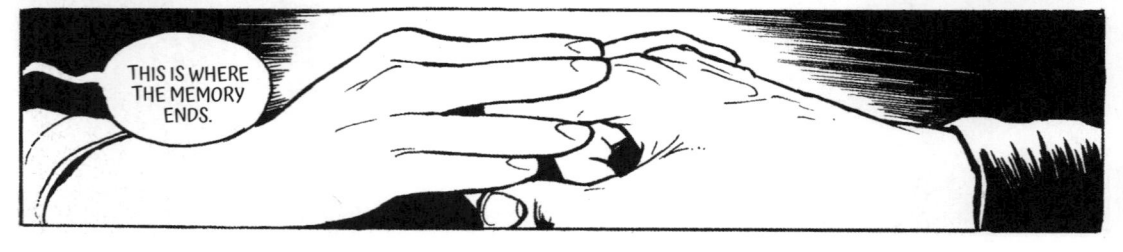

HERE COMES SATINA AGAIN.

RUMOR HAS IT YOU START WORSHIPPING JUN ONCE YOU GET A TASTE OF THAT DRUG HE MAKES.

AS LONG AS YOU DON'T LOSE YOUR MIND IN THE PROCESS...

AS SHE APPROACHED, THINGS TURNED DARK.

THIS IS WHERE THE MEMORY ENDS.

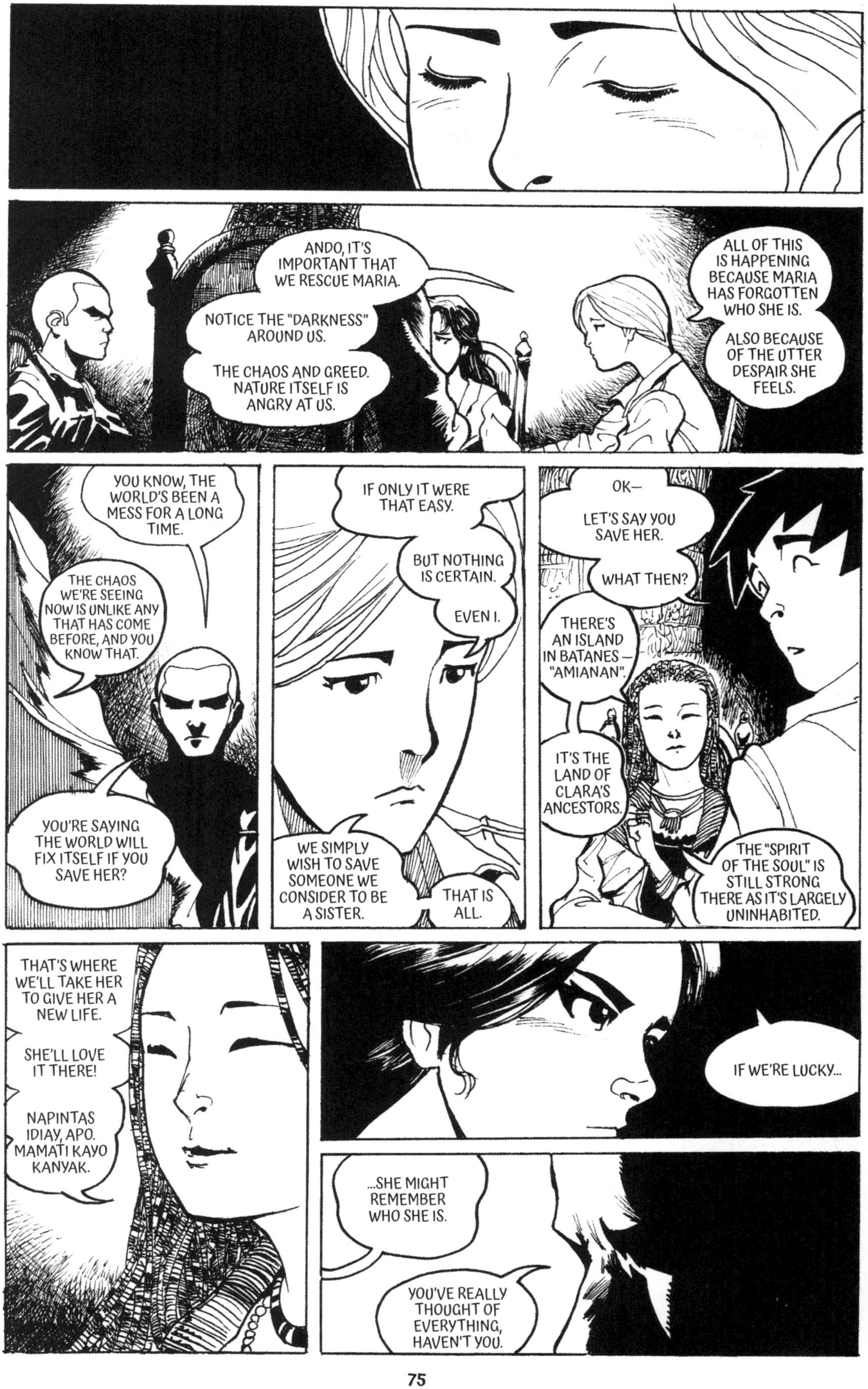

ANDO, IT'S IMPORTANT THAT WE RESCUE MARIA.
NOTICE THE "DARKNESS" AROUND US.
THE CHAOS AND GREED. NATURE ITSELF IS ANGRY AT US.
ALL OF THIS IS HAPPENING BECAUSE MARIA HAS FORGOTTEN WHO SHE IS.
ALSO BECAUSE OF THE UTTER DESPAIR SHE FEELS.
YOU KNOW, THE WORLD'S BEEN A MESS FOR A LONG TIME.
THE CHAOS WE'RE SEEING NOW IS UNLIKE ANY THAT HAS COME BEFORE, AND YOU KNOW THAT.
YOU'RE SAYING THE WORLD WILL FIX ITSELF IF YOU SAVE HER?
IF ONLY IT WERE THAT EASY.
BUT NOTHING IS CERTAIN.
EVEN I.
WE SIMPLY WISH TO SAVE SOMEONE WE CONSIDER TO BE A SISTER.
THAT IS ALL.
OK—
LET'S SAY YOU SAVE HER.
WHAT THEN?
THERE'S AN ISLAND IN BATANES—"AMIANAN".
IT'S THE LAND OF CLARA'S ANCESTORS.
THE "SPIRIT OF THE SOUL" IS STILL STRONG THERE AS IT'S LARGELY UNINHABITED.
THAT'S WHERE WE'LL TAKE HER TO GIVE HER A NEW LIFE.
SHE'LL LOVE IT THERE!
NAPINTAS IDIAY, APO. MAMATI KAYO KANYAK.
IF WE'RE LUCKY...
...SHE MIGHT REMEMBER WHO SHE IS.
YOU'VE REALLY THOUGHT OF EVERYTHING, HAVEN'T YOU.

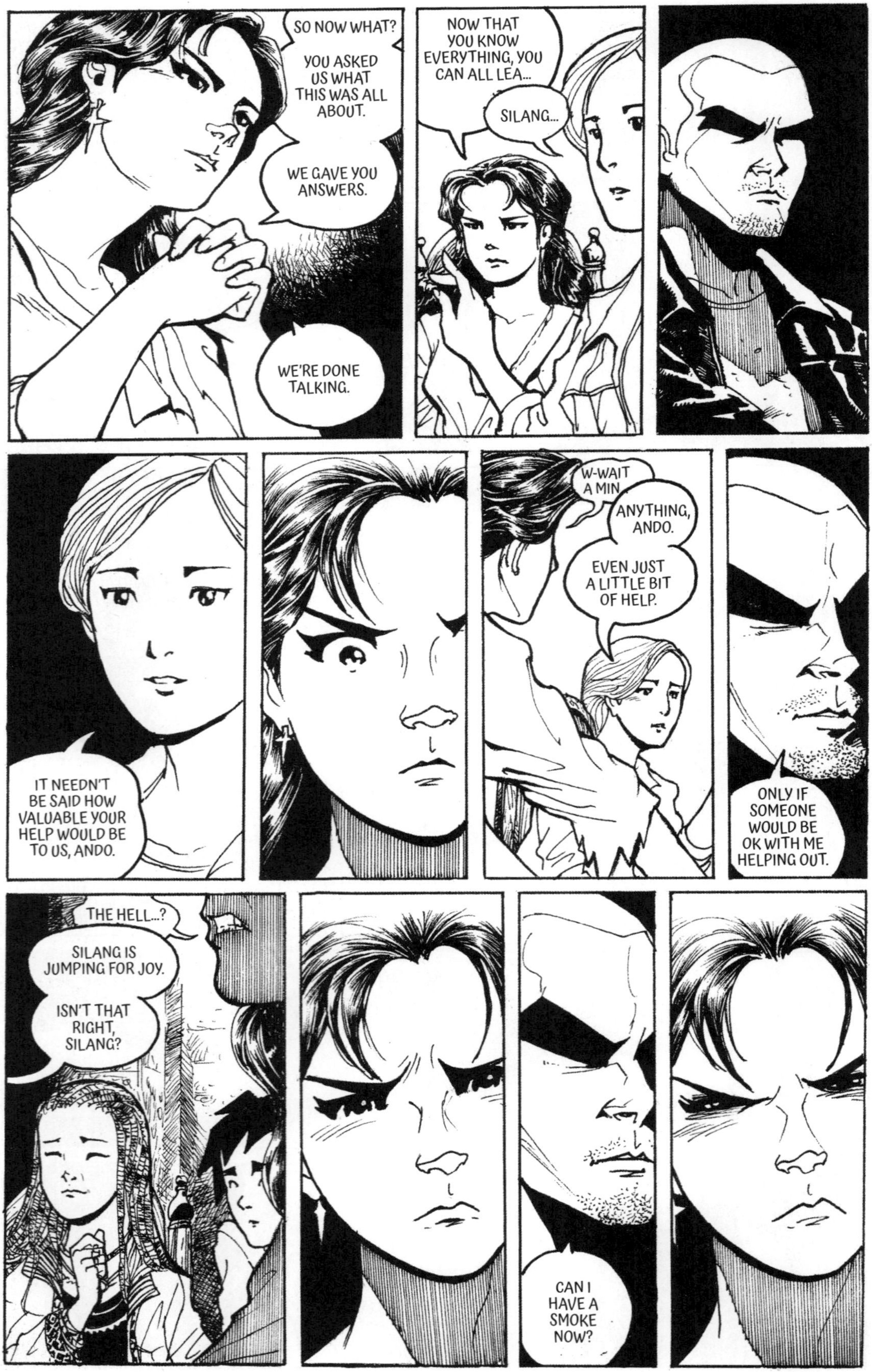
SO NOW WHAT?
YOU ASKED US WHAT THIS WAS ALL ABOUT.
WE GAVE YOU ANSWERS.
WE'RE DONE TALKING.
NOW THAT YOU KNOW EVERYTHING, YOU CAN ALL LEA...
SILANG...
IT NEEDN'T BE SAID HOW VALUABLE YOUR HELP WOULD BE TO US, ANDO.
W-WAIT A MIN
ANYTHING, ANDO.
EVEN JUST A LITTLE BIT OF HELP.
ONLY IF SOMEONE WOULD BE OK WITH ME HELPING OUT.
THE HELL...?
SILANG IS JUMPING FOR JOY.
ISN'T THAT RIGHT, SILANG?
CAN I HAVE A SMOKE NOW?

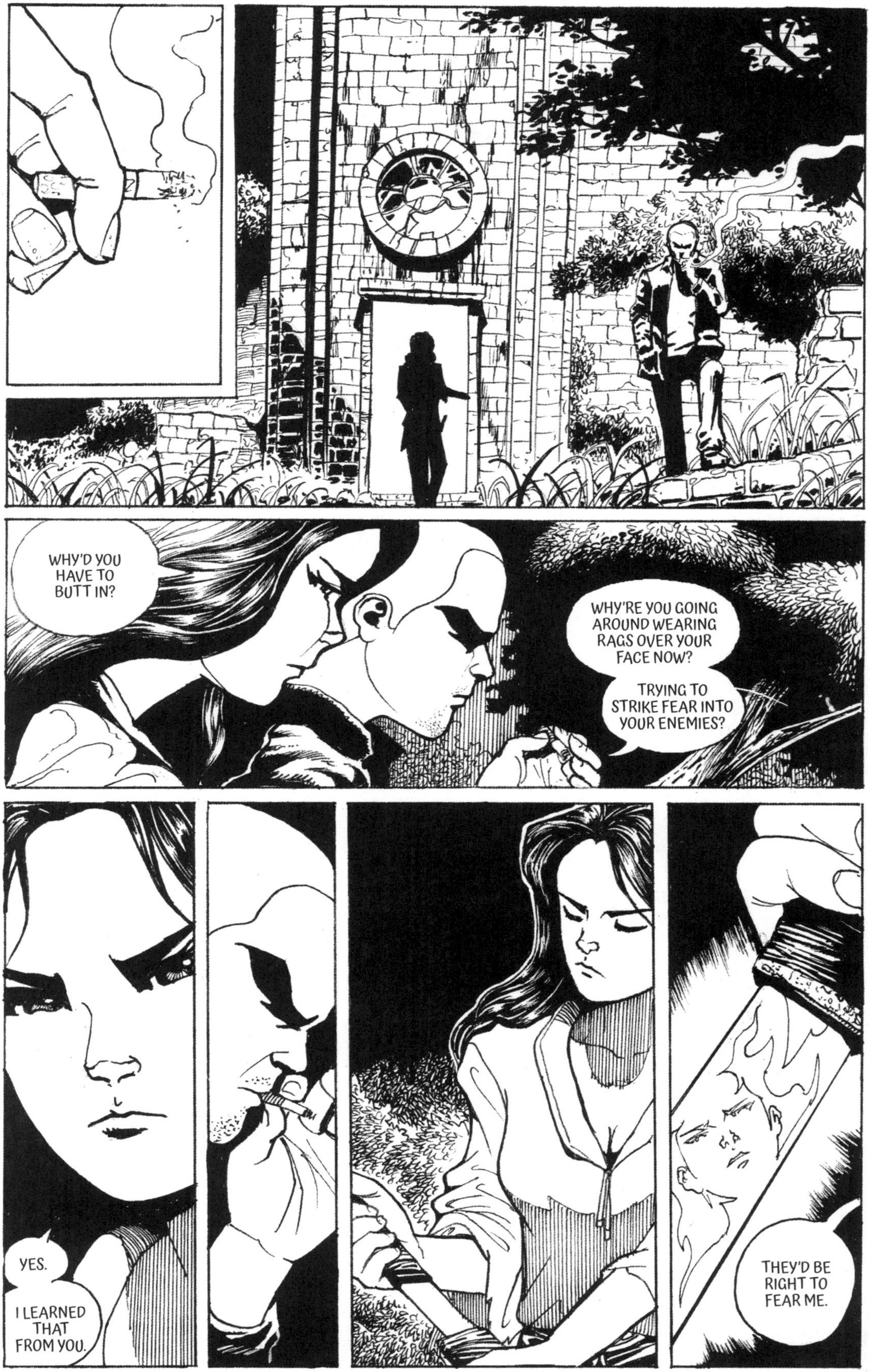
WHY'D YOU HAVE TO BUTT IN?
WHY'RE YOU GOING AROUND WEARING RAGS OVER YOUR FACE NOW?
TRYING TO STRIKE FEAR INTO YOUR ENEMIES?
YES.
I LEARNED THAT FROM YOU.
THEY'D BE RIGHT TO FEAR ME.

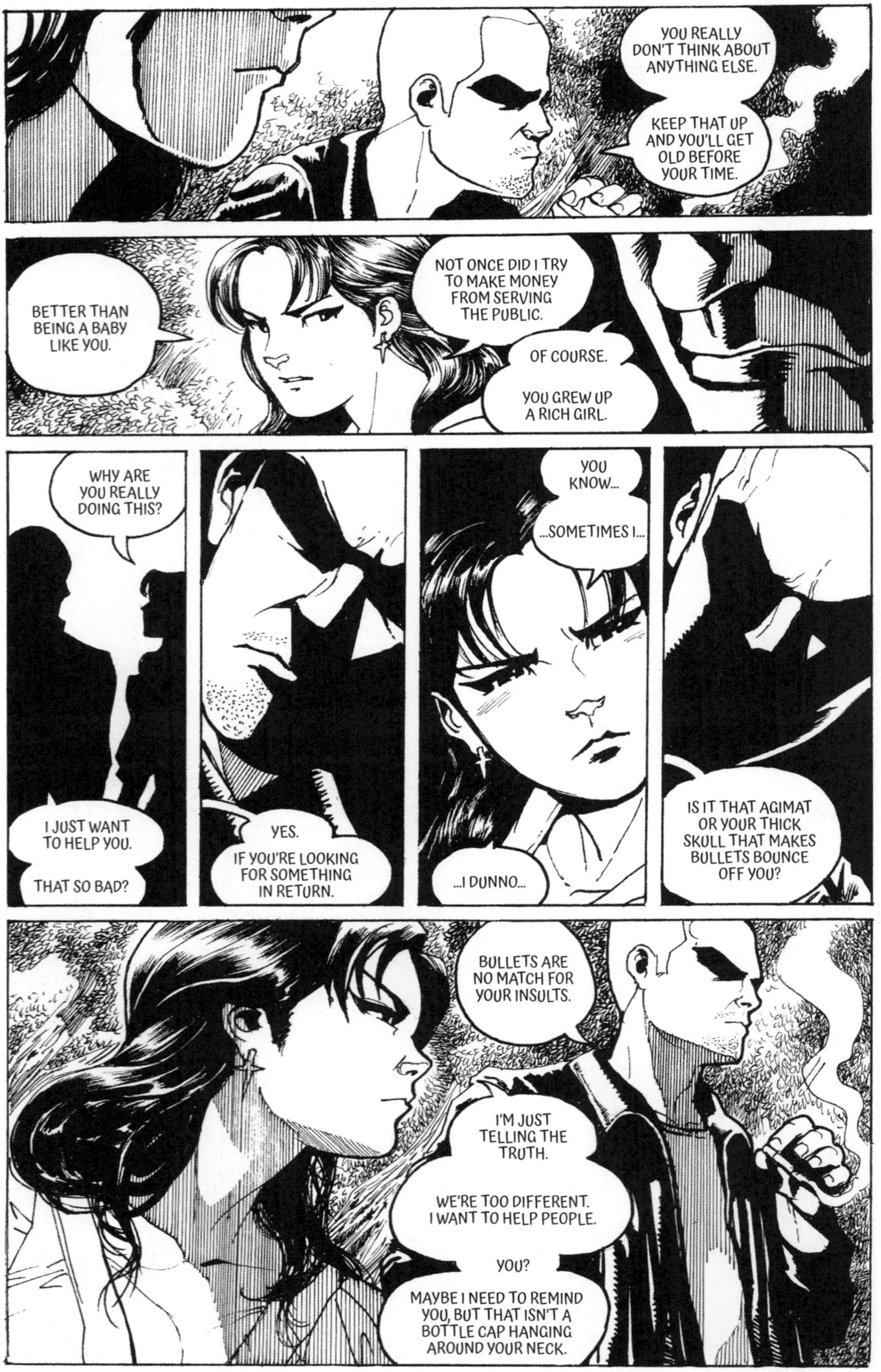
YOU REALLY DON'T THINK ABOUT ANYTHING ELSE.
KEEP THAT UP AND YOU'LL GET OLD BEFORE YOUR TIME.
BETTER THAN BEING A BABY LIKE YOU.
NOT ONCE DID I TRY TO MAKE MONEY FROM SERVING THE PUBLIC.
OF COURSE.
YOU GREW UP A RICH GIRL.
WHY ARE YOU REALLY DOING THIS?
I JUST WANT TO HELP YOU.
THAT SO BAD?
YES.
IF YOU'RE LOOKING FOR SOMETHING IN RETURN.
YOU KNOW...
...SOMETIMES I...
...I DUNNO...
IS IT THAT AGIMAT OR YOUR THICK SKULL THAT MAKES BULLETS BOUNCE OFF YOU?
BULLETS ARE NO MATCH FOR YOUR INSULTS.
I'M JUST TELLING THE TRUTH.
WE'RE TOO DIFFERENT. I WANT TO HELP PEOPLE.
YOU?
MAYBE I NEED TO REMIND YOU, BUT THAT ISN'T A BOTTLE CAP HANGING AROUND YOUR NECK.

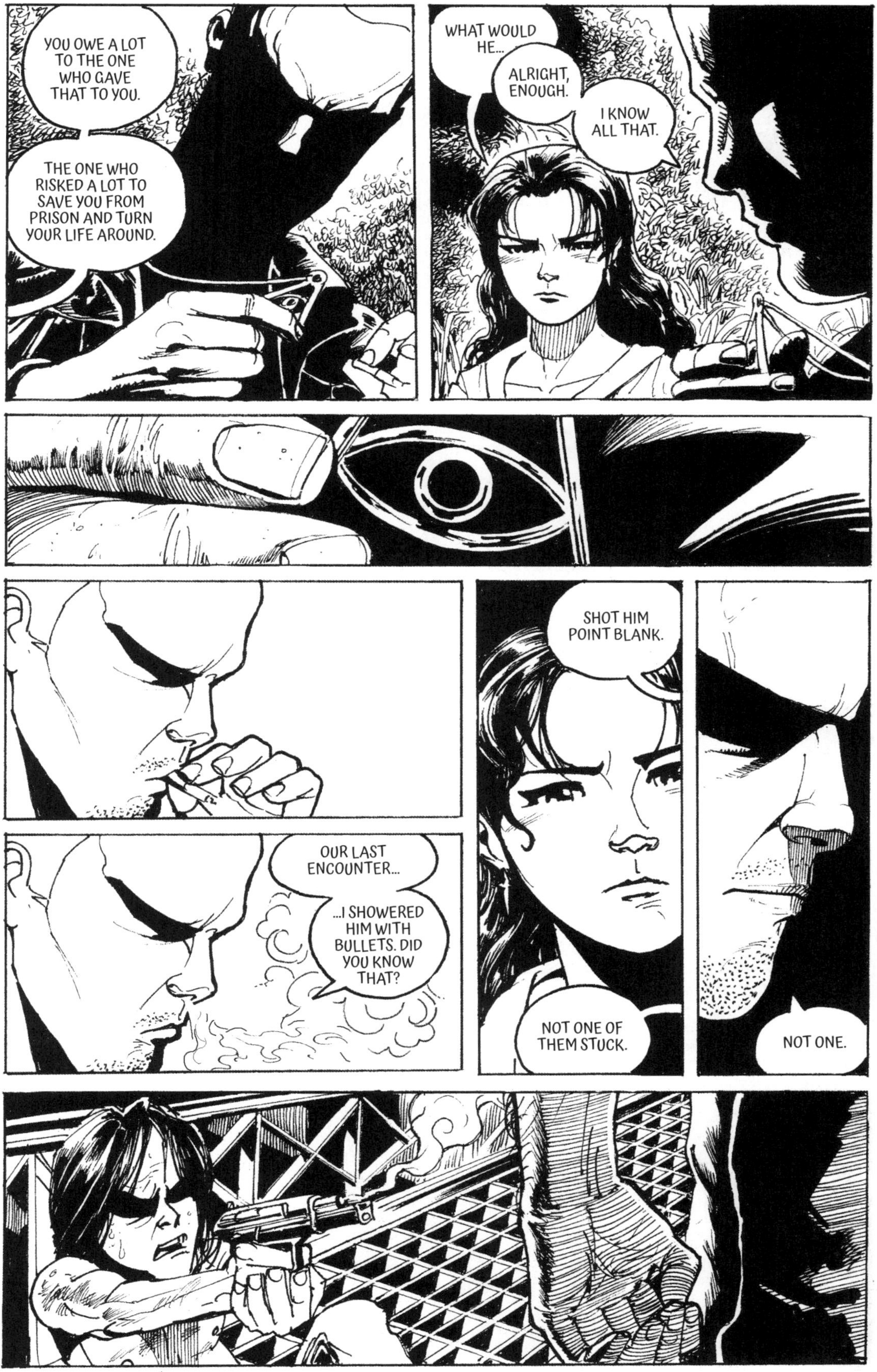
YOU OWE A LOT TO THE ONE WHO GAVE THAT TO YOU.
THE ONE WHO RISKED A LOT TO SAVE YOU FROM PRISON AND TURN YOUR LIFE AROUND.
WHAT WOULD HE...
ALRIGHT, ENOUGH.
I KNOW ALL THAT.
OUR LAST ENCOUNTER...
...I SHOWERED HIM WITH BULLETS. DID YOU KNOW THAT?
SHOT HIM POINT BLANK.
NOT ONE OF THEM STUCK.
NOT ONE.

I WAS THE ONLY ONE HE SHOWED HIS SECRET TO.

ERNESTO WAS A SAINT.

PEOPLE LIKE THAT..

MEN LIKE HIM ARE RARE THESE DAYS

...THEY'RE SAYING SOMETHING IMPORTANT.

HE SAID SOMETHING.

HE SAID...

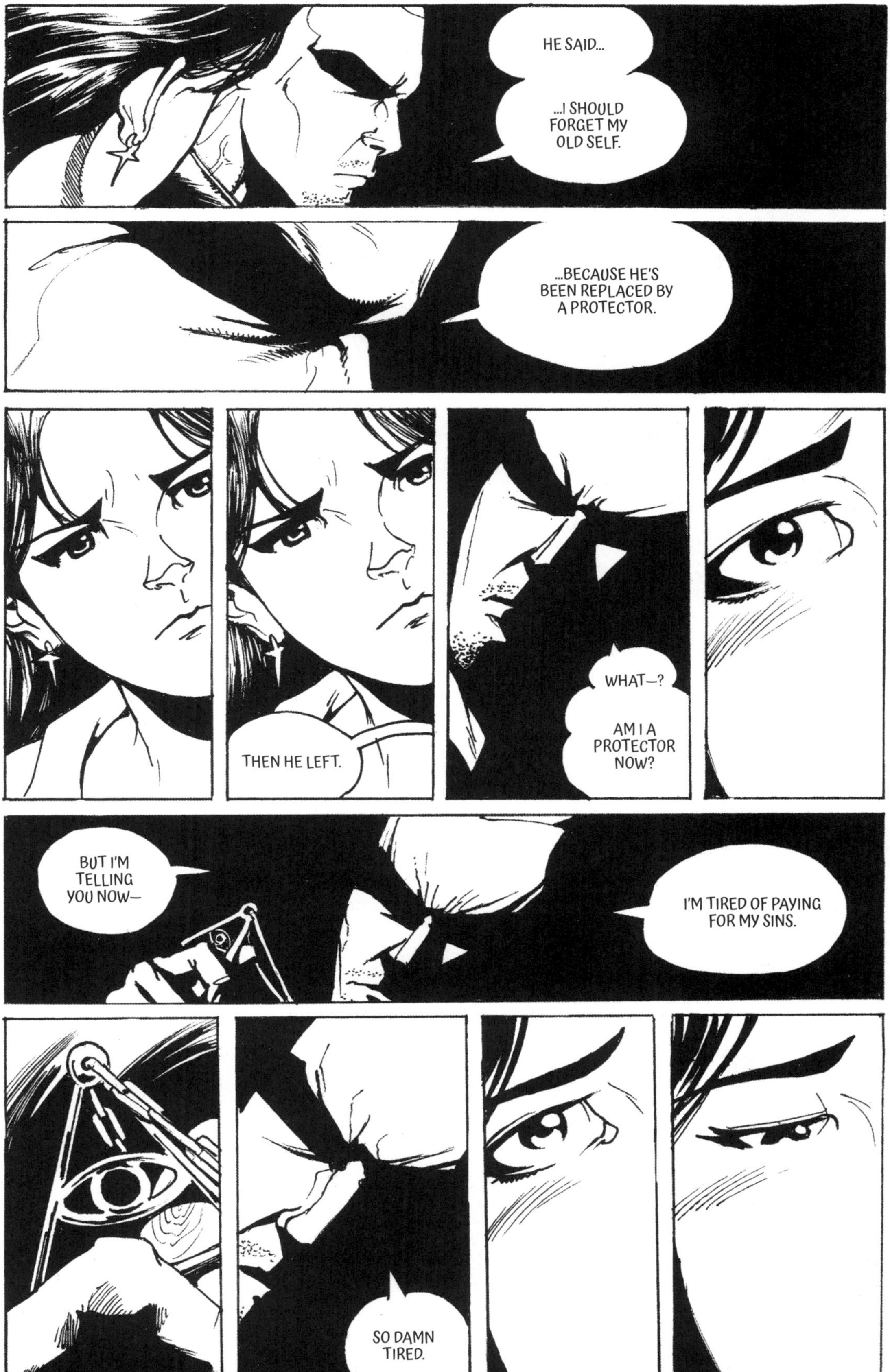
HE SAID...
...I SHOULD FORGET MY OLD SELF.
...BECAUSE HE'S BEEN REPLACED BY A PROTECTOR.
THEN HE LEFT.
WHAT—?
AM I A PROTECTOR NOW?
BUT I'M TELLING YOU NOW—
I'M TIRED OF PAYING FOR MY SINS.
SO DAMN TIRED.

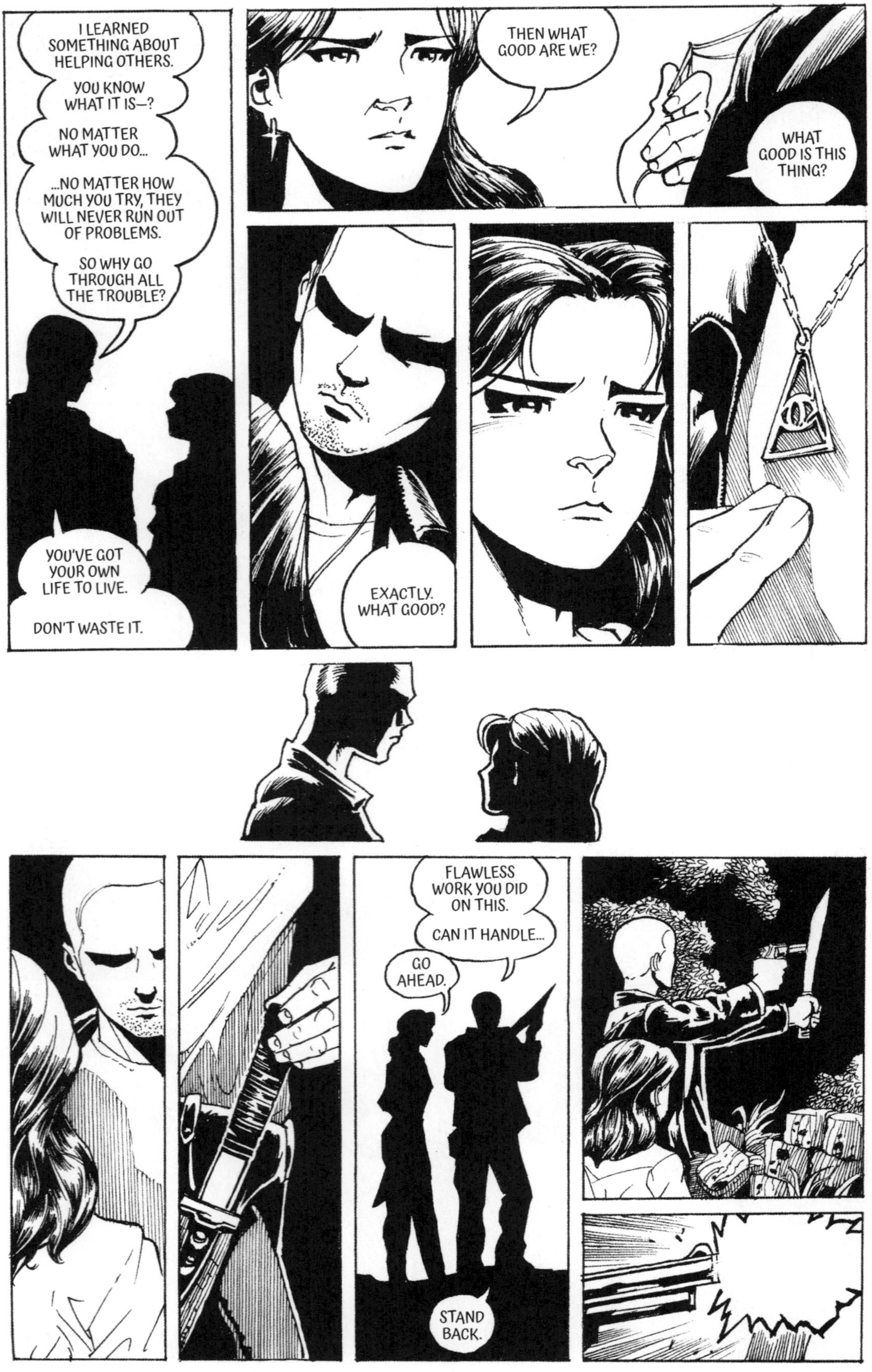

I LEARNED SOMETHING ABOUT HELPING OTHERS.
YOU KNOW WHAT IT IS—?
NO MATTER WHAT YOU DO...
...NO MATTER HOW MUCH YOU TRY, THEY WILL NEVER RUN OUT OF PROBLEMS.
SO WHY GO THROUGH ALL THE TROUBLE?
YOU'VE GOT YOUR OWN LIFE TO LIVE.
DON'T WASTE IT.
THEN WHAT GOOD ARE WE?
WHAT GOOD IS THIS THING?
EXACTLY. WHAT GOOD?
FLAWLESS WORK YOU DID ON THIS.
CAN IT HANDLE...
GO AHEAD.
STAND BACK.

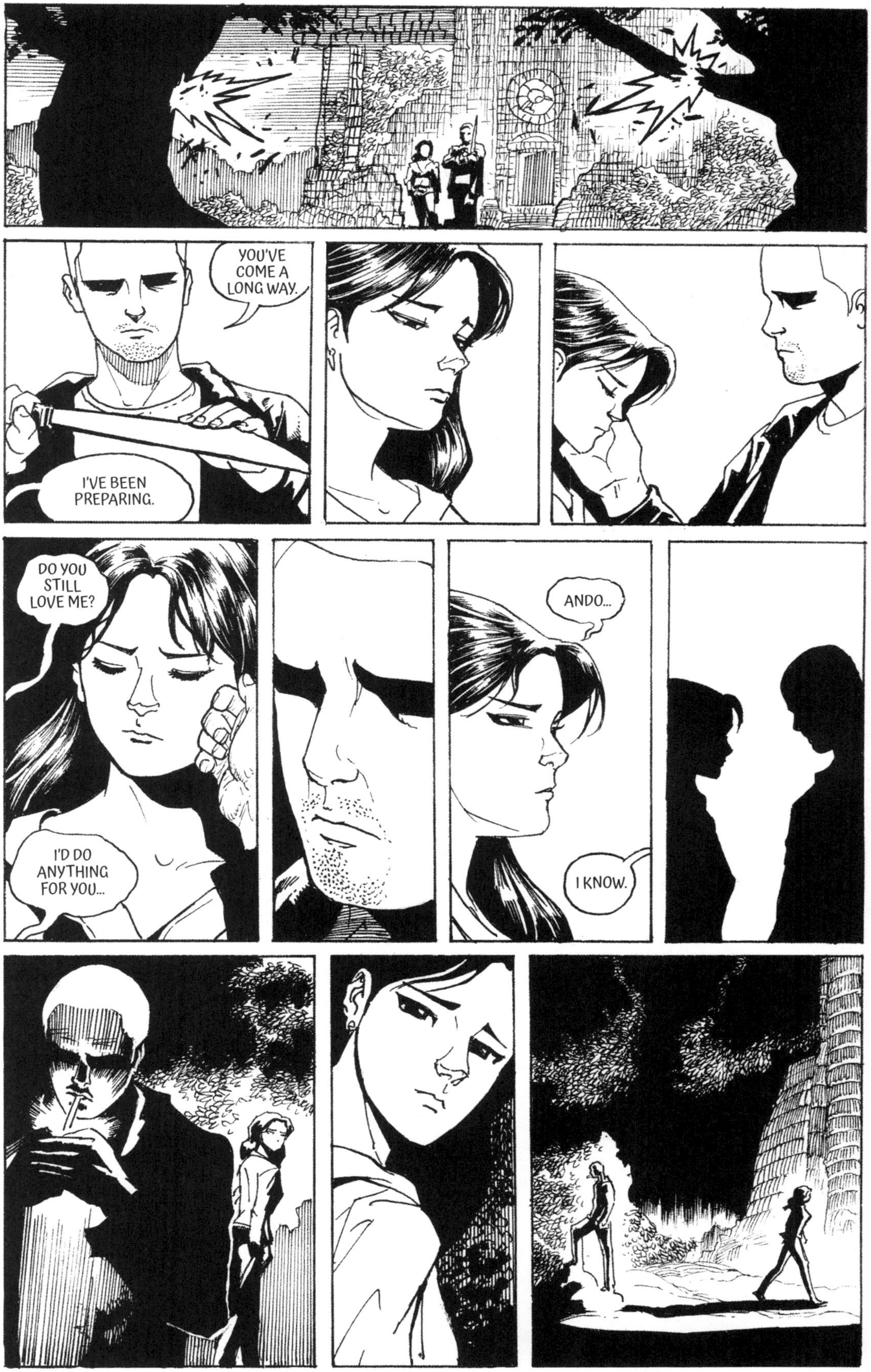
YOU'VE COME A LONG WAY.
I'VE BEEN PREPARING.
DO YOU STILL LOVE ME?
I'D DO ANYTHING FOR YOU...
ANDO...
I KNOW.

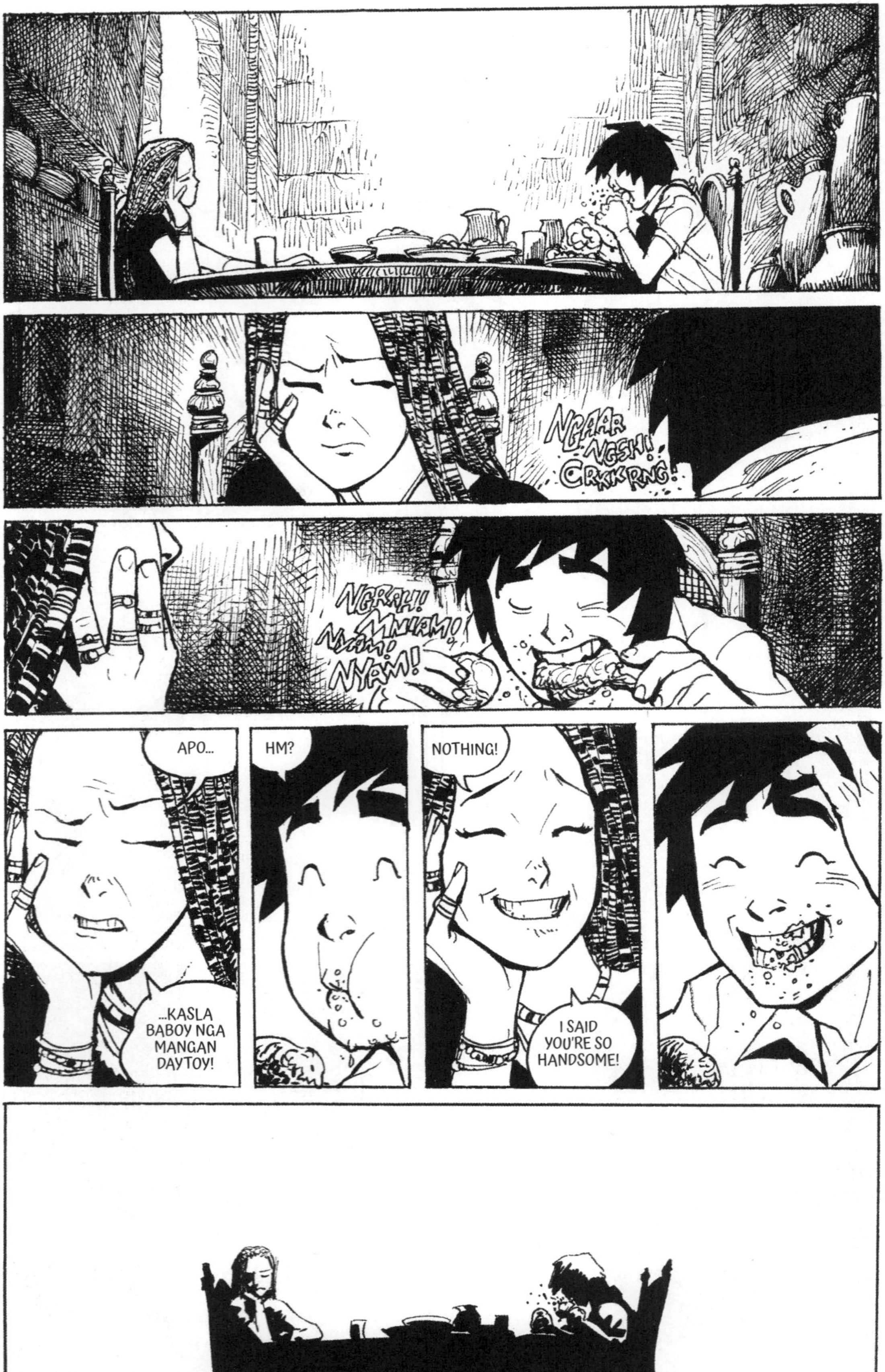
NGAAR NGSH!
CRKKRNG!
NGRAH! MNIRM! NYAM! NYAM!
APO...
...KASLA BABOY NGA MANGAN DAYTOY!
HM?
NOTHING!
I SAID YOU'RE SO HANDSOME!

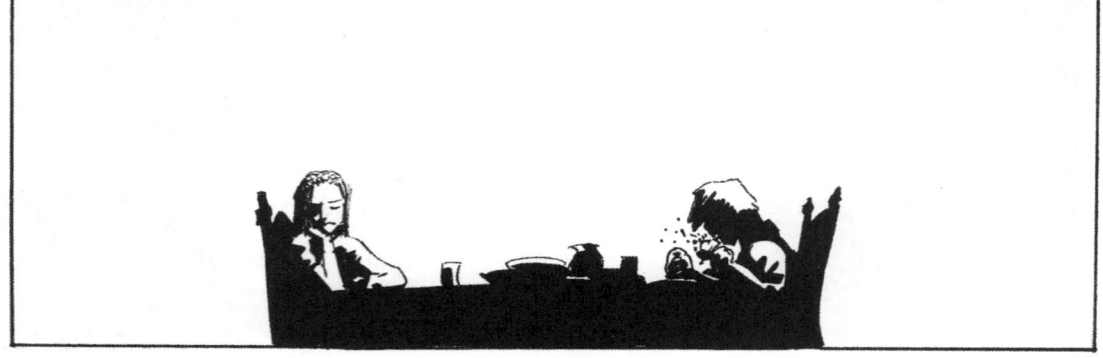

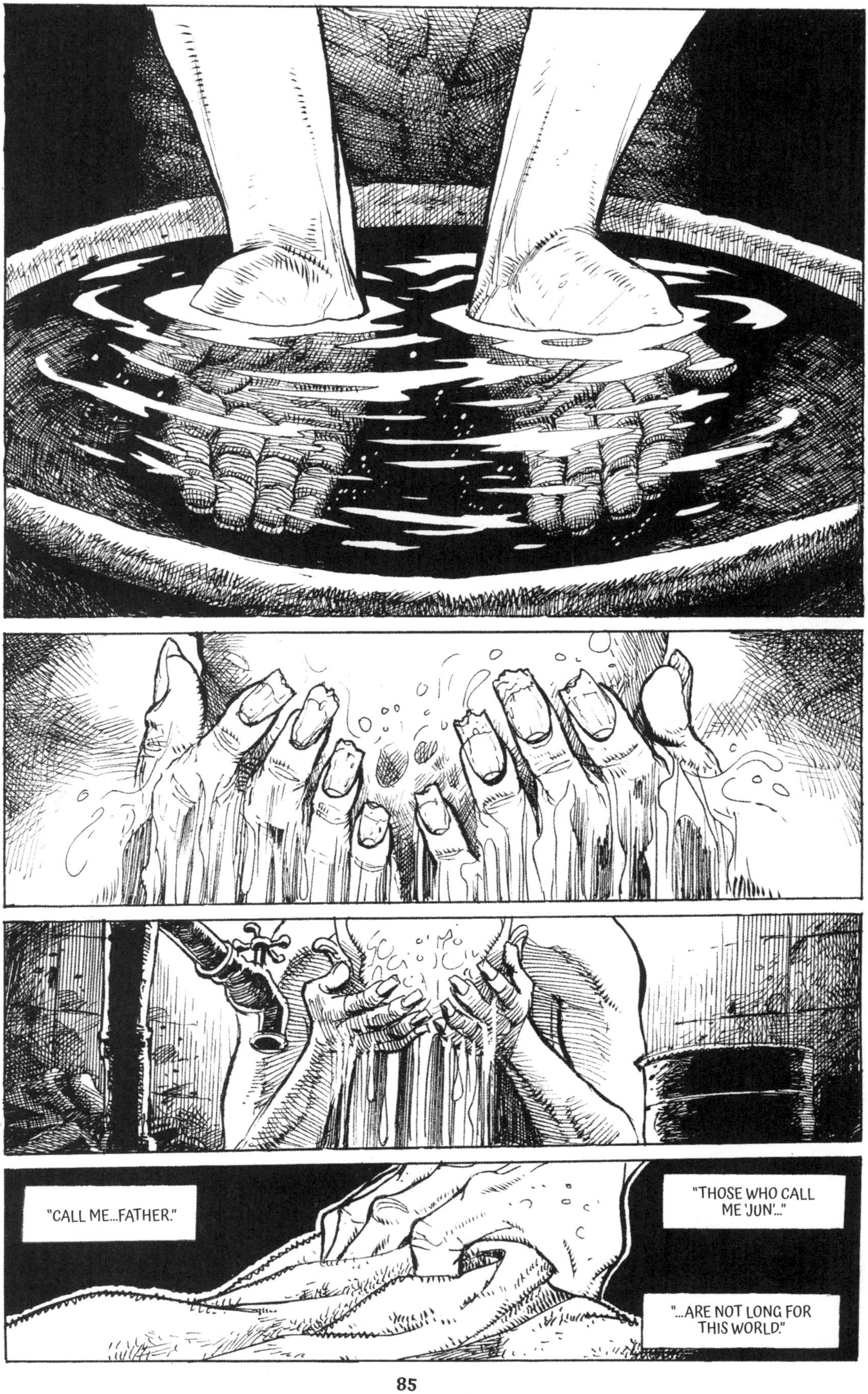
"CALL ME...FATHER."
"THOSE WHO CALL ME 'JUN'..."
"...ARE NOT LONG FOR THIS WORLD."

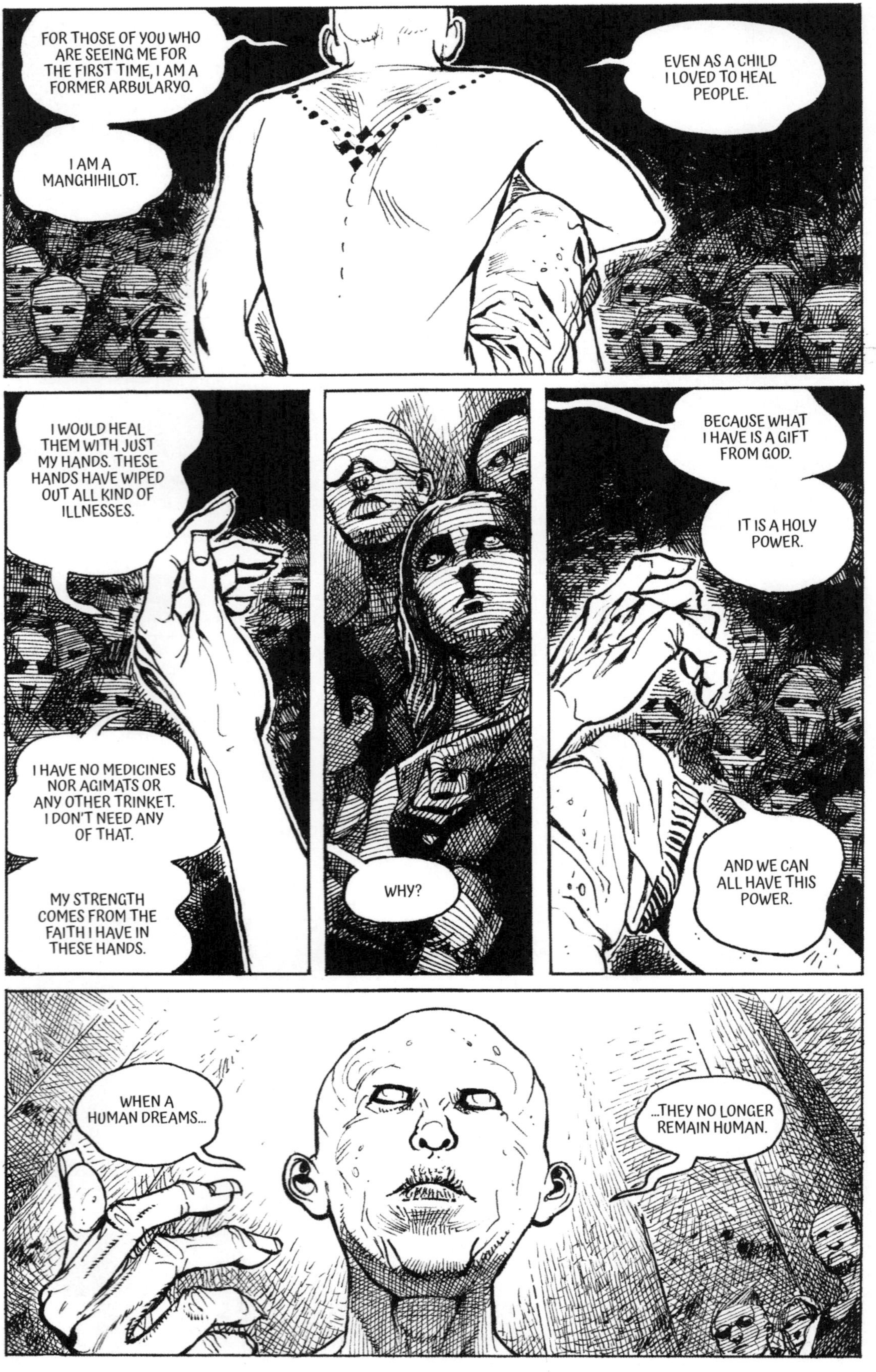
FOR THOSE OF YOU WHO ARE SEEING ME FOR THE FIRST TIME, I AM A FORMER ARBULARYO.
I AM A MANGHIHILOT.
EVEN AS A CHILD I LOVED TO HEAL PEOPLE.
I WOULD HEAL THEM WITH JUST MY HANDS. THESE HANDS HAVE WIPED OUT ALL KIND OF ILLNESSES.
I HAVE NO MEDICINES NOR AGIMATS OR ANY OTHER TRINKET. I DON'T NEED ANY OF THAT.
MY STRENGTH COMES FROM THE FAITH I HAVE IN THESE HANDS.
WHY?
BECAUSE WHAT I HAVE IS A GIFT FROM GOD.
IT IS A HOLY POWER.
AND WE CAN ALL HAVE THIS POWER.
WHEN A HUMAN DREAMS...
...THEY NO LONGER REMAIN HUMAN.

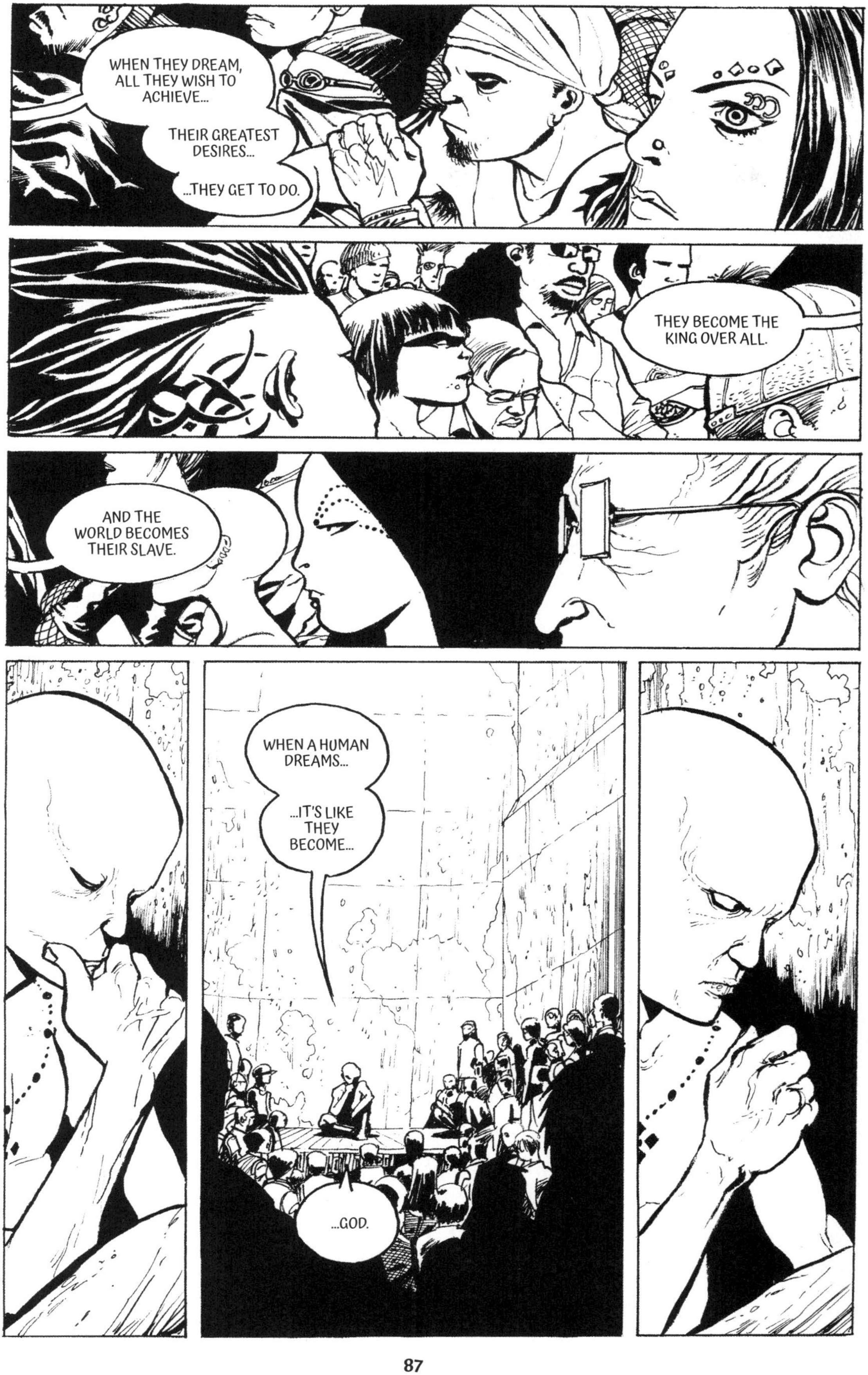
WHEN THEY DREAM, ALL THEY WISH TO ACHIEVE...
THEIR GREATEST DESIRES...
...THEY GET TO DO.
THEY BECOME THE KING OVER ALL.
AND THE WORLD BECOMES THEIR SLAVE.
WHEN A HUMAN DREAMS...
...IT'S LIKE THEY BECOME...
...GOD.

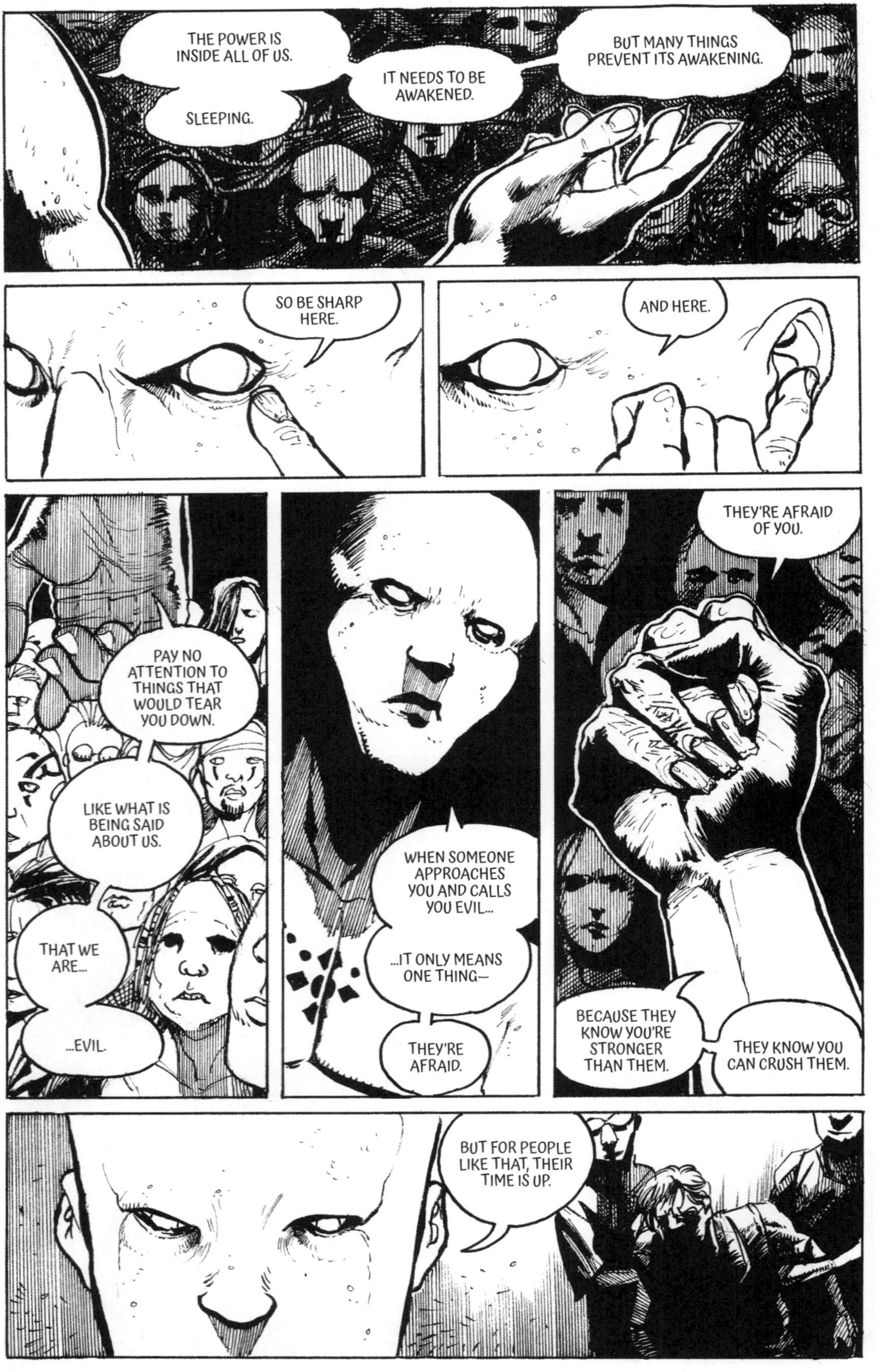
THE POWER IS INSIDE ALL OF US.
SLEEPING.
IT NEEDS TO BE AWAKENED.
BUT MANY THINGS PREVENT ITS AWAKENING.
SO BE SHARP HERE.
AND HERE.
PAY NO ATTENTION TO THINGS THAT WOULD TEAR YOU DOWN.
LIKE WHAT IS BEING SAID ABOUT US.
THAT WE ARE...
...EVIL.
WHEN SOMEONE APPROACHES YOU AND CALLS YOU EVIL...
...IT ONLY MEANS ONE THING—
THEY'RE AFRAID.
THEY'RE AFRAID OF YOU.
BECAUSE THEY KNOW YOU'RE STRONGER THAN THEM.
THEY KNOW YOU CAN CRUSH THEM.
BUT FOR PEOPLE LIKE THAT, THEIR TIME IS UP.

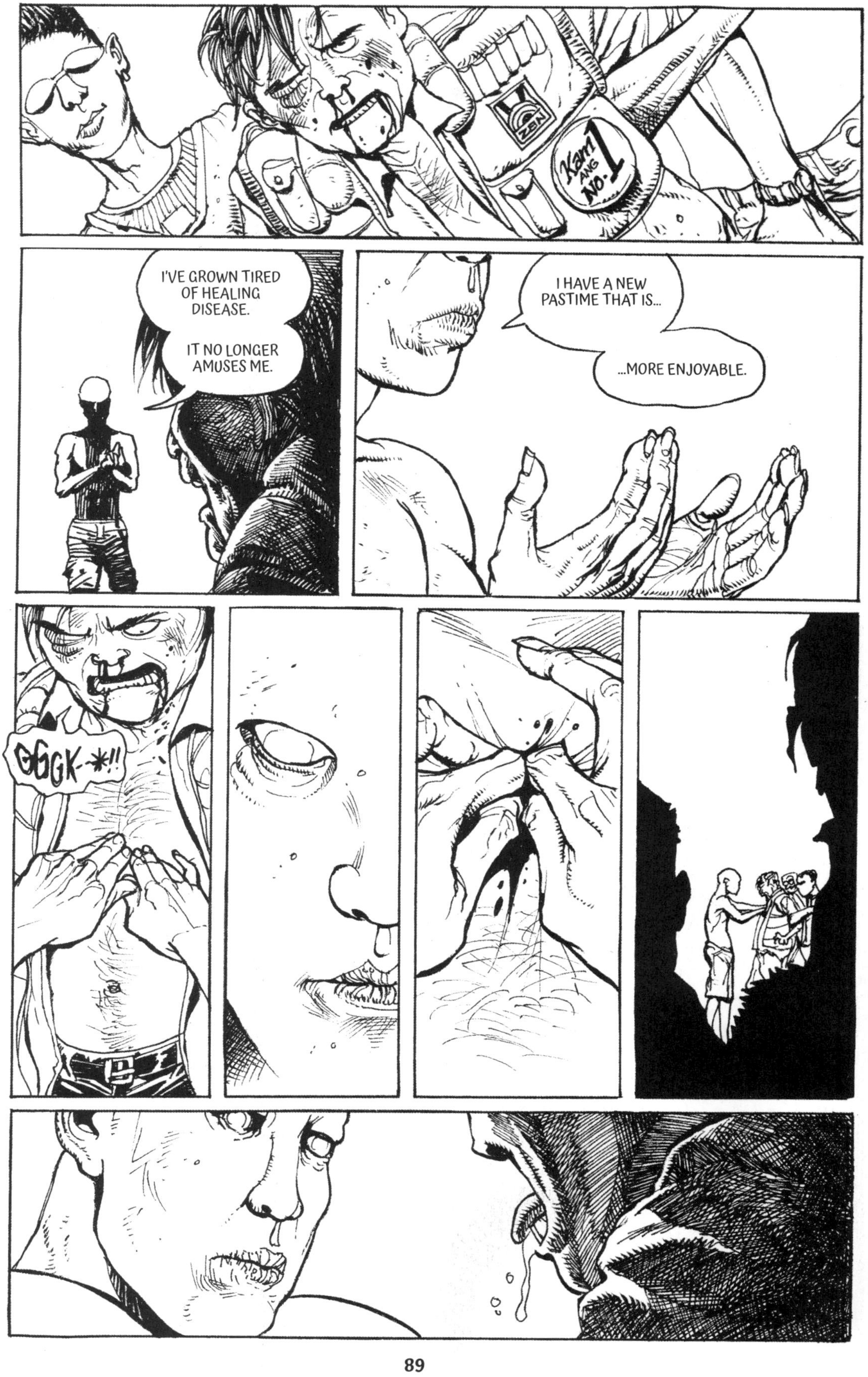
ZEN
Kami ANG No. 1
I'VE GROWN TIRED OF HEALING DISEASE.
IT NO LONGER AMUSES ME.
I HAVE A NEW PASTIME THAT IS...
...MORE ENJOYABLE.
OGGK-*!!

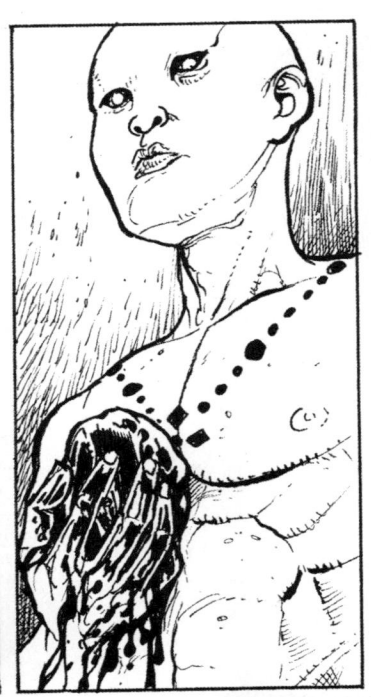

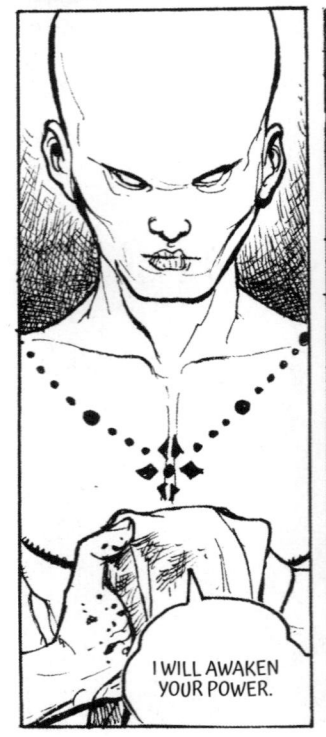

FROM NOW ON...

...YOU NO LONGER NEED TO DREAM.

I WILL TEACH YOU THE PATH.

I WILL AWAKEN YOUR POWER.

THE GODDESS OF NATURE...

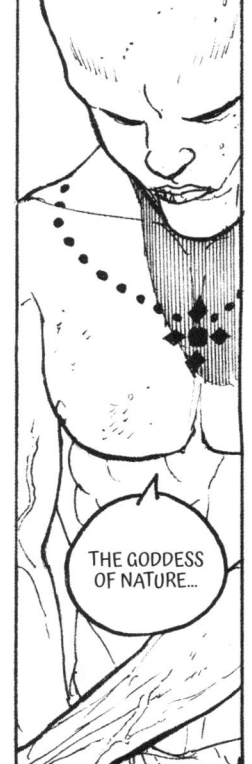

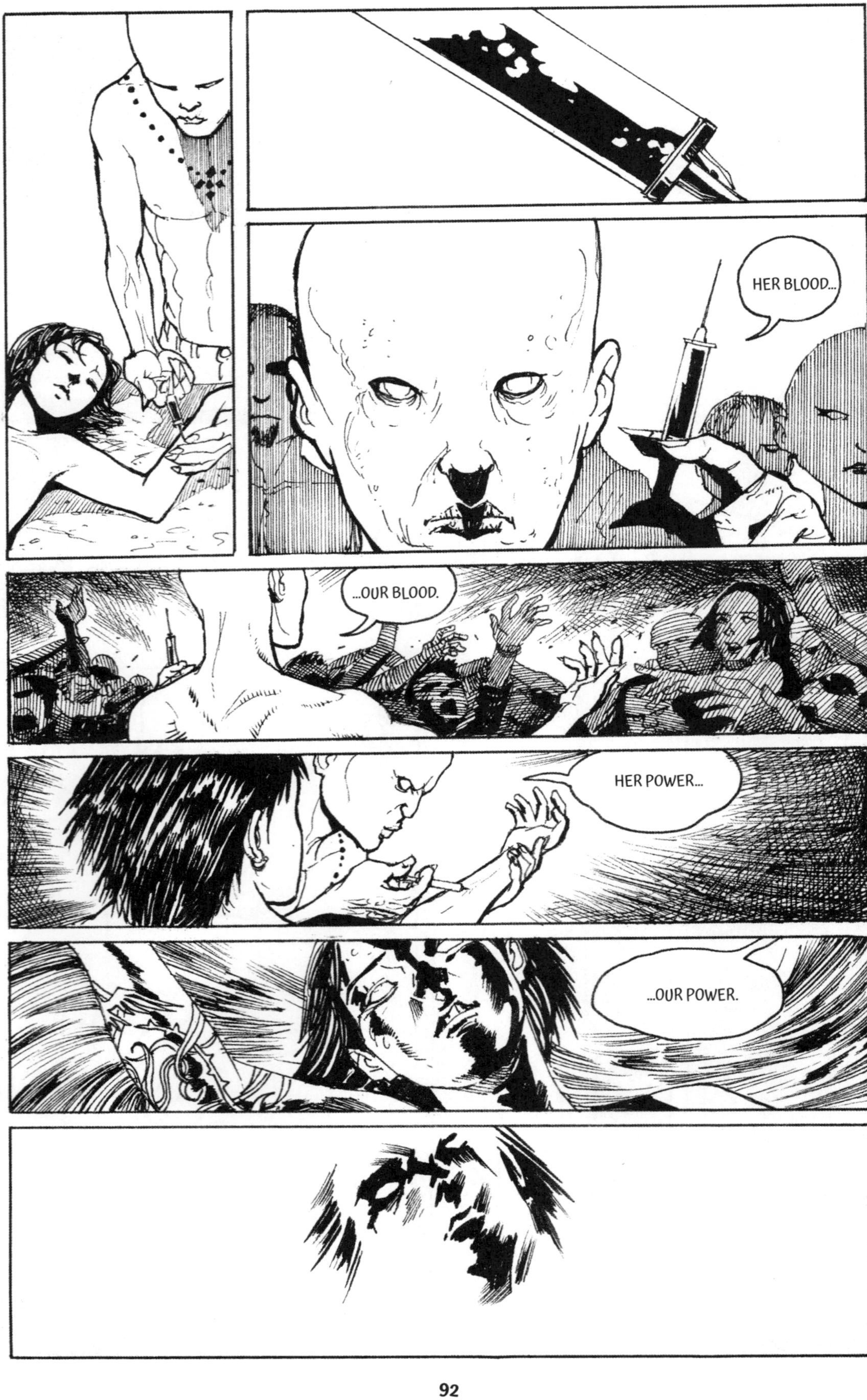
HER BLOOD...
...OUR BLOOD.
HER POWER...
...OUR POWER.

THE CITY.

IT WAS IN THE CITY WHERE SHE ENDED UP.

WHO WOULD'VE THOUGHT.

OVER A HUNDRED YEARS OF SEARCHING HAS FINALLY PAID OFF.

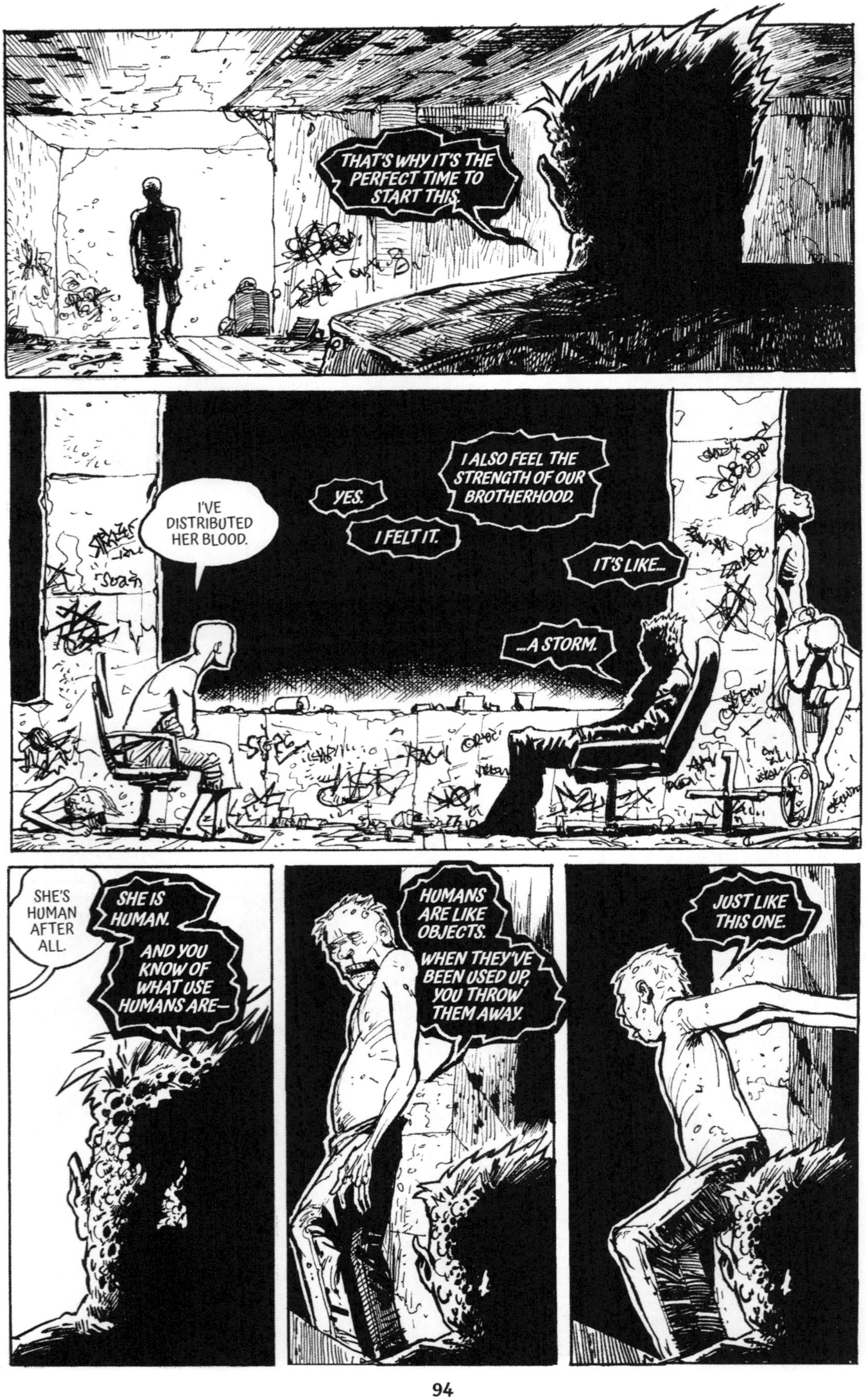
THAT'S WHY IT'S THE PERFECT TIME TO START THIS.
I'VE DISTRIBUTED HER BLOOD.
YES.
I FELT IT.
I ALSO FEEL THE STRENGTH OF OUR BROTHERHOOD.
IT'S LIKE...
...A STORM.
SHE'S HUMAN AFTER ALL.
SHE IS HUMAN.
AND YOU KNOW OF WHAT USE HUMANS ARE—
HUMANS ARE LIKE OBJECTS.
WHEN THEY'VE BEEN USED UP, YOU THROW THEM AWAY.
JUST LIKE THIS ONE.

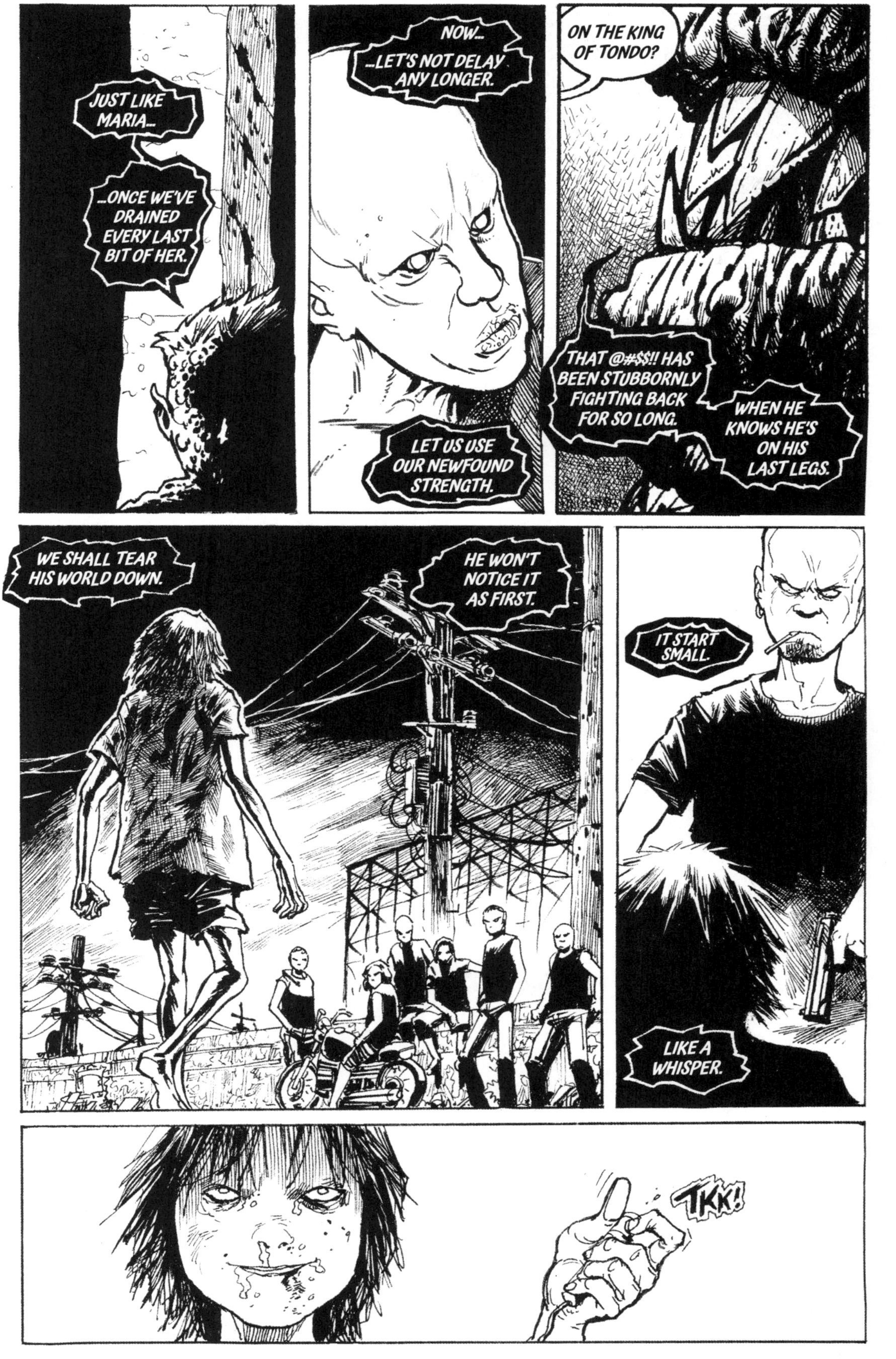

JUST LIKE MARIA...
...ONCE WE'VE DRAINED EVERY LAST BIT OF HER.
NOW... ...LET'S NOT DELAY ANY LONGER.
LET US USE OUR NEWFOUND STRENGTH.
ON THE KING OF TONDO?
THAT @#$$!! HAS BEEN STUBBORNLY FIGHTING BACK FOR SO LONG.
WHEN HE KNOWS HE'S ON HIS LAST LEGS.
WE SHALL TEAR HIS WORLD DOWN.
HE WON'T NOTICE IT AS FIRST.
IT START SMALL.
LIKE A WHISPER.
TKK!

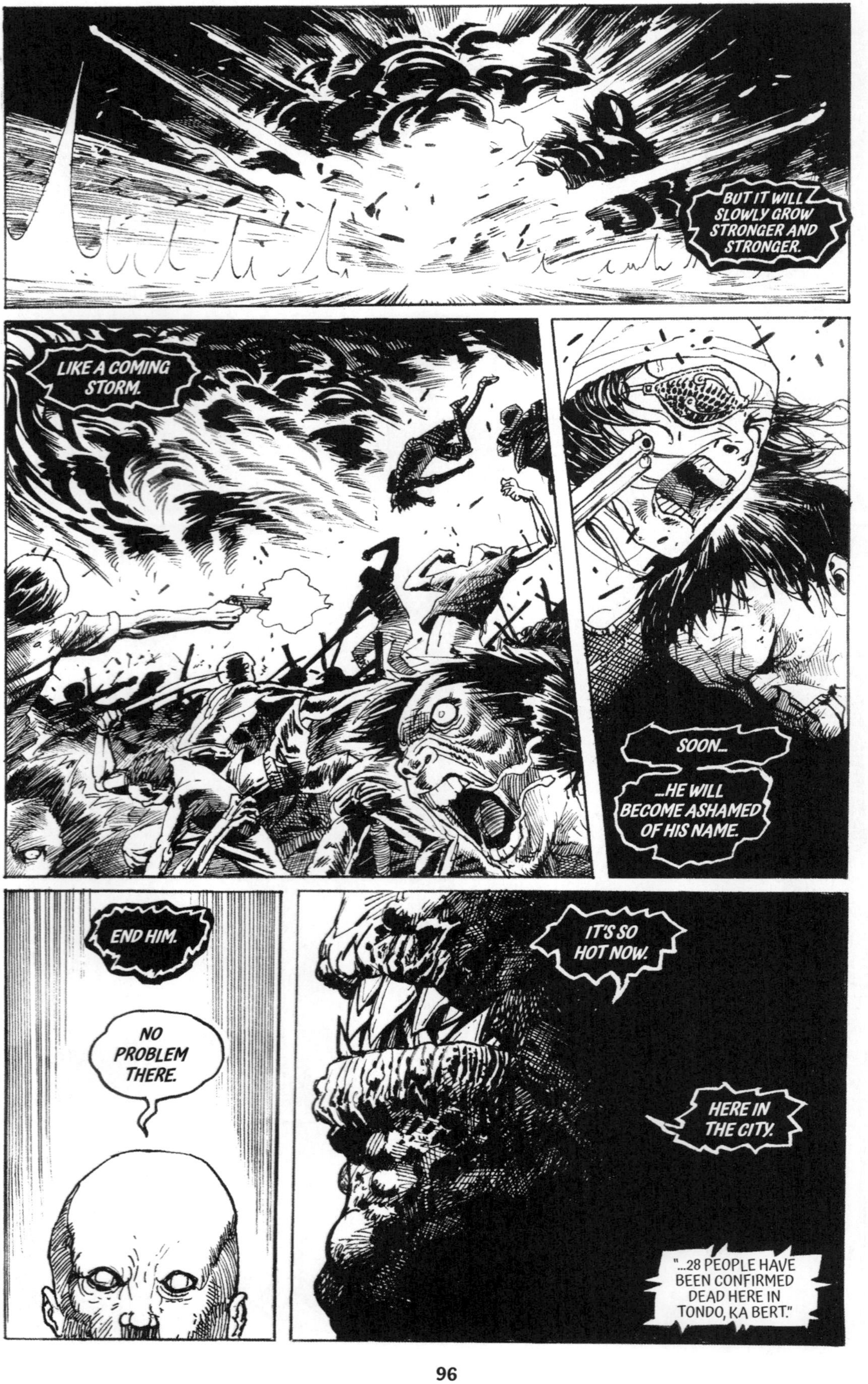
BUT IT WILL SLOWLY GROW STRONGER AND STRONGER.
LIKE A COMING STORM.
SOON...
...HE WILL BECOME ASHAMED OF HIS NAME.
END HIM.
NO PROBLEM THERE.
IT'S SO HOT NOW.
HERE IN THE CITY.
"...28 PEOPLE HAVE BEEN CONFIRMED DEAD HERE IN TONDO, KA BERT."

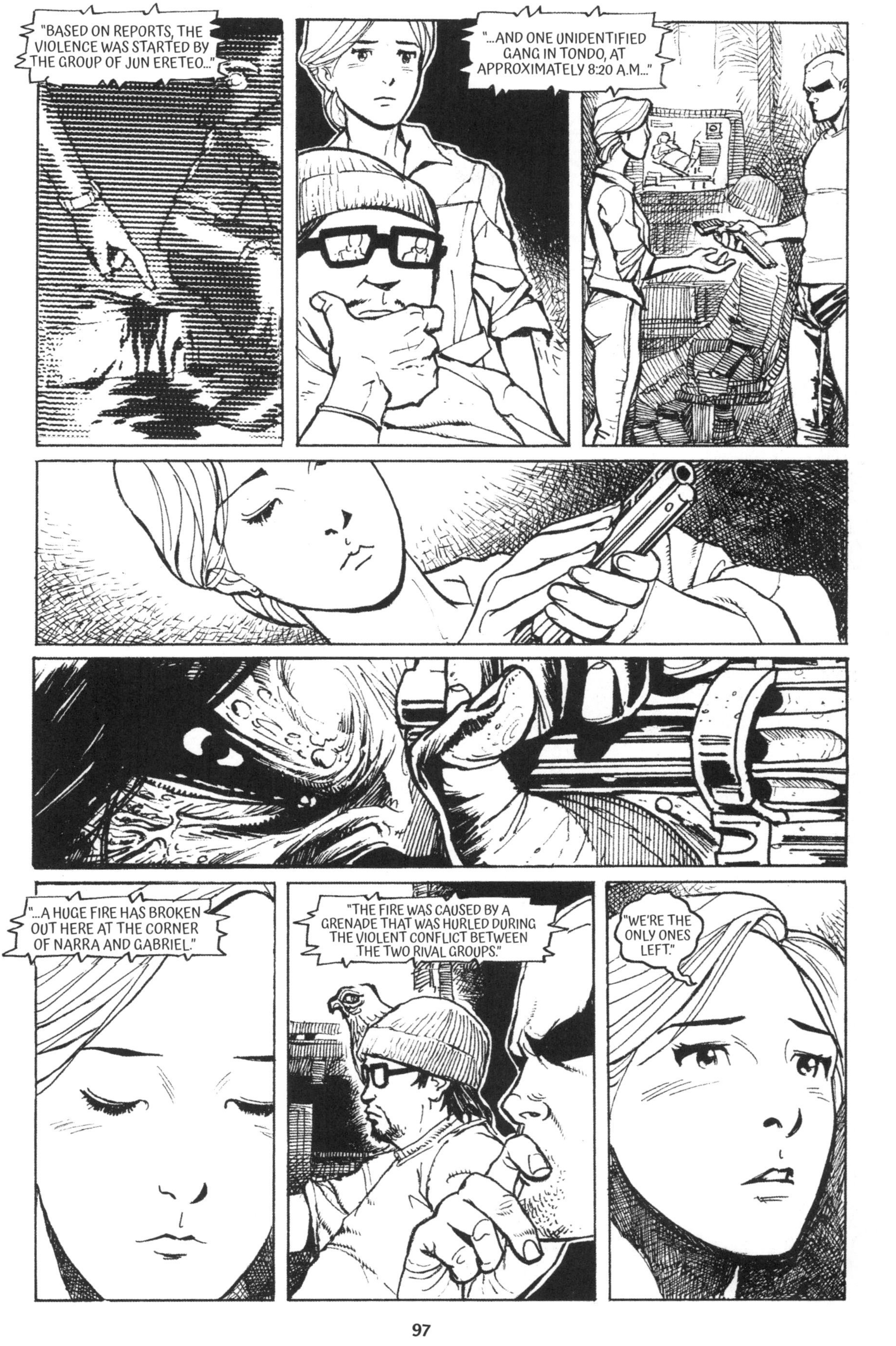
"BASED ON REPORTS, THE VIOLENCE WAS STARTED BY THE GROUP OF JUN ERETEO..."
"...AND ONE UNIDENTIFIED GANG IN TONDO, AT APPROXIMATELY 8:20 A.M..."
"...A HUGE FIRE HAS BROKEN OUT HERE AT THE CORNER OF NARRA AND GABRIEL."
"THE FIRE WAS CAUSED BY A GRENADE THAT WAS HURLED DURING THE VIOLENT CONFLICT BETWEEN THE TWO RIVAL GROUPS."
"WE'RE THE ONLY ONES LEFT."

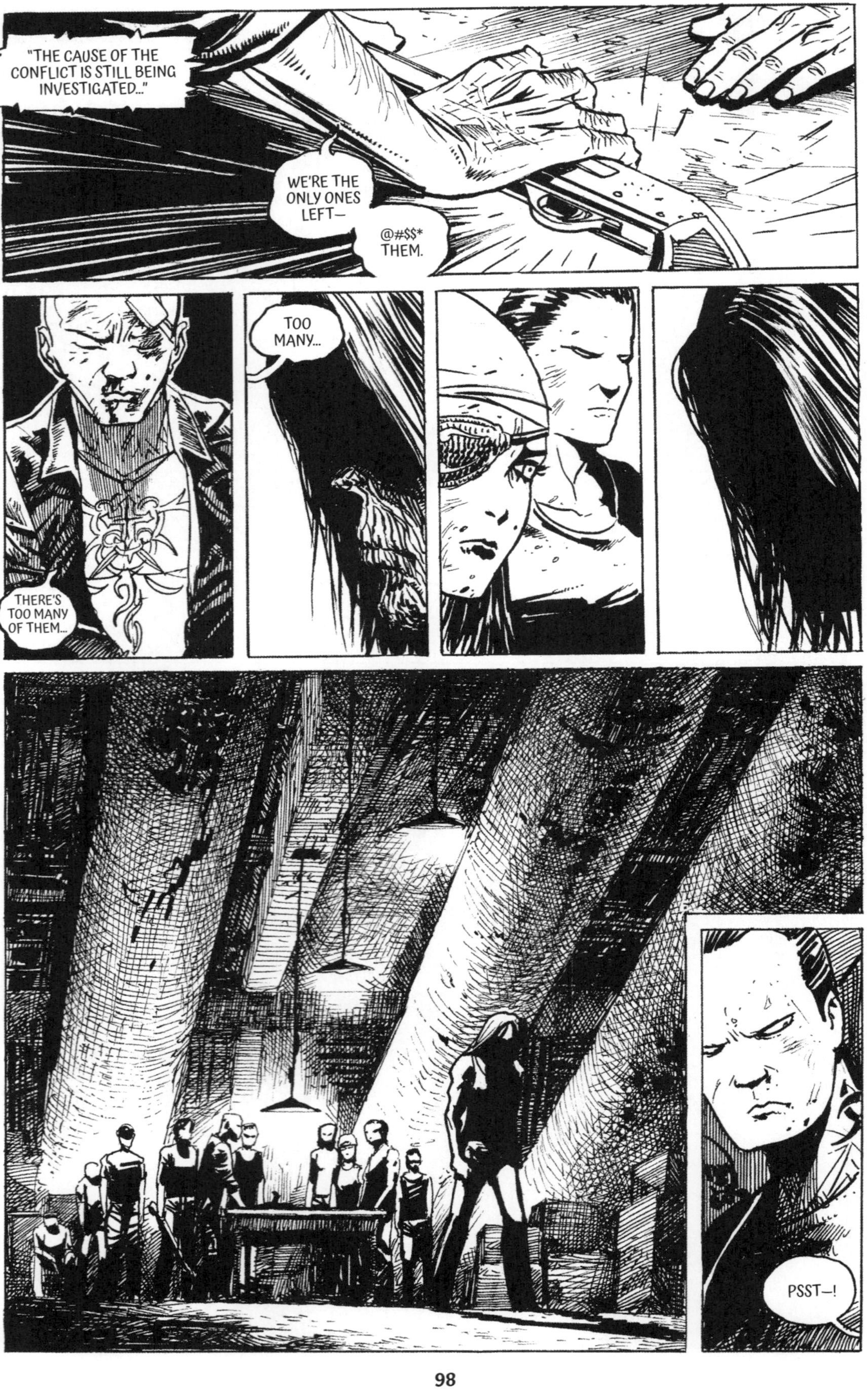
"THE CAUSE OF THE CONFLICT IS STILL BEING INVESTIGATED..."
WE'RE THE ONLY ONES LEFT—
@#$$* THEM.
THERE'S TOO MANY OF THEM...
TOO MANY...
PSST—!

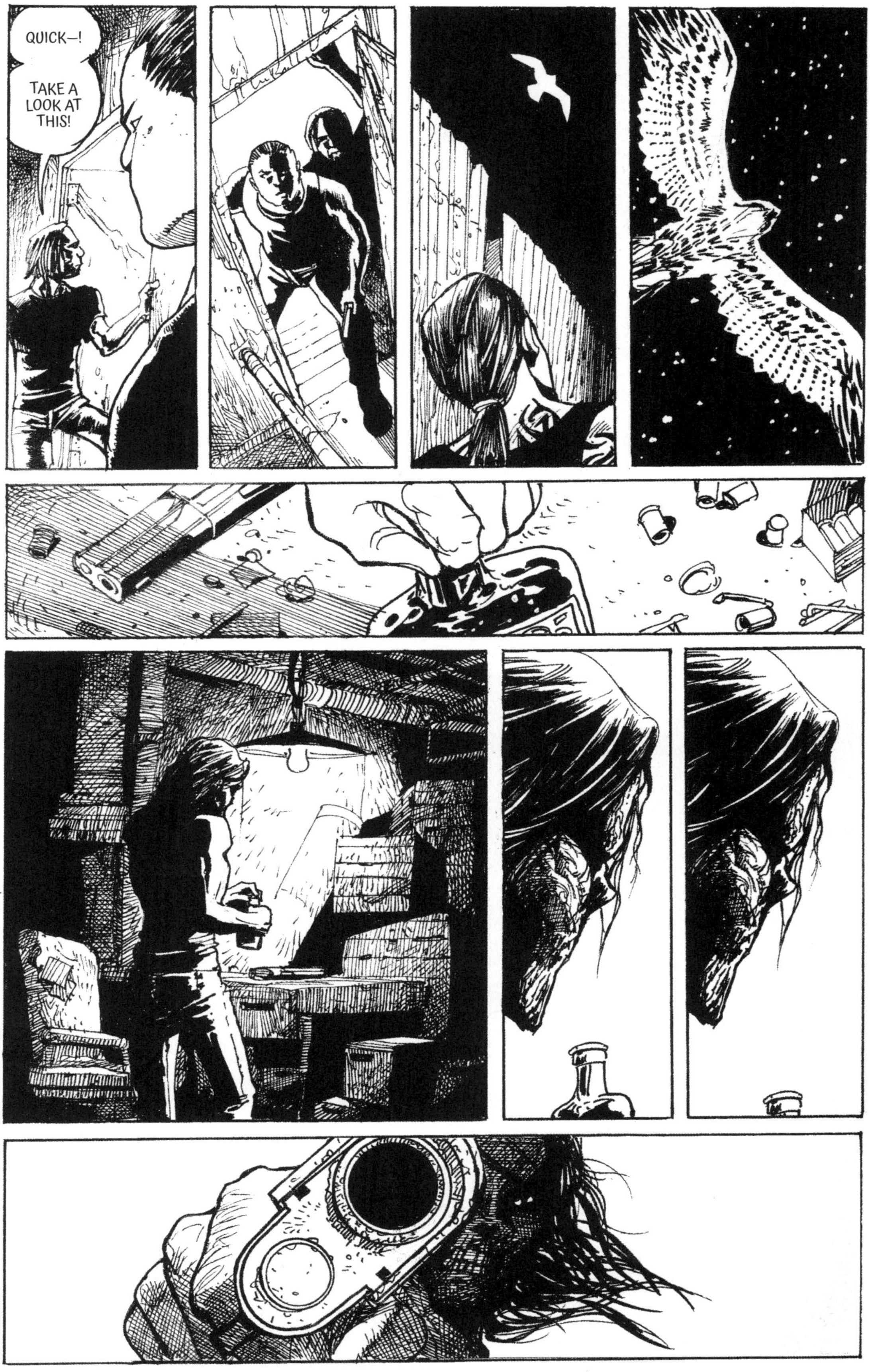
QUICK—!
TAKE A LOOK AT THIS!

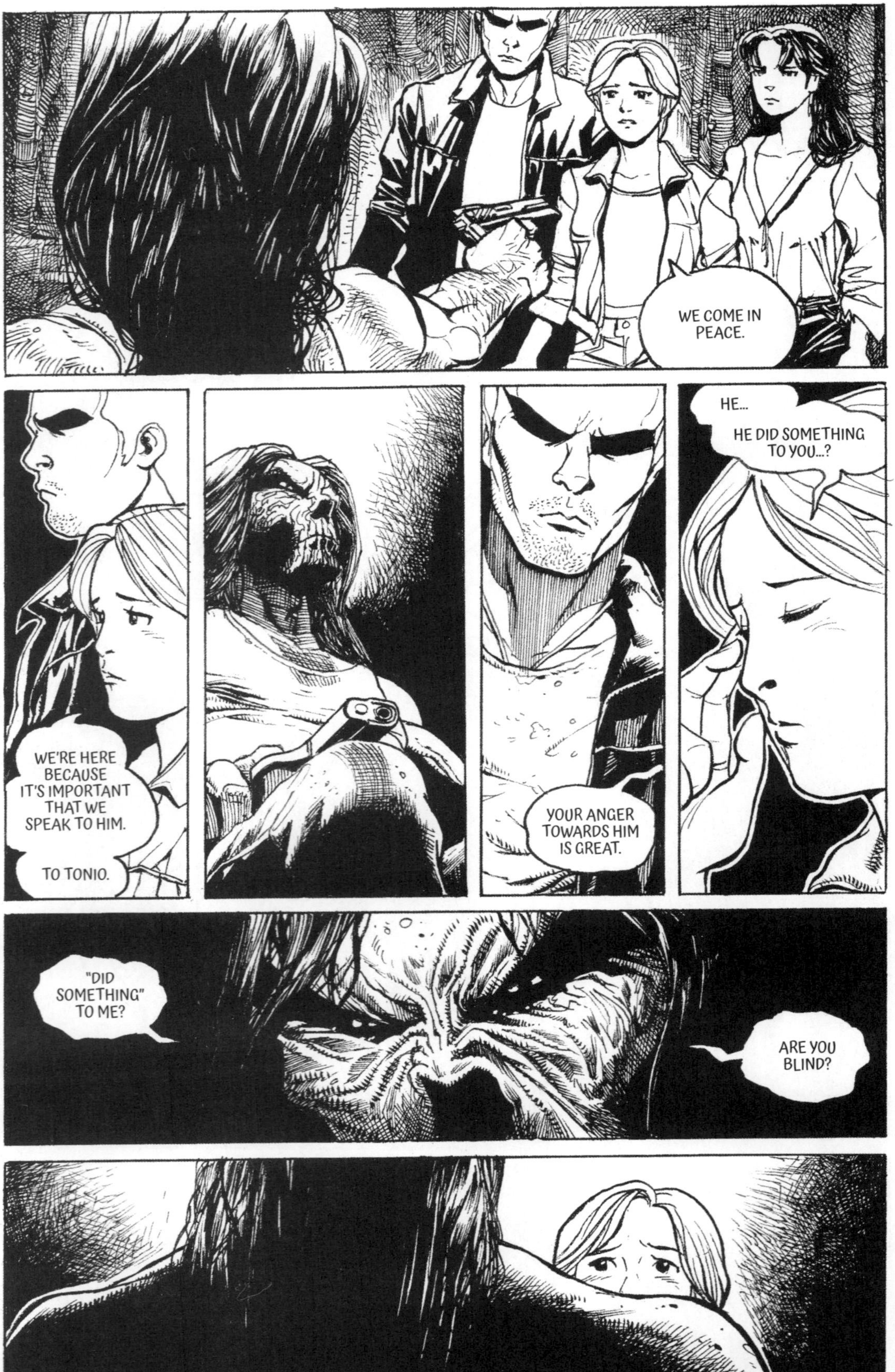
WE COME IN PEACE.
WE'RE HERE BECAUSE IT'S IMPORTANT THAT WE SPEAK TO HIM.
TO TONIO.
YOUR ANGER TOWARDS HIM IS GREAT.
HE...
HE DID SOMETHING TO YOU...?
"DID SOMETHING" TO ME?
ARE YOU BLIND?

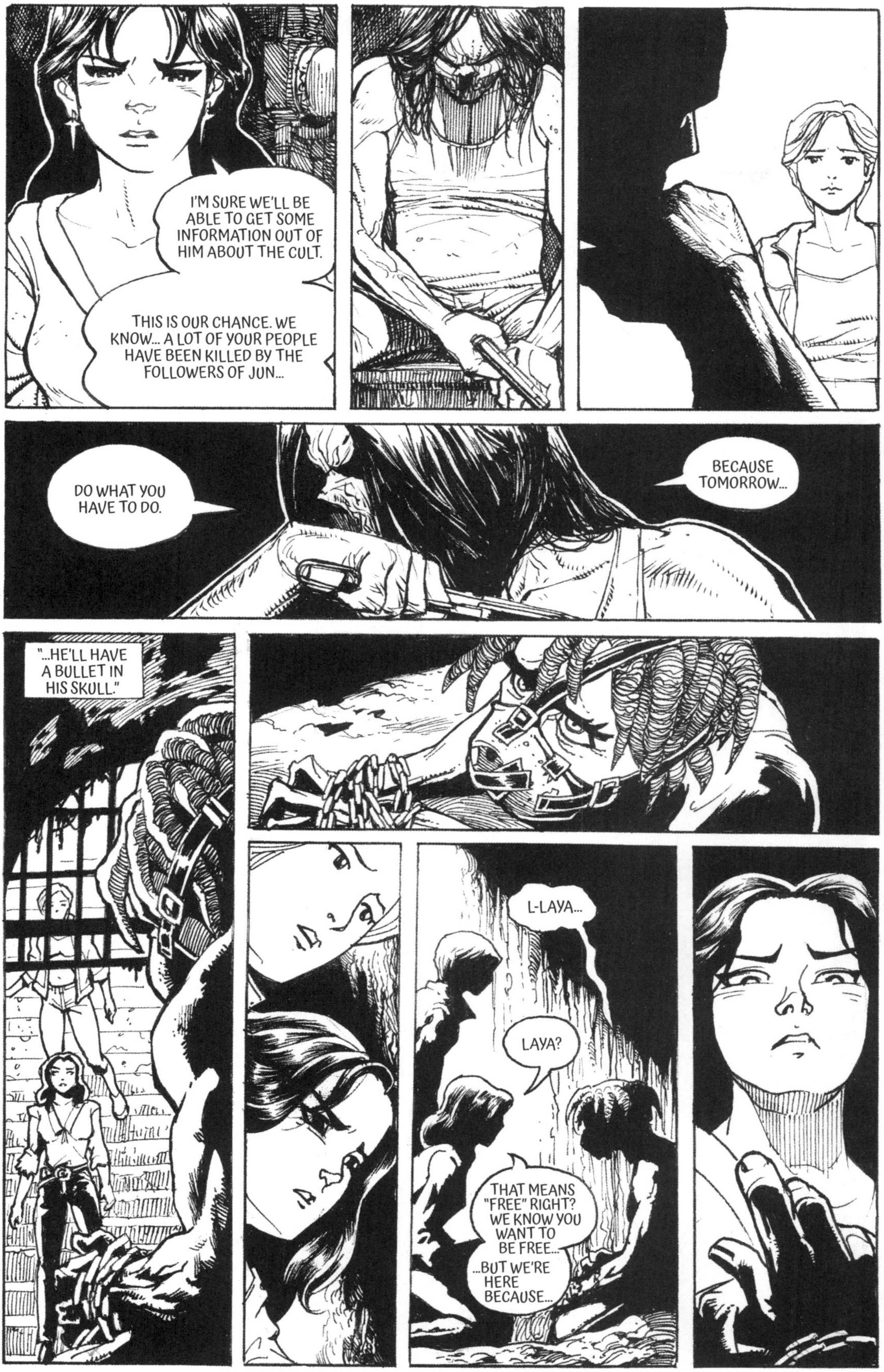
I'M SURE WE'LL BE ABLE TO GET SOME INFORMATION OUT OF HIM ABOUT THE CULT.
THIS IS OUR CHANCE. WE KNOW... A LOT OF YOUR PEOPLE HAVE BEEN KILLED BY THE FOLLOWERS OF JUN...
DO WHAT YOU HAVE TO DO.
BECAUSE TOMORROW...
"...HE'LL HAVE A BULLET IN HIS SKULL."
L-LAYA...
LAYA?
THAT MEANS "FREE" RIGHT? WE KNOW YOU WANT TO BE FREE...
...BUT WE'RE HERE BECAUSE...

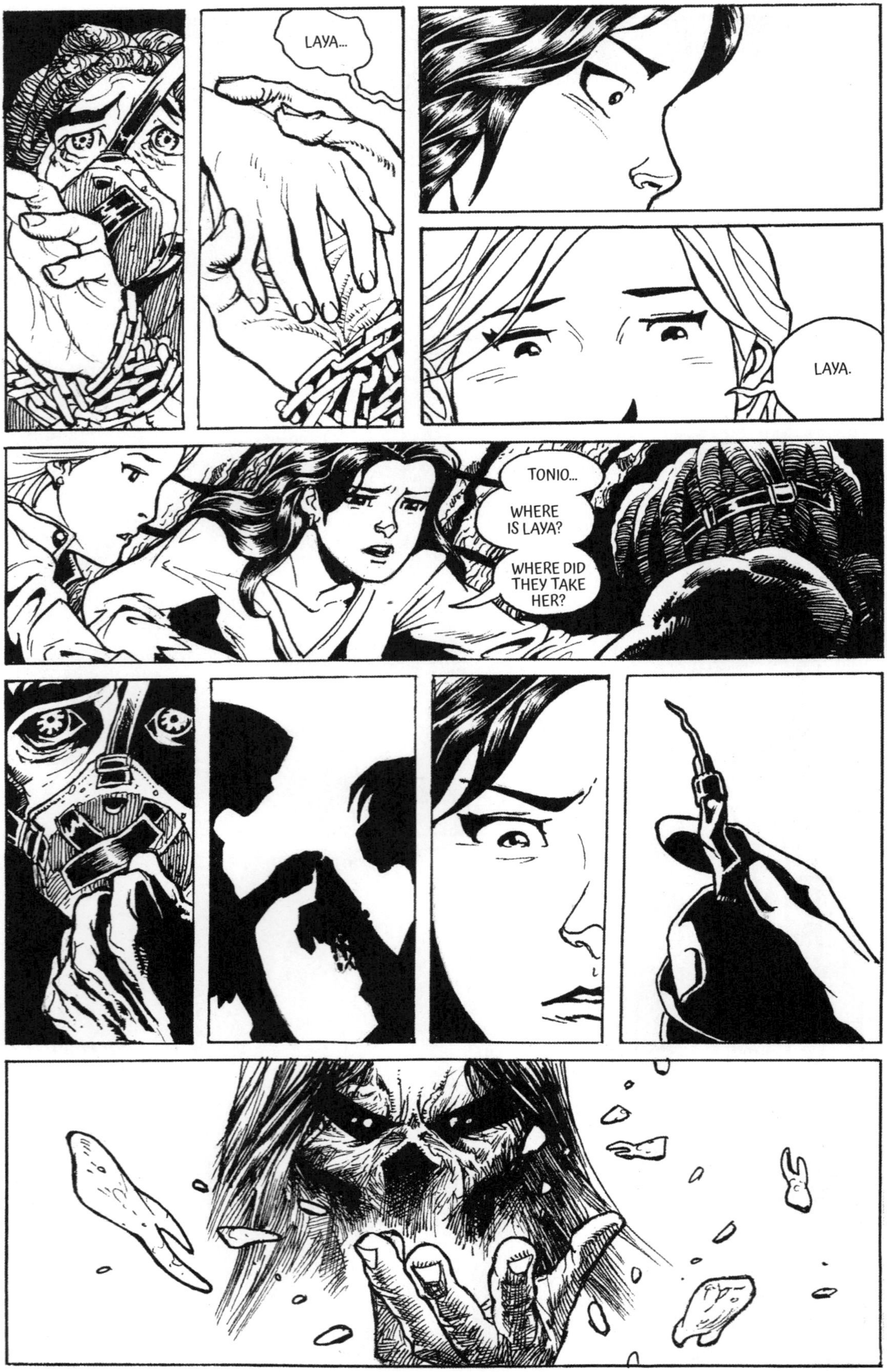
LAYA...
LAYA.
TONIO...
WHERE IS LAYA?
WHERE DID THEY TAKE HER?

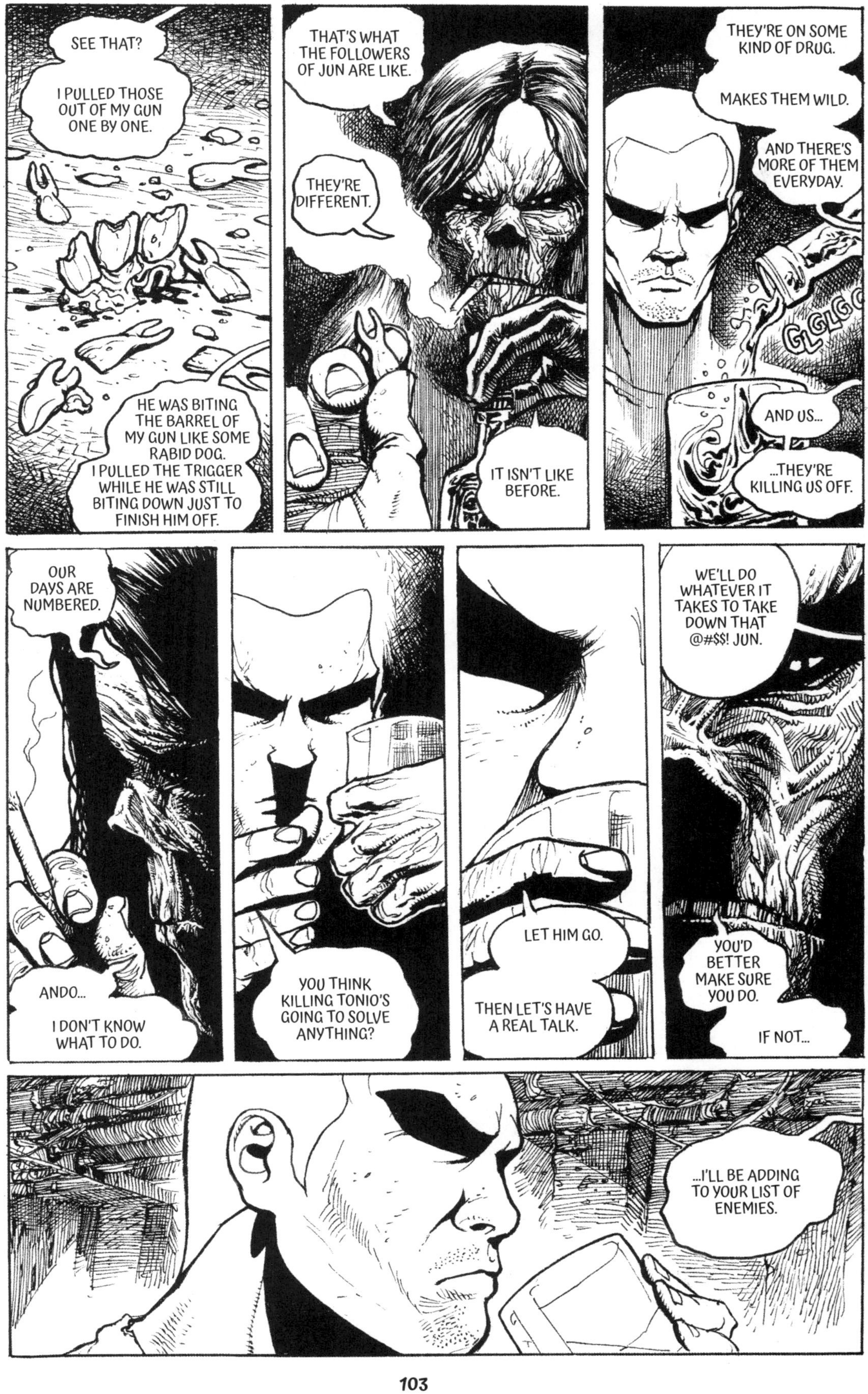

SEE THAT?
I PULLED THOSE OUT OF MY GUN ONE BY ONE.
HE WAS BITING THE BARREL OF MY GUN LIKE SOME RABID DOG. I PULLED THE TRIGGER WHILE HE WAS STILL BITING DOWN JUST TO FINISH HIM OFF.
THAT'S WHAT THE FOLLOWERS OF JUN ARE LIKE.
THEY'RE DIFFERENT.
IT ISN'T LIKE BEFORE.
THEY'RE ON SOME KIND OF DRUG.
MAKES THEM WILD.
AND THERE'S MORE OF THEM EVERYDAY.
GLGLG
AND US...
...THEY'RE KILLING US OFF.
OUR DAYS ARE NUMBERED.
ANDO...
I DON'T KNOW WHAT TO DO.
YOU THINK KILLING TONIO'S GOING TO SOLVE ANYTHING?
LET HIM GO.
THEN LET'S HAVE A REAL TALK.
WE'LL DO WHATEVER IT TAKES TO TAKE DOWN THAT @#$$! JUN.
YOU'D BETTER MAKE SURE YOU DO.
IF NOT...
...I'LL BE ADDING TO YOUR LIST OF ENEMIES.

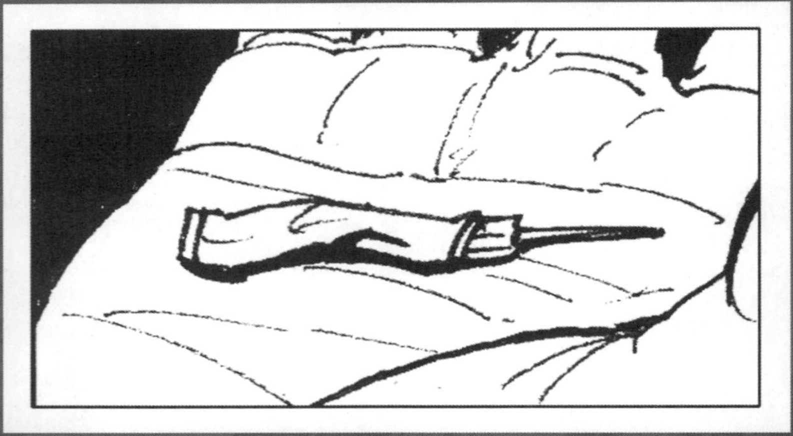

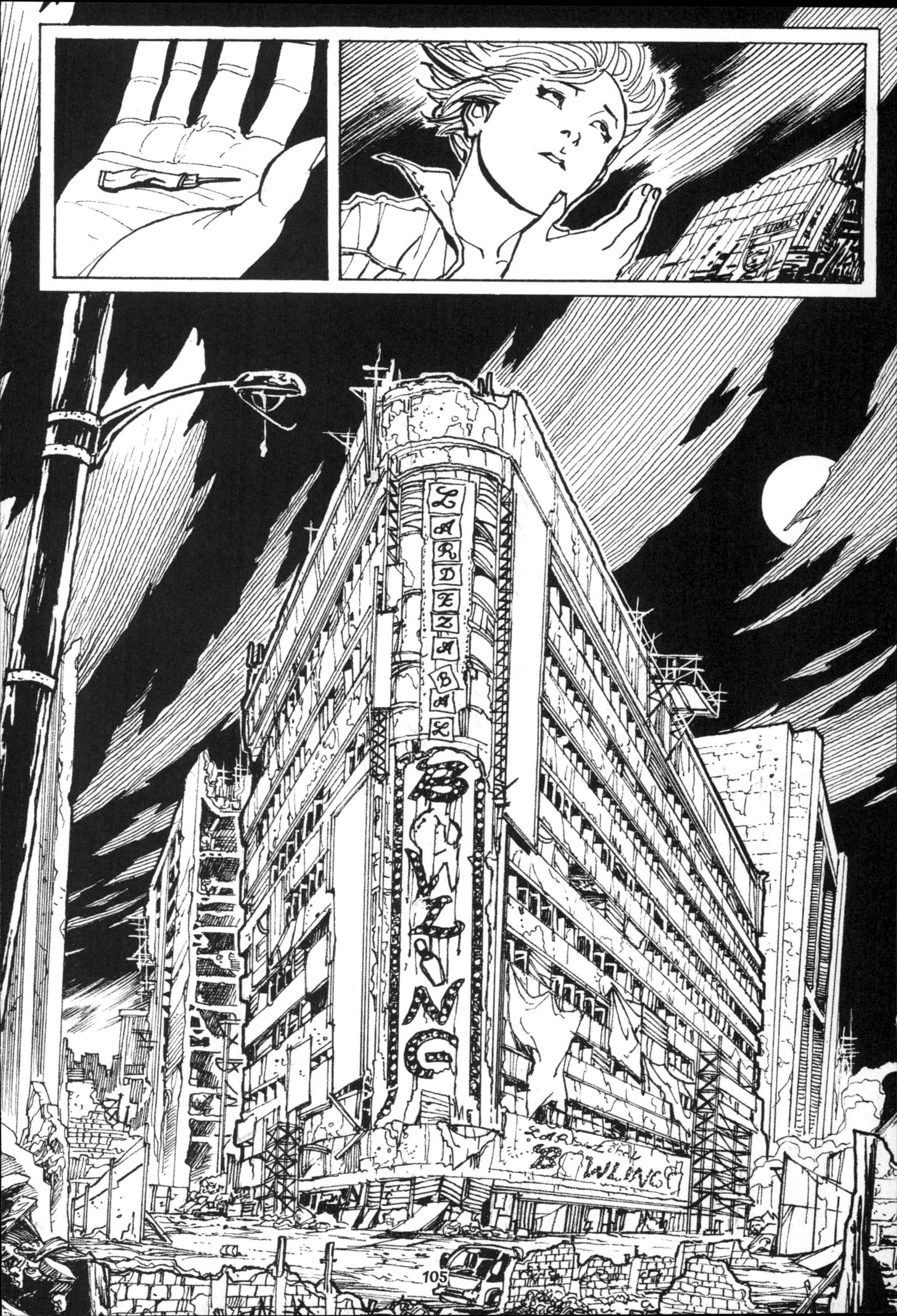
LARDEZZABAL

— DO YOU HAVE THE STRENGTH FOR THIS? WE'RE NOT IN PALAWAN ANYMORE.

— I'M STRONG ENOUGH TO WATCH YOU WORK.

— AND SO I CAN TALK TO THAT @#$$! PEDRO.

— YOU'VE GOT A JOB FOR HIM?

— I WANT HIM TO GO NUTS ON THIS CITY.

— AS MUCH AS HE WANTS.

"AHH...311, JUST A ROUTINE CHECK. HOW'S THE CARGO? OVER."

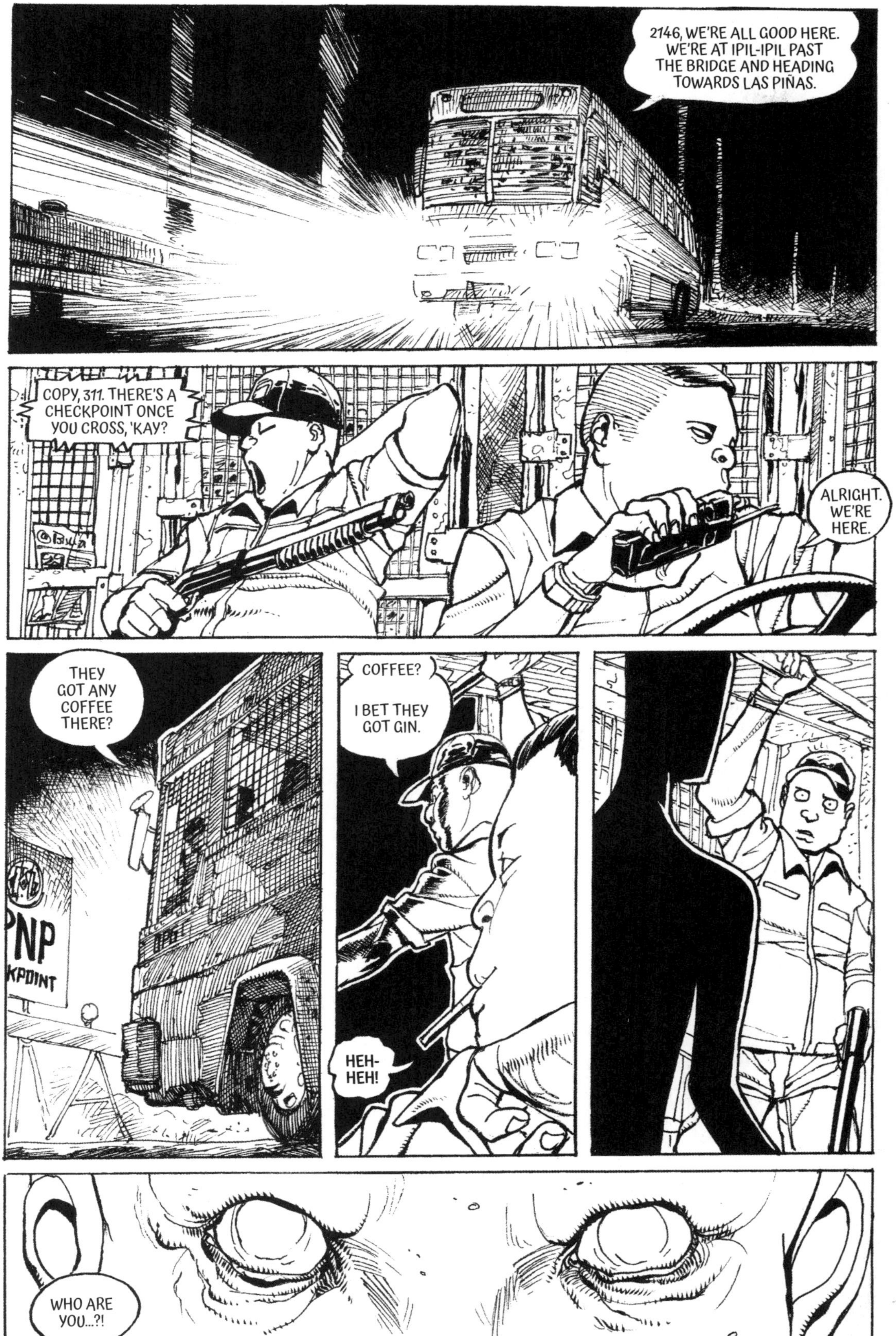
2146, WE'RE ALL GOOD HERE. WE'RE AT IPIL-IPIL PAST THE BRIDGE AND HEADING TOWARDS LAS PIÑAS.
COPY, 311. THERE'S A CHECKPOINT ONCE YOU CROSS, 'KAY?
ALRIGHT. WE'RE HERE.
THEY GOT ANY COFFEE THERE?
PNP
KPOINT
COFFEE?
I BET THEY GOT GIN.
HEH-HEH!
WHO ARE YOU...?!

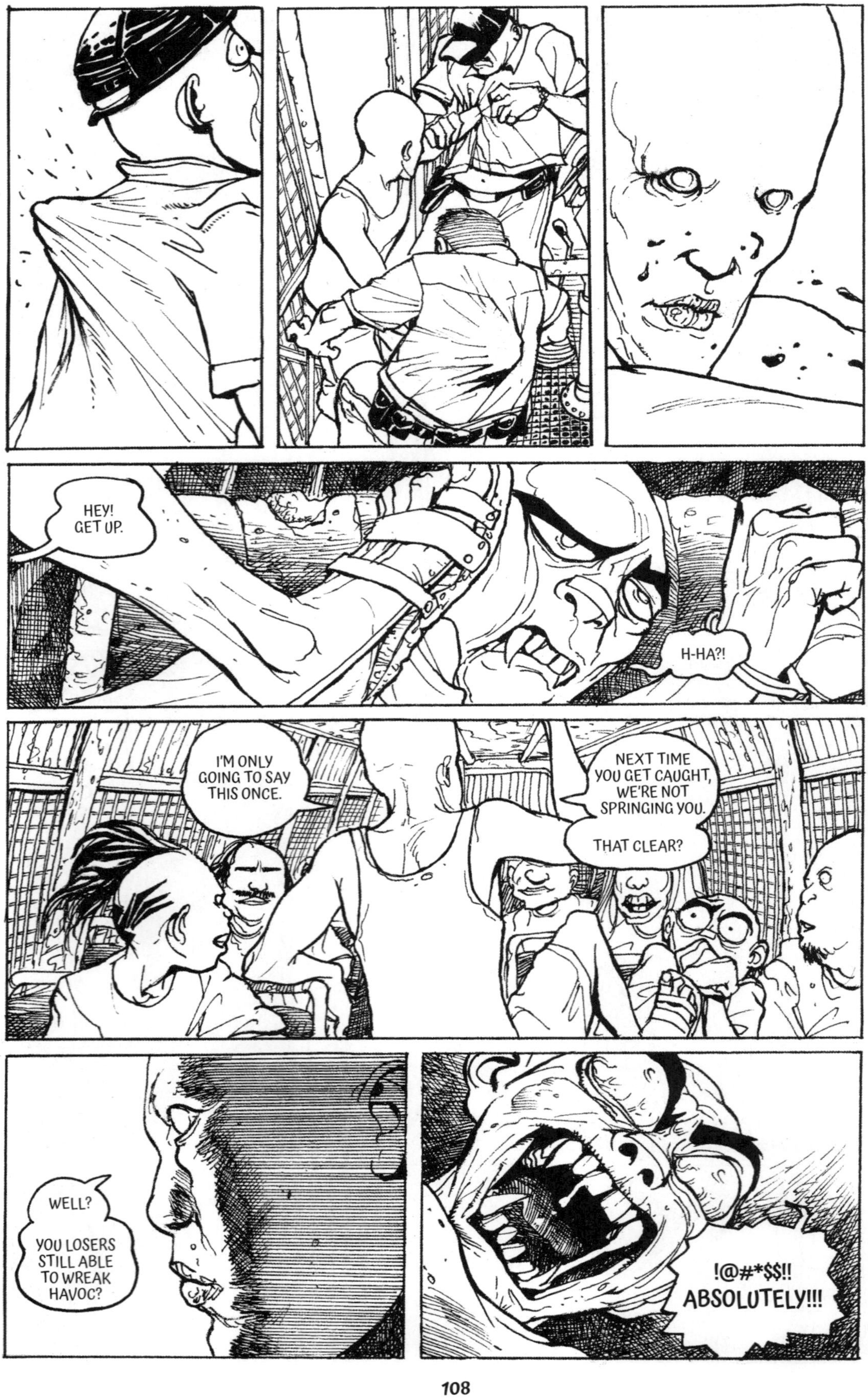
HEY! GET UP.
H-HA?!
I'M ONLY GOING TO SAY THIS ONCE.
NEXT TIME YOU GET CAUGHT, WE'RE NOT SPRINGING YOU.
THAT CLEAR?
WELL?
YOU LOSERS STILL ABLE TO WREAK HAVOC?
!@#*$$!! ABSOLUTELY!!!

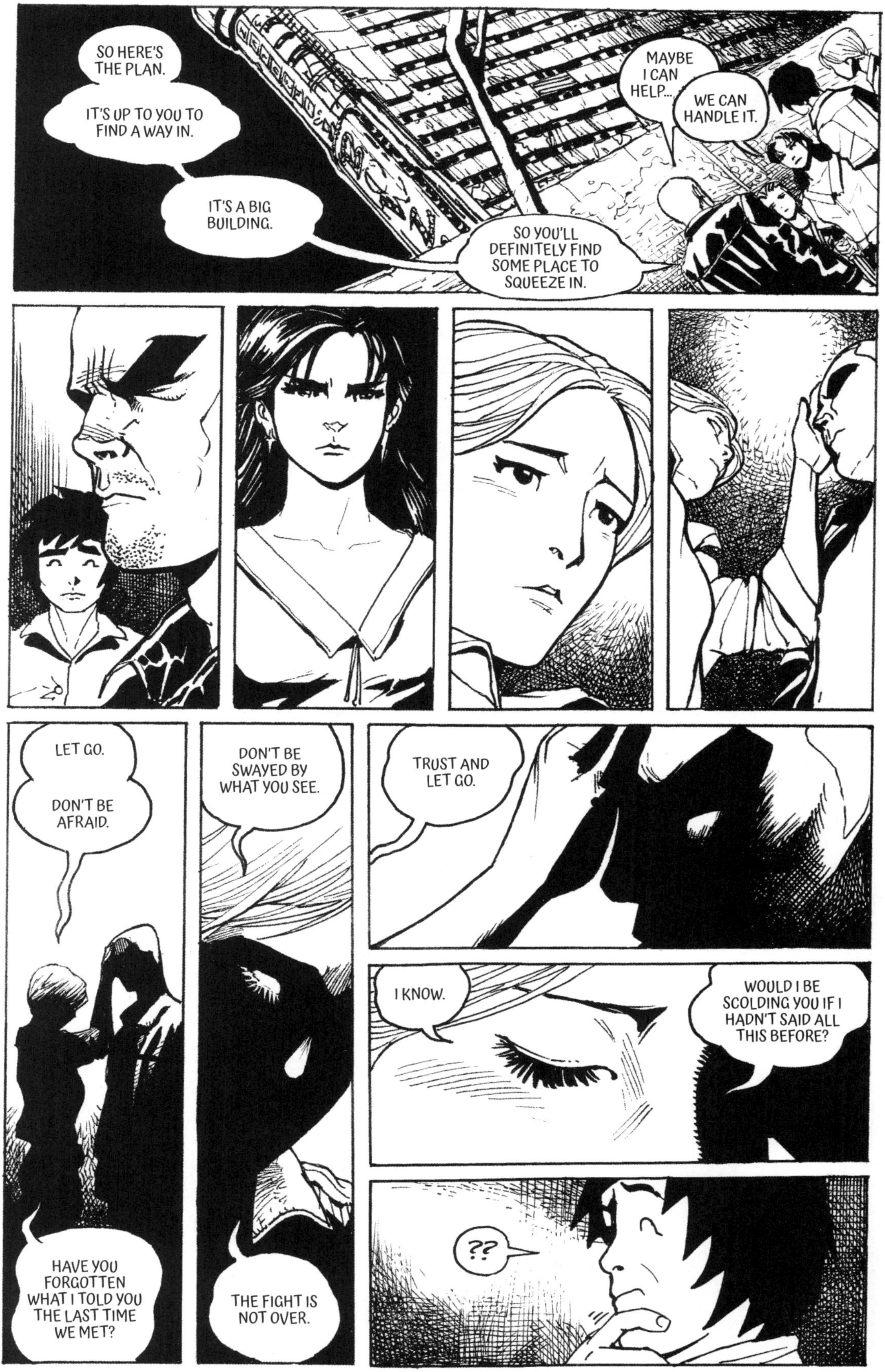
SO HERE'S THE PLAN.
IT'S UP TO YOU TO FIND A WAY IN.
IT'S A BIG BUILDING.
SO YOU'LL DEFINITELY FIND SOME PLACE TO SQUEEZE IN.
MAYBE I CAN HELP...
WE CAN HANDLE IT.
LET GO.
DON'T BE AFRAID.
HAVE YOU FORGOTTEN WHAT I TOLD YOU THE LAST TIME WE MET?
DON'T BE SWAYED BY WHAT YOU SEE.
THE FIGHT IS NOT OVER.
TRUST AND LET GO.
I KNOW.
WOULD I BE SCOLDING YOU IF I HADN'T SAID ALL THIS BEFORE?
??

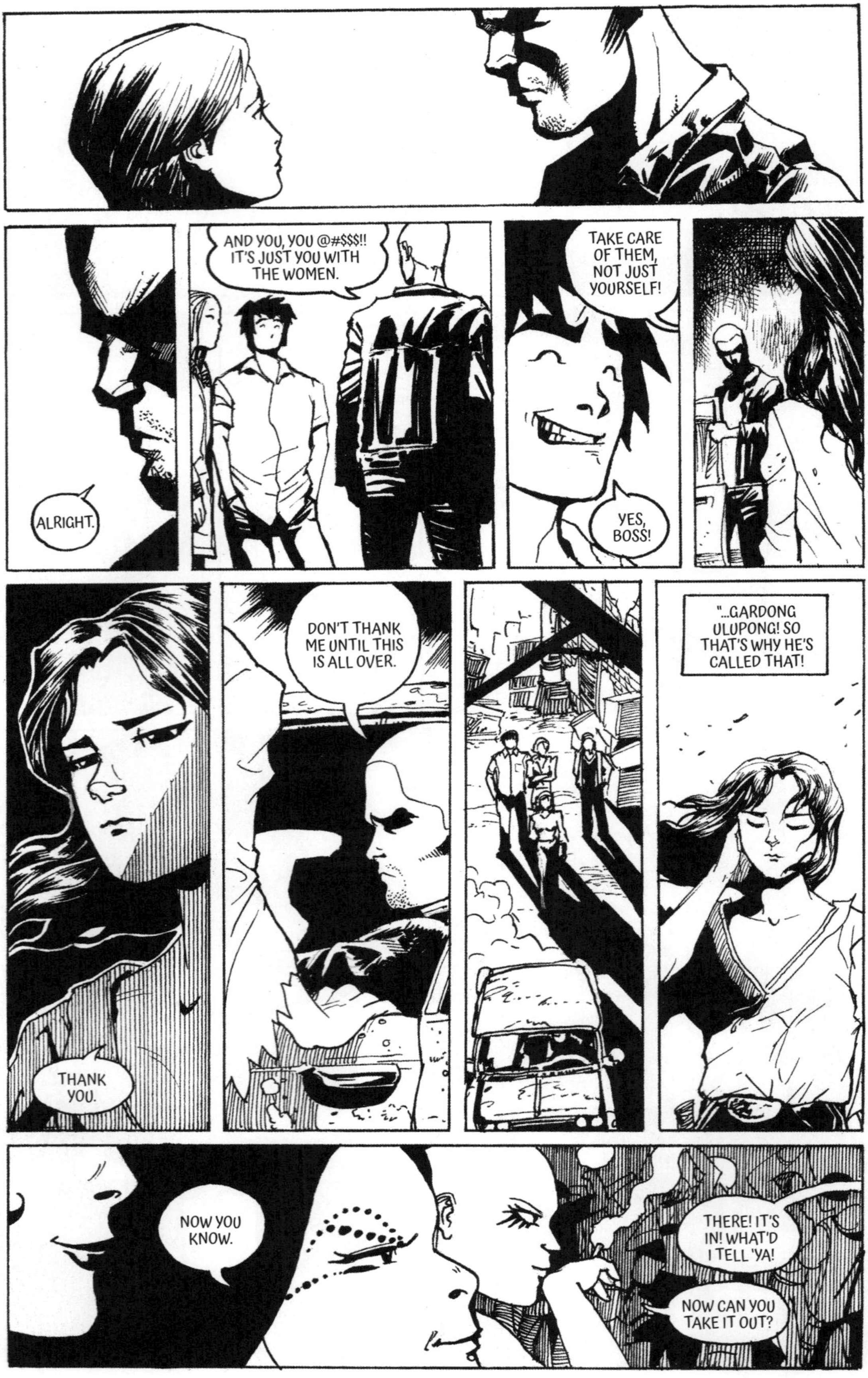
ALRIGHT.
AND YOU, YOU @#$$$!! IT'S JUST YOU WITH THE WOMEN.
TAKE CARE OF THEM, NOT JUST YOURSELF!
YES, BOSS!
THANK YOU.
DON'T THANK ME UNTIL THIS IS ALL OVER.
"...GARDONG ULUPONG! SO THAT'S WHY HE'S CALLED THAT!
NOW YOU KNOW.
THERE! IT'S IN! WHAT'D I TELL 'YA!
NOW CAN YOU TAKE IT OUT?

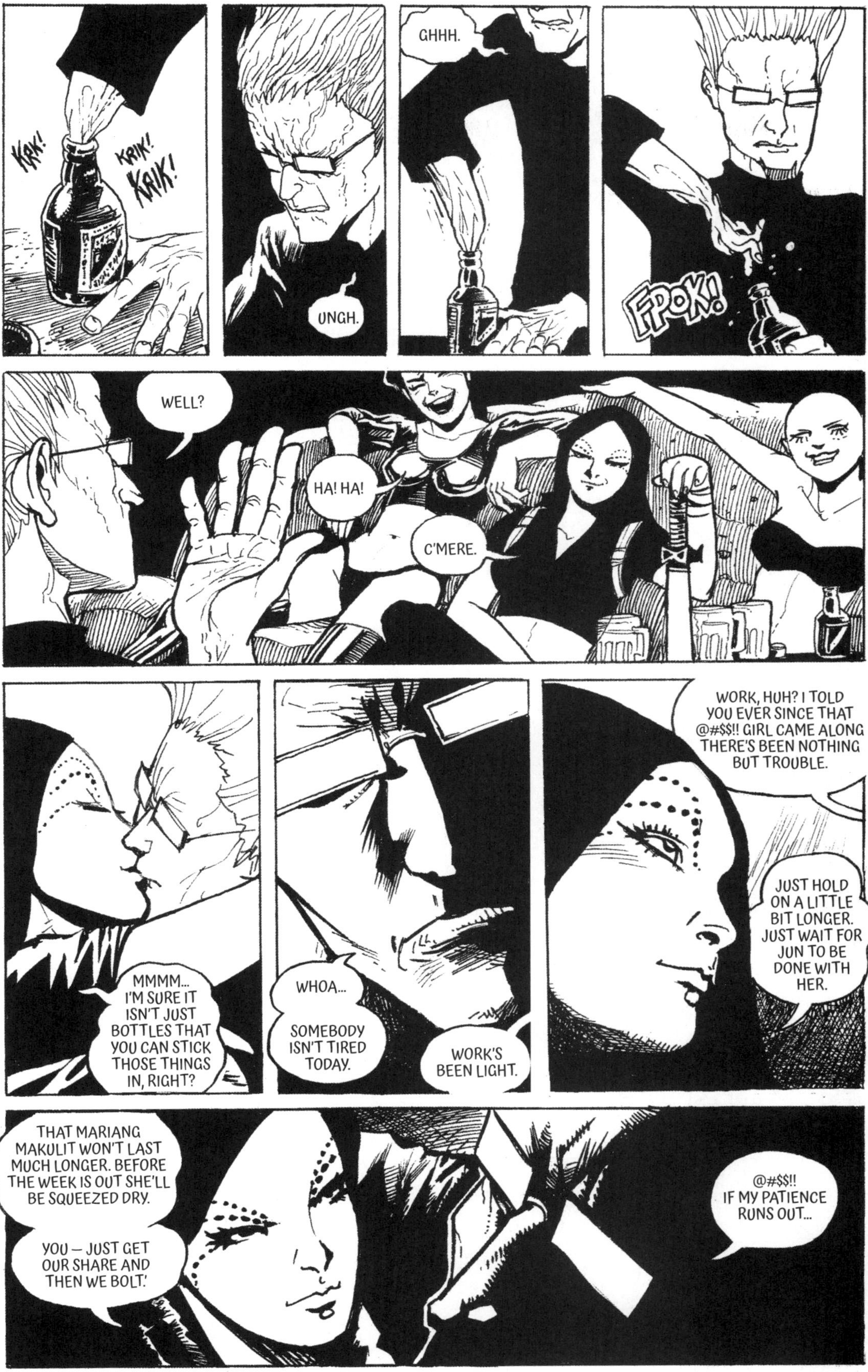
KRIK!
KRIK!
KRIK!
UNGH.
GHHH.
FPOK!
WELL?
HA! HA!
C'MERE.
MMMM... I'M SURE IT ISN'T JUST BOTTLES THAT YOU CAN STICK THOSE THINGS IN, RIGHT?
WHOA...
SOMEBODY ISN'T TIRED TODAY.
WORK'S BEEN LIGHT.
WORK, HUH? I TOLD YOU EVER SINCE THAT @#$$!! GIRL CAME ALONG THERE'S BEEN NOTHING BUT TROUBLE.
JUST HOLD ON A LITTLE BIT LONGER. JUST WAIT FOR JUN TO BE DONE WITH HER.
THAT MARIANG MAKULIT WON'T LAST MUCH LONGER. BEFORE THE WEEK IS OUT SHE'LL BE SQUEEZED DRY.
YOU — JUST GET OUR SHARE AND THEN WE BOLT.'
@#$$!! IF MY PATIENCE RUNS OUT...

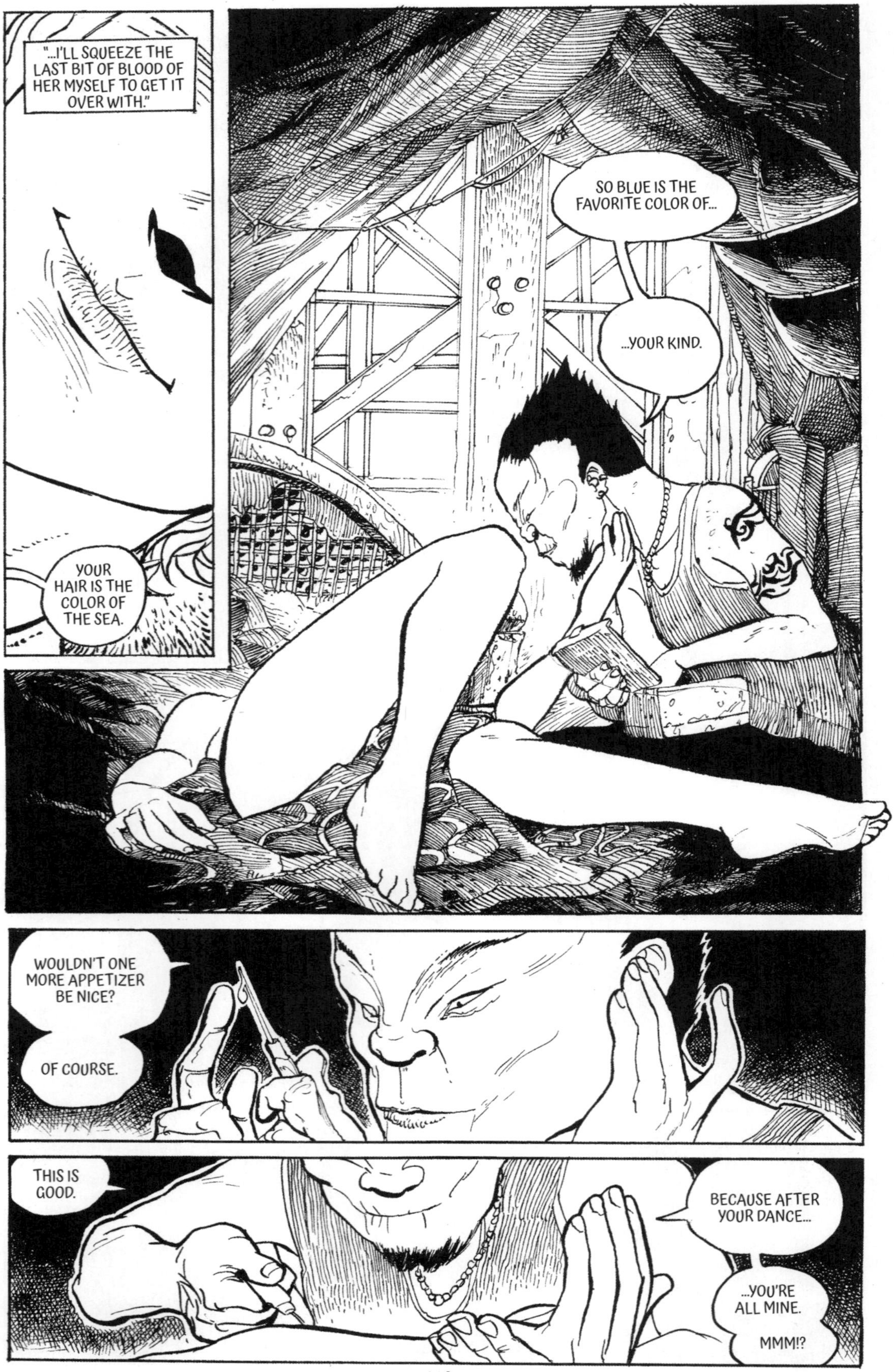
"...I'LL SQUEEZE THE LAST BIT OF BLOOD OF HER MYSELF TO GET IT OVER WITH."
SO BLUE IS THE FAVORITE COLOR OF...
...YOUR KIND.
YOUR HAIR IS THE COLOR OF THE SEA.
WOULDN'T ONE MORE APPETIZER BE NICE?
OF COURSE.
THIS IS GOOD.
BECAUSE AFTER YOUR DANCE...
...YOU'RE ALL MINE.
MMM!?

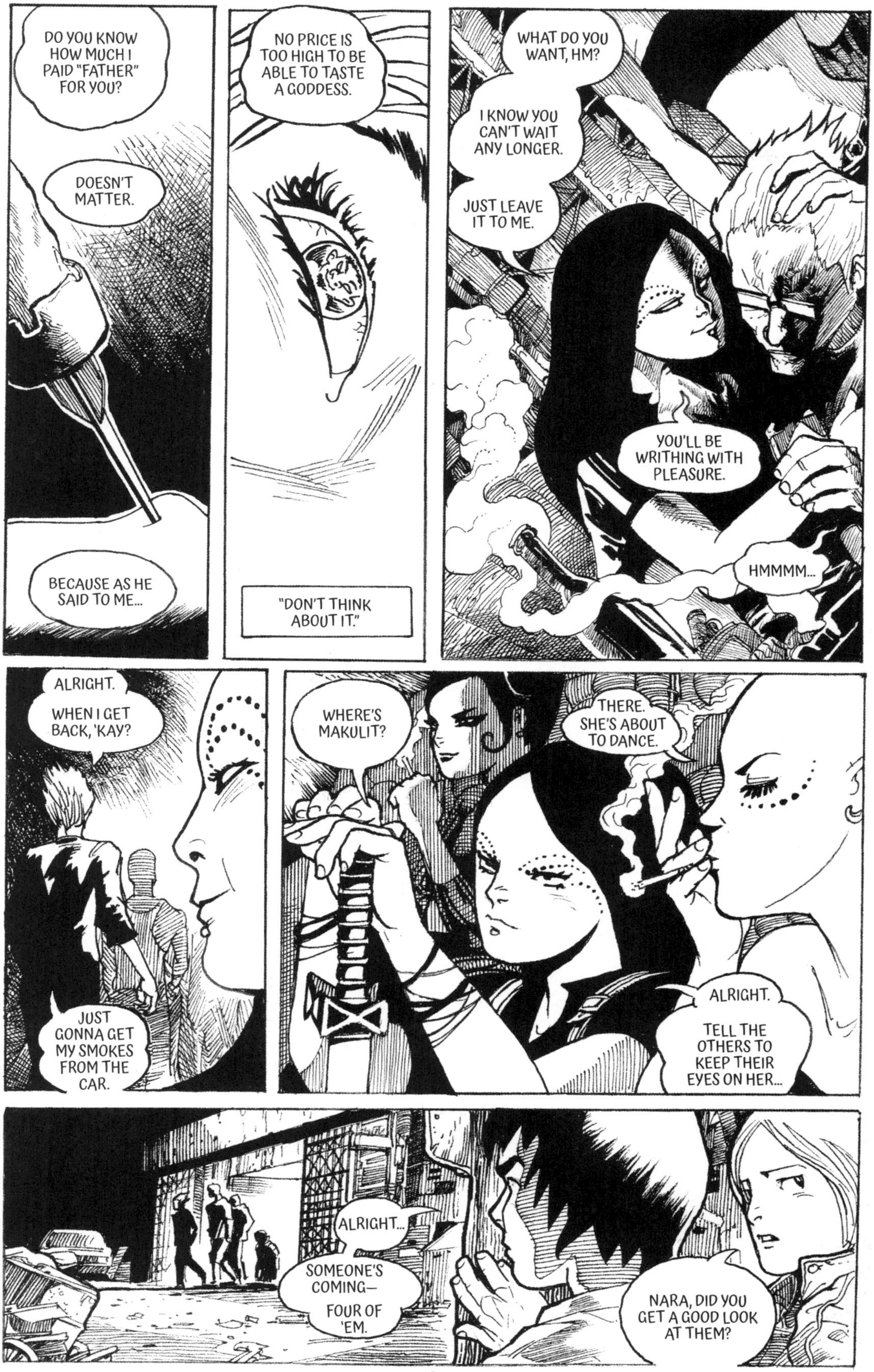
DO YOU KNOW HOW MUCH I PAID "FATHER" FOR YOU?
DOESN'T MATTER.
BECAUSE AS HE SAID TO ME...
NO PRICE IS TOO HIGH TO BE ABLE TO TASTE A GODDESS.
"DON'T THINK ABOUT IT."
WHAT DO YOU WANT, HM?
I KNOW YOU CAN'T WAIT ANY LONGER.
JUST LEAVE IT TO ME.
YOU'LL BE WRITHING WITH PLEASURE.
HMMMM...
ALRIGHT.
WHEN I GET BACK, 'KAY?
JUST GONNA GET MY SMOKES FROM THE CAR.
WHERE'S MAKULIT?
THERE. SHE'S ABOUT TO DANCE.
ALRIGHT.
TELL THE OTHERS TO KEEP THEIR EYES ON HER...
ALRIGHT...
SOMEONE'S COMING—
FOUR OF 'EM.
NARA, DID YOU GET A GOOD LOOK AT THEM?

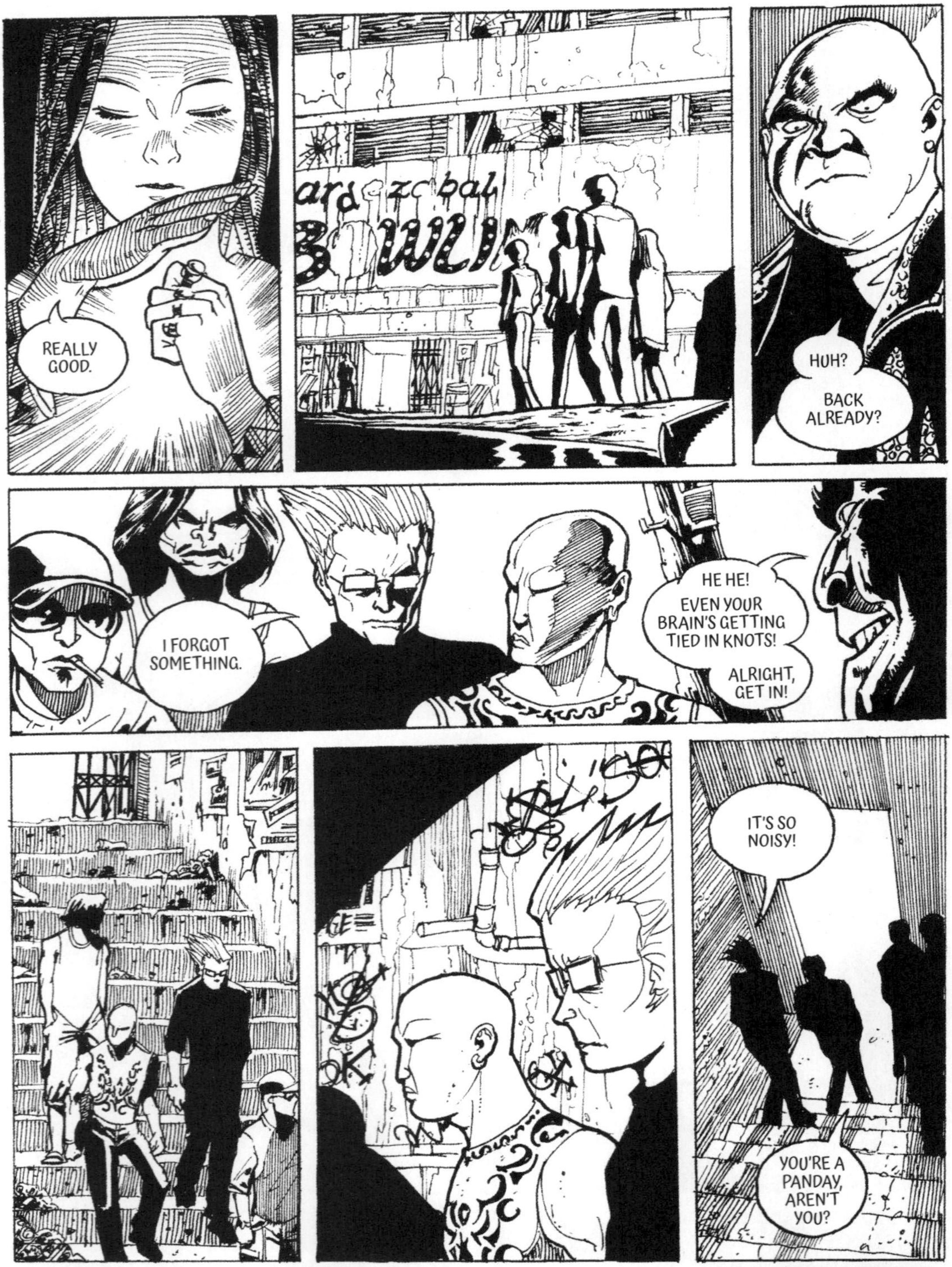
REALLY GOOD.
ard zobal
BOWLI
HUH?
BACK ALREADY?
I FORGOT SOMETHING.
HE HE!
EVEN YOUR BRAIN'S GETTING TIED IN KNOTS!
ALRIGHT, GET IN!
IT'S SO NOISY!
YOU'RE A PANDAY, AREN'T YOU?
YOU SHOULD BE USED TO THIS.
YEAH. YEAH.

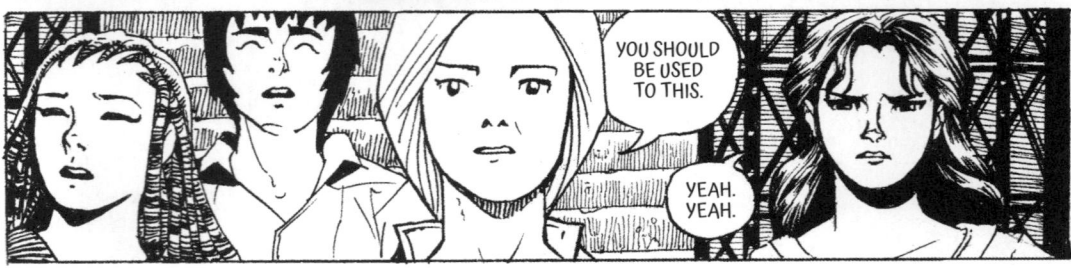

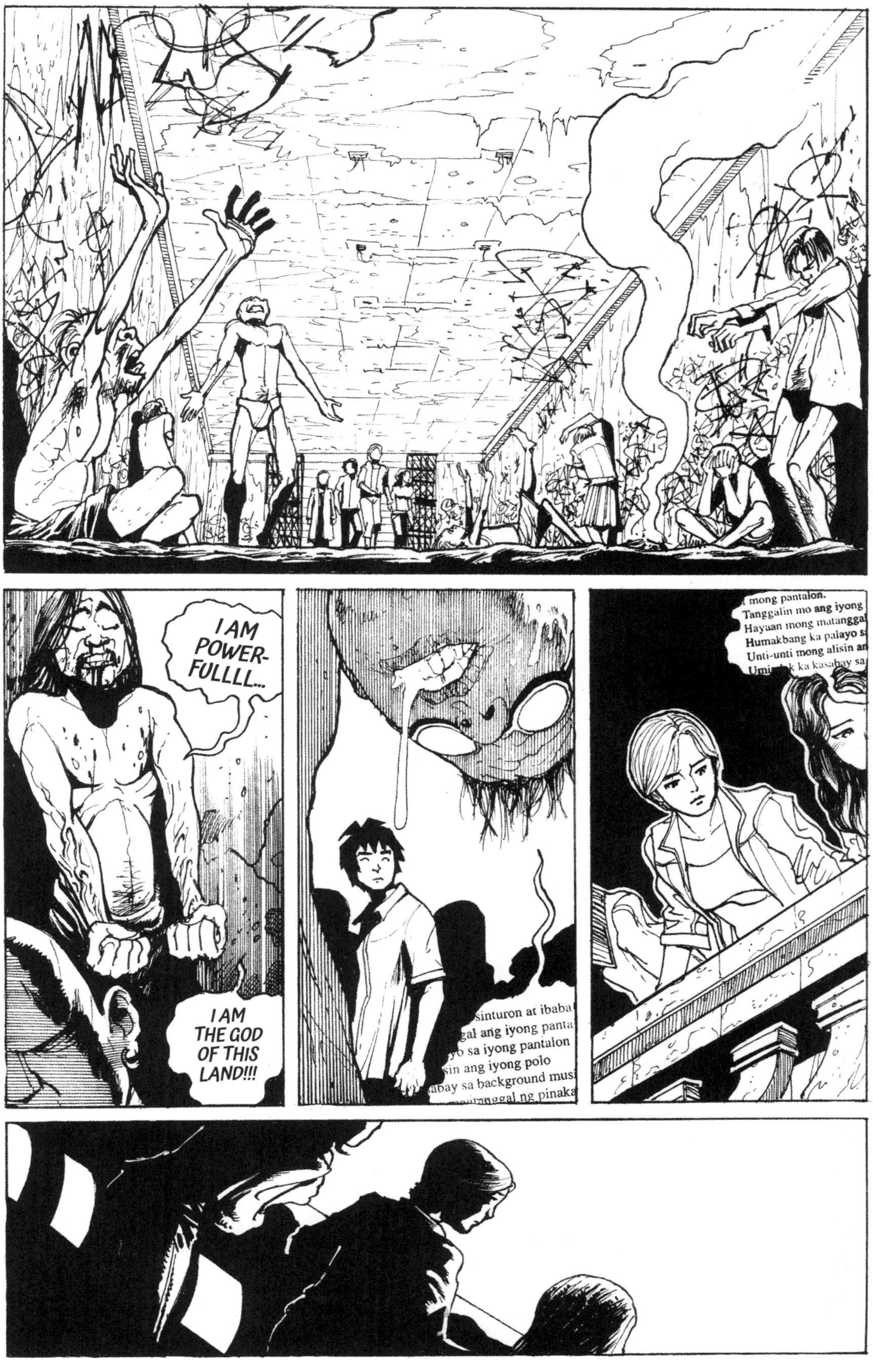

I AM POWER-FULLLL...
I AM THE GOD OF THIS LAND!!!
sinturon at ibaba
gal ang iyong panta
yo sa iyong pantalon
sin ang iyong polo
abay sa background musi
mong pantalon.
Tanggalin mo ang iyong
Hayaan mong matangga
Humakbang ka palayo sa
Unti-unti mong alisin an

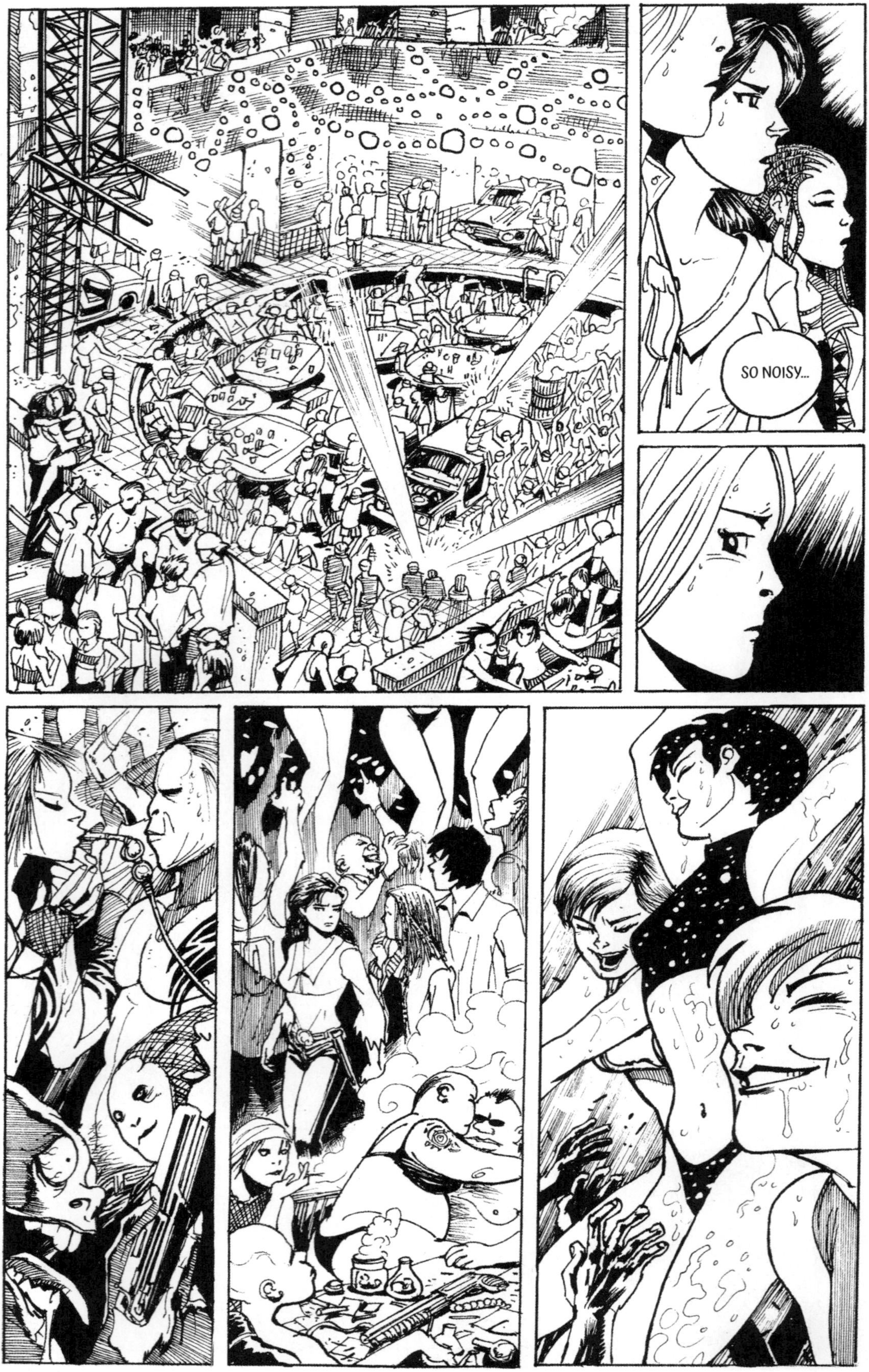
SO NOISY...

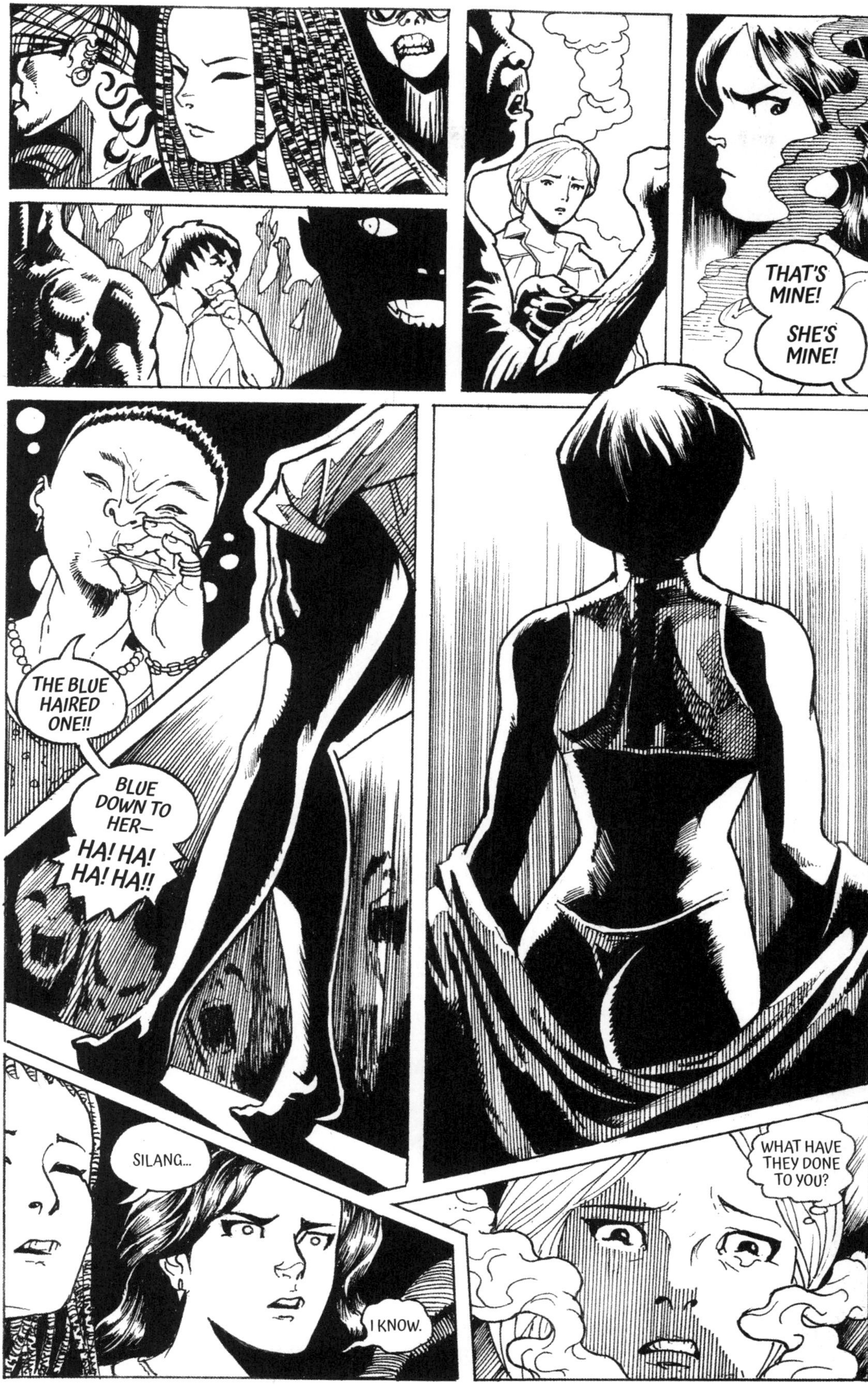
THAT'S MINE!
SHE'S MINE!
THE BLUE HAIRED ONE!!
BLUE DOWN TO HER—
HA! HA! HA! HA!!
SILANG...
I KNOW.
WHAT HAVE THEY DONE TO YOU?

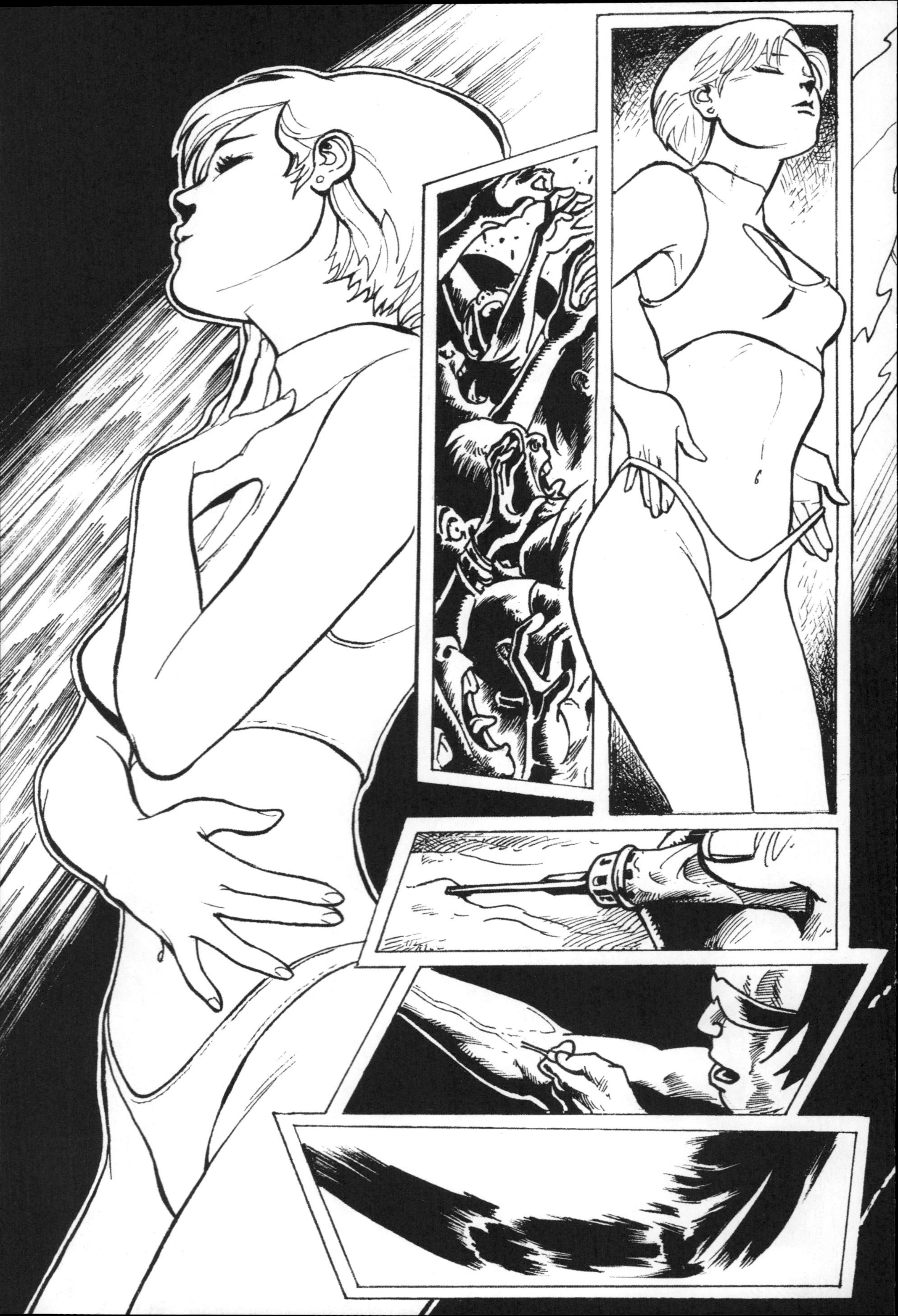

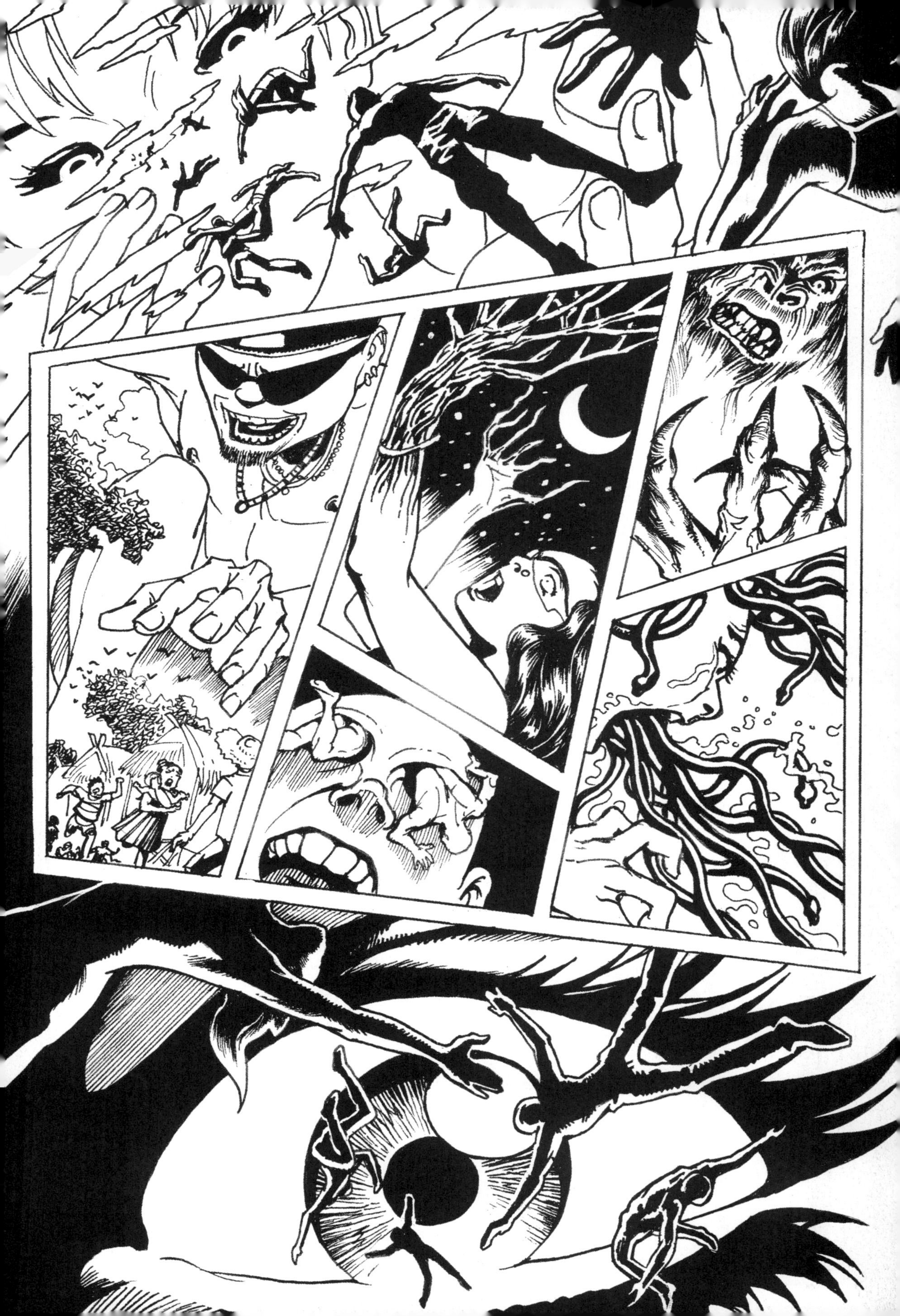

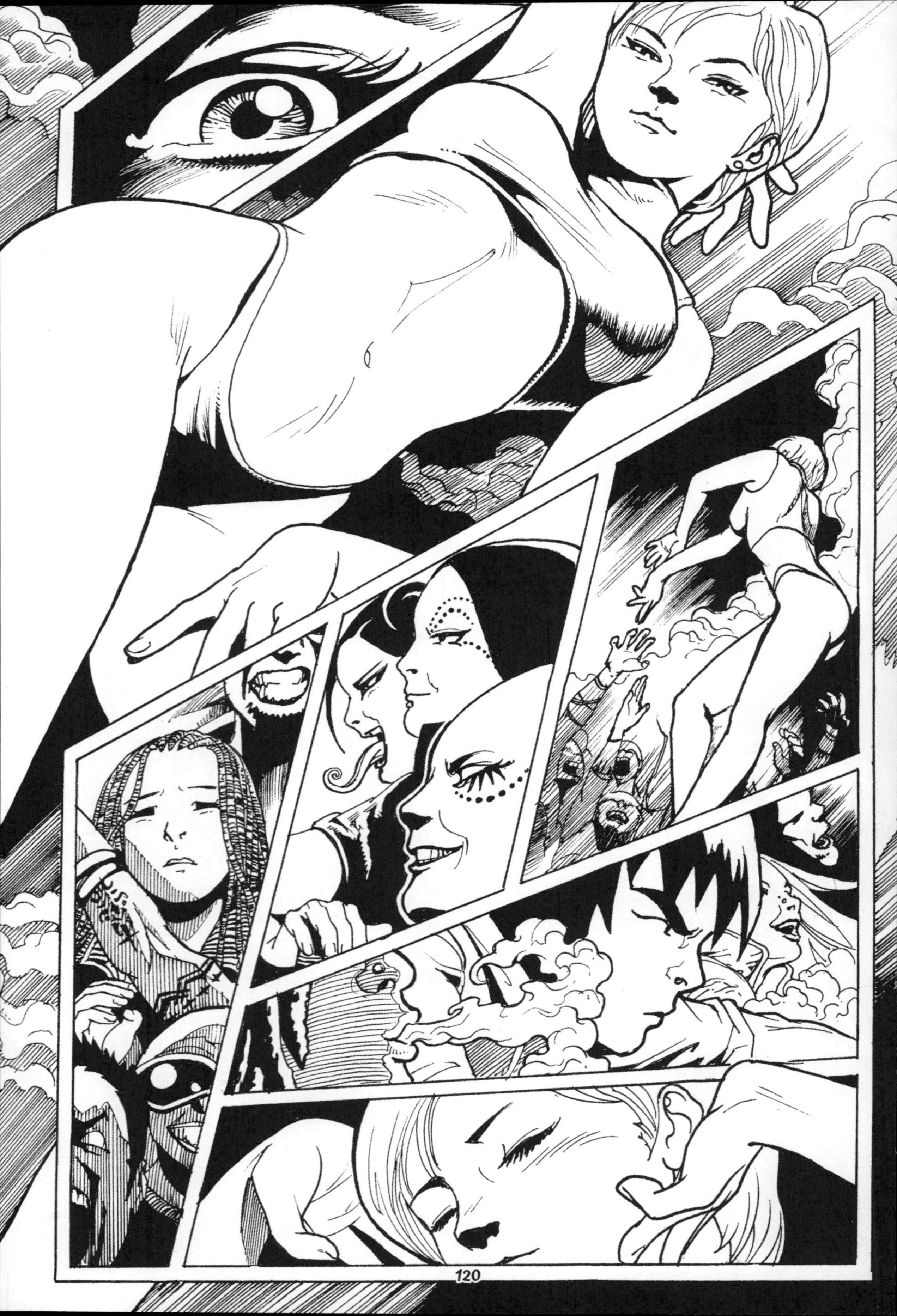

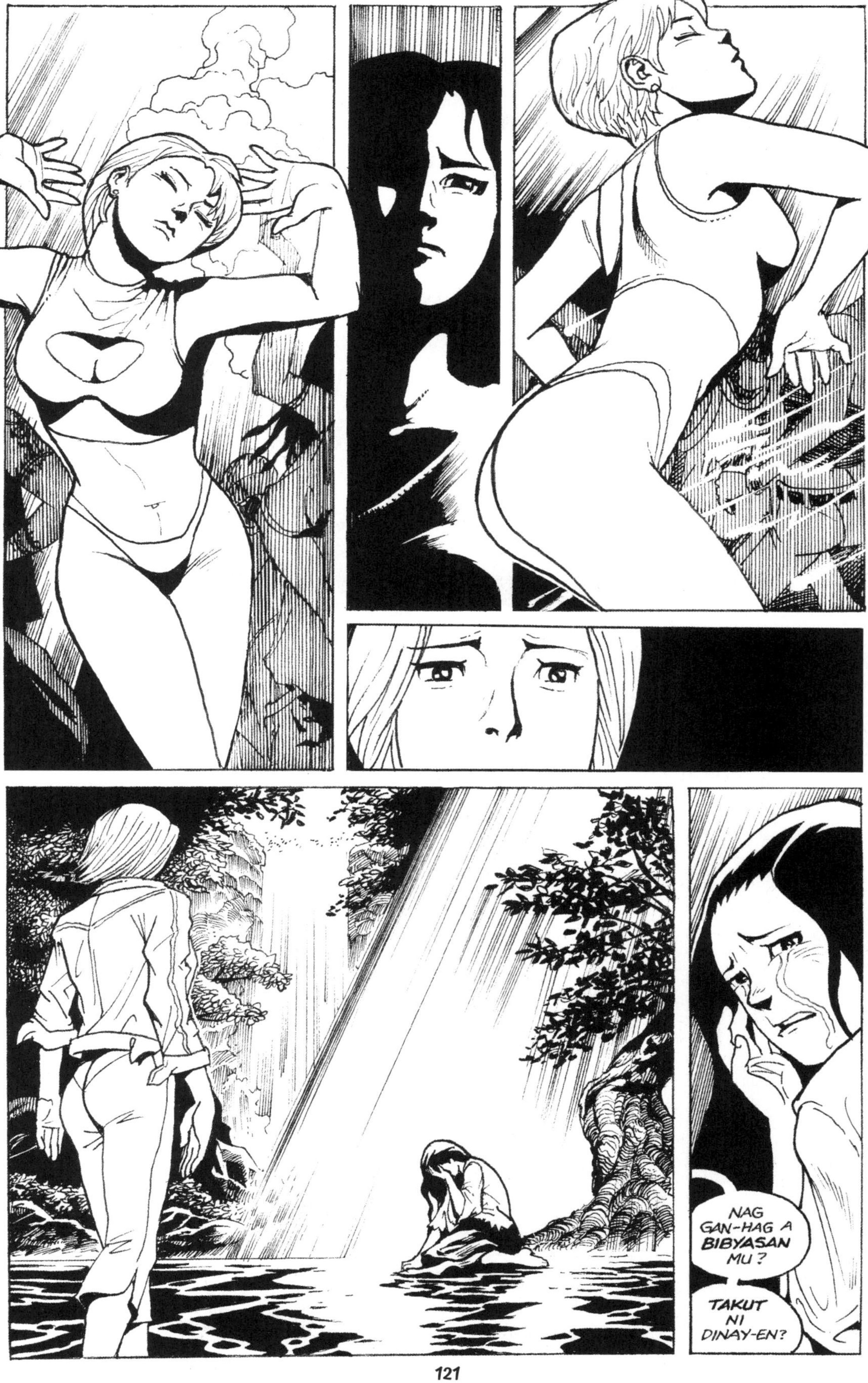
NAG GAN-HAG A BIBYASAN MU?
TAKUT NI DINAY-EN?

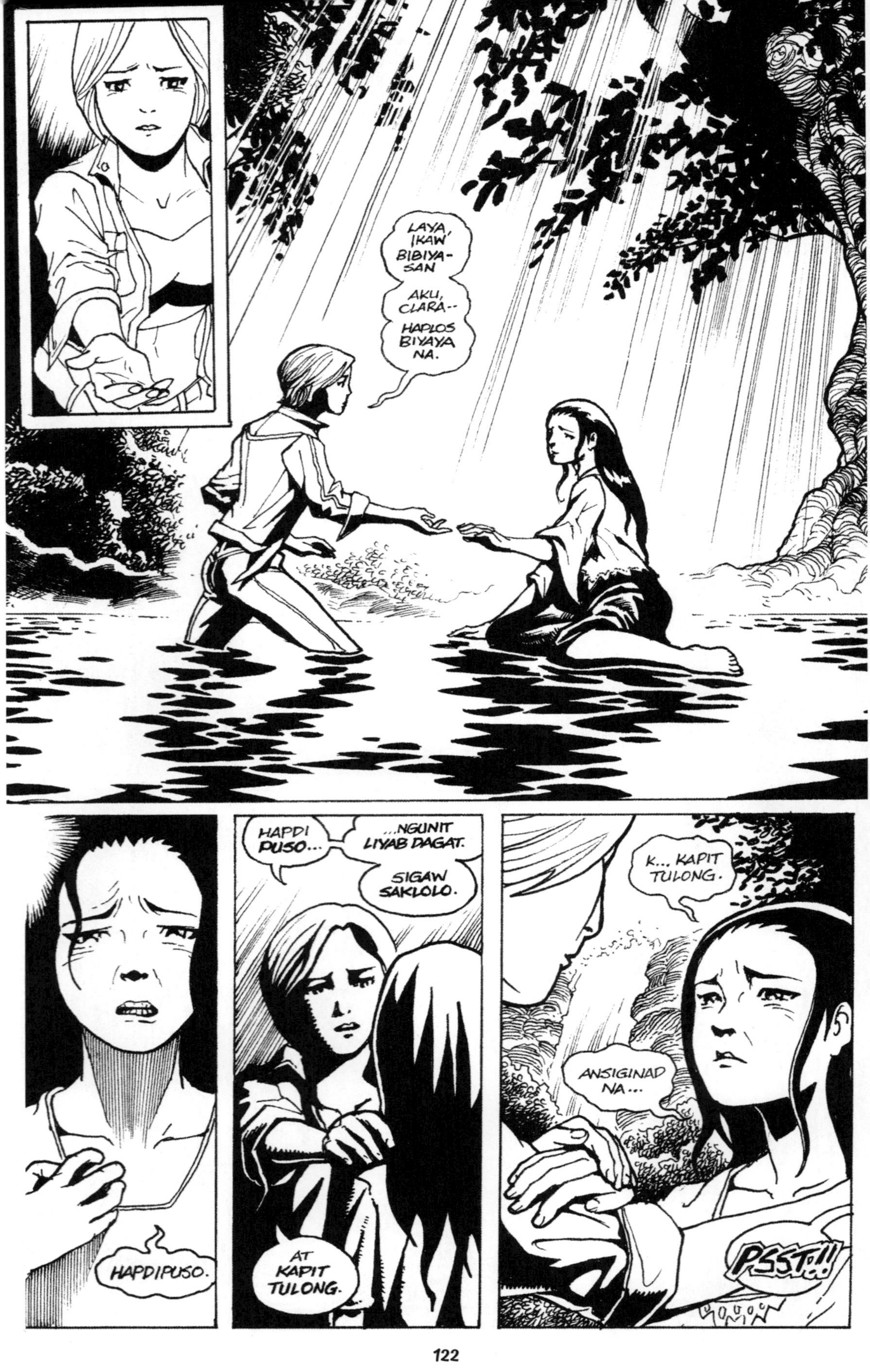
LAYA, IKAW BIBIYASAN
AKU, CLARA--
HAPLOS BIYAYA NA.
HAPDIPUSO.
HAPDI PUSO...
...NGUNIT LIYAB DAGAT.
SIGAW SAKLOLO.
AT KAPIT TULONG.
K... KAPIT TULONG.
ANSIGINAD NA...
PSST!!!

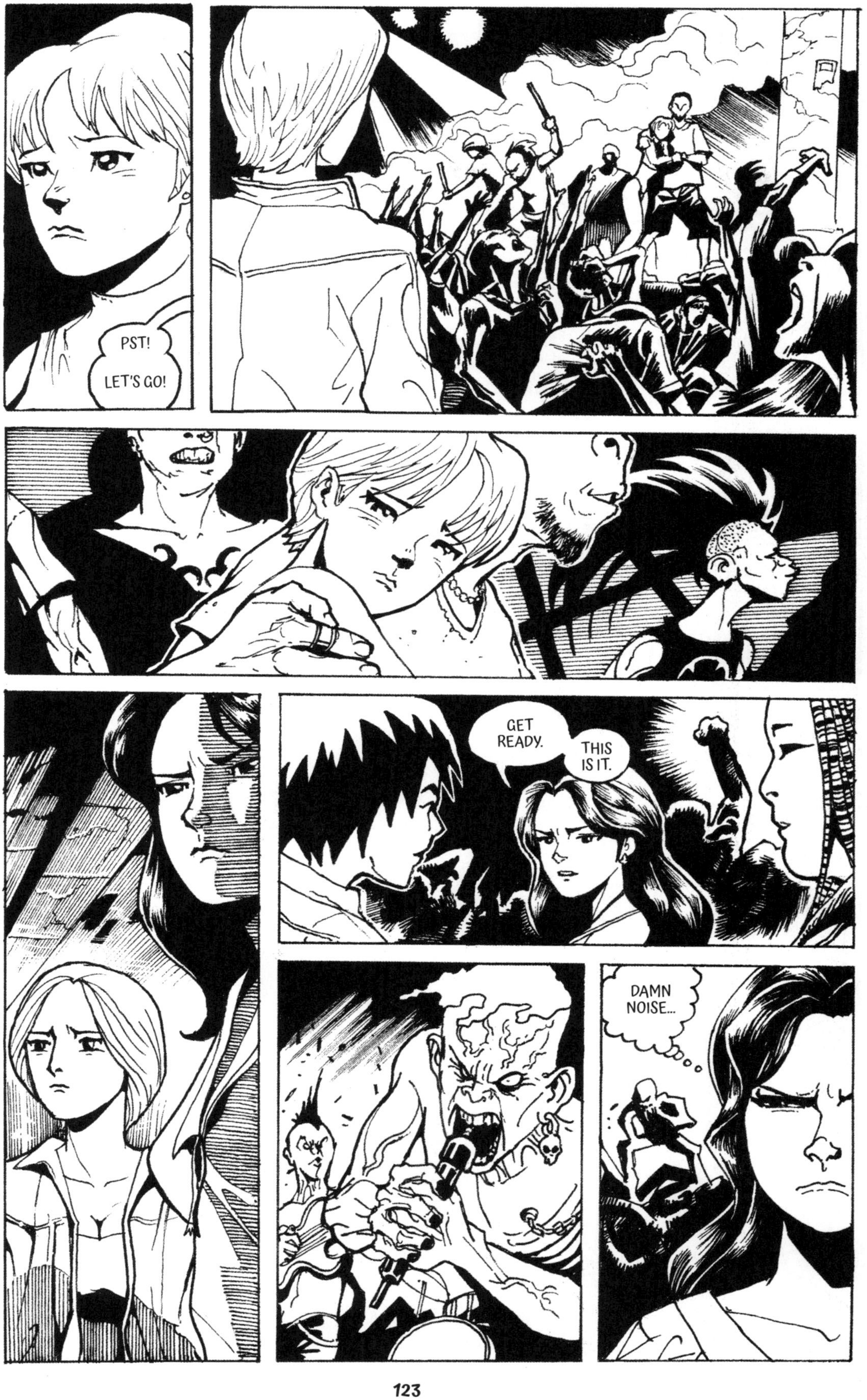
PST!
LET'S GO!
GET READY.
THIS IS IT.
DAMN NOISE...

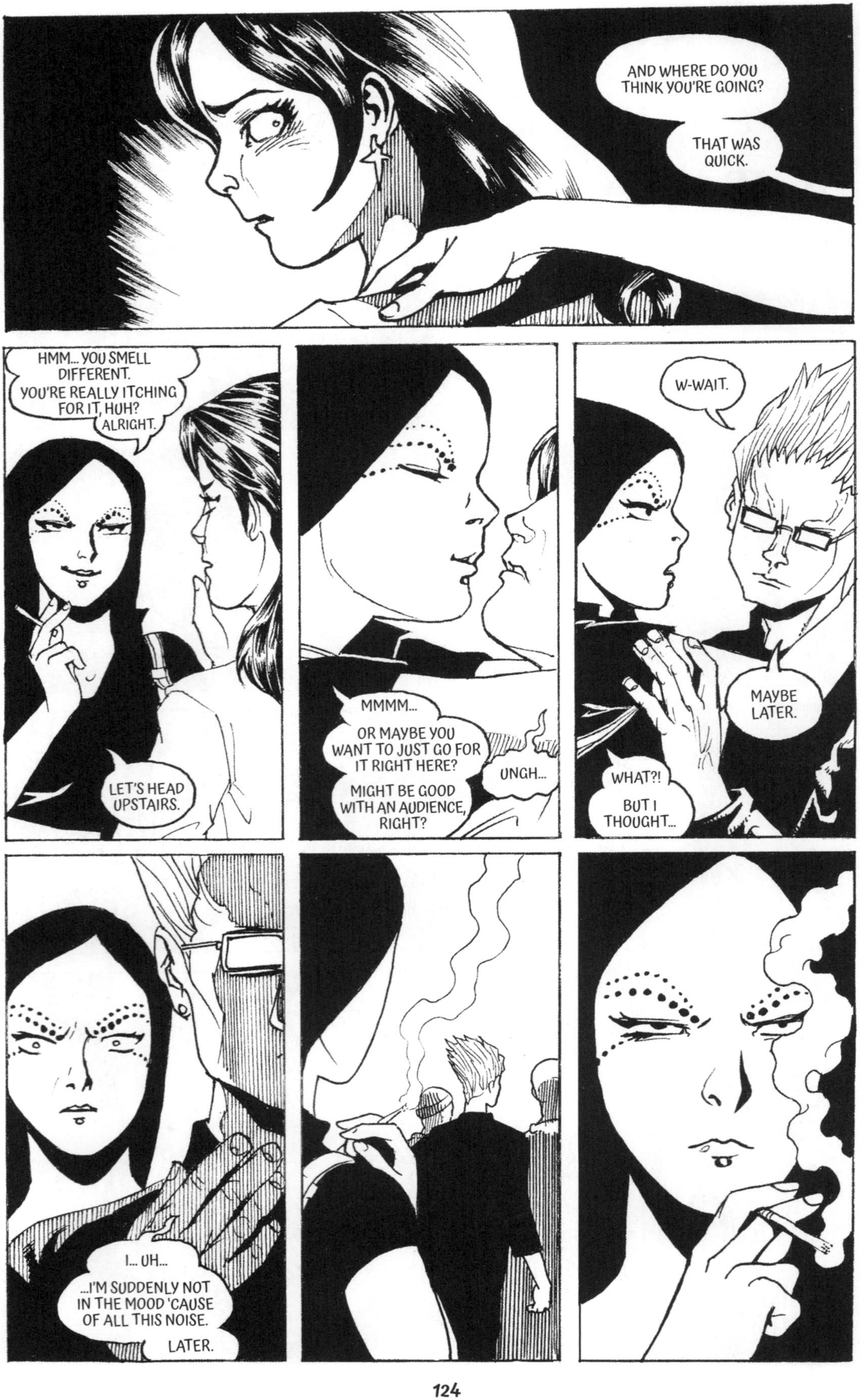
AND WHERE DO YOU THINK YOU'RE GOING?
THAT WAS QUICK.
HMM... YOU SMELL DIFFERENT. YOU'RE REALLY ITCHING FOR IT, HUH? ALRIGHT.
LET'S HEAD UPSTAIRS.
MMMM...
OR MAYBE YOU WANT TO JUST GO FOR IT RIGHT HERE?
MIGHT BE GOOD WITH AN AUDIENCE, RIGHT?
UNGH...
W-WAIT.
MAYBE LATER.
WHAT?!
BUT I THOUGHT...
I... UH...
...I'M SUDDENLY NOT IN THE MOOD 'CAUSE OF ALL THIS NOISE.
LATER.

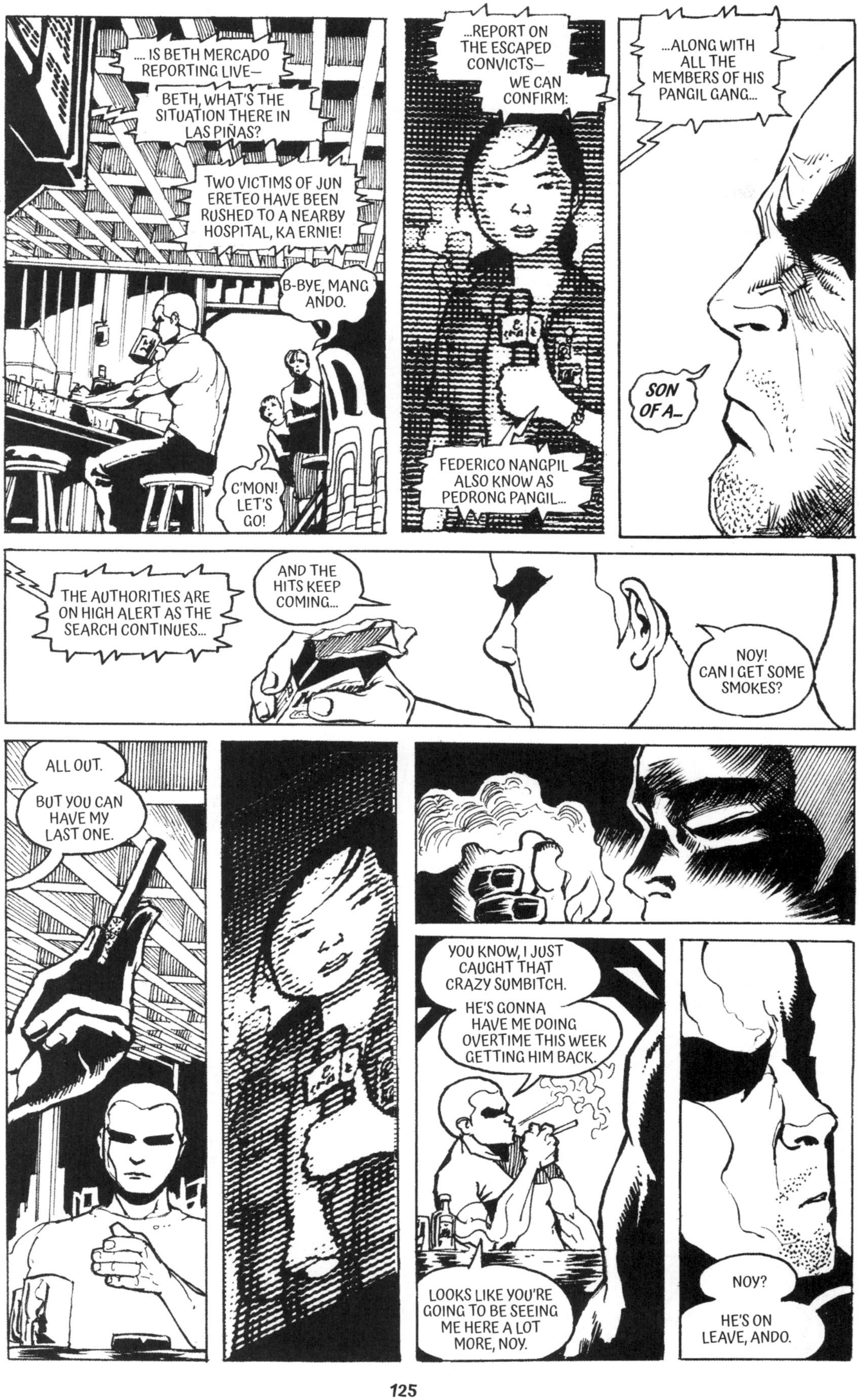
.... IS BETH MERCADO REPORTING LIVE—
BETH, WHAT'S THE SITUATION THERE IN LAS PIÑAS?
TWO VICTIMS OF JUN ERETEO HAVE BEEN RUSHED TO A NEARBY HOSPITAL, KA ERNIE!
B-BYE, MANG ANDO.
C'MON! LET'S GO!
...REPORT ON THE ESCAPED CONVICTS—
WE CAN CONFIRM:
FEDERICO NANGPIL ALSO KNOW AS PEDRONG PANGIL...
...ALONG WITH ALL THE MEMBERS OF HIS PANGIL GANG...
SON OF A...
THE AUTHORITIES ARE ON HIGH ALERT AS THE SEARCH CONTINUES...
AND THE HITS KEEP COMING...
NOY! CAN I GET SOME SMOKES?
ALL OUT.
BUT YOU CAN HAVE MY LAST ONE.
YOU KNOW, I JUST CAUGHT THAT CRAZY SUMBITCH.
HE'S GONNA HAVE ME DOING OVERTIME THIS WEEK GETTING HIM BACK.
LOOKS LIKE YOU'RE GOING TO BE SEEING ME HERE A LOT MORE, NOY.
NOY?
HE'S ON LEAVE, ANDO.

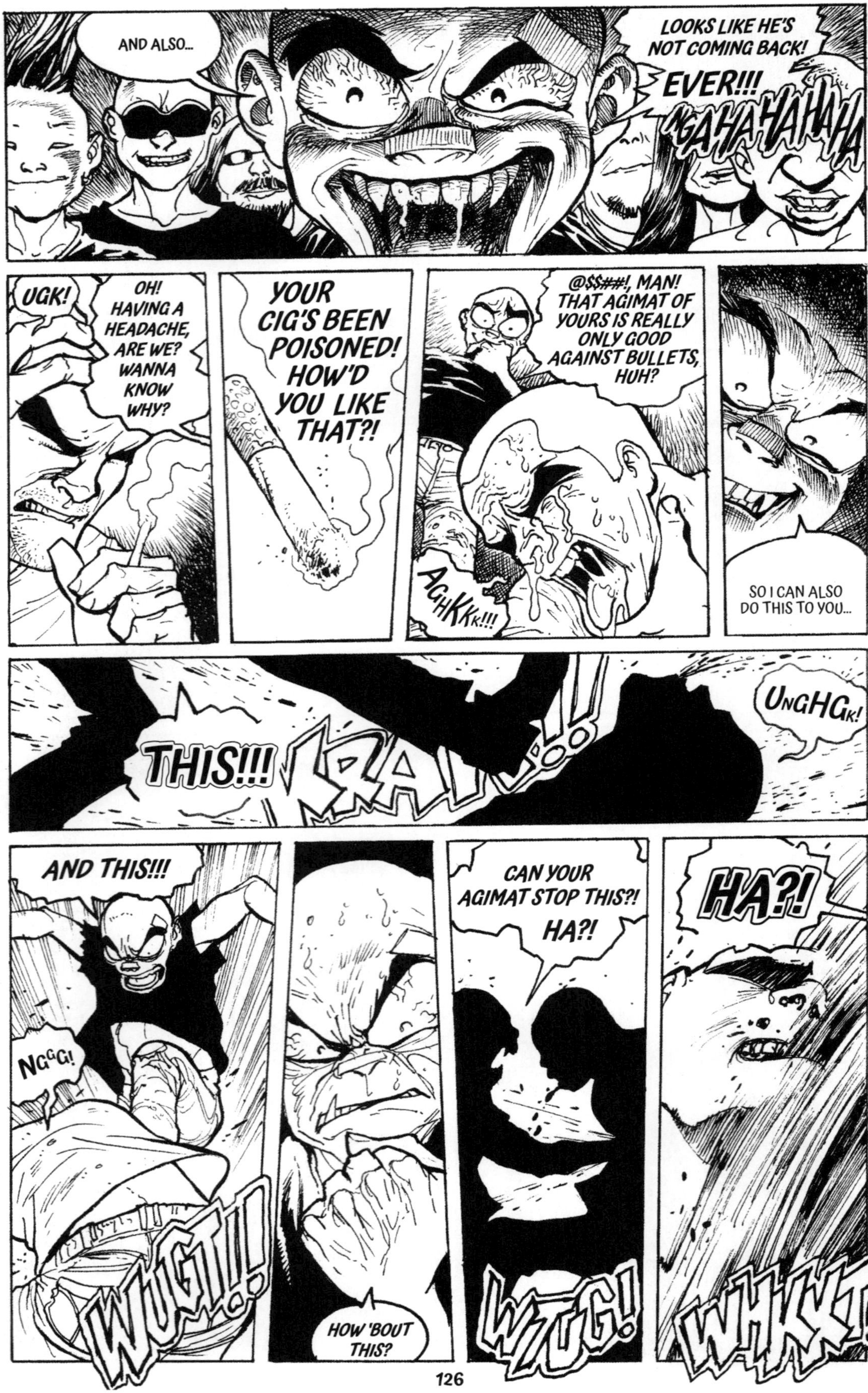
AND ALSO...
LOOKS LIKE HE'S NOT COMING BACK!
EVER!!!
NGAHAHAHAHAHA
UGK!
OH! HAVING A HEADACHE, ARE WE? WANNA KNOW WHY?
YOUR CIG'S BEEN POISONED! HOW'D YOU LIKE THAT?!
@$$##!, MAN! THAT AGIMAT OF YOURS IS REALLY ONLY GOOD AGAINST BULLETS, HUH?
AGHKKK!!!
SO I CAN ALSO DO THIS TO YOU...
THIS!!!
UNGHGK!
AND THIS!!!
NGGG!
WUGT!!
HOW 'BOUT THIS?
CAN YOUR AGIMAT STOP THIS?!
HA?!
WTUG!
HA?!
WHKT!

!@##$$! DUDES, YOU KNOW THIS @##$$!! ALMOST RIPPED MY NOSE OFF?

NOW WHO'S ON THEIR KNEES?!

HUH?! WHO, YOU @##$$!!

KRSS....SSHHH!!!

WGKT!

ONCE I'M DONE WITH YOU, WE'RE GOING TO TEAR THIS TOWN APART ALL NIGHT! THEN HE'S GOING TO GIVE US POWER! THAT'S RIGHT!

AND I'M NOT TALKING ABOUT JUN. I MEAN HIS MASTER!

THAT'S ZOLGO, MAN!

AWESOME!!!

THAT'S JUN'S DEMON BOSS! HE'S CRAZY POWERFUL, MAN! UNBELIEVABLE!!!

THAT'S WHY YOU...

YOU'RE FINISHED!!!

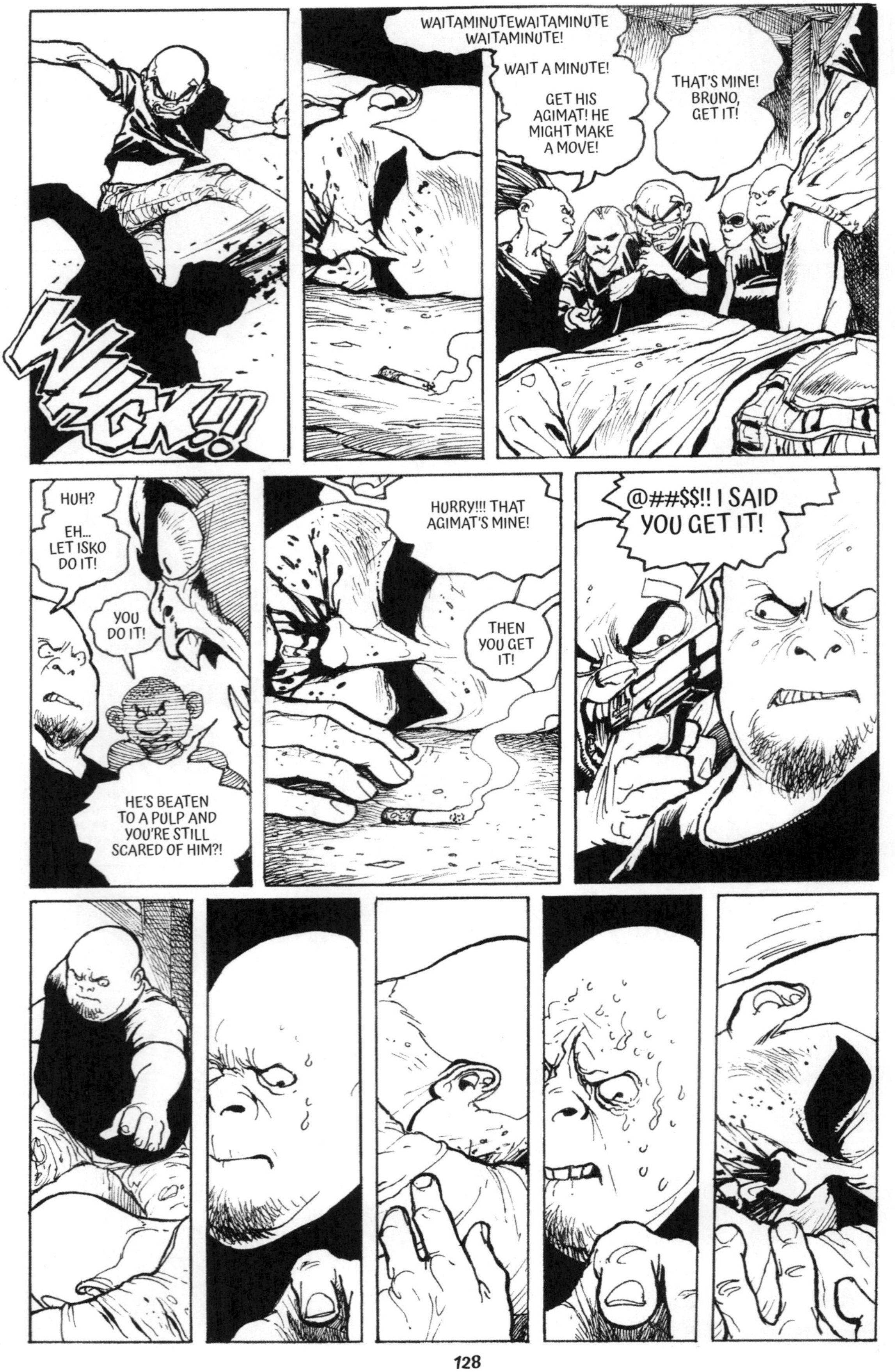
WUGK!!
WAITAMINUTEWAITAMINUTE WAITAMINUTE!
WAIT A MINUTE!
GET HIS AGIMAT! HE MIGHT MAKE A MOVE!
THAT'S MINE! BRUNO, GET IT!
HUH?
EH... LET ISKO DO IT!
YOU DO IT!
HE'S BEATEN TO A PULP AND YOU'RE STILL SCARED OF HIM?!
HURRY!!! THAT AGIMAT'S MINE!
THEN YOU GET IT!
@##$$!! I SAID YOU GET IT!

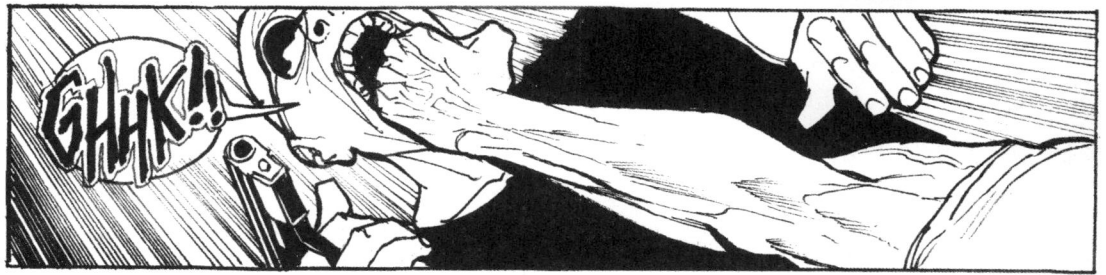

NGYAAA AAAH!!

@#*$$!! ANDOOOO...

@#*$$!! IT!

KNOCK HIM OUT!!!

KRIIIKT!!!

GHHK!!

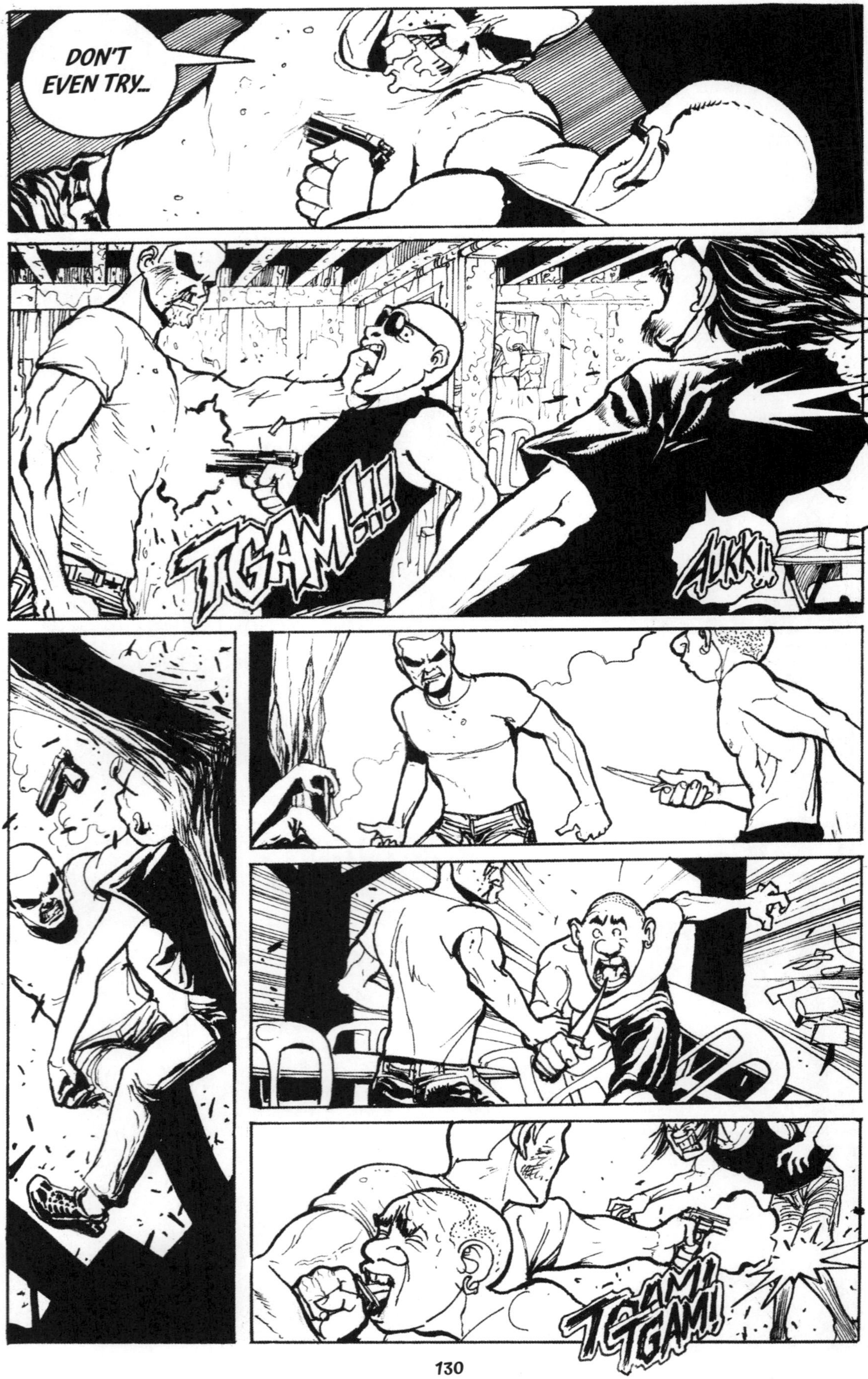
DON'T EVEN TRY...
TGAM!!!
AUKK!!
TGAM! TGAM!

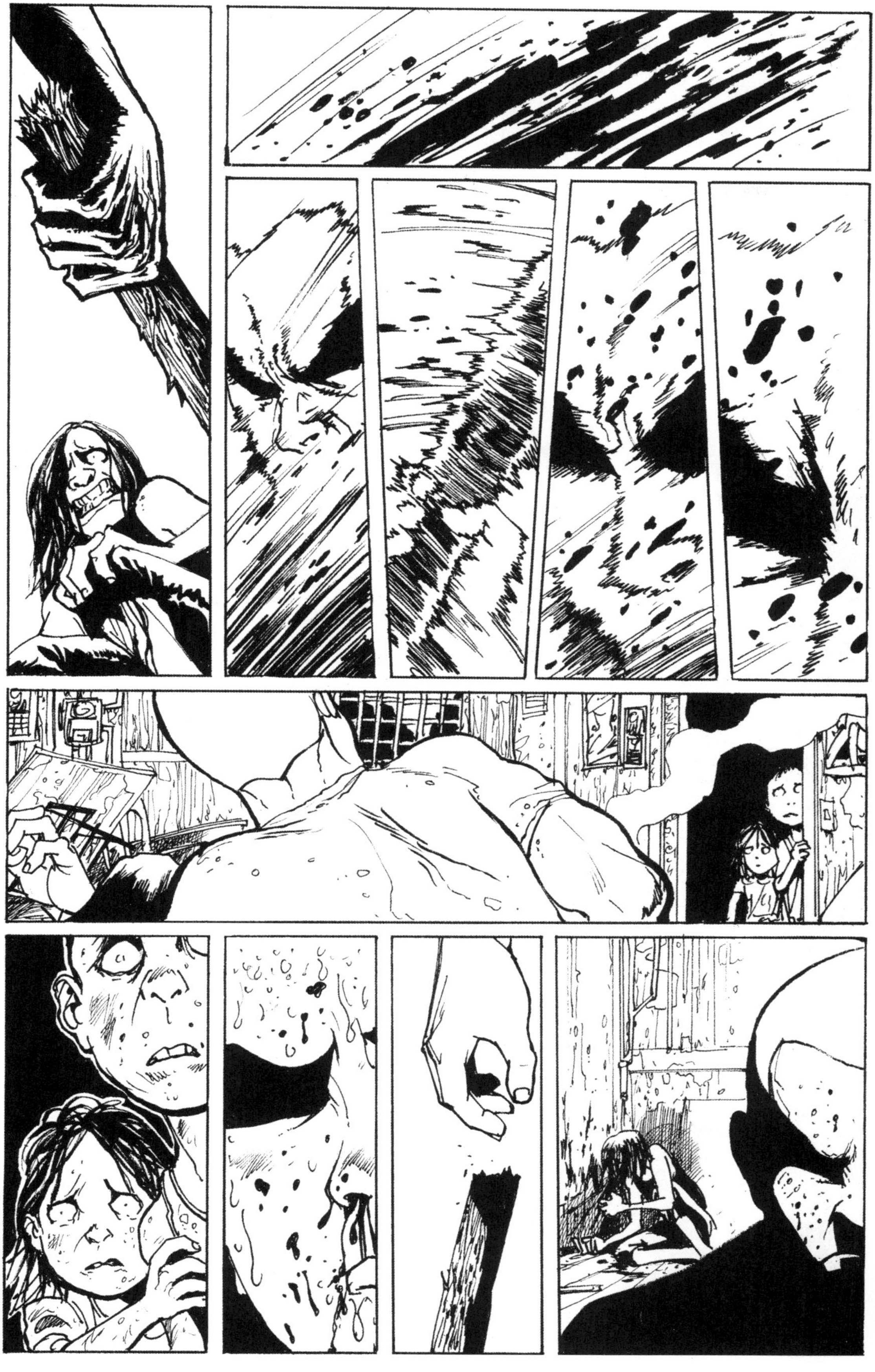

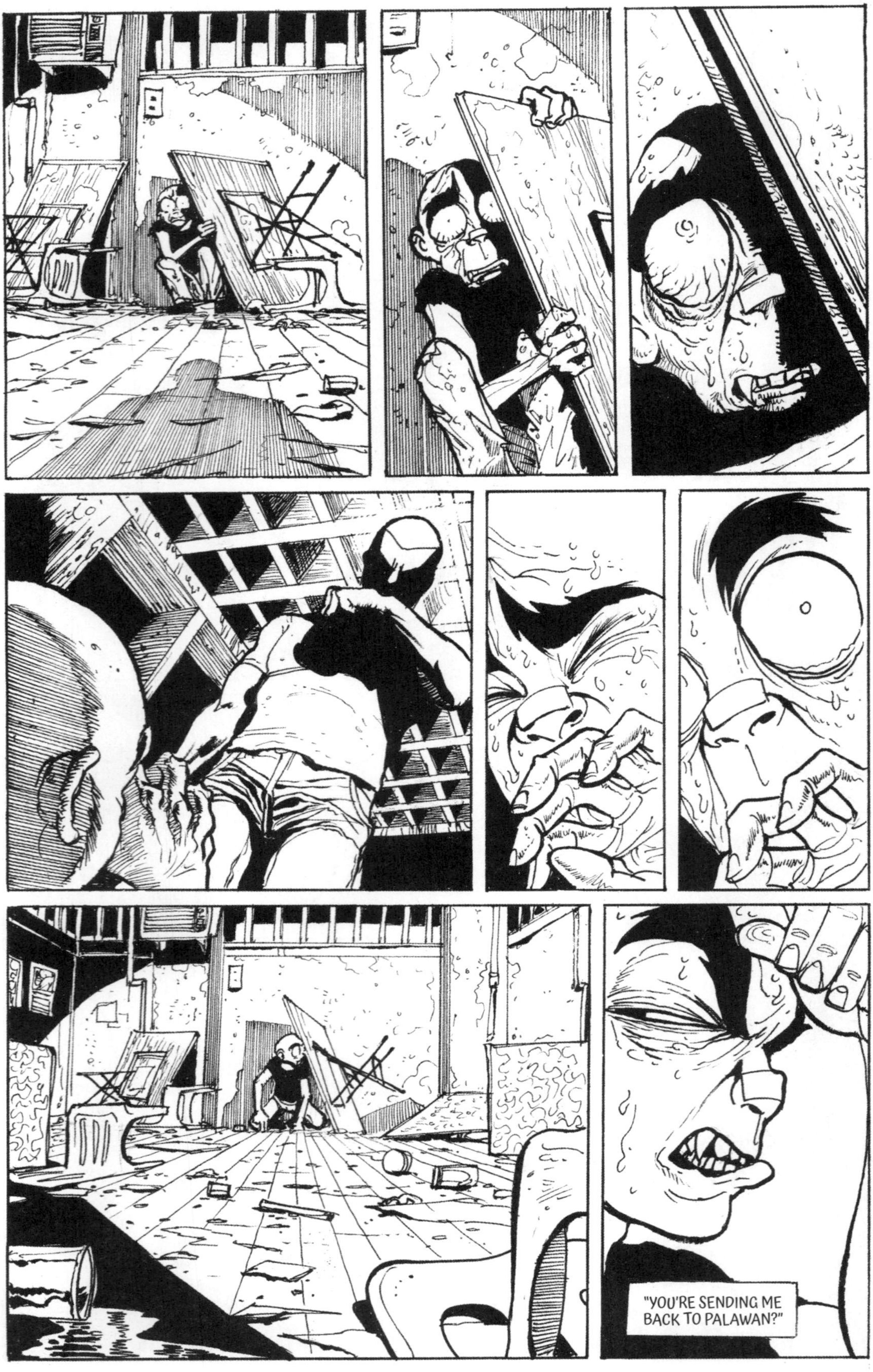
"YOU'RE SENDING ME BACK TO PALAWAN?"

"WATCH OVER CAREFULLY MY POSSESSIONS. YOUR WORK HERE IS DONE."

"WHAT WILL YOU DO NOW?"

"I'M GOING TO TAKE A TOUR..."

"...AROUND MY CITY."

"ONE YEAR WENT BY FAST."

"FIVE HUNDRED YEARS."

YAAAAAA--!!!

YOU BITCH—

YOU'RE GONNA GET IT FROM ME!

LOOK AT ME AND STOP SQUIRMING! IT'LL BE OVER QUICKLY IF YOU JUST BEHAVE!

YOU'D BETTER DO WHAT I TELL YOU OR ELSE...

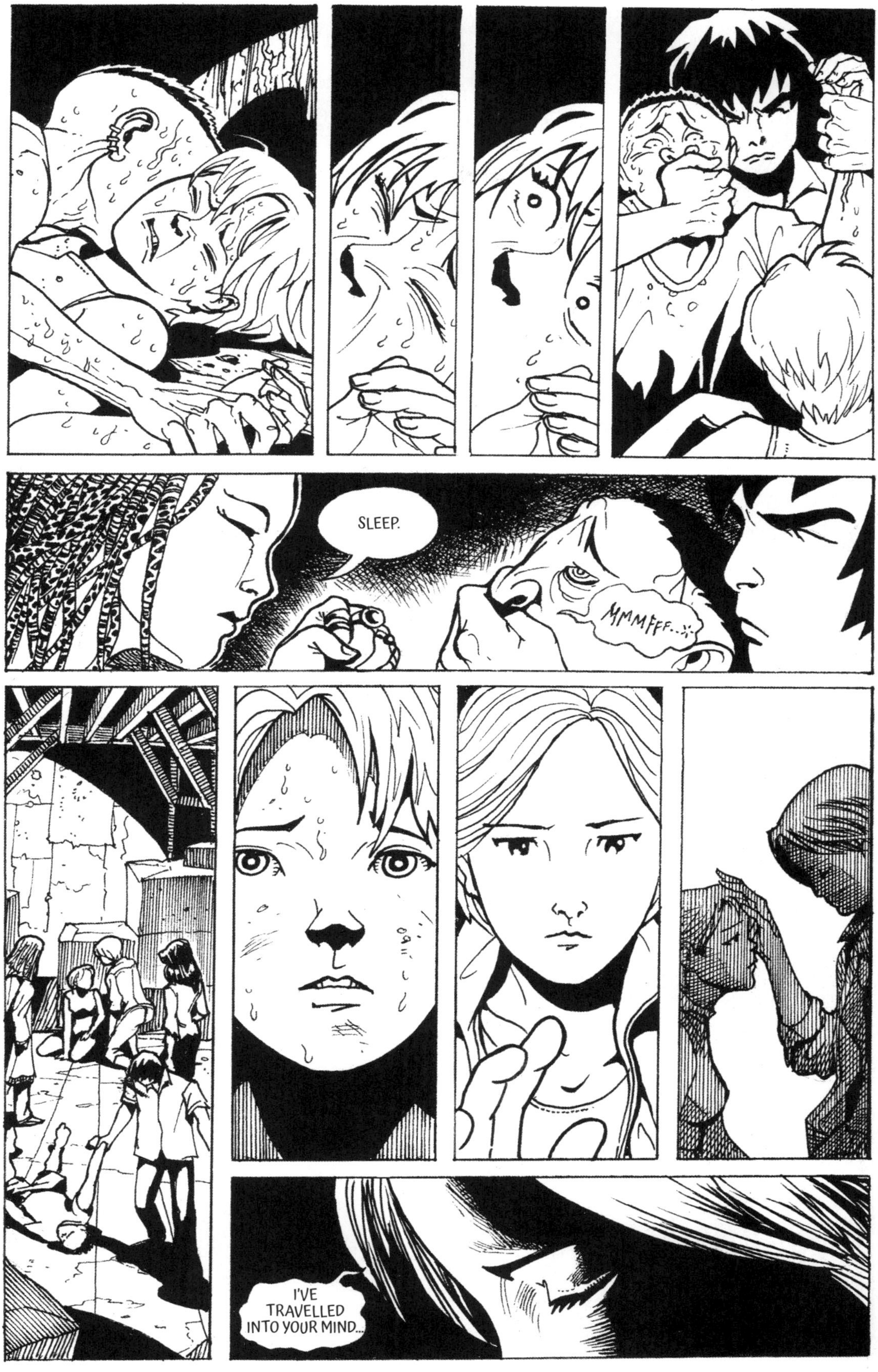
SLEEP.
MMMFFF...
I'VE TRAVELLED INTO YOUR MIND...

"...AND THIS IS WHERE I DISCOVERED THE TRUTH."

"YOU'D BEEN HIDING FOR SO LONG FROM THE SPANISH WHO WERE **HIS** SERVANTS."

"ALL THAT SUFFERING JUST BECAUSE YOU REFUSED TO JOIN HIM — AN ALLY OF DARKNESS."

"AND IT COST YOU YOUR LOVE."

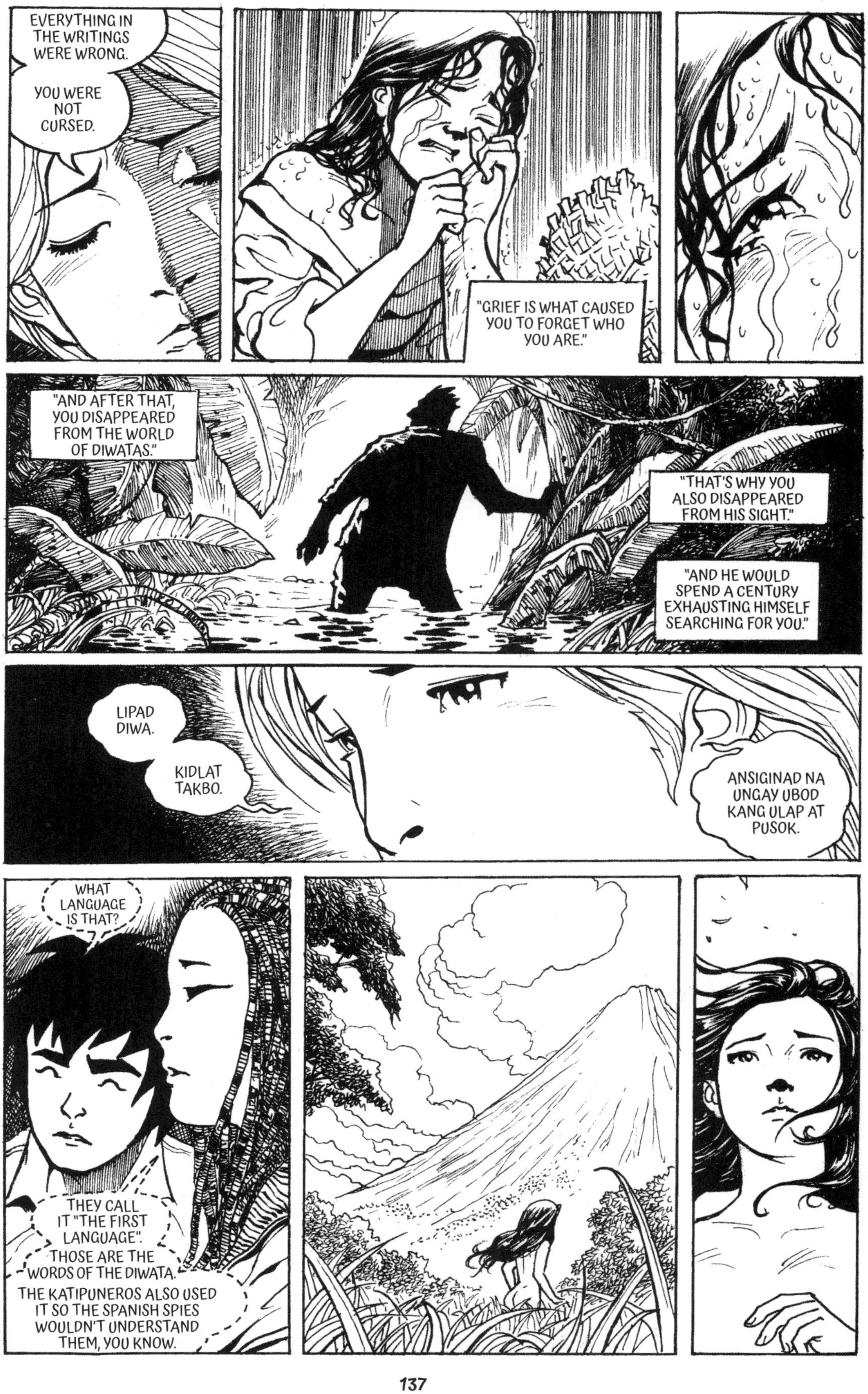
EVERYTHING IN THE WRITINGS WERE WRONG.
YOU WERE NOT CURSED.
"GRIEF IS WHAT CAUSED YOU TO FORGET WHO YOU ARE."
"AND AFTER THAT, YOU DISAPPEARED FROM THE WORLD OF DIWATAS."
"THAT'S WHY YOU ALSO DISAPPEARED FROM HIS SIGHT."
"AND HE WOULD SPEND A CENTURY EXHAUSTING HIMSELF SEARCHING FOR YOU."
LIPAD DIWA.
KIDLAT TAKBO.
ANSIGINAD NA UNGAY UBOD KANG ULAP AT PUSOK.
WHAT LANGUAGE IS THAT?
THEY CALL IT "THE FIRST LANGUAGE".
THOSE ARE THE WORDS OF THE DIWATA.
THE KATIPUNEROS ALSO USED IT SO THE SPANISH SPIES WOULDN'T UNDERSTAND THEM, YOU KNOW.

"THE YEARS PASSED."

"YOU WITNESSED LIKE THE RISING OF THE SUN..."

"...THE CHANGES HAPPENING IN THE WORLD."

"AFTER SOME TIME, YOU EVENTUALLY ENDED UP IN THE CITY."

"YOU BECAME CLOSE TO THE STREET CHILDREN."

"AND AT TIMES, WHEN NEEDED, YOU RELEASED YOUR FORMER POWERS."

"YOU COULD RELEASE THEM."

"USE THEM."

"BUT DID NOT UNDERSTAND THEM."

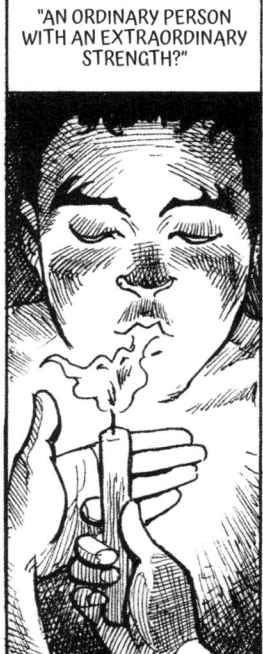

"EVEN LESS SO THOSE WHO WERE NARROW OF MIND."

"THAT IS WHY WORD QUICKLY REACHED HIS HENCHMEN."

"DESPITE ALL THIS, YOU STILL FOUND TIME TO LOVE."

"AN ORDINARY PERSON WITH AN EXTRAORDINARY STRENGTH?"

"WHAT DID YOU WANT FROM THIS KIND OF PERSON?"

"WAS IT RIGHT FOR YOU TO BE TOGETHER?"

"PERHAPS IT DID NOT MATTER."

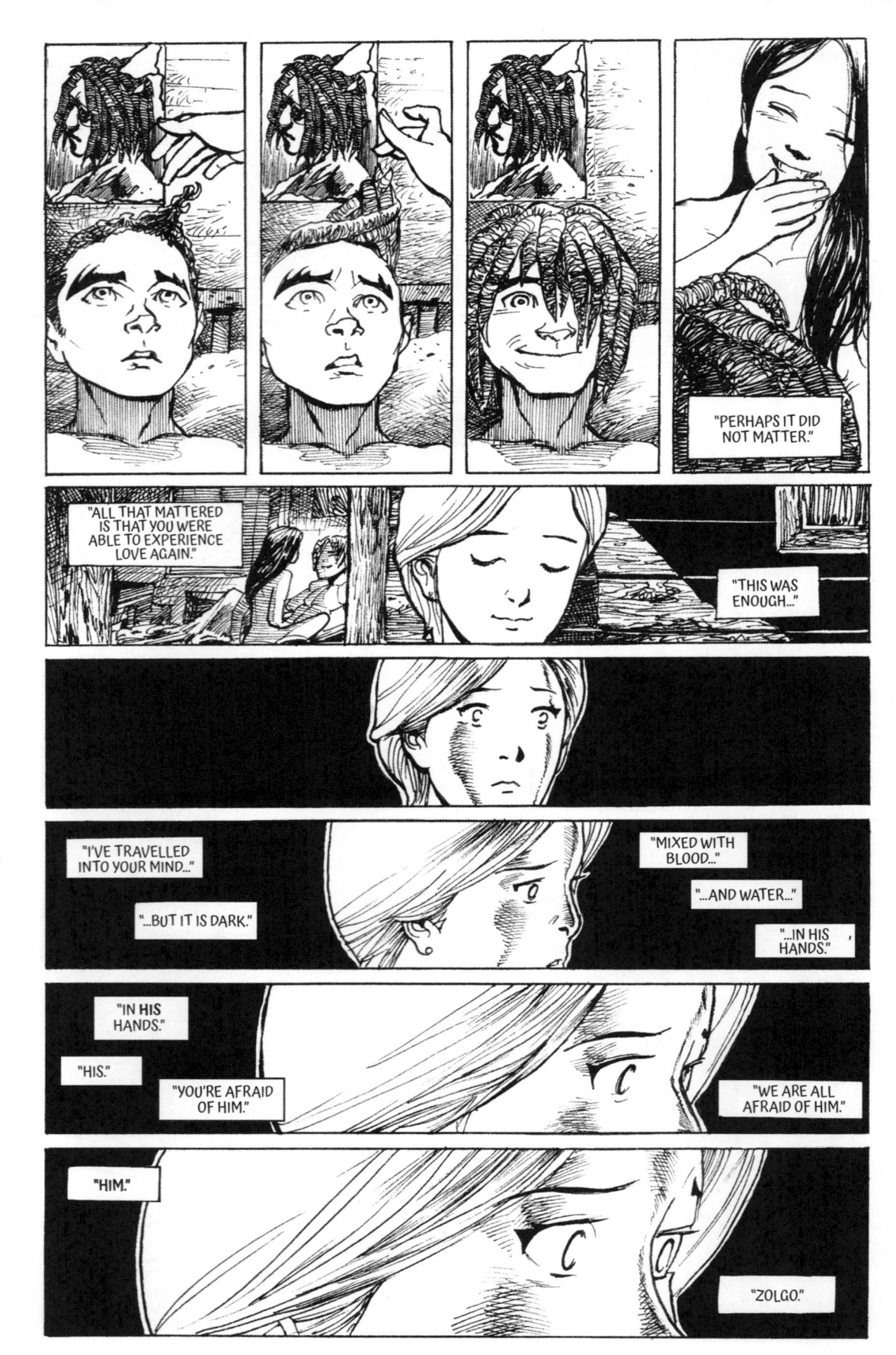

"ALL THAT MATTERED IS THAT YOU WERE ABLE TO EXPERIENCE LOVE AGAIN."

"THIS WAS ENOUGH..."

"I'VE TRAVELLED INTO YOUR MIND..."

"...BUT IT IS DARK."

"MIXED WITH BLOOD..."

"...AND WATER..."

"...IN HIS HANDS."

"IN HIS HANDS."

"HIS."

"YOU'RE AFRAID OF HIM."

"WE ARE ALL AFRAID OF HIM."

"HIM."

"ZOLGO."

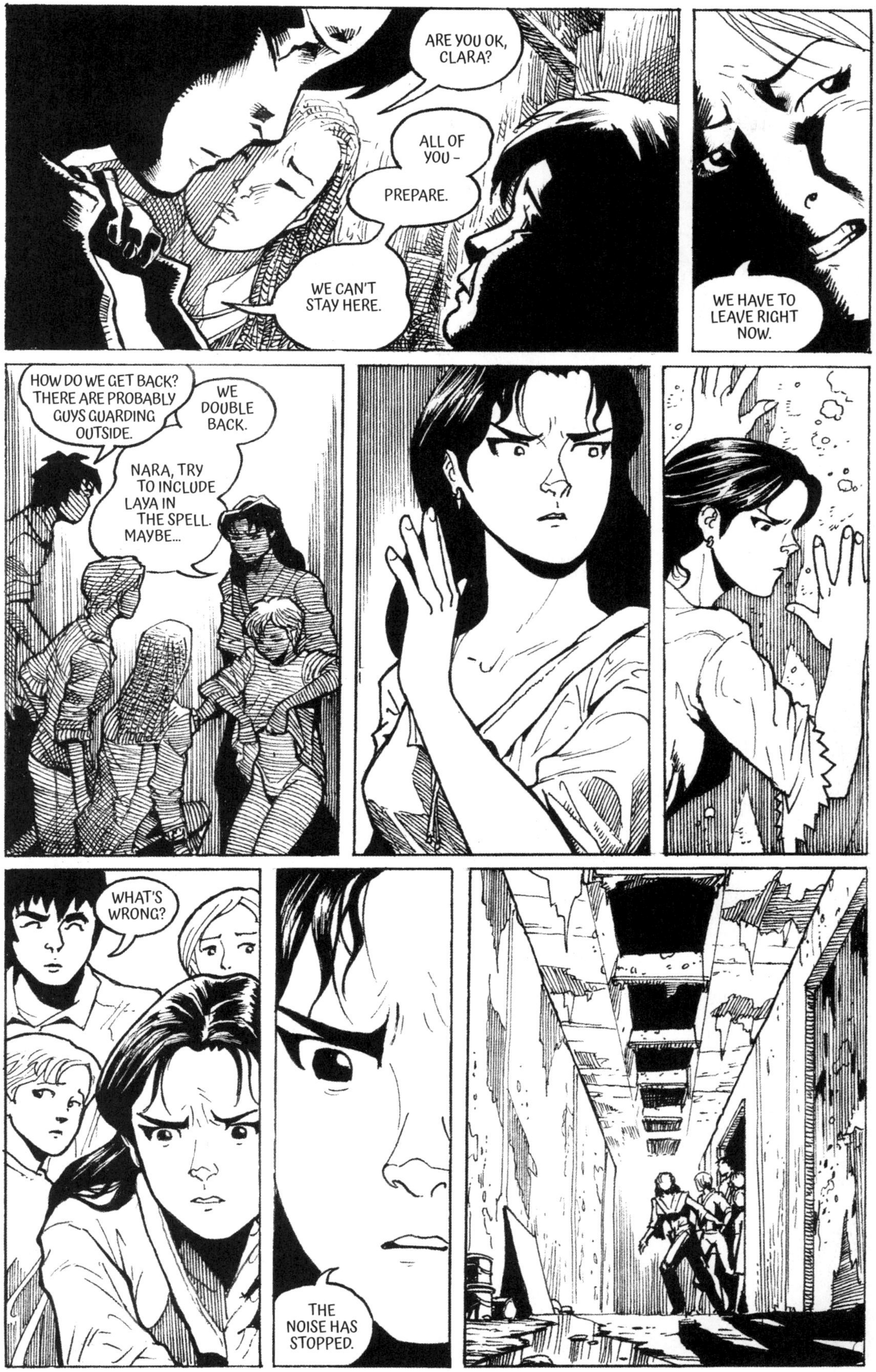
ARE YOU OK, CLARA?
ALL OF YOU -
PREPARE.
WE CAN'T STAY HERE.
WE HAVE TO LEAVE RIGHT NOW.
HOW DO WE GET BACK? THERE ARE PROBABLY GUYS GUARDING OUTSIDE.
WE DOUBLE BACK.
NARA, TRY TO INCLUDE LAYA IN THE SPELL. MAYBE...
WHAT'S WRONG?
THE NOISE HAS STOPPED.

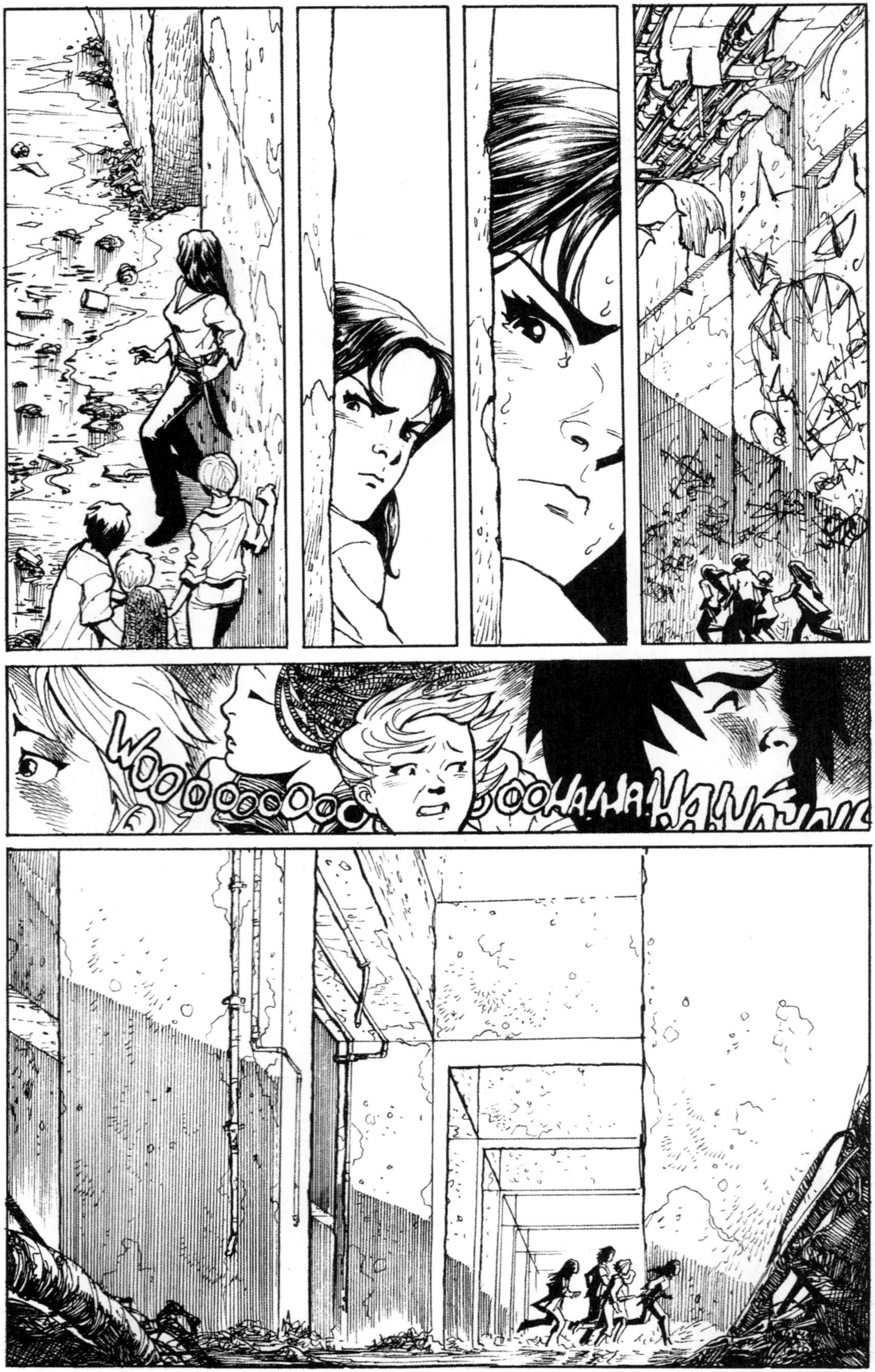
WOOOOOOOOOOOOOOOHAHAHA

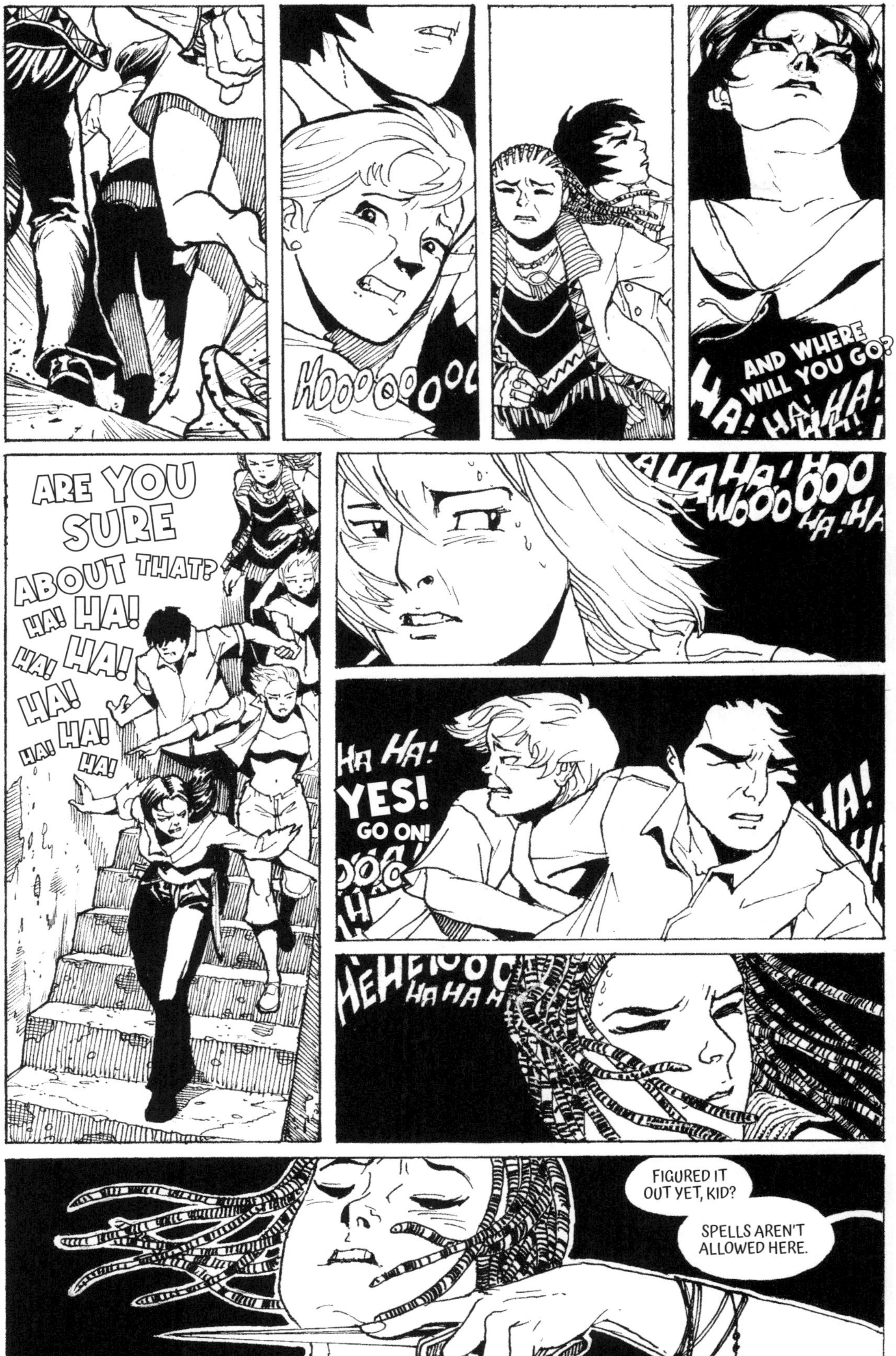
HOOOOOOOOO
AND WHERE WILL YOU GO?
HA! HA! HA! HA!
ARE YOU SURE ABOUT THAT?
HA! HA! HA! HA! HA! HA! HA! HA!
HA HA! HA! HOO WOOOOOOO HA! HA
HA HA!
YES!
GO ON!
HA!
HEHEHOOO HA HA H
FIGURED IT OUT YET, KID?
SPELLS AREN'T ALLOWED HERE.

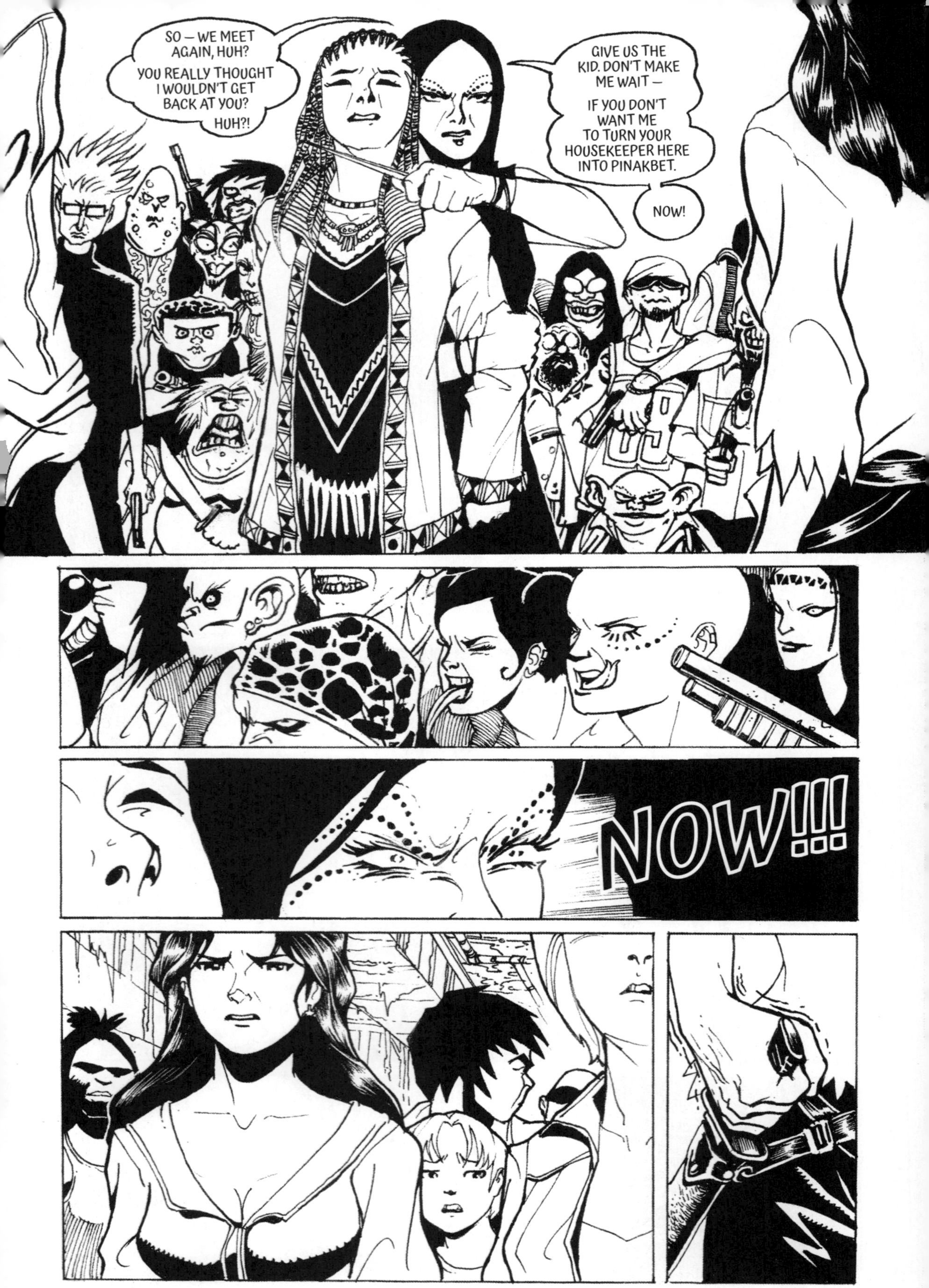
SO — WE MEET AGAIN, HUH?
YOU REALLY THOUGHT I WOULDN'T GET BACK AT YOU?
HUH?!
GIVE US THE KID. DON'T MAKE ME WAIT —
IF YOU DON'T WANT ME TO TURN YOUR HOUSEKEEPER HERE INTO PINAKBET.
NOW!
NOW!!!

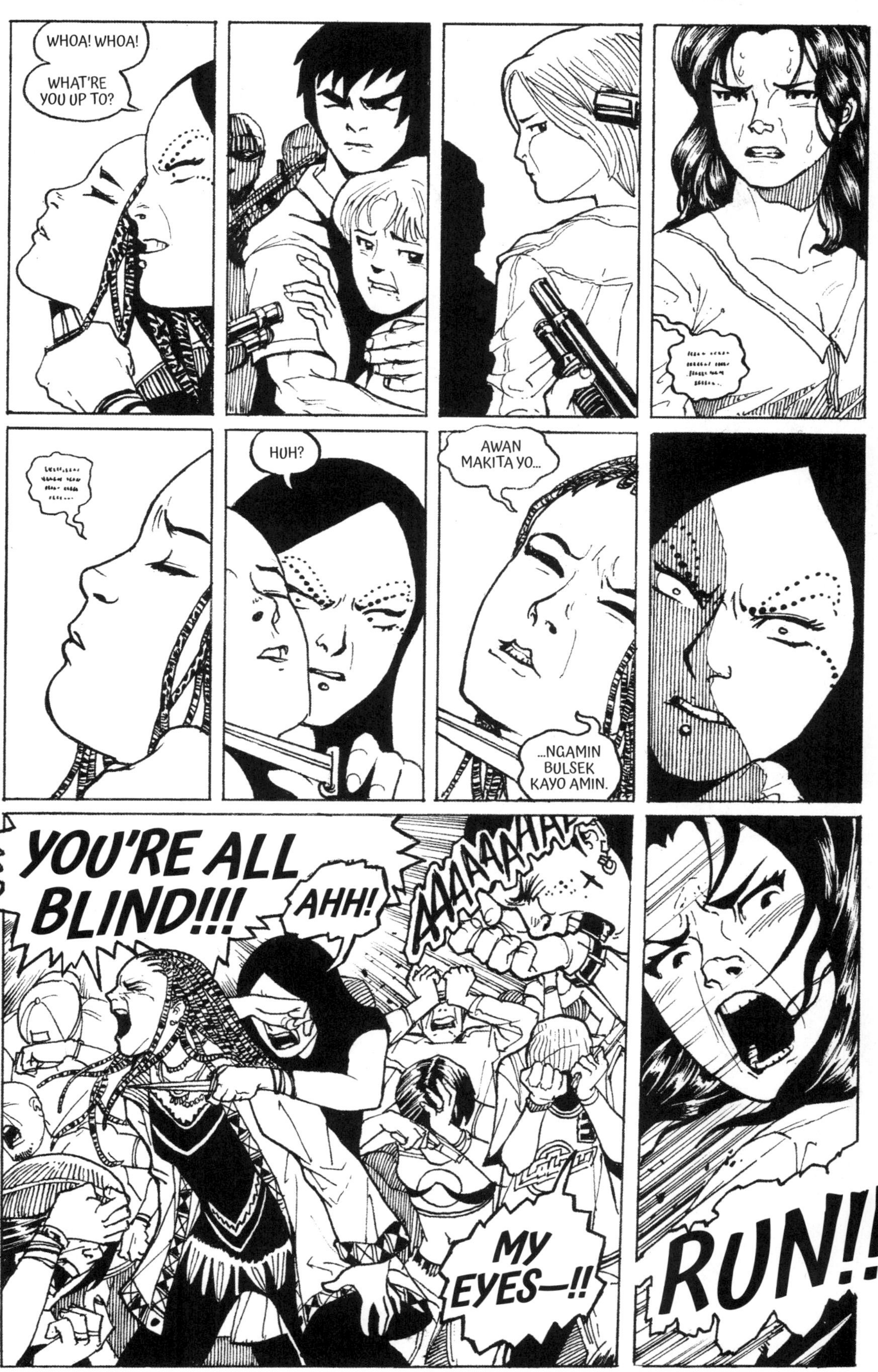
WHOA! WHOA!
WHAT'RE YOU UP TO?
HUH?
AWAN MAKITA YO...
...NGAMIN BULSEK KAYO AMIN.
YOU'RE ALL BLIND!!!
AHH!
AAAAAAHH!
MY EYES—!!
RUN!!

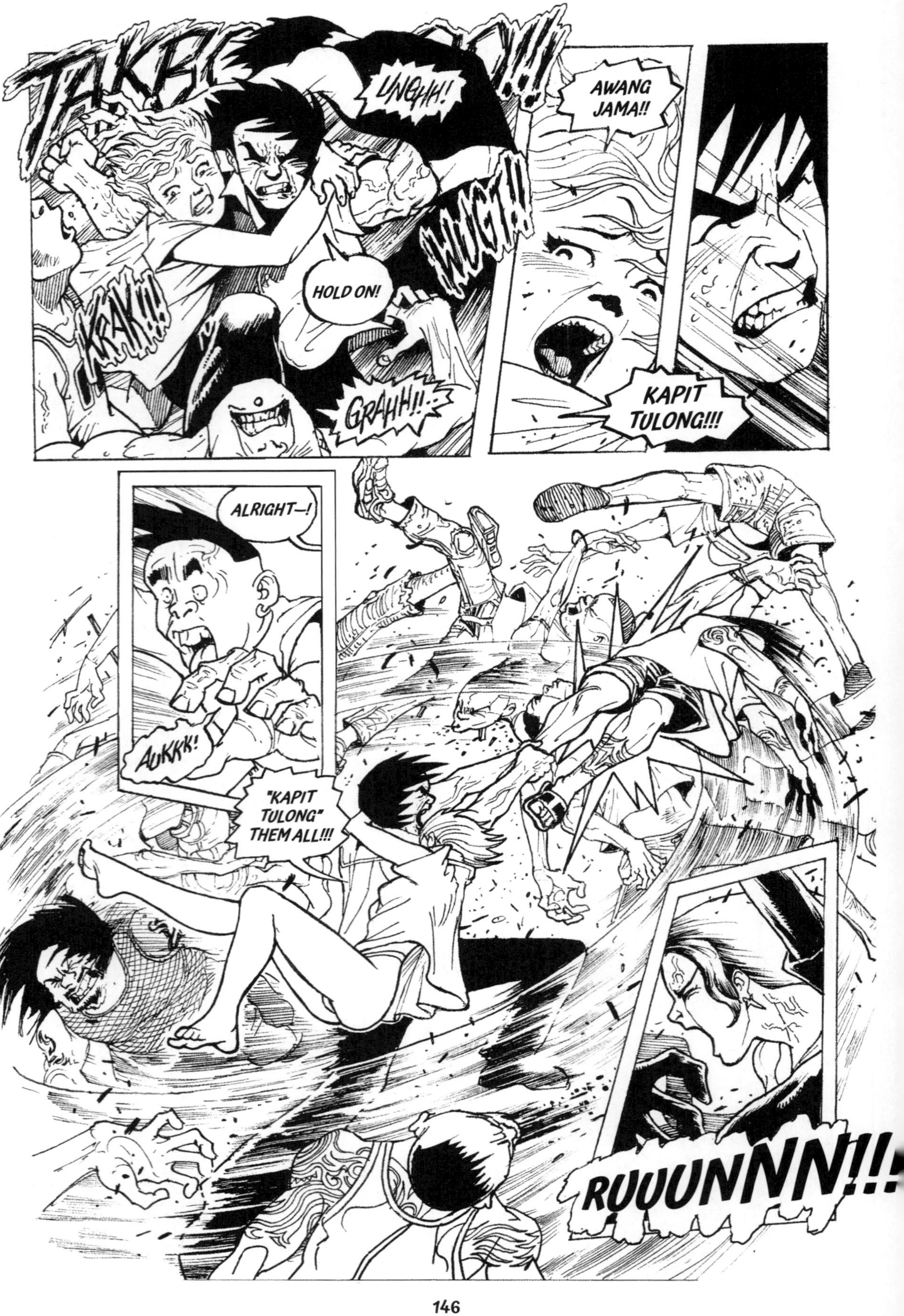
TAKBO...!!
UNGHH!
WUGH!!
KRAK!!!
HOLD ON!
GRAHH!!
AWANG JAMA!!
KAPIT TULONG!!!
ALRIGHT—!
AUKKK!
"KAPIT TULONG" THEM ALL!!!
RUUUNNN!!!

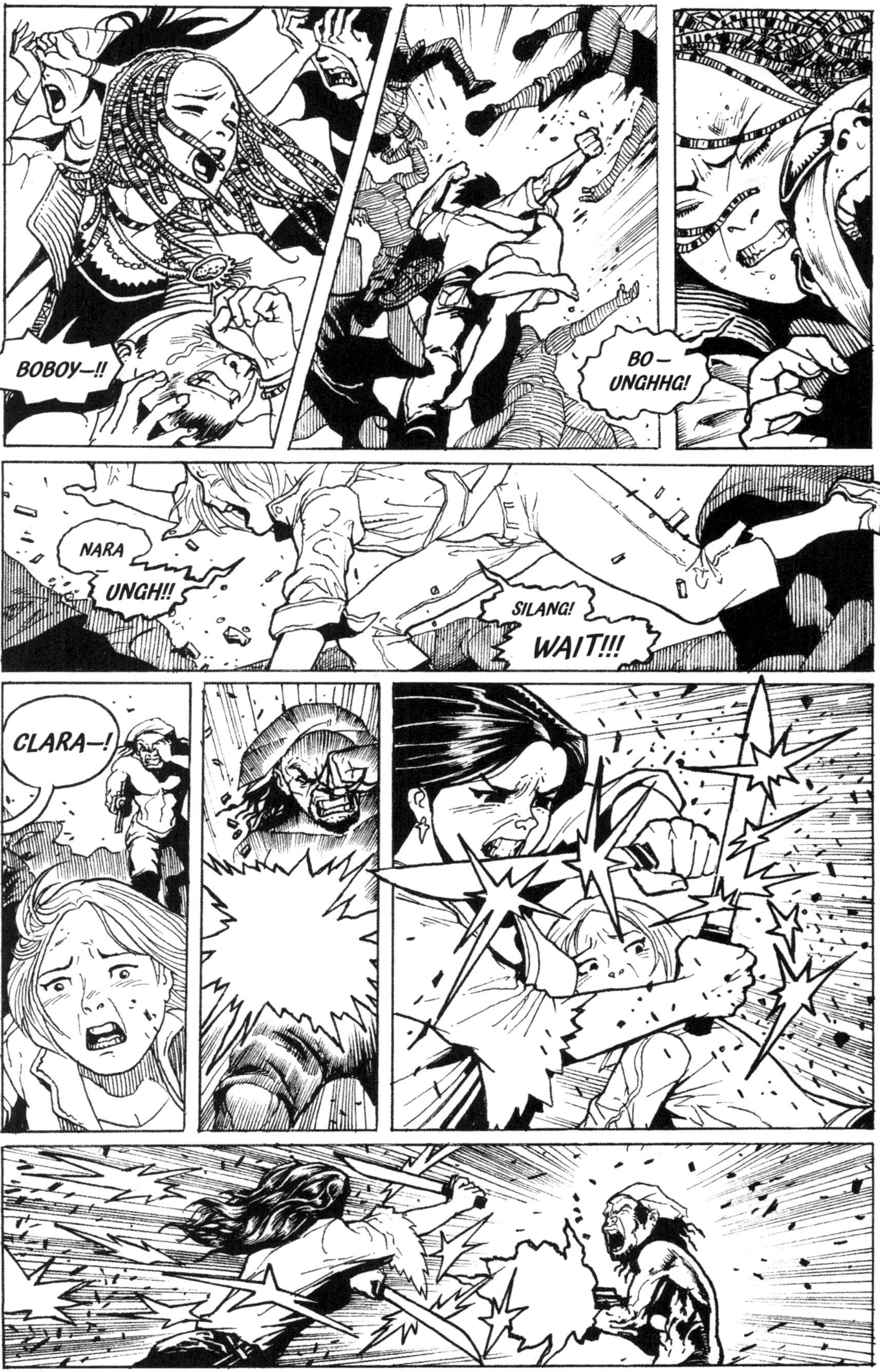
BOBOY—!!
BO—
UNGHHG!
NARA
UNGH!!
SILANG!
WAIT!!!
CLARA—!

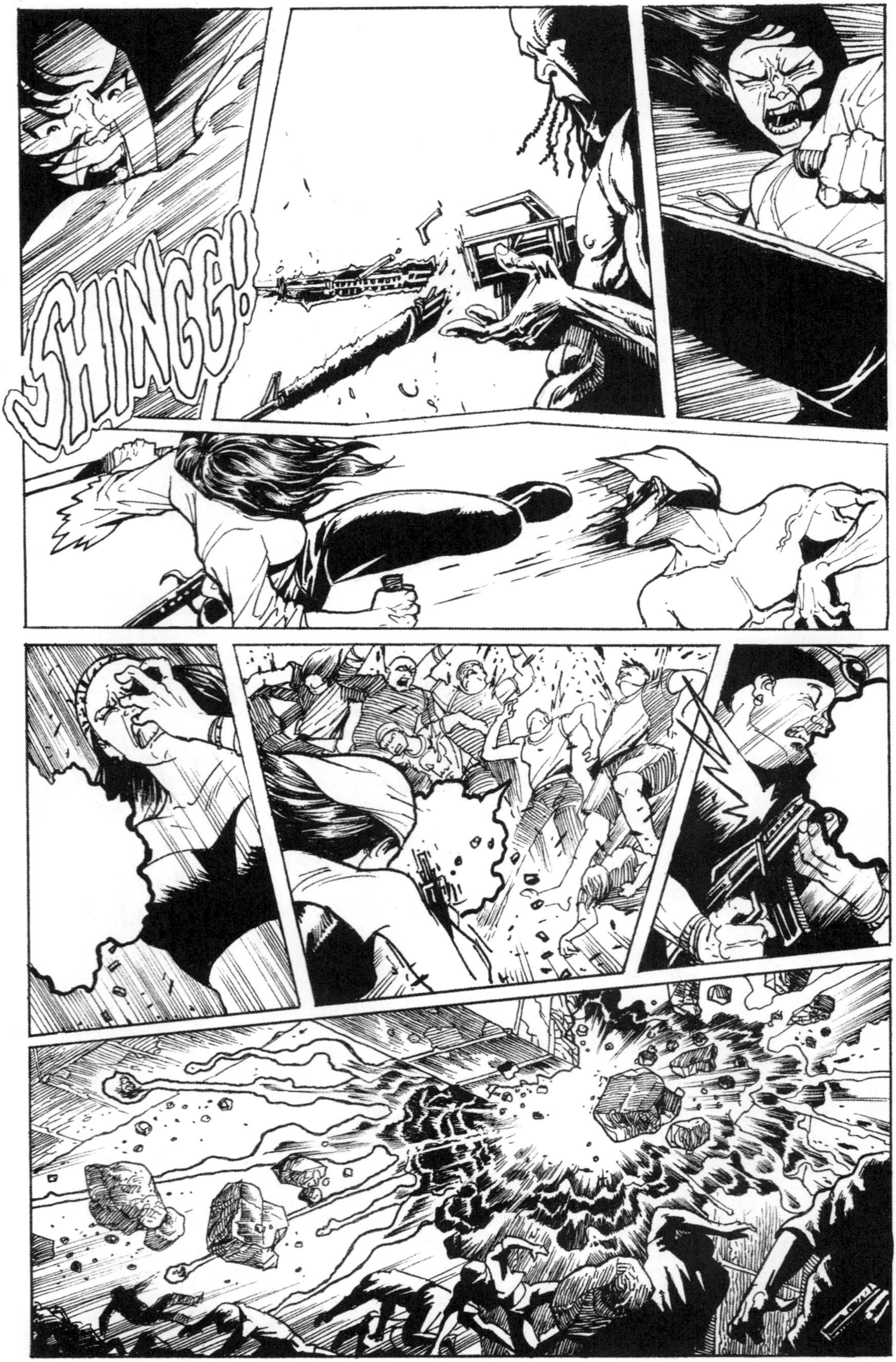
SHINGG!

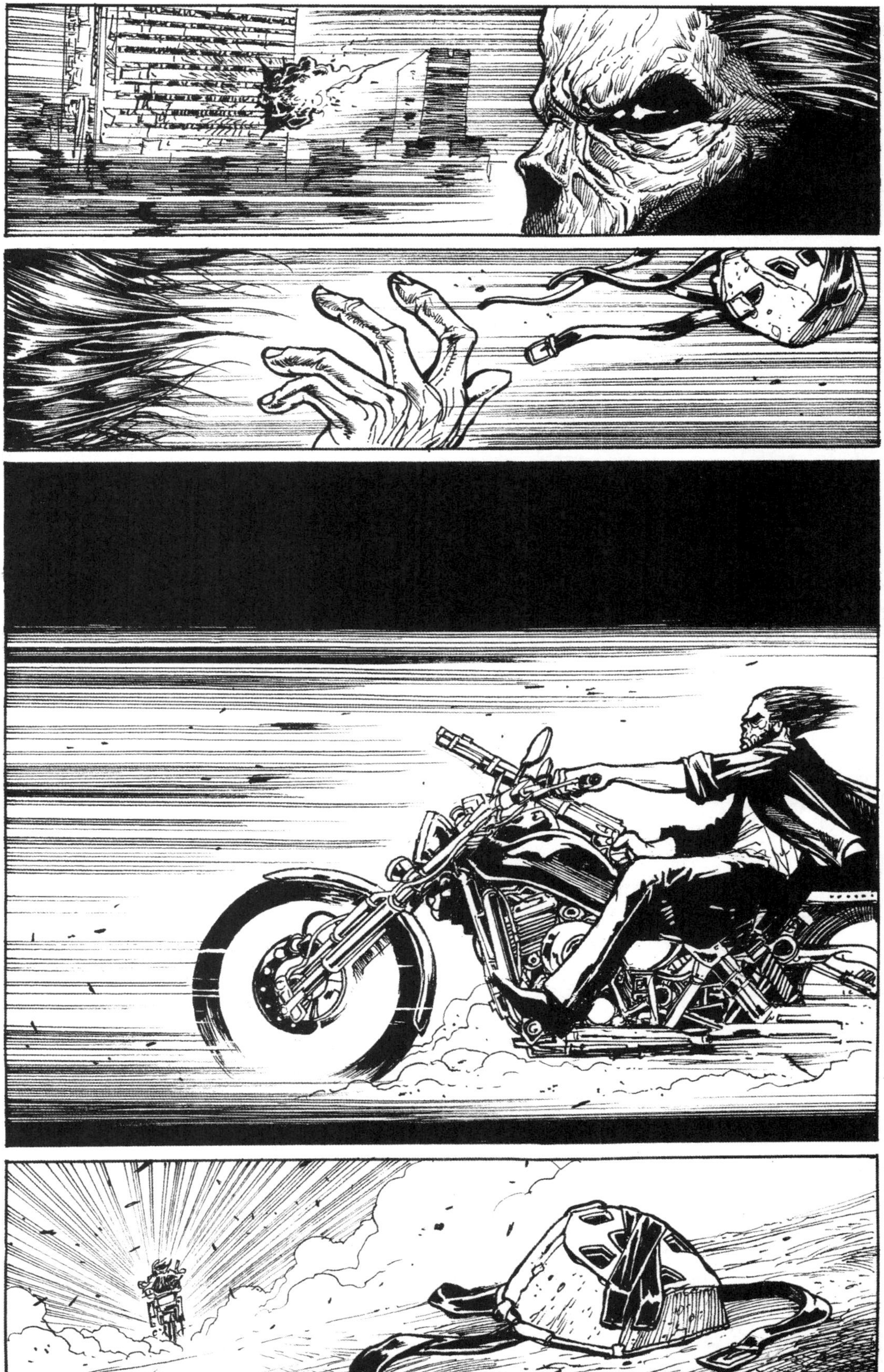

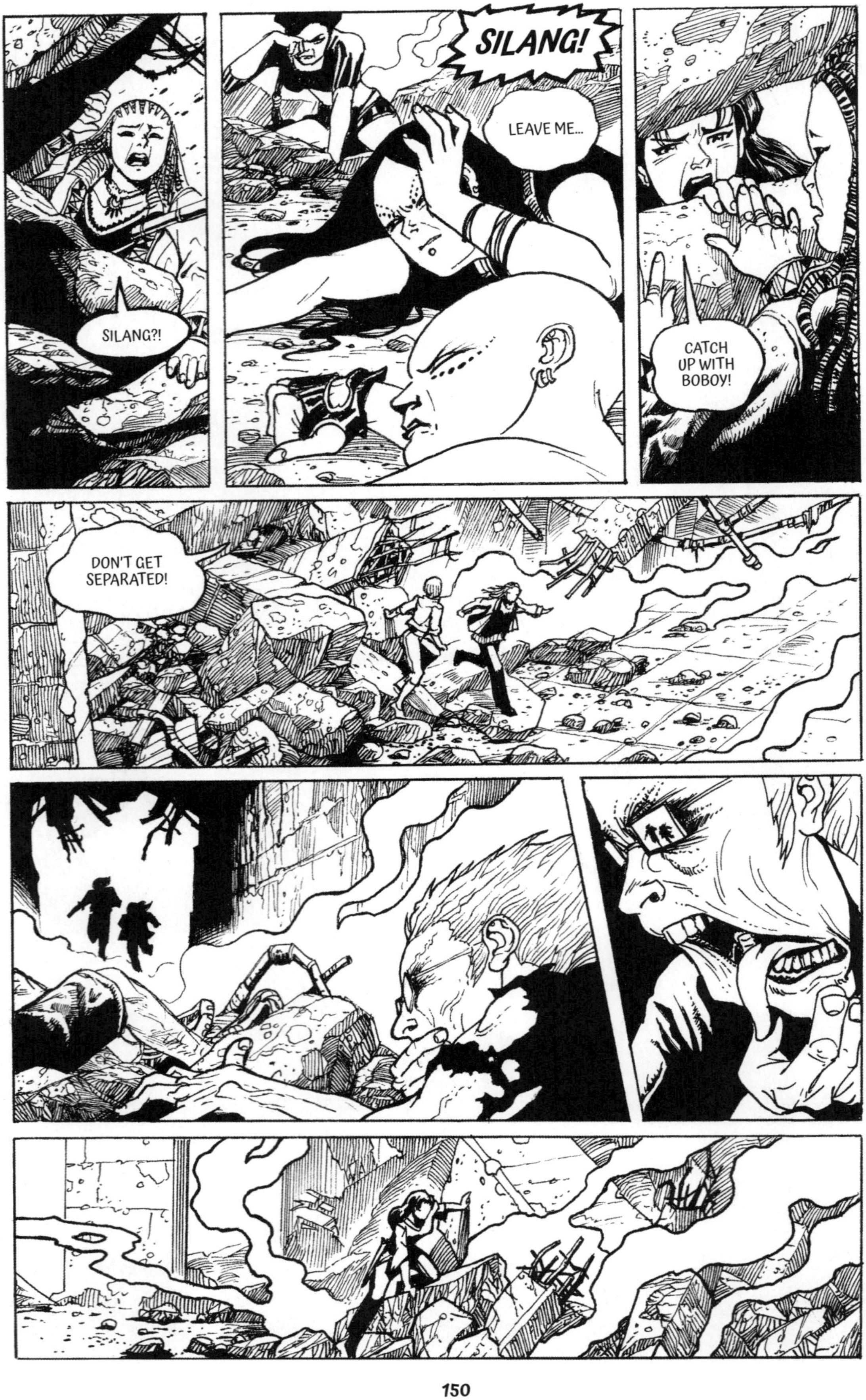
SILANG?!
SILANG!
LEAVE ME...
CATCH UP WITH BOBOY!
DON'T GET SEPARATED!

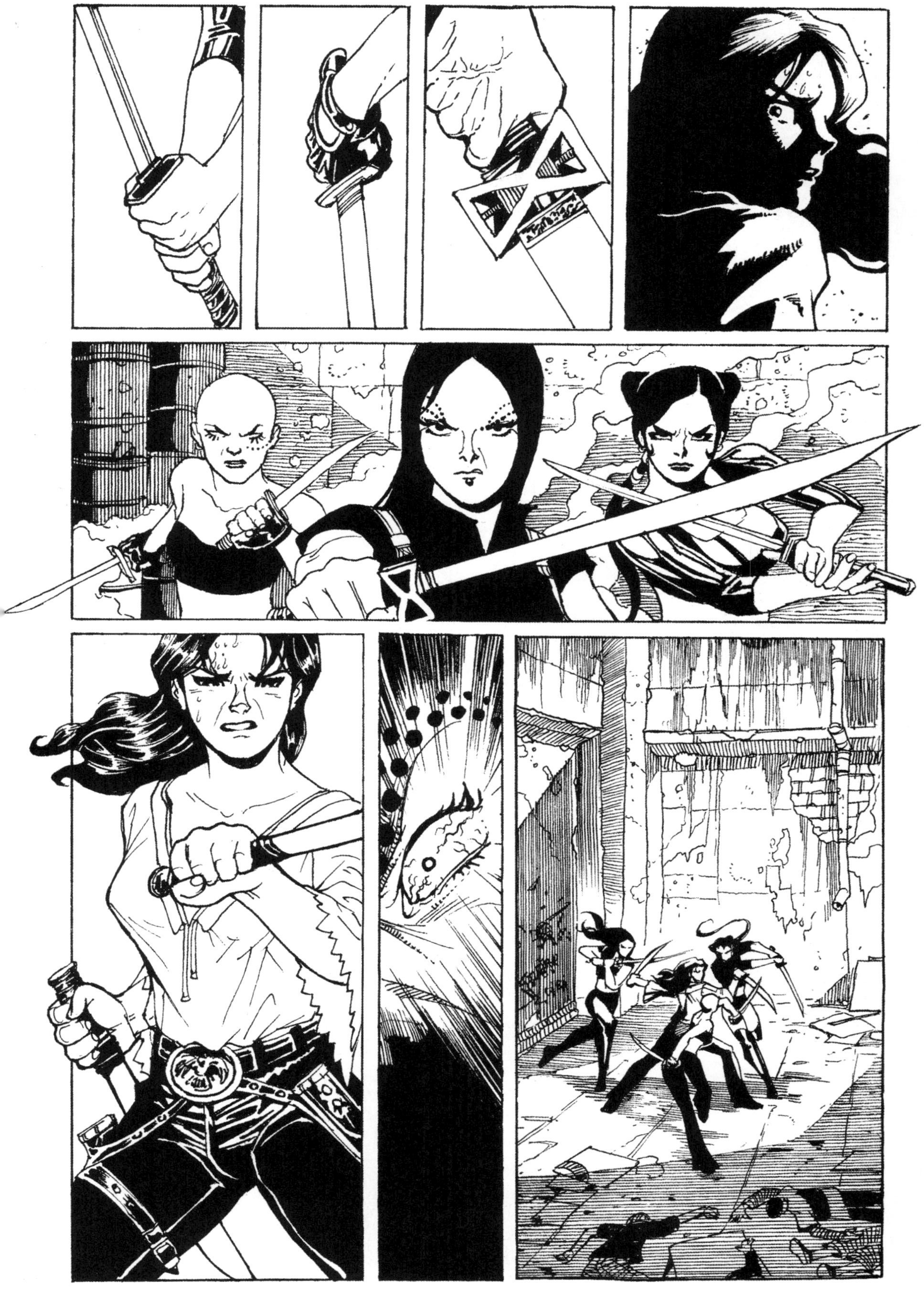

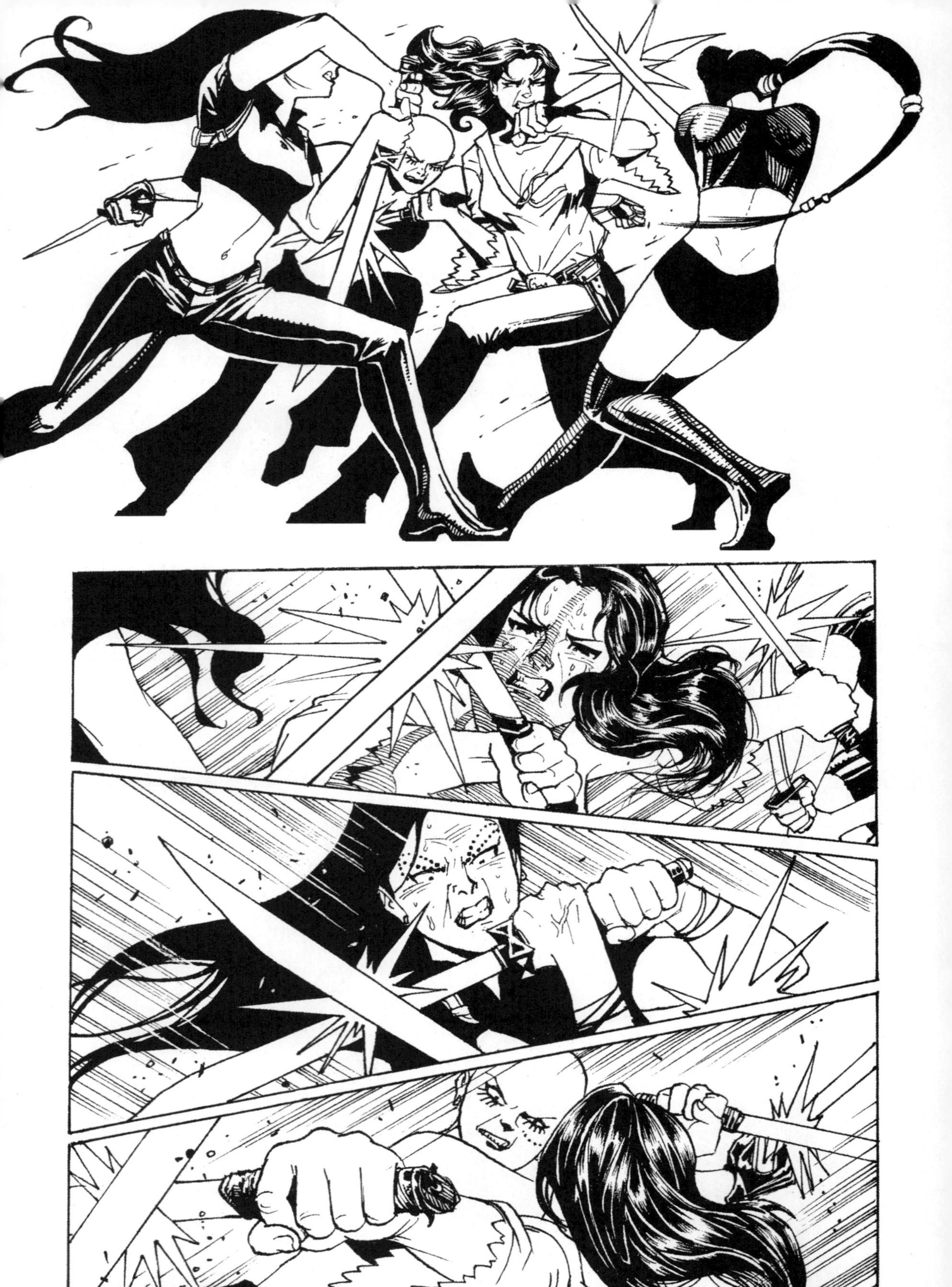

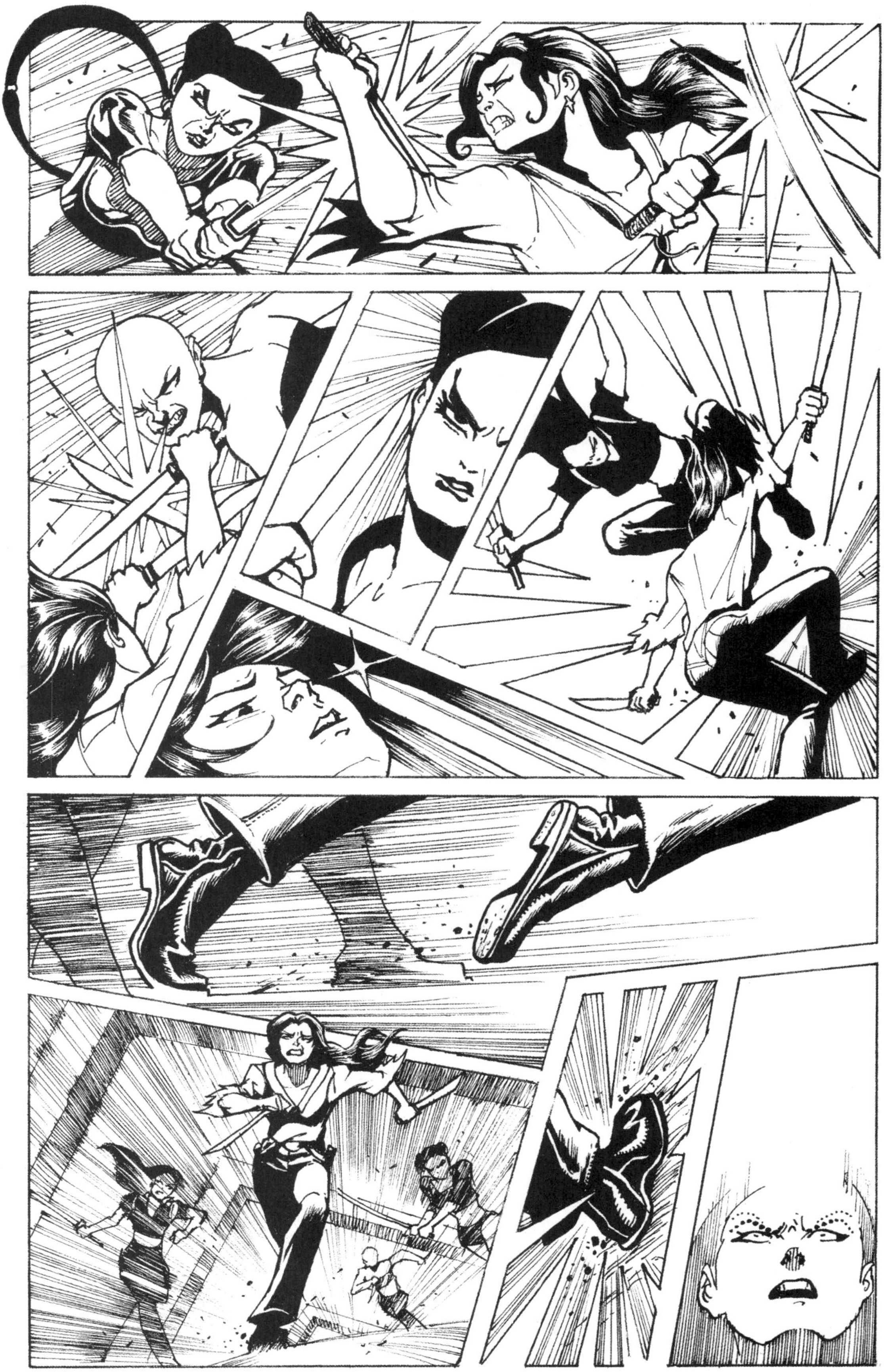

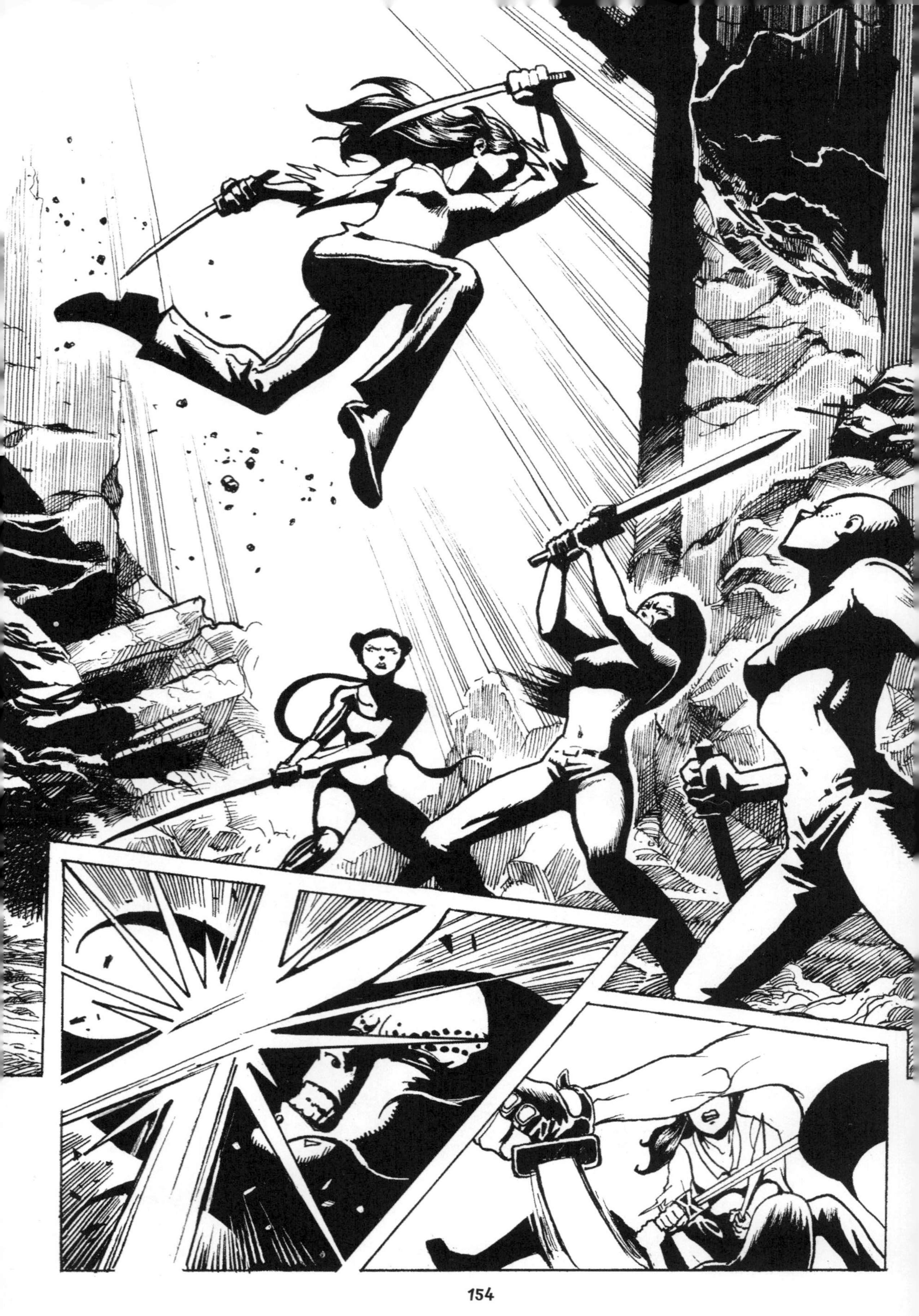

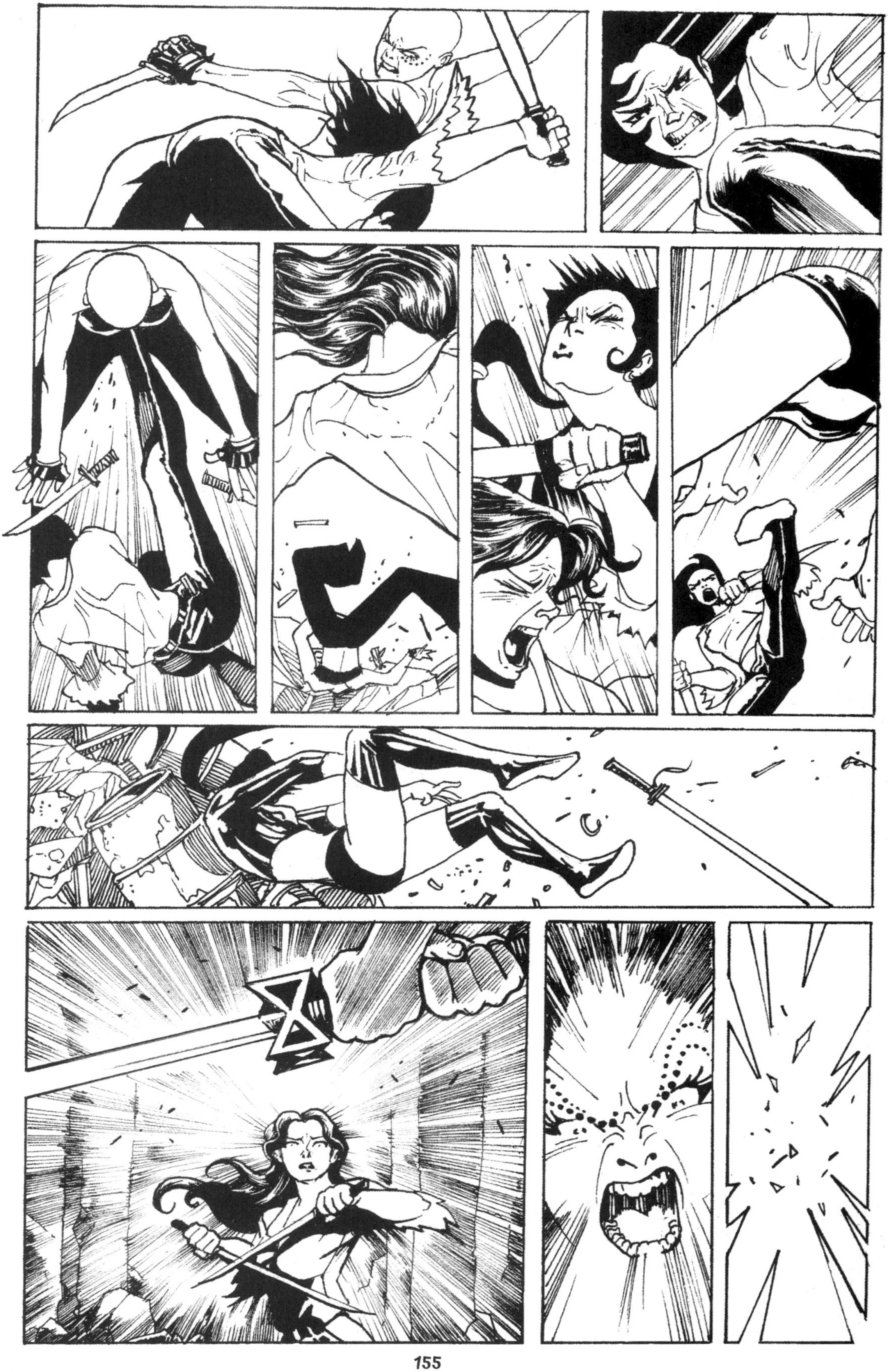

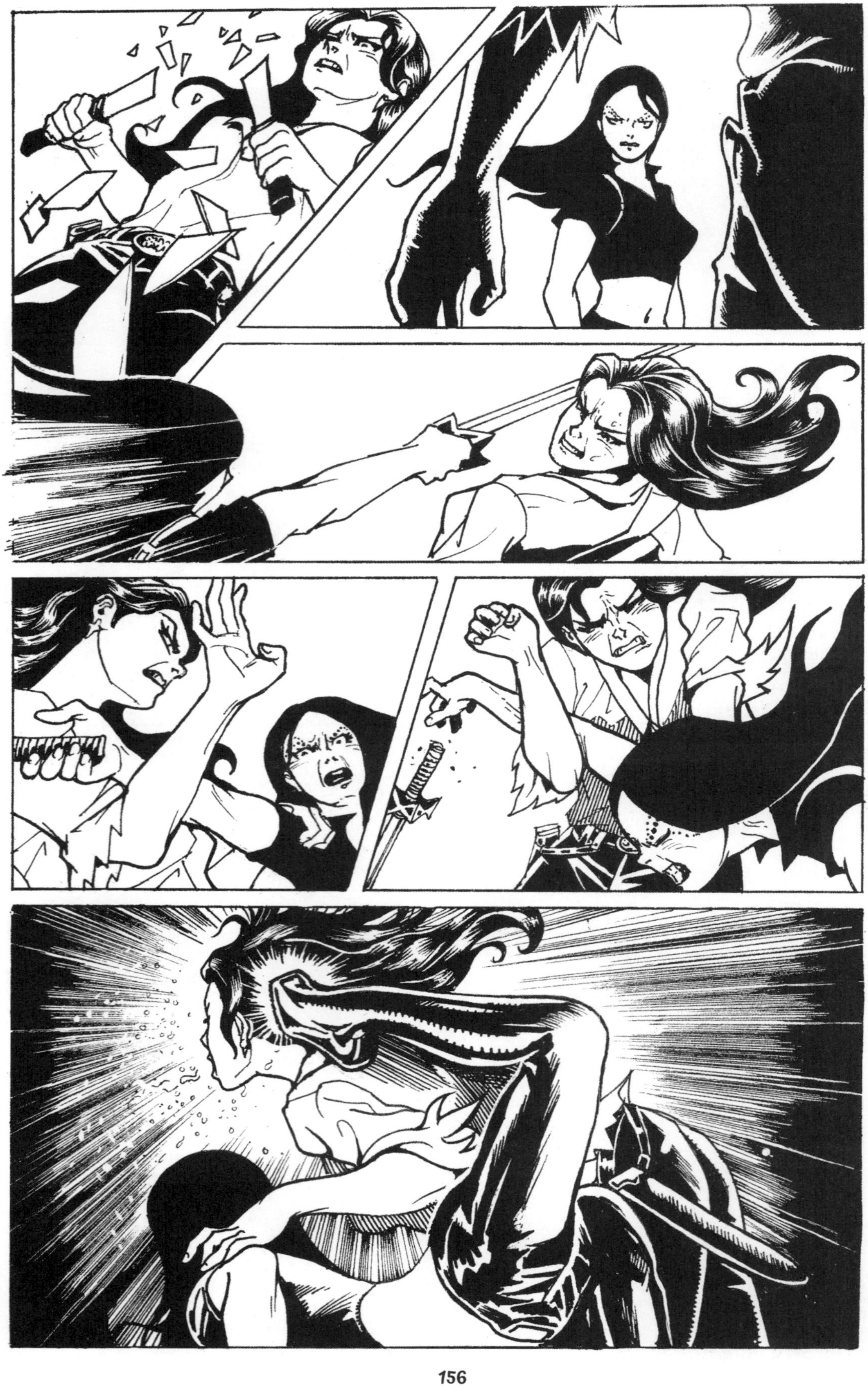

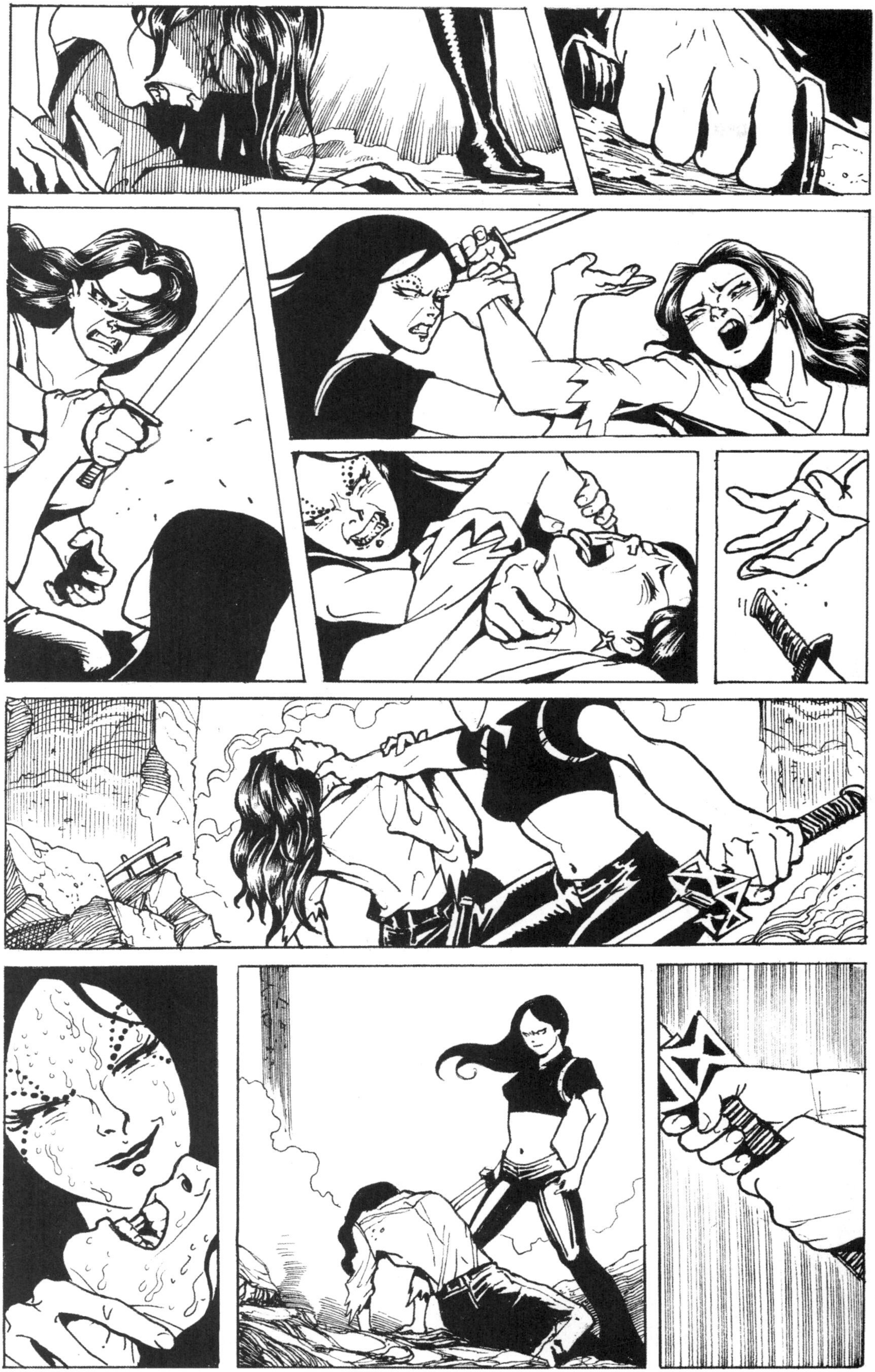

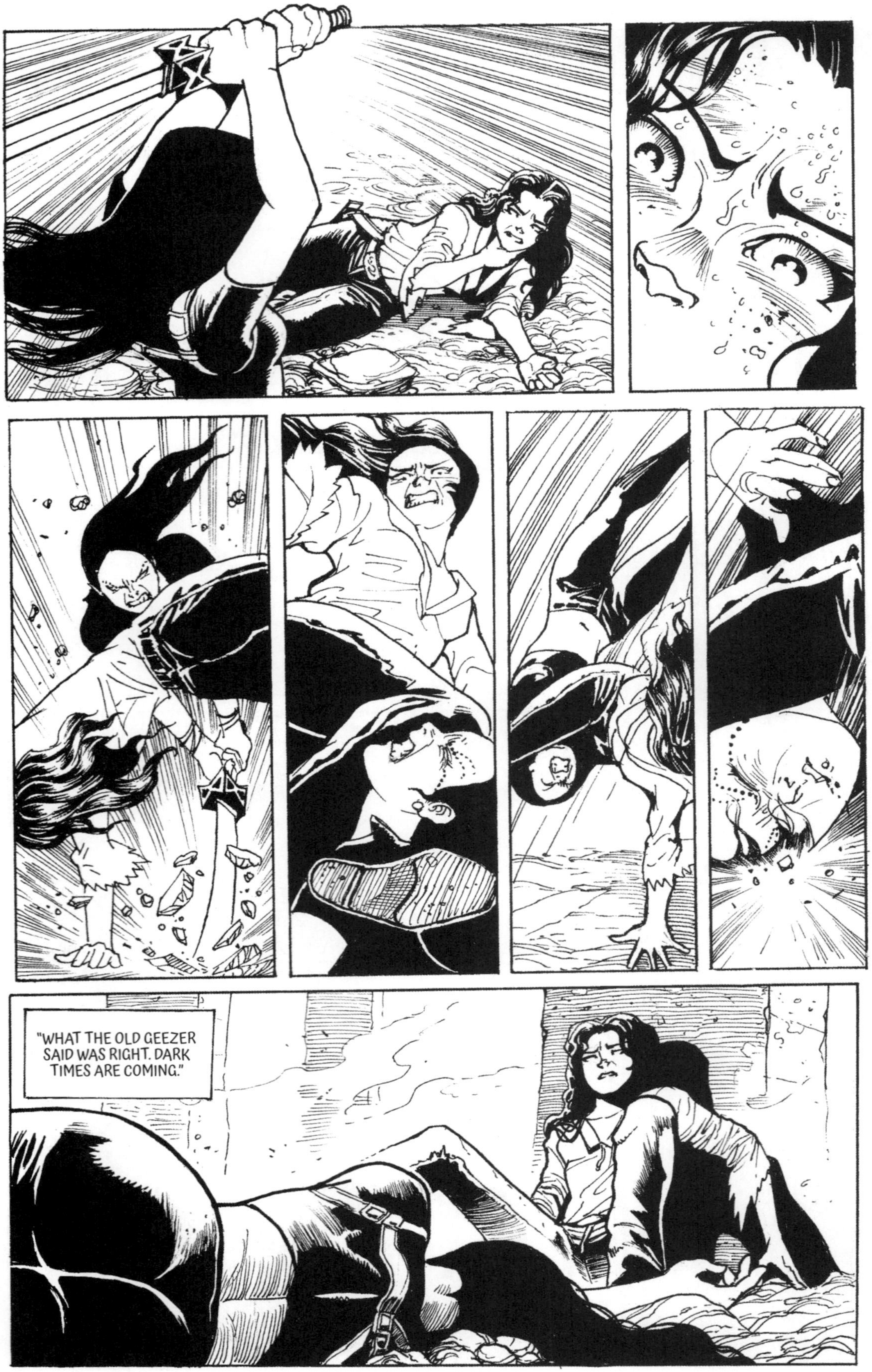
"WHAT THE OLD GEEZER SAID WAS RIGHT. DARK TIMES ARE COMING."

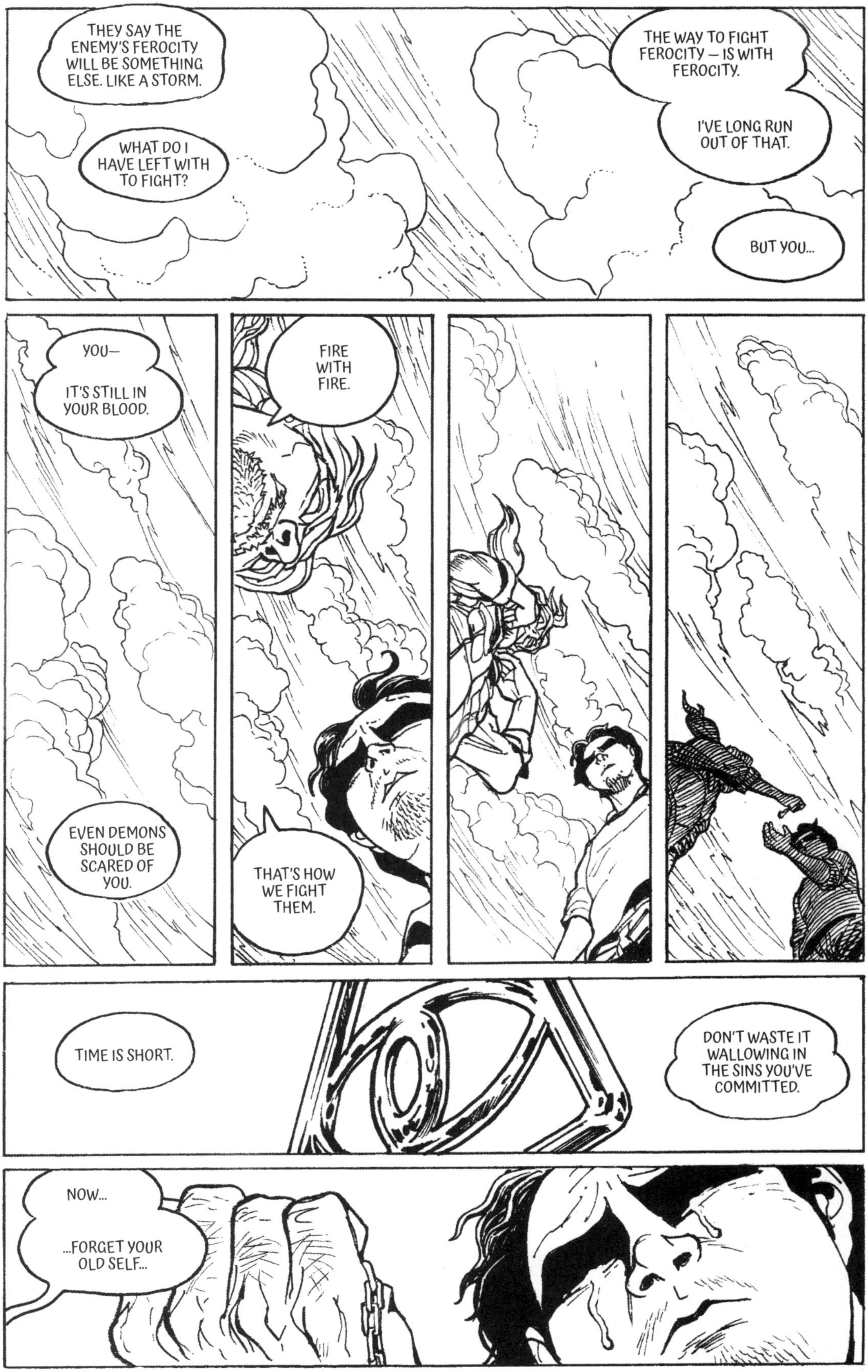
THEY SAY THE ENEMY'S FEROCITY WILL BE SOMETHING ELSE. LIKE A STORM.
WHAT DO I HAVE LEFT WITH TO FIGHT?
THE WAY TO FIGHT FEROCITY — IS WITH FEROCITY.
I'VE LONG RUN OUT OF THAT.
BUT YOU...
YOU—
IT'S STILL IN YOUR BLOOD.
EVEN DEMONS SHOULD BE SCARED OF YOU.
FIRE WITH FIRE.
THAT'S HOW WE FIGHT THEM.
TIME IS SHORT.
DON'T WASTE IT WALLOWING IN THE SINS YOU'VE COMMITTED.
NOW...
...FORGET YOUR OLD SELF...

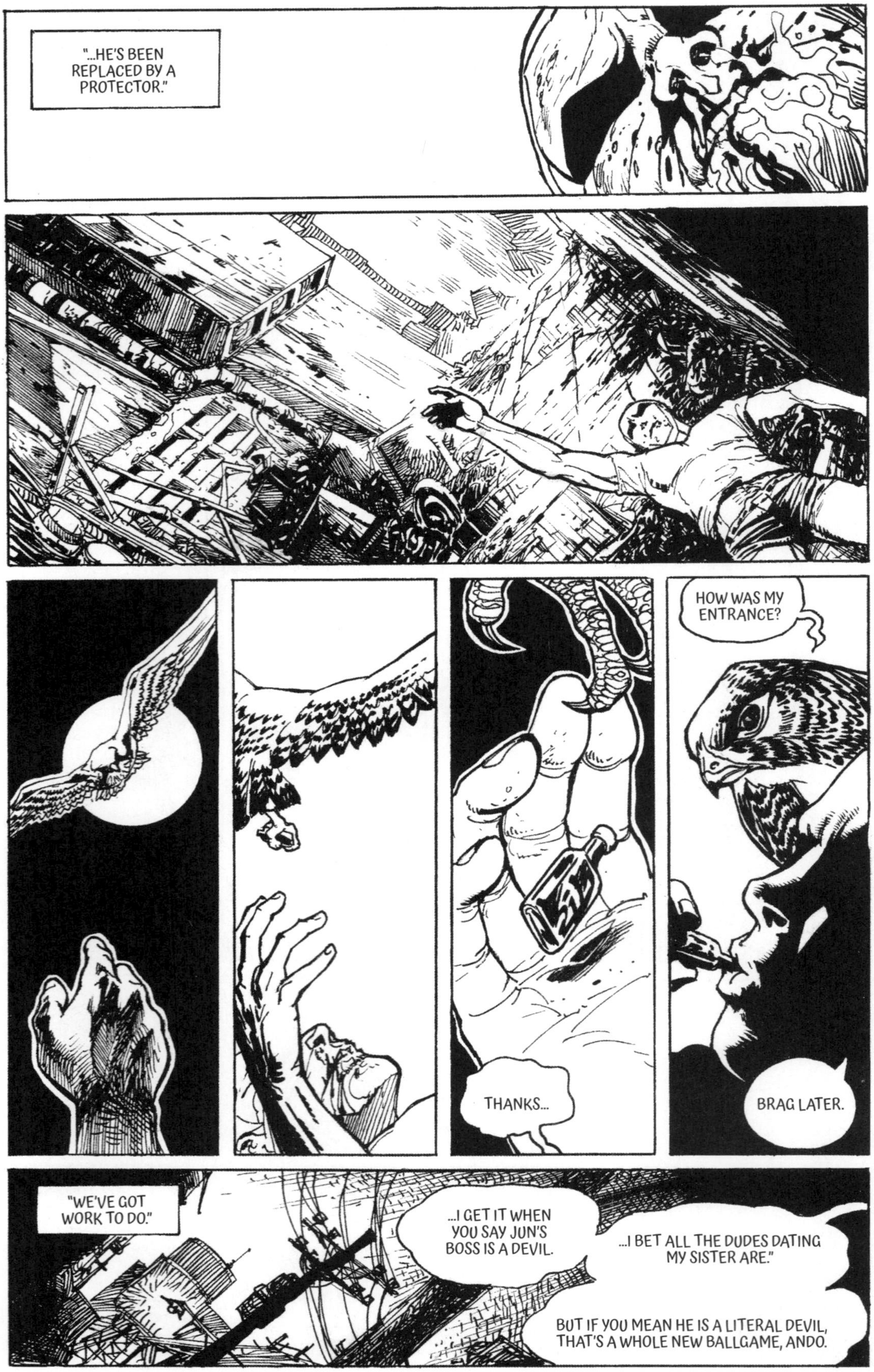
"...HE'S BEEN REPLACED BY A PROTECTOR."
HOW WAS MY ENTRANCE?
THANKS...
BRAG LATER.
"WE'VE GOT WORK TO DO."
...I GET IT WHEN YOU SAY JUN'S BOSS IS A DEVIL.
...I BET ALL THE DUDES DATING MY SISTER ARE."
BUT IF YOU MEAN HE IS A LITERAL DEVIL, THAT'S A WHOLE NEW BALLGAME, ANDO.

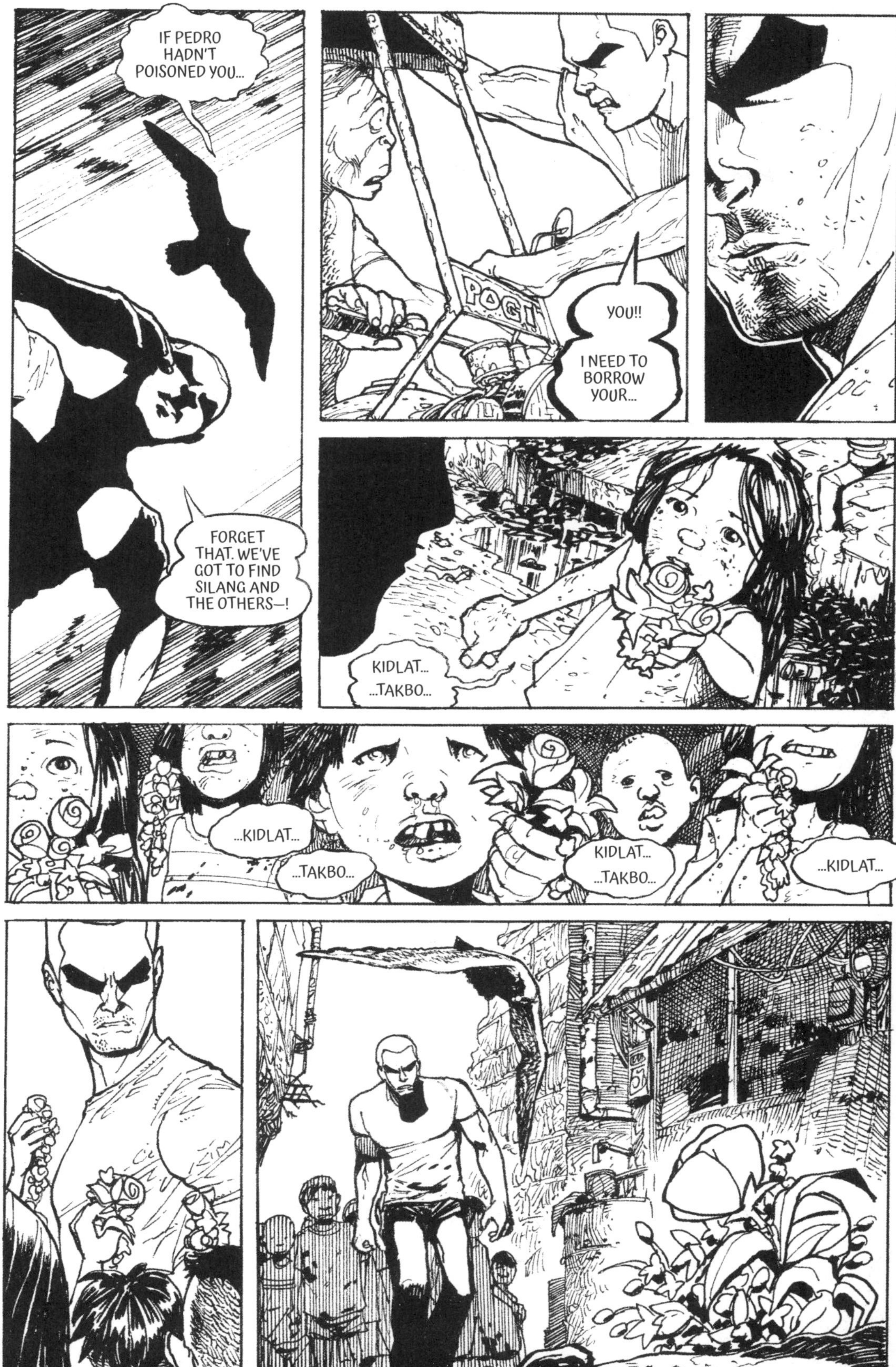
IF PEDRO HADN'T POISONED YOU...
FORGET THAT. WE'VE GOT TO FIND SILANG AND THE OTHERS—!
YOU!!
I NEED TO BORROW YOUR...
POGI
KIDLAT... ...TAKBO...
...KIDLAT...
...TAKBO...
KIDLAT... ...TAKBO...
...KIDLAT...

THEY'RE LIKE FOOTPRINTS.

DID SHE MAKE THESE?

ANDO...
...WAIT...
...COMING.

SOMEONE'S...

HUMID.
DRY EARTH.
ROTTING.
NOT ALIVE.

HE'S NEAR.

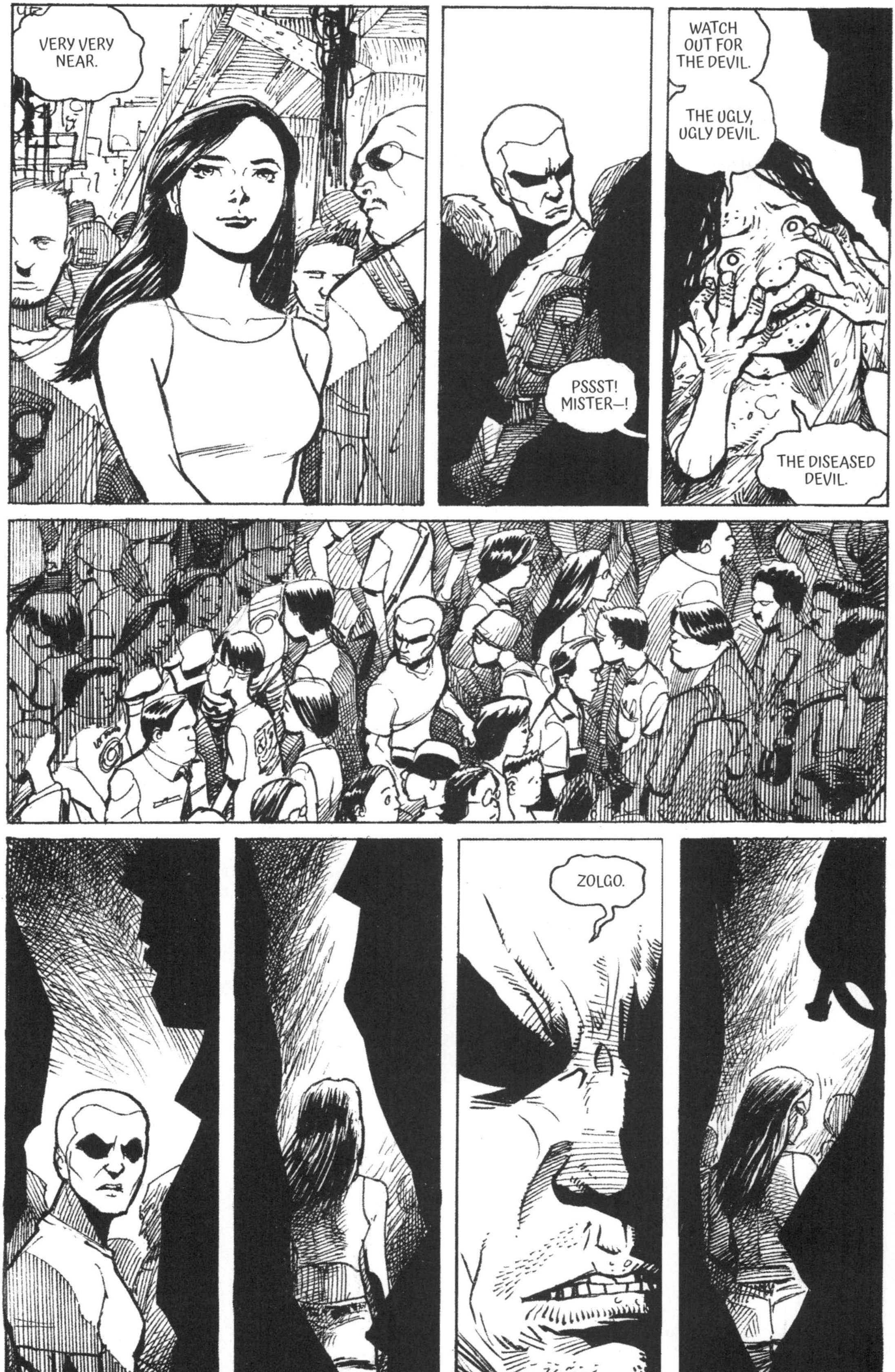
VERY VERY NEAR.
PSSST! MISTER—!
WATCH OUT FOR THE DEVIL.
THE UGLY, UGLY DEVIL.
THE DISEASED DEVIL.
ZOLGO.

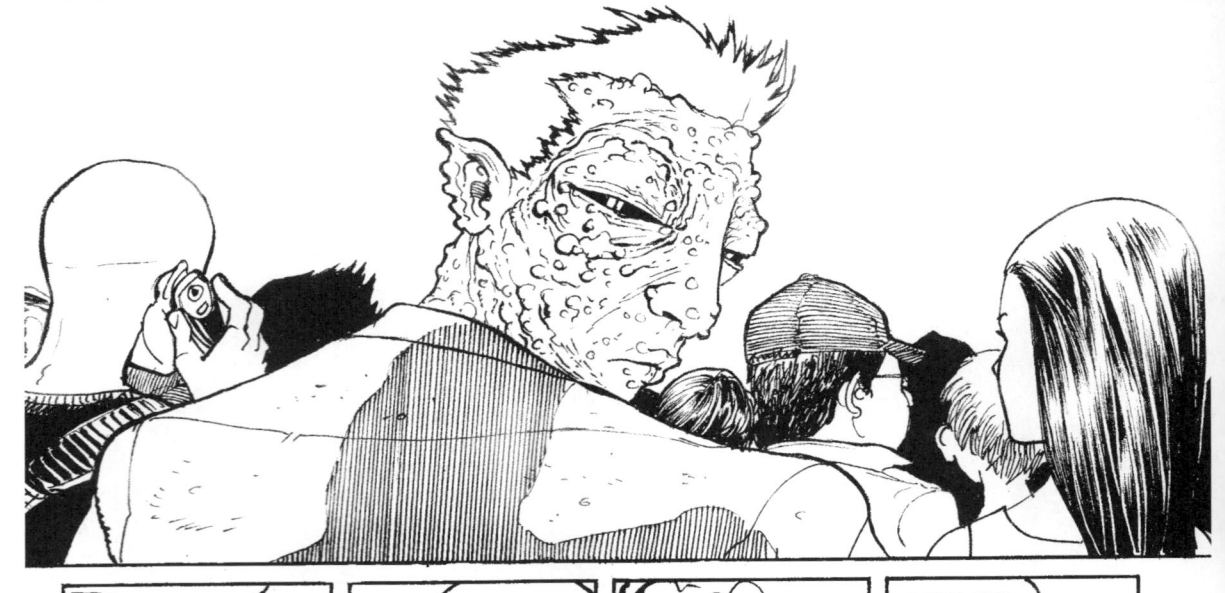

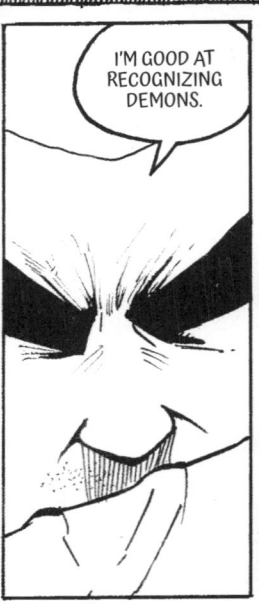

YOU KNOW ME?

I'M GOOD AT RECOGNIZING DEMONS.

AREN'T YOU HORRIFIED BY WHAT YOU'RE DOING?

WE'RE USED TO THAT.

SUCH A STOP BLABBERING. @#$$!! THAT'S WHAT TICKS ME OFF. YOU'VE GOT A LOT TO ANSWER FOR SO JUST FOLLOW ME IF YOU STILL WANT TO KEEP YOUR SORES INTACT.

WAAIITT... ...YOU... I KNOW YOU...

ASEDILLIO... ...THE FORMER TERROR OF MANILA.

THAT'S RIGHT. THAT'S WHY I'M THE ONE YOU SHOULD BE AFRAID OF.

I'M AFRAID OF NOTHING.

164

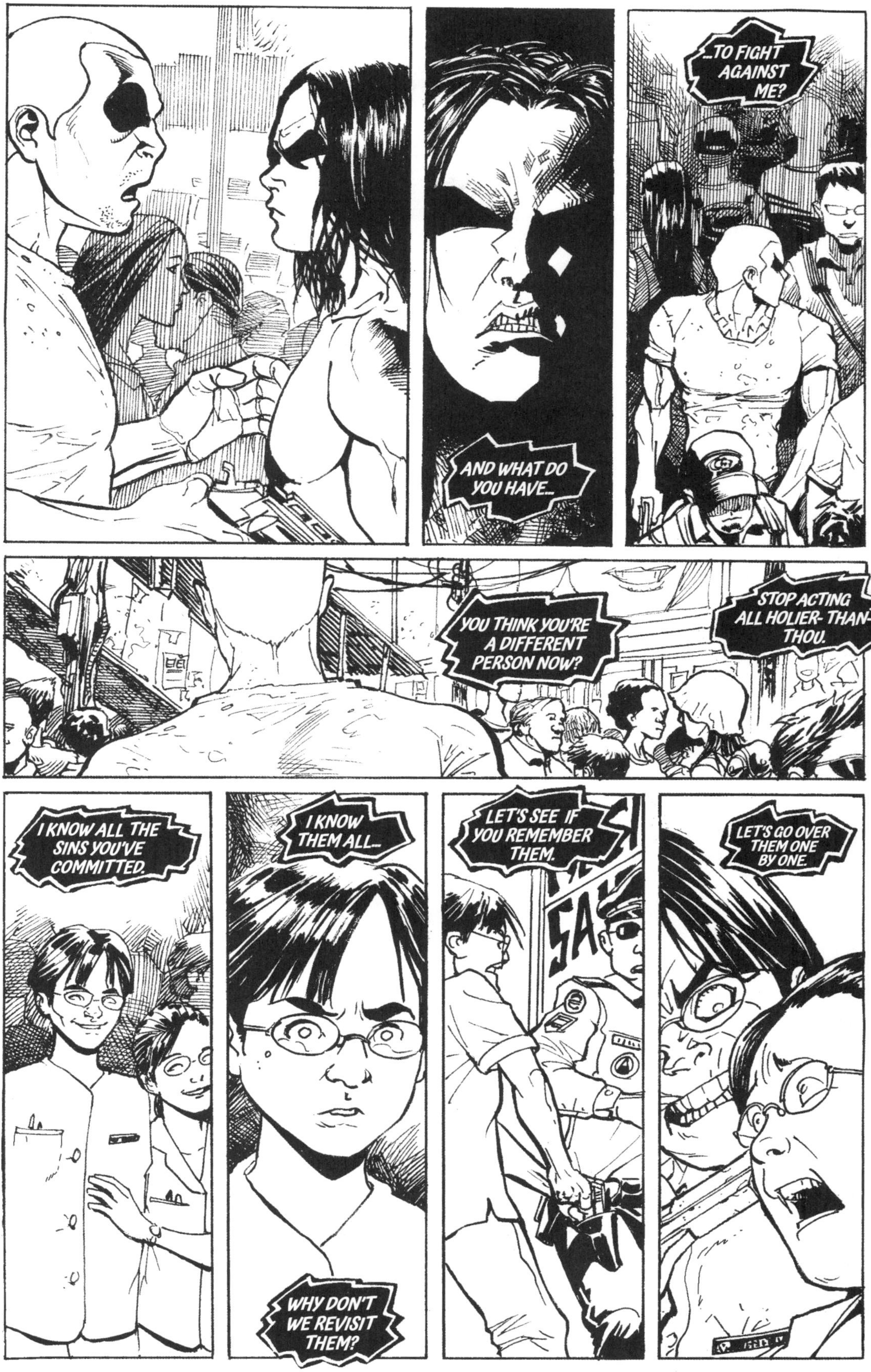
AND WHAT DO YOU HAVE...
...TO FIGHT AGAINST ME?
YOU THINK YOU'RE A DIFFERENT PERSON NOW?
STOP ACTING ALL HOLIER-THAN-THOU.
I KNOW ALL THE SINS YOU'VE COMMITTED.
I KNOW THEM ALL...
WHY DON'T WE REVISIT THEM?
LET'S SEE IF YOU REMEMBER THEM.
LET'S GO OVER THEM ONE BY ONE.

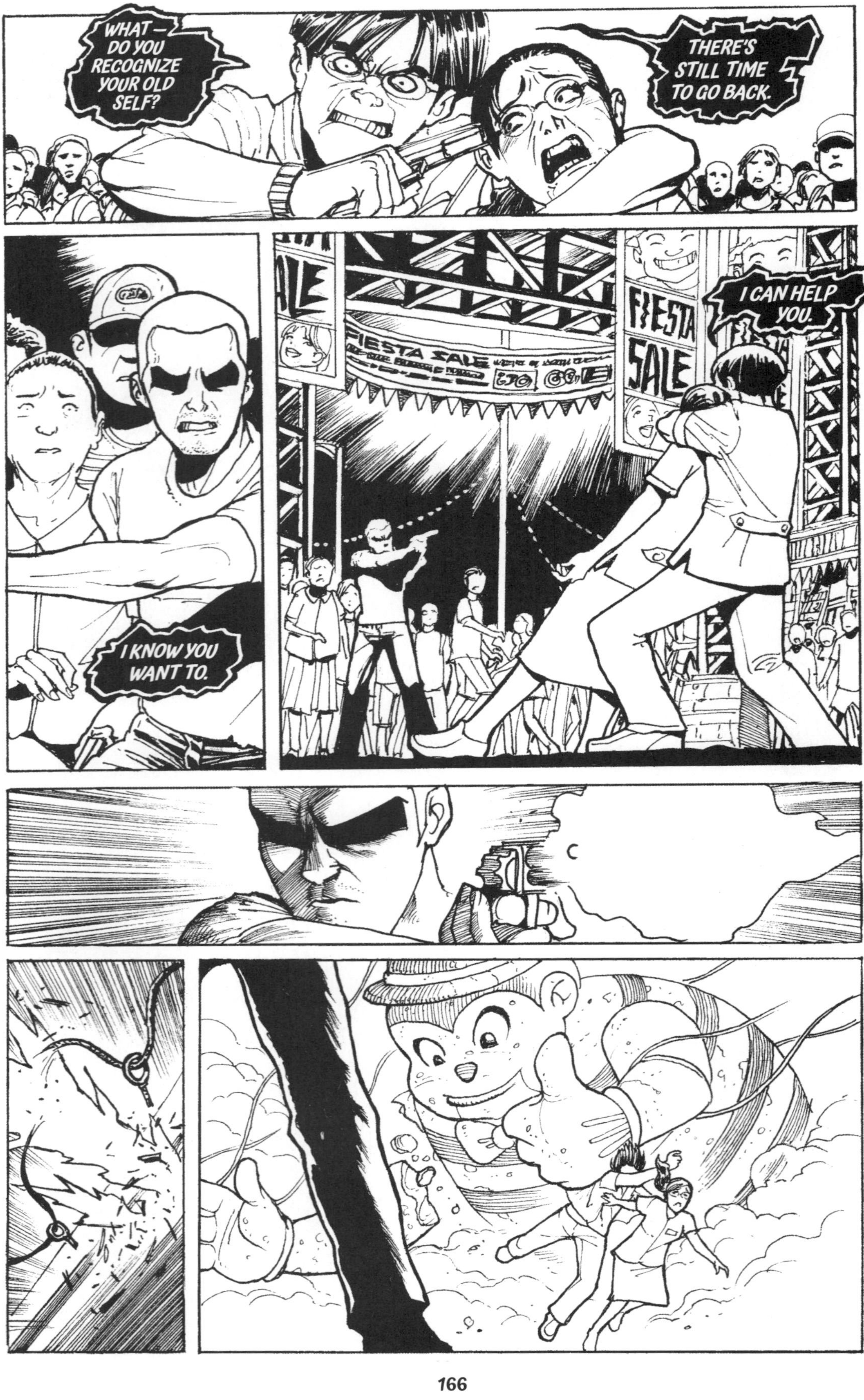
WHAT— DO YOU RECOGNIZE YOUR OLD SELF?
THERE'S STILL TIME TO GO BACK.
FIESTA SALE
I CAN HELP YOU.
I KNOW YOU WANT TO.

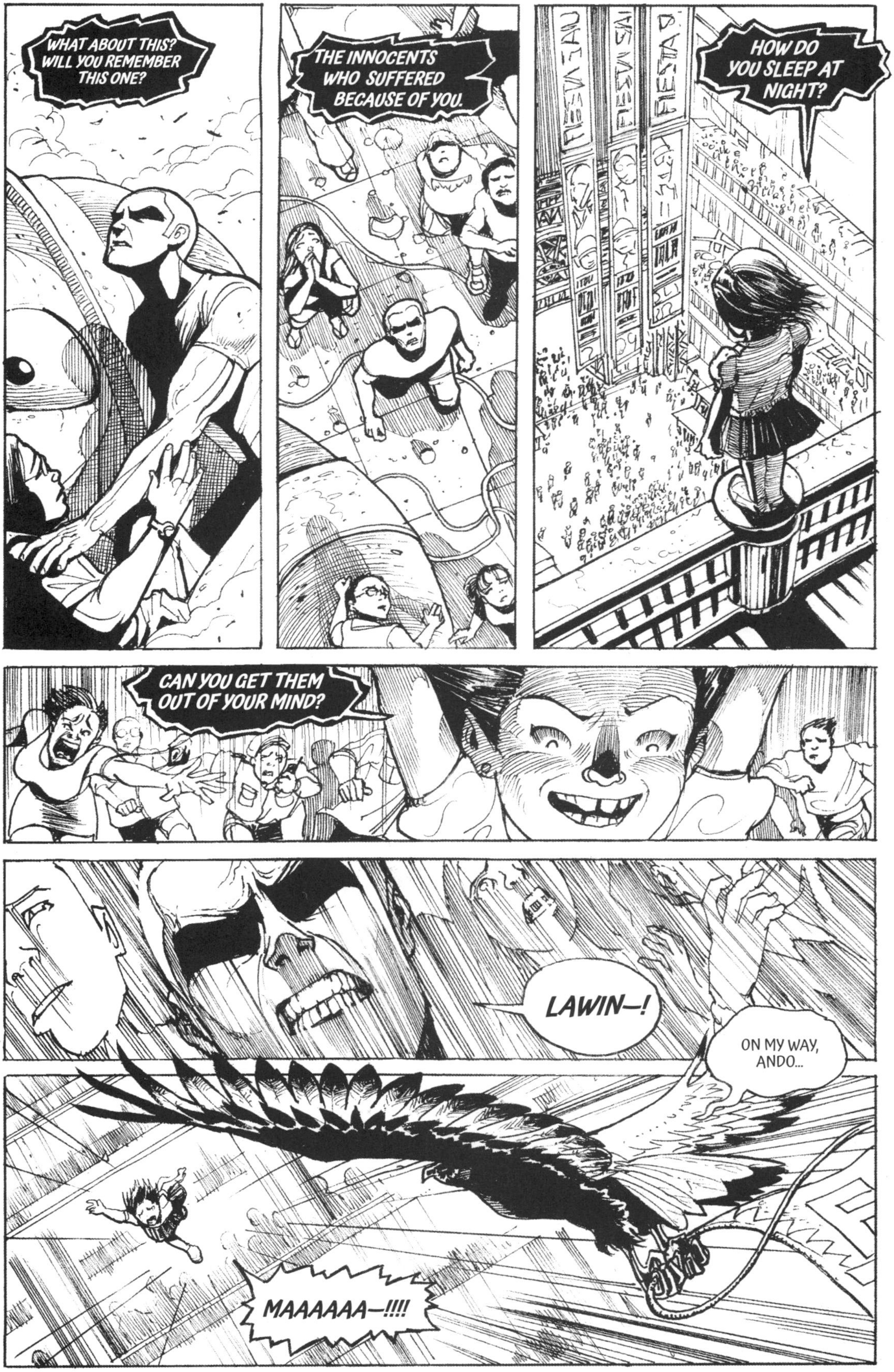
WHAT ABOUT THIS? WILL YOU REMEMBER THIS ONE?
THE INNOCENTS WHO SUFFERED BECAUSE OF YOU.
HOW DO YOU SLEEP AT NIGHT?
CAN YOU GET THEM OUT OF YOUR MIND?
LAWIN—!
ON MY WAY, ANDO...
MAAAAAA—!!!!

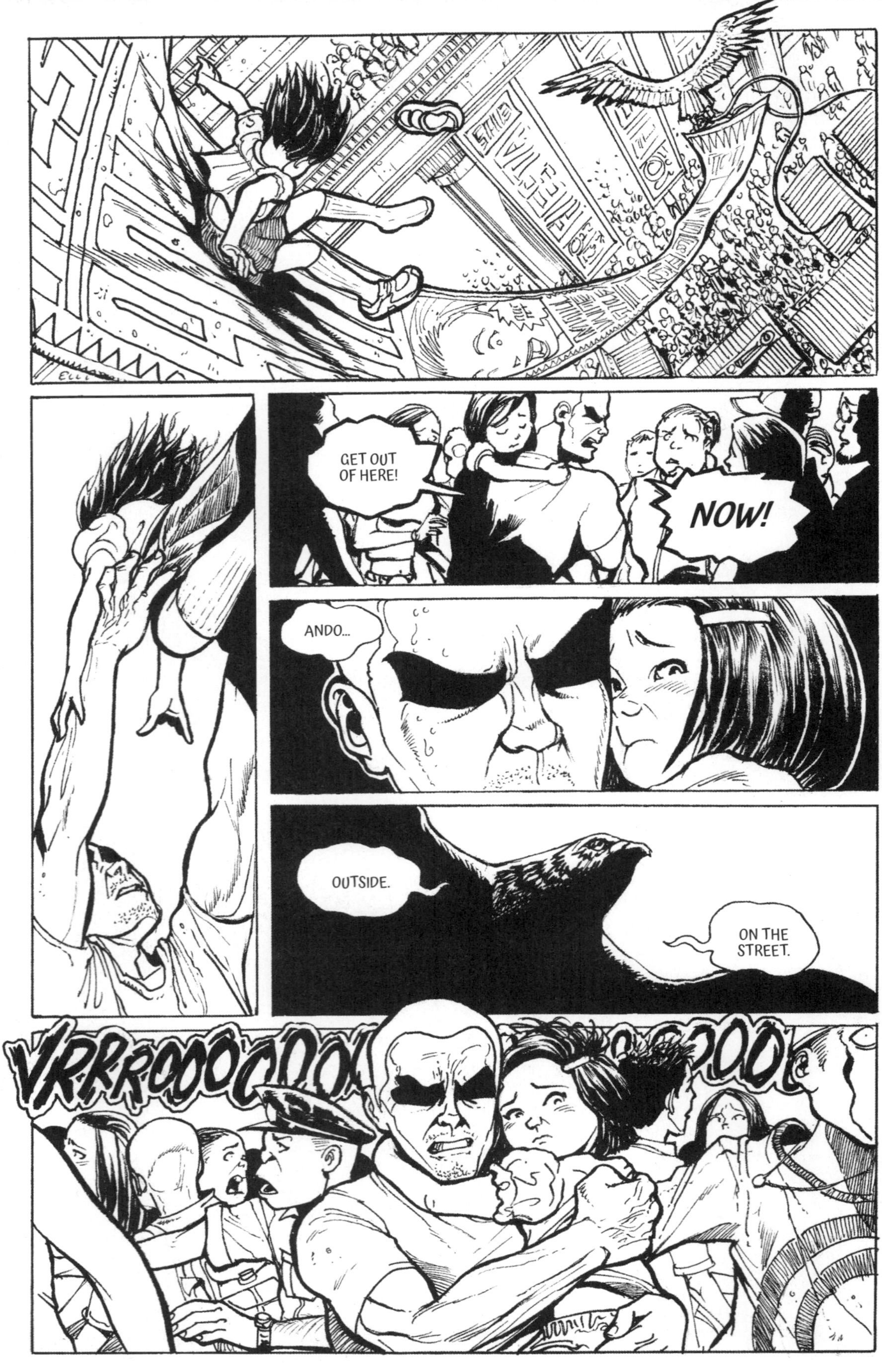
GET OUT OF HERE!
NOW!
ANDO...
OUTSIDE.
ON THE STREET.
VRRROOOOOOOOOOOOOO

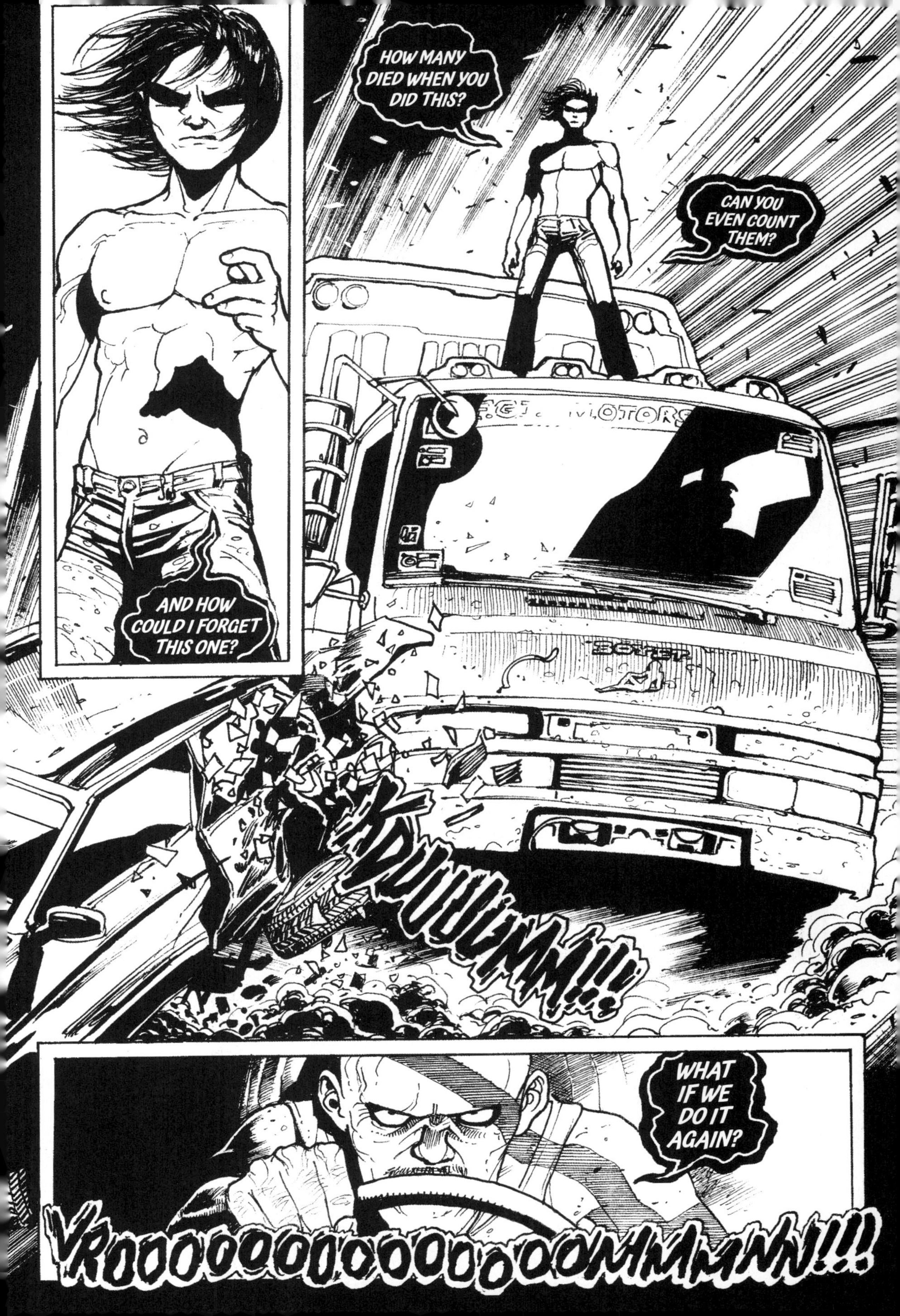
AND HOW COULD I FORGET THIS ONE?
HOW MANY DIED WHEN YOU DID THIS?
CAN YOU EVEN COUNT THEM?
MOTORS
KDUUUMM!!
WHAT IF WE DO IT AGAIN?
VROOOOOOOOOOOOOOOOMMMMNN!!!

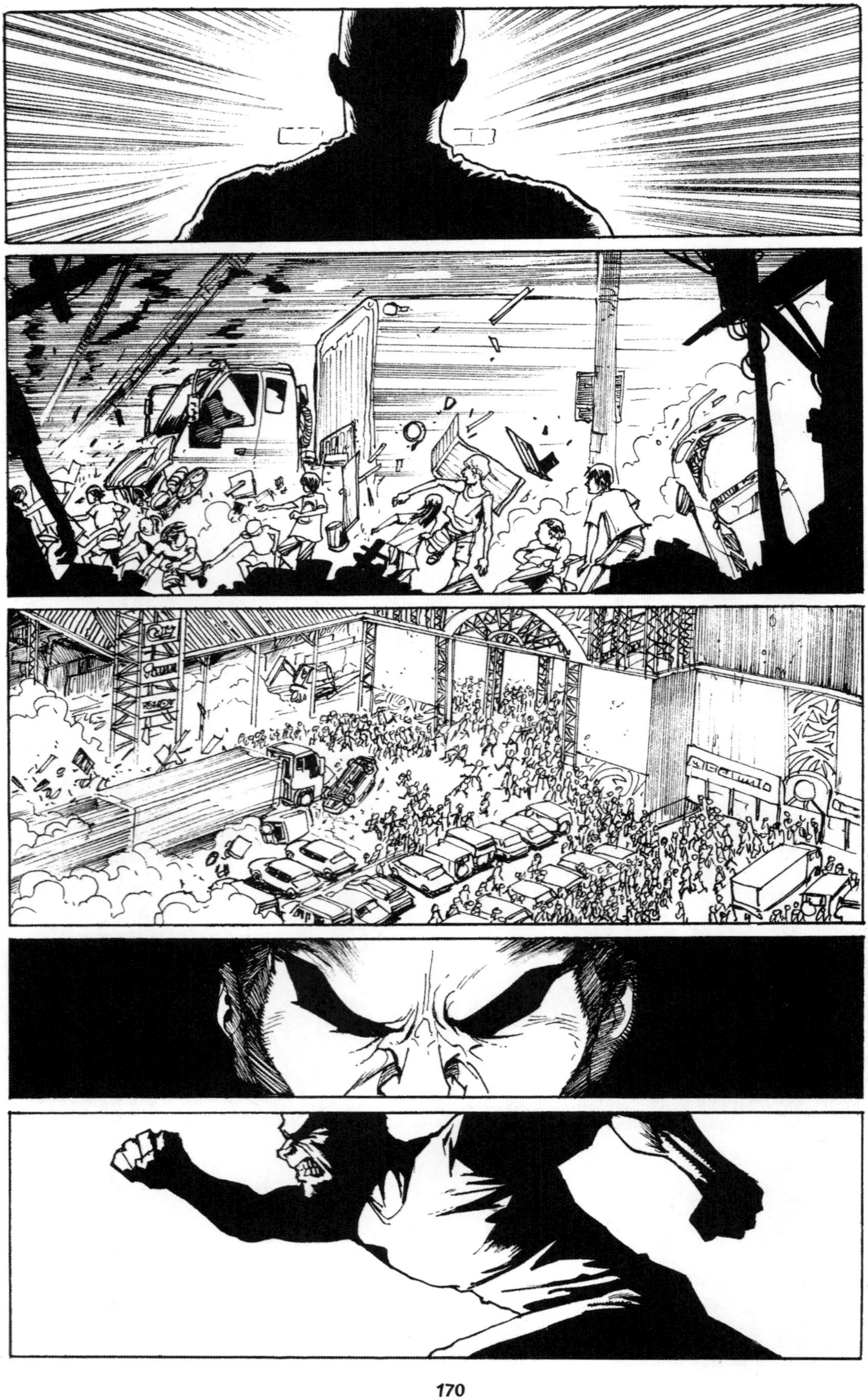

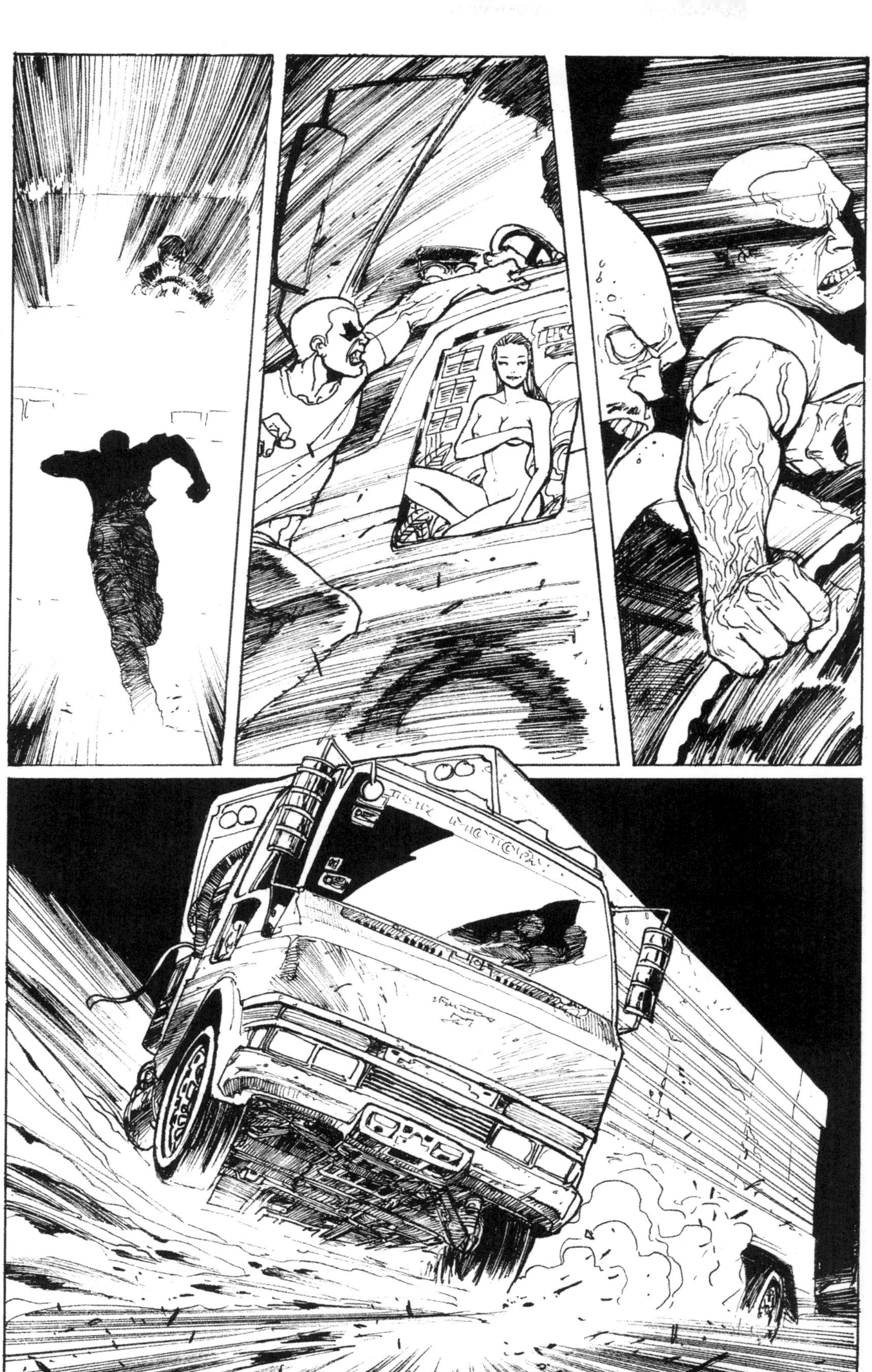

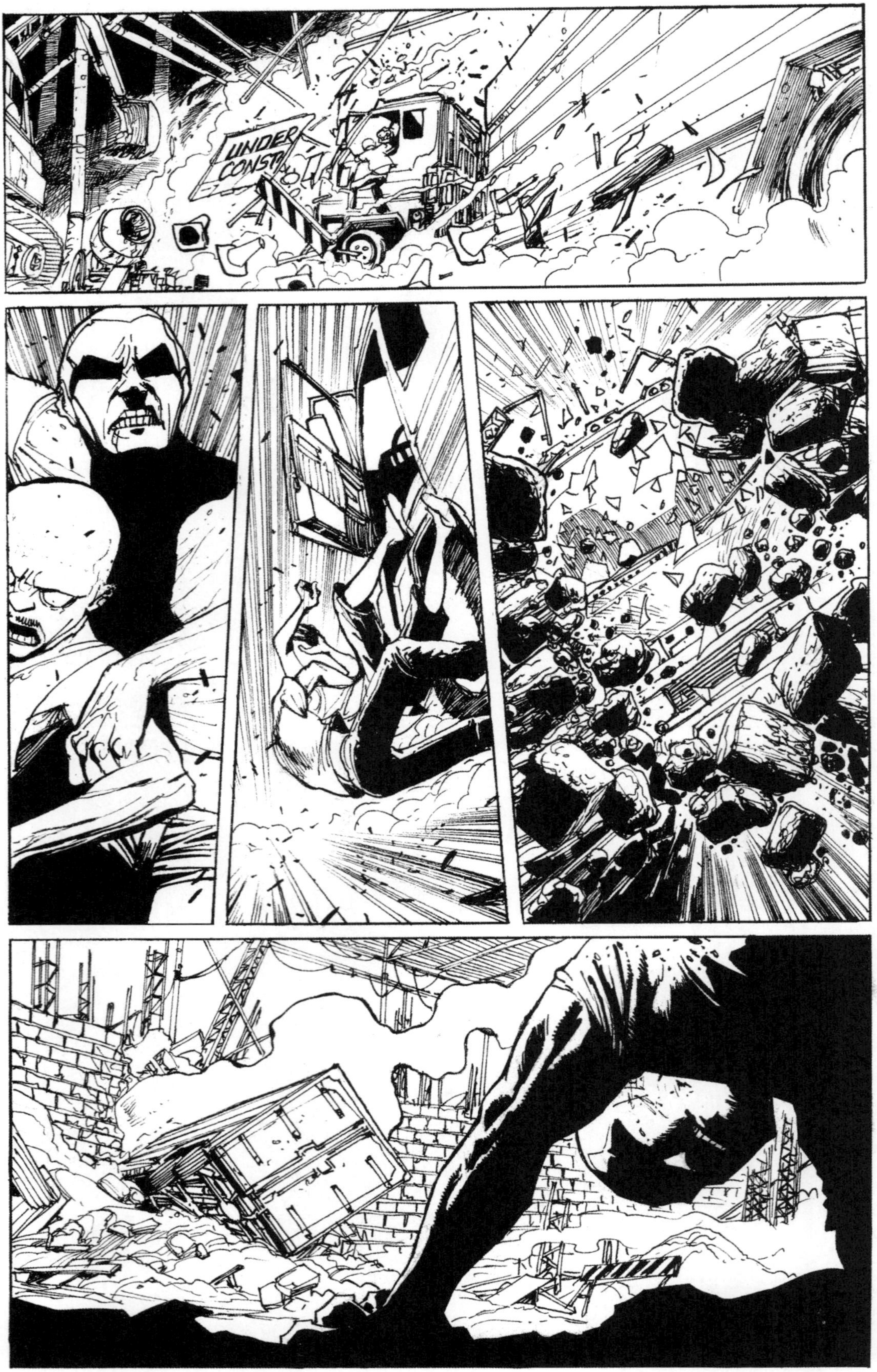
UNDER
CONSTR

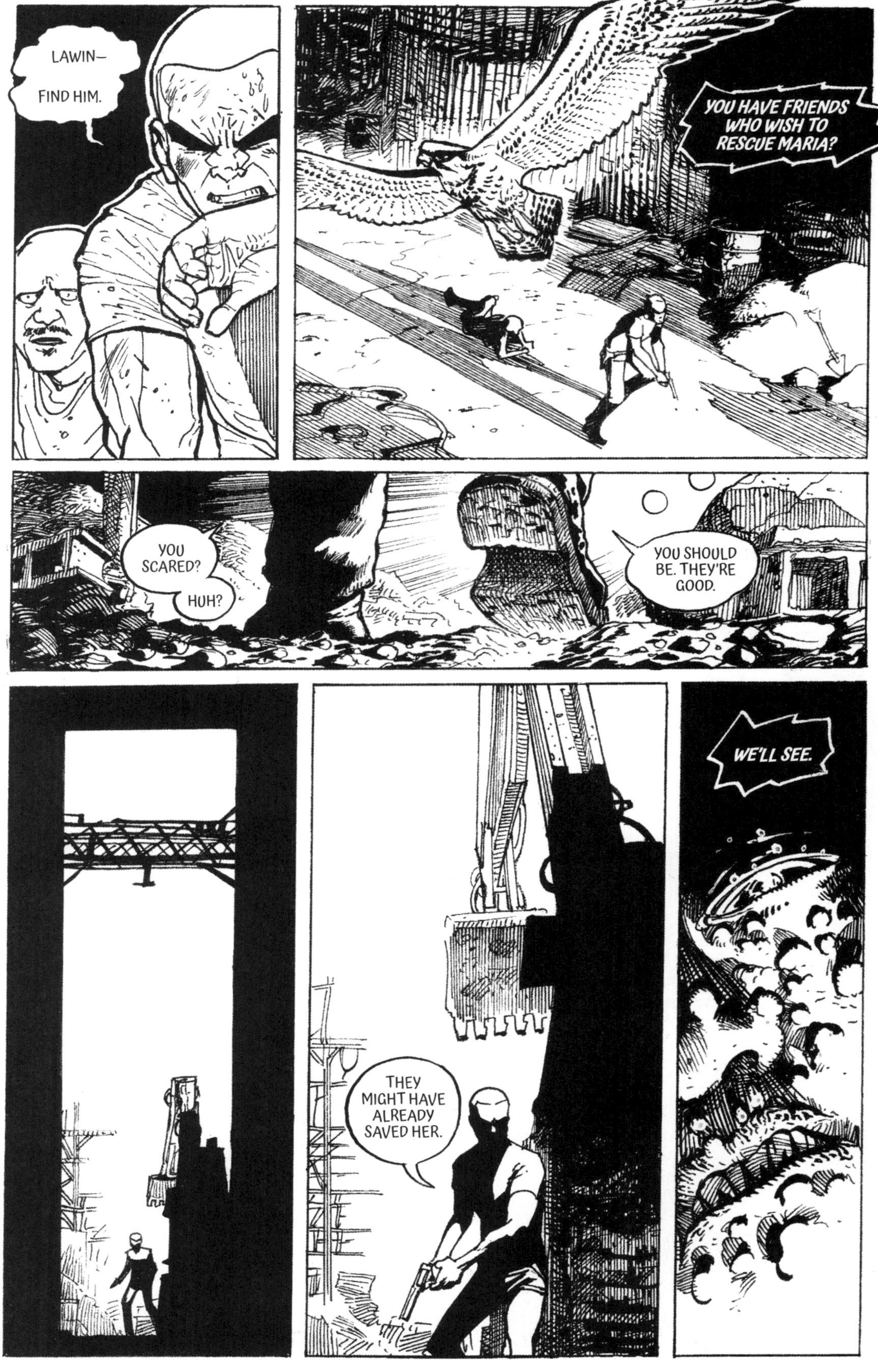
LAWIN—
FIND HIM.
YOU HAVE FRIENDS WHO WISH TO RESCUE MARIA?
YOU SCARED?
HUH?
YOU SHOULD BE. THEY'RE GOOD.
THEY MIGHT HAVE ALREADY SAVED HER.
WE'LL SEE.

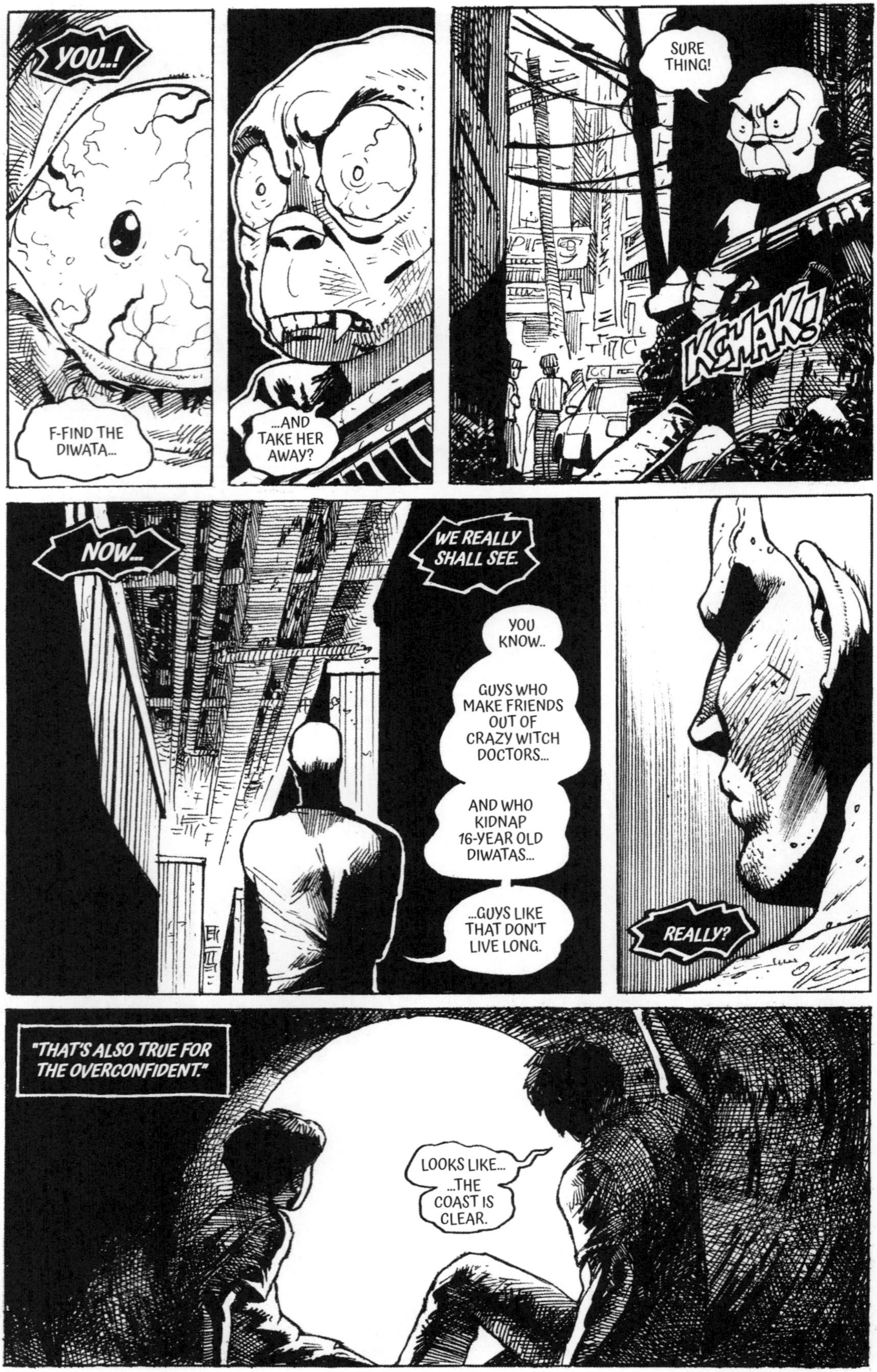
YOU..!
F-FIND THE DIWATA...
...AND TAKE HER AWAY?
SURE THING!
KCHAK!
NOW...
WE REALLY SHALL SEE.
YOU KNOW..
GUYS WHO MAKE FRIENDS OUT OF CRAZY WITCH DOCTORS...
AND WHO KIDNAP 16-YEAR OLD DIWATAS...
...GUYS LIKE THAT DON'T LIVE LONG.
REALLY?
"THAT'S ALSO TRUE FOR THE OVERCONFIDENT."
LOOKS LIKE...
...THE COAST IS CLEAR.

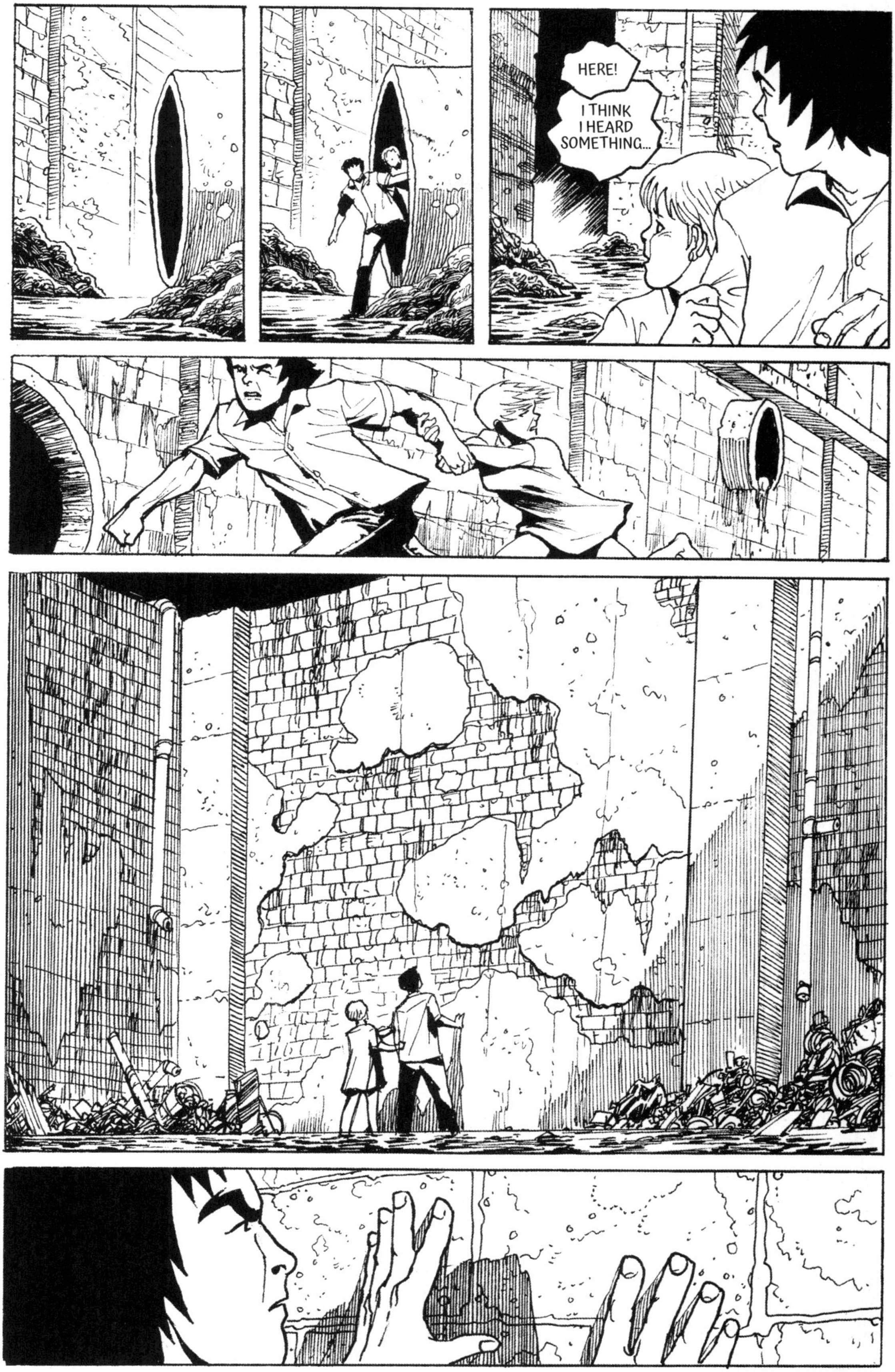
HERE!
I THINK I HEARD SOMETHING...

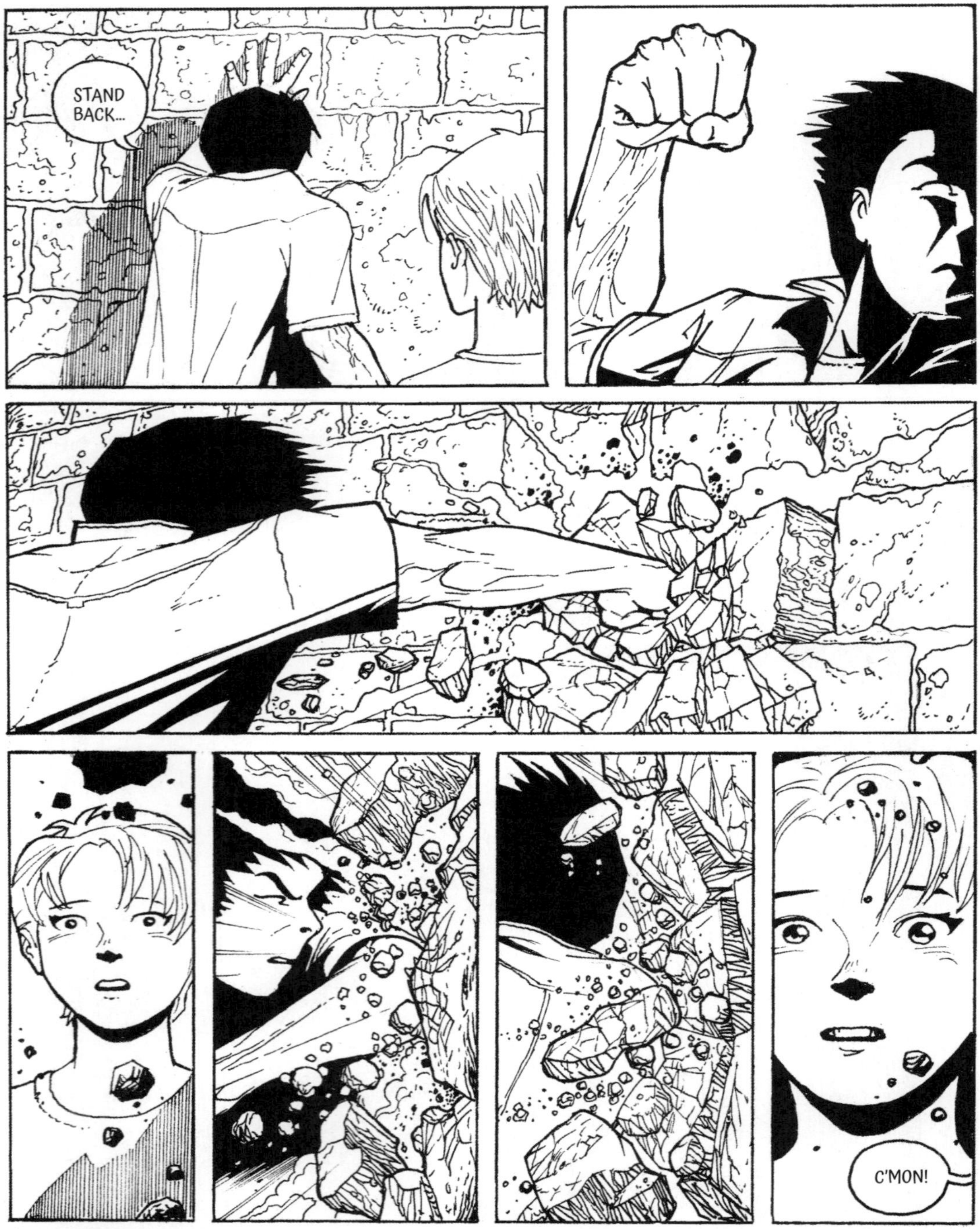
STAND BACK...
C'MON!

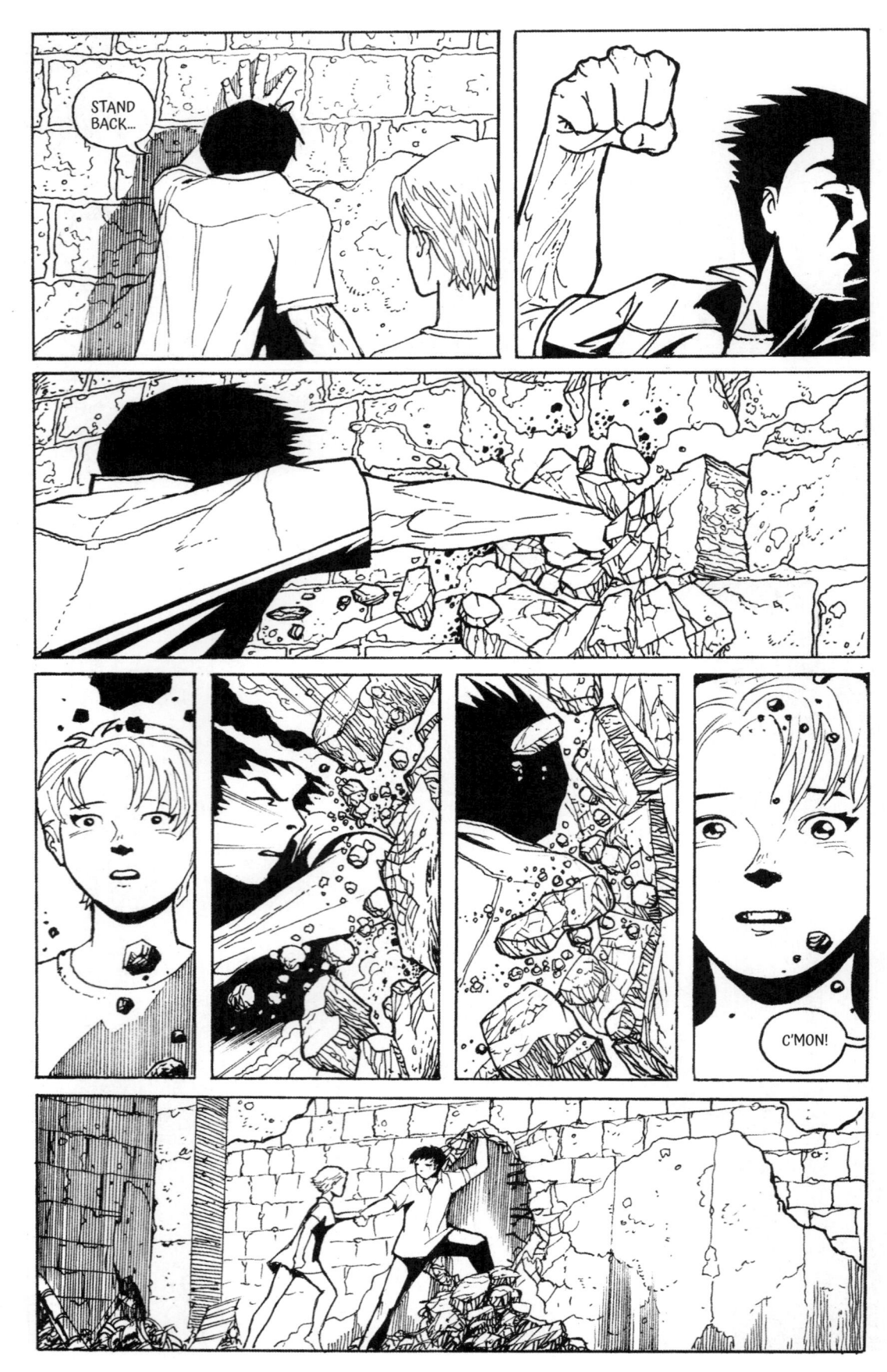

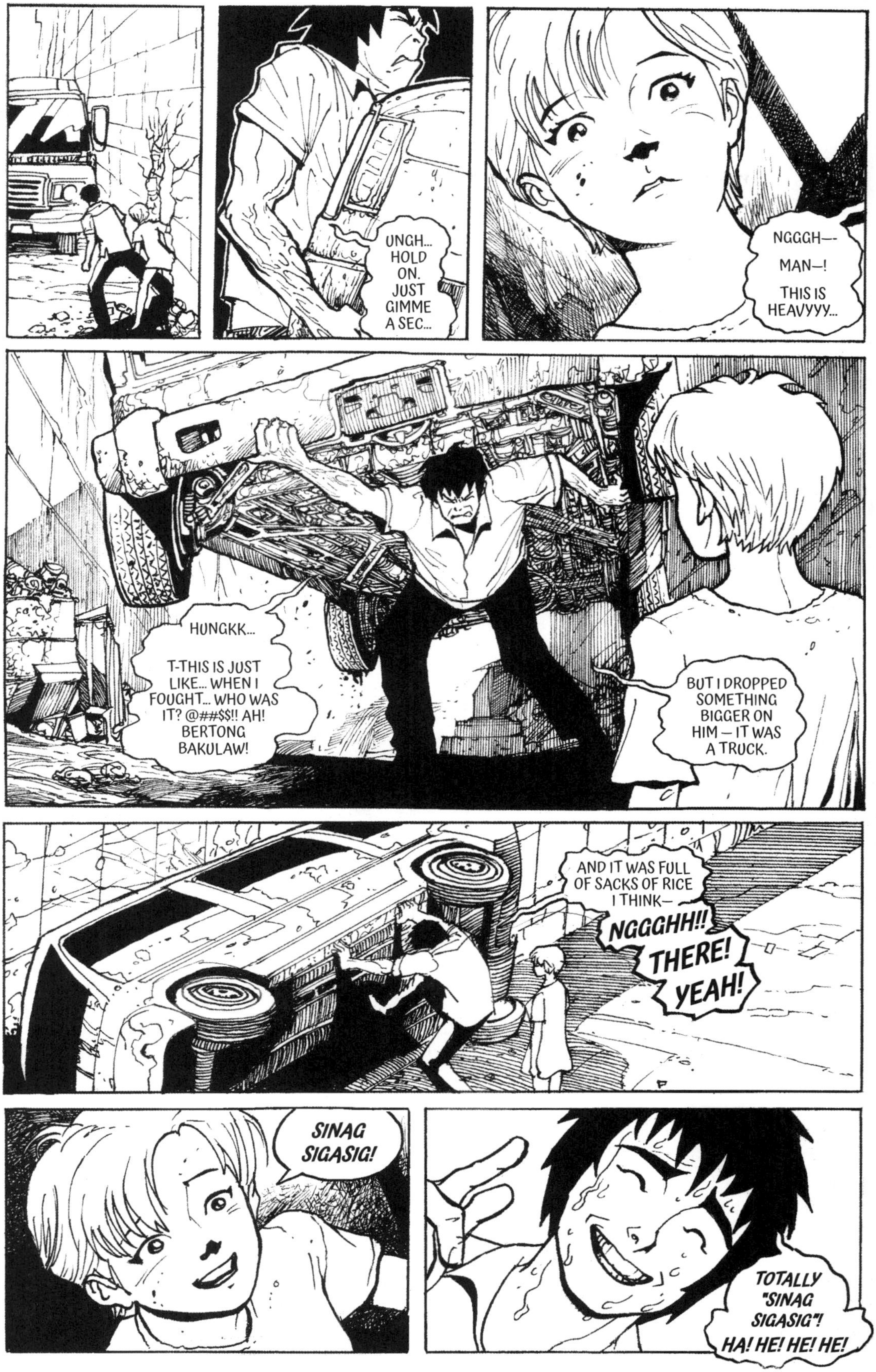
UNGH... HOLD ON. JUST GIMME A SEC...
NGGGH-- MAN-! THIS IS HEAVYYY...
HUNGKK... T-THIS IS JUST LIKE... WHEN I FOUGHT... WHO WAS IT? @##$$!! AH! BERTONG BAKULAW!
BUT I DROPPED SOMETHING BIGGER ON HIM — IT WAS A TRUCK.
AND IT WAS FULL OF SACKS OF RICE I THINK—
NGGGHH!! THERE! YEAH!
SINAG SIGASIG!
TOTALLY "SINAG SIGASIG"! HA! HE! HE! HE!

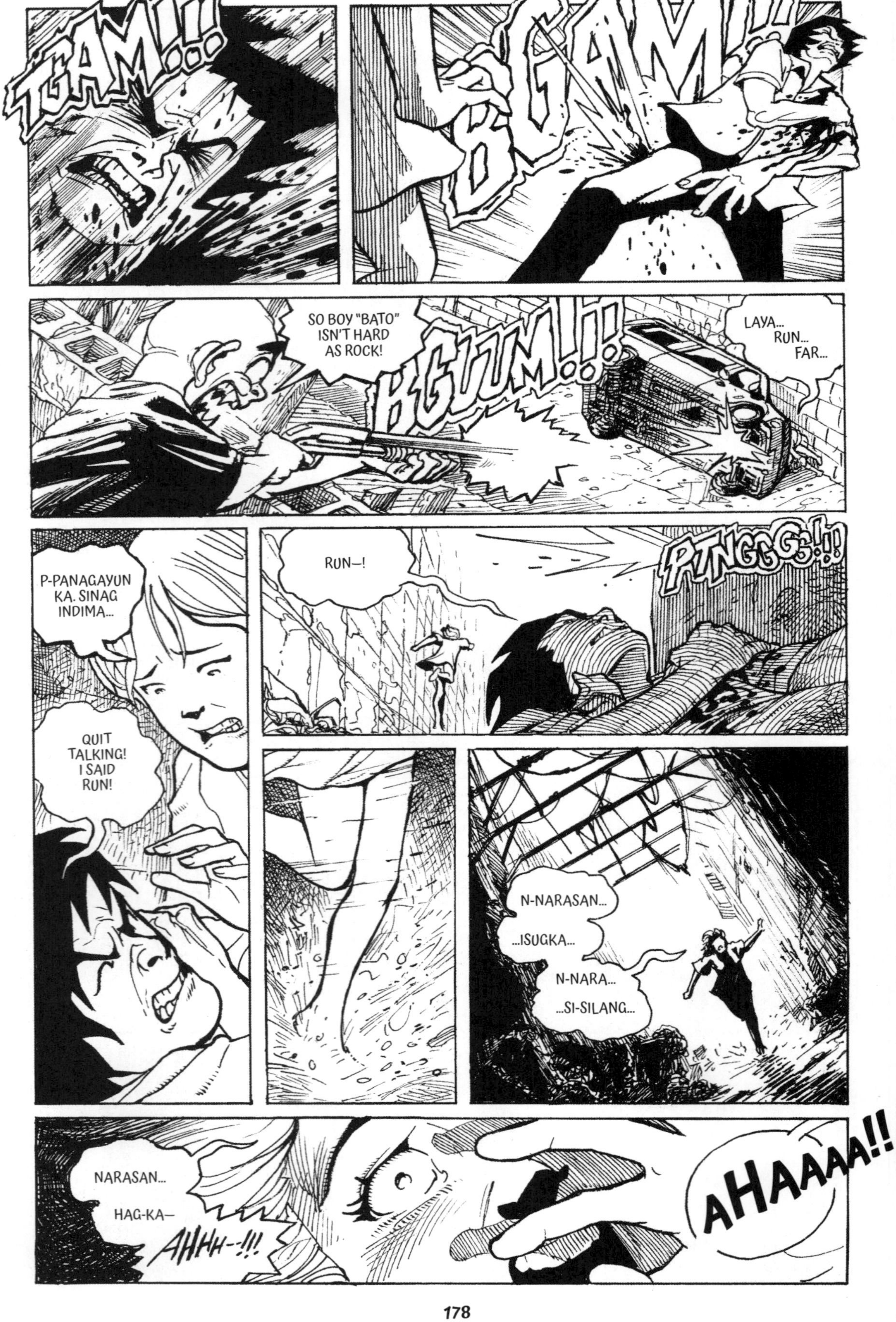
TGAM!!
BGAM!!
SO BOY "BATO" ISN'T HARD AS ROCK!
HGUUM!!
LAYA... RUN... FAR...
P-PANAGAYUN KA. SINAG INDIMA...
QUIT TALKING! I SAID RUN!
RUN—!
PTNGGGS!!
N-NARASAN...
...ISUGKA...
N-NARA...
...SI-SILANG...
NARASAN...
HAG-KA—
AHHH--!!!
AHAAAA!!

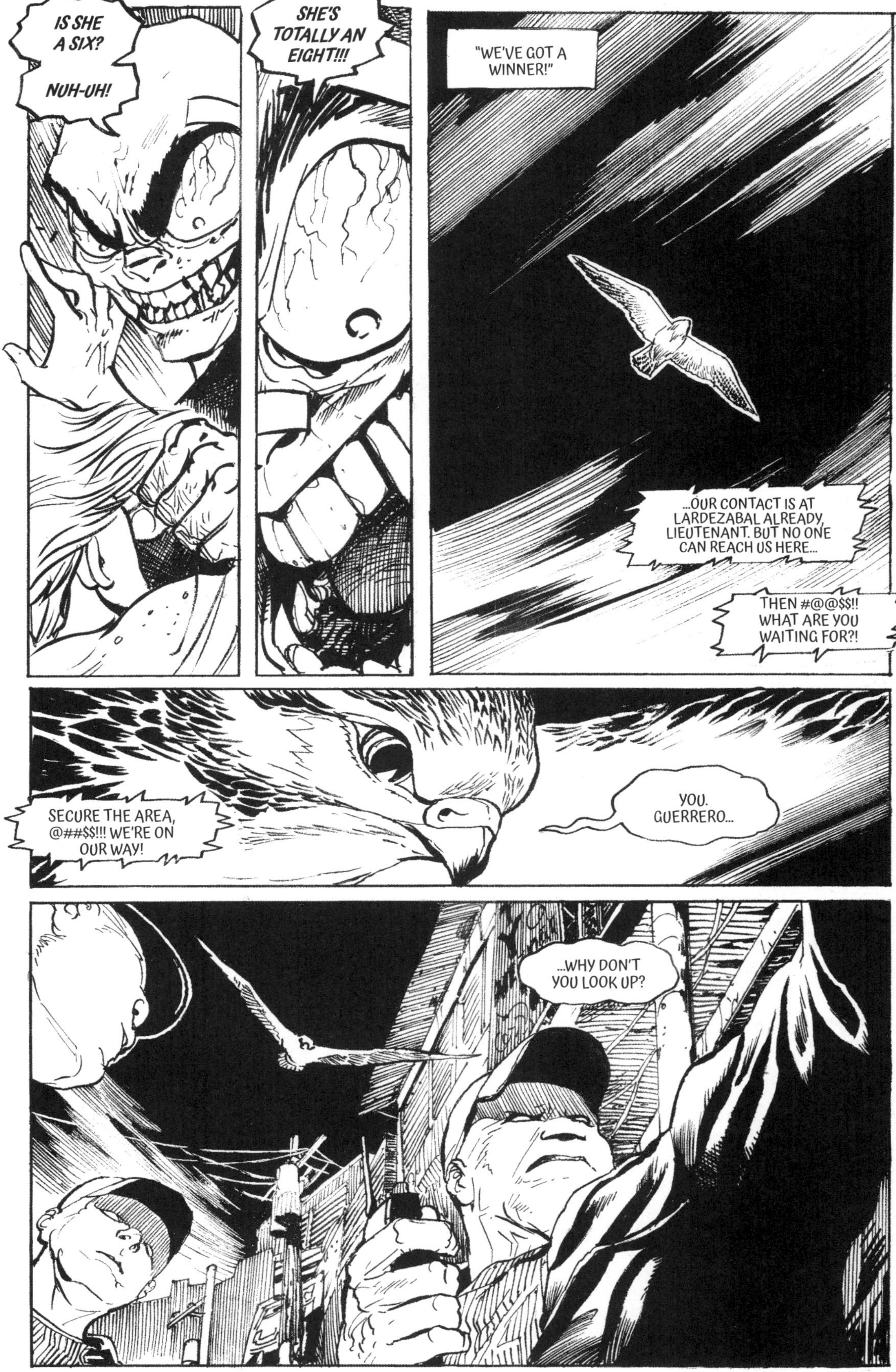
IS SHE A SIX?
NUH-UH!
SHE'S TOTALLY AN EIGHT!!!
"WE'VE GOT A WINNER!"
...OUR CONTACT IS AT LARDEZABAL ALREADY, LIEUTENANT. BUT NO ONE CAN REACH US HERE...
THEN #@@$$!! WHAT ARE YOU WAITING FOR?!
SECURE THE AREA, @##$$!!! WE'RE ON OUR WAY!
YOU. GUERRERO...
...WHY DON'T YOU LOOK UP?

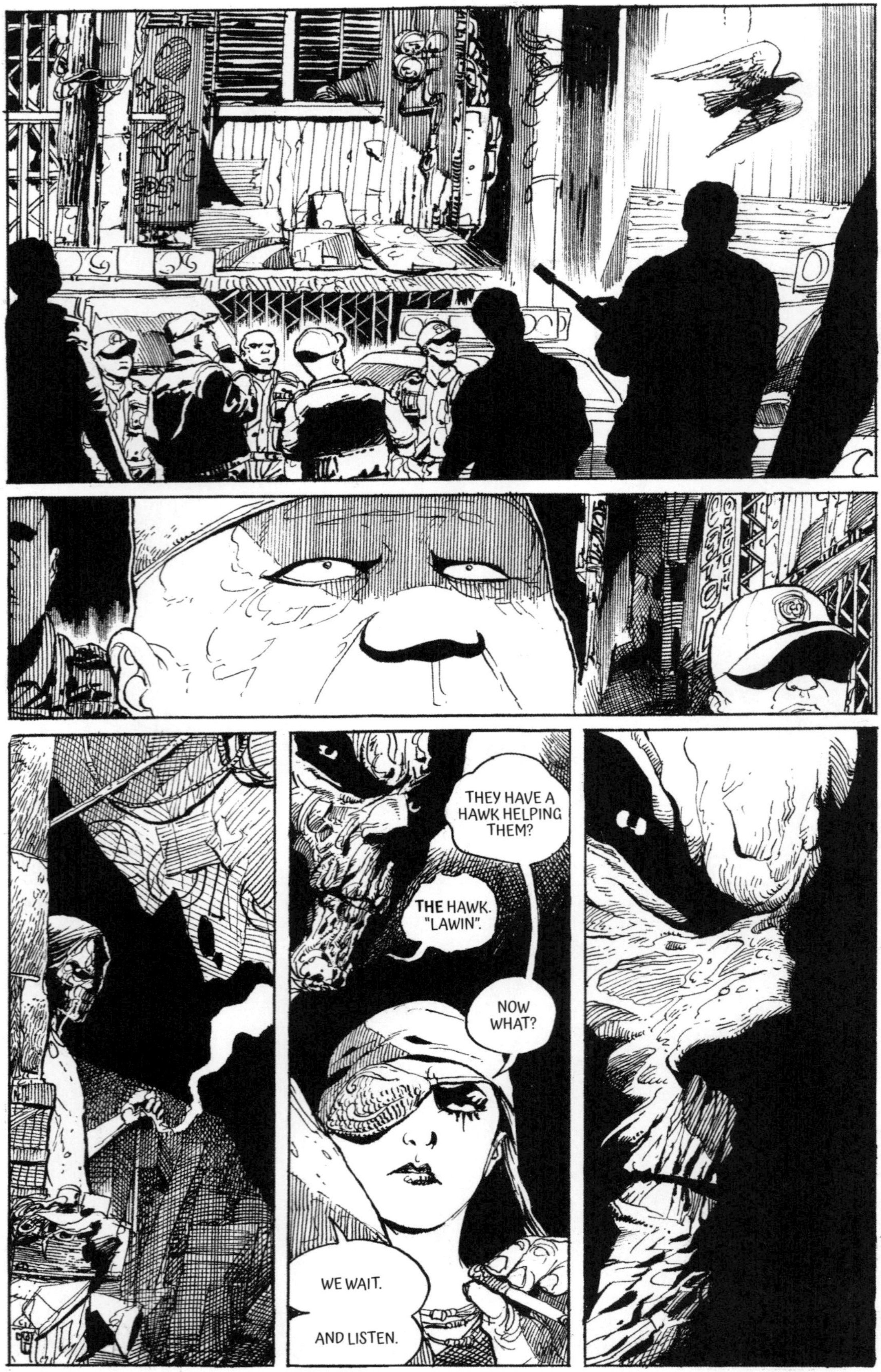
THEY HAVE A HAWK HELPING THEM?
THE HAWK. "LAWIN".
NOW WHAT?
WE WAIT.
AND LISTEN.

ARAY!! I SAID IT HURTS!!!

W... WHAT HAPPENED? WHERE'S LAYA?

SILANG!

DON'T BE SUCH A BABY! I'M JUST WIPING IT...

S-SILANG... L-LAYA... ...LAYA IS...

PEDRONG PANGIL GOT HER... ...I DUNNO WHERE — GHH!!

@#$$!! JUST SPILL IT!

IT'S OVER! FORGET IT! WE'LL NEVER CATCH UP TO THEM.

NO.

WE STILL CAN.

THERE'S STILL TIME.

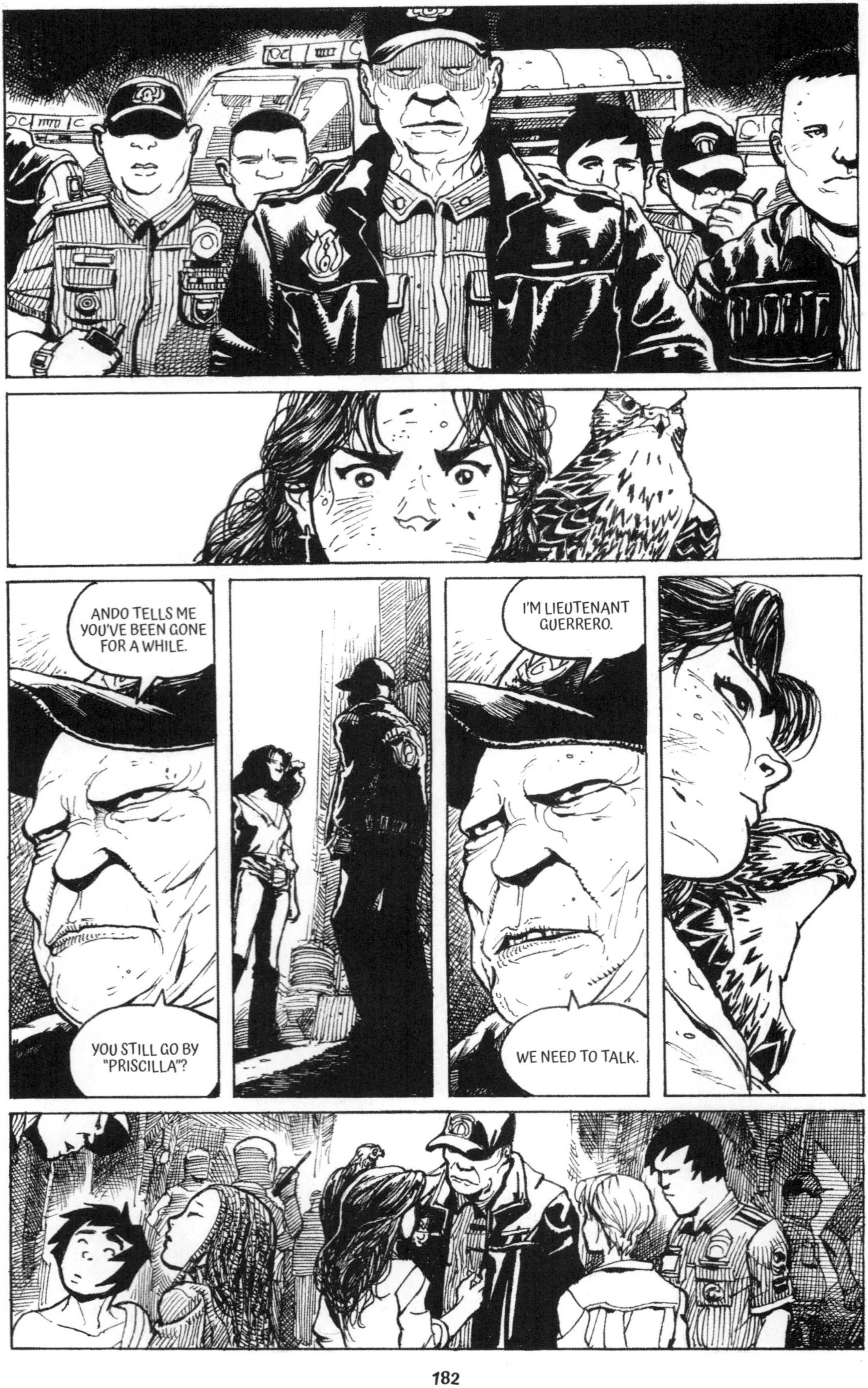
ANDO TELLS ME YOU'VE BEEN GONE FOR A WHILE.
YOU STILL GO BY "PRISCILLA"?
I'M LIEUTENANT GUERRERO.
WE NEED TO TALK.

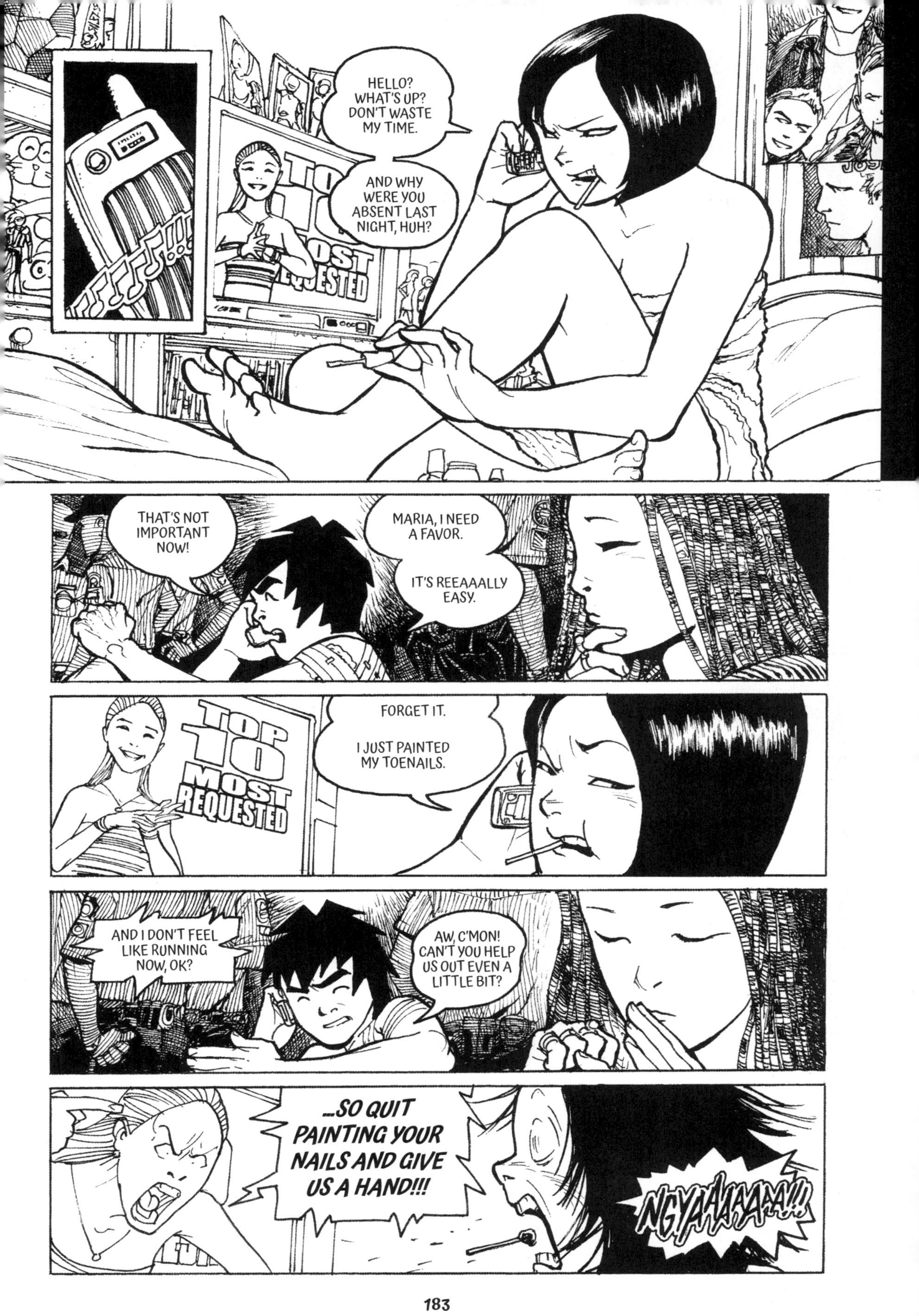

HELLO? WHAT'S UP? DON'T WASTE MY TIME.
AND WHY WERE YOU ABSENT LAST NIGHT, HUH?
TOP 10 MOST REQUESTED
THAT'S NOT IMPORTANT NOW!
MARIA, I NEED A FAVOR.
IT'S REEAAALLY EASY.
TOP 10 MOST REQUESTED
FORGET IT.
I JUST PAINTED MY TOENAILS.
AND I DON'T FEEL LIKE RUNNING NOW, OK?
AW, C'MON! CAN'T YOU HELP US OUT EVEN A LITTLE BIT?
...SO QUIT PAINTING YOUR NAILS AND GIVE US A HAND!!!
NGYAAAAAAA!!!

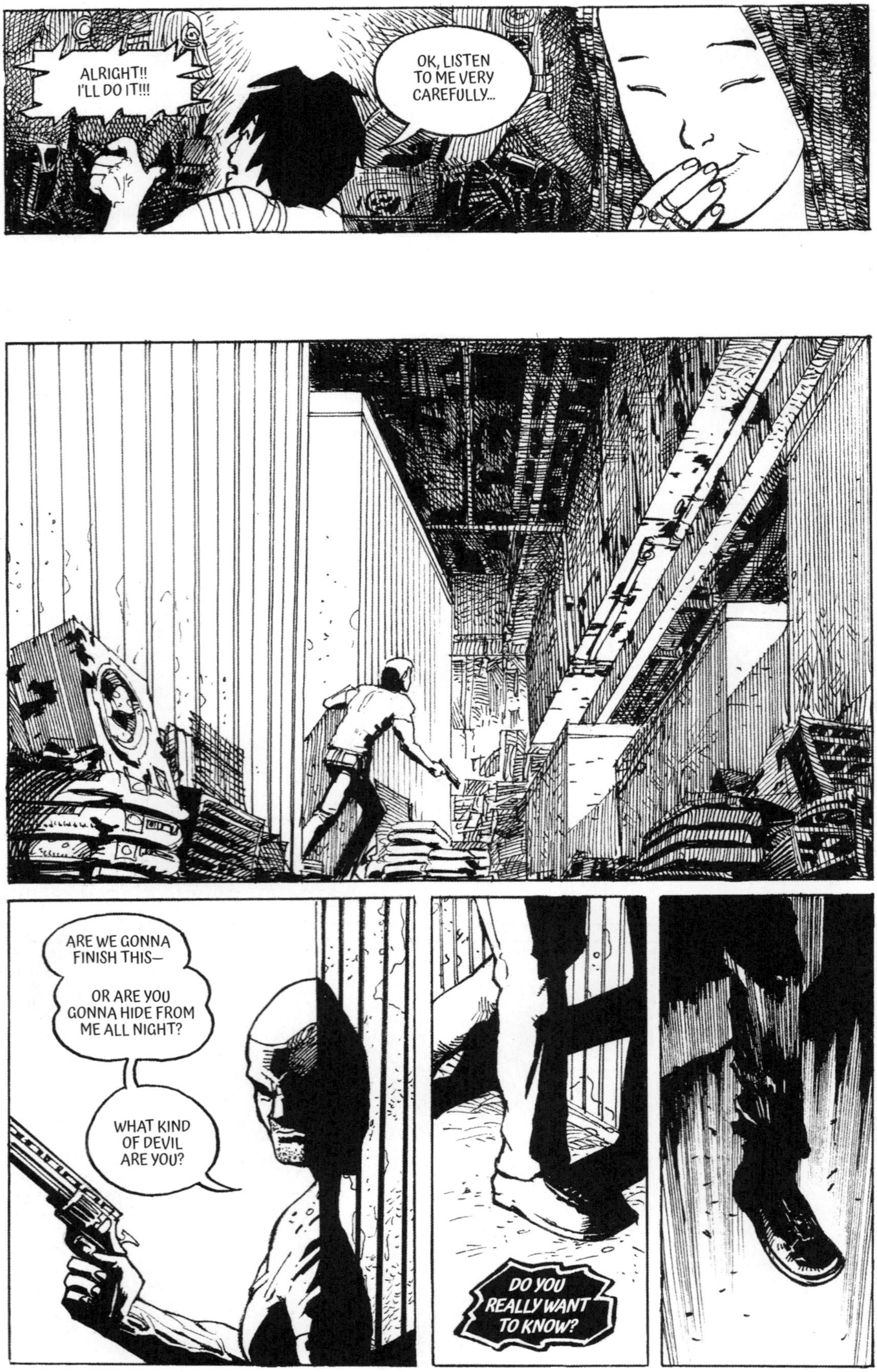
ALRIGHT!!
I'LL DO IT!!!
OK, LISTEN
TO ME VERY
CAREFULLY...
ARE WE GONNA
FINISH THIS—
OR ARE YOU
GONNA HIDE FROM
ME ALL NIGHT?
WHAT KIND
OF DEVIL
ARE YOU?
DO YOU
REALLY WANT
TO KNOW?

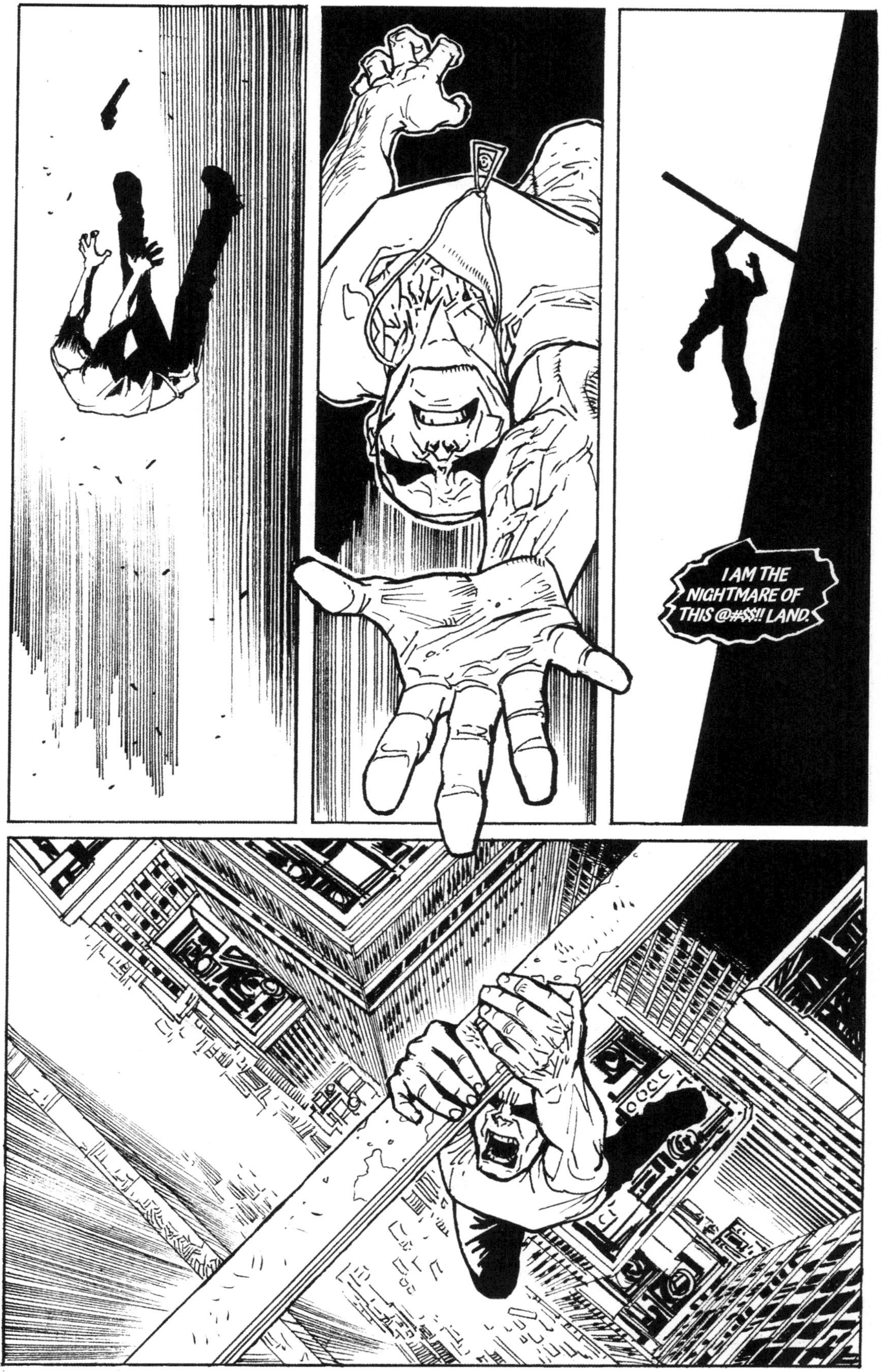
I AM THE NIGHTMARE OF THIS @#$$!! LAND.

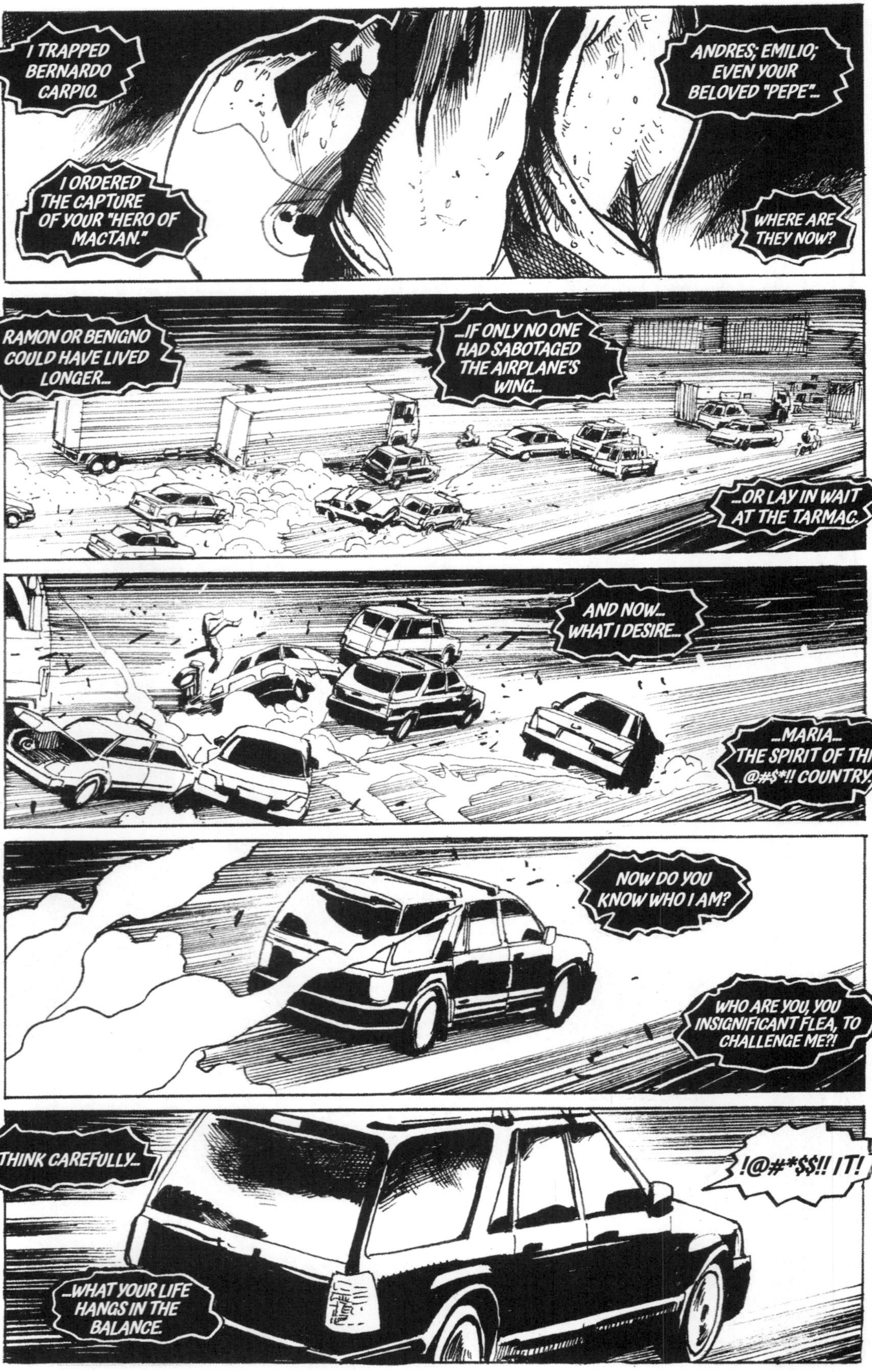
I TRAPPED BERNARDO CARPIO.
I ORDERED THE CAPTURE OF YOUR "HERO OF MACTAN."
ANDRES; EMILIO; EVEN YOUR BELOVED "PEPE"...
WHERE ARE THEY NOW?
RAMON OR BENIGNO COULD HAVE LIVED LONGER...
...IF ONLY NO ONE HAD SABOTAGED THE AIRPLANE'S WING...
...OR LAY IN WAIT AT THE TARMAC.
AND NOW... WHAT I DESIRE...
...MARIA... THE SPIRIT OF THIS @#$*!! COUNTRY.
NOW DO YOU KNOW WHO I AM?
WHO ARE YOU, YOU INSIGNIFICANT FLEA, TO CHALLENGE ME?!
THINK CAREFULLY...
...WHAT YOUR LIFE HANGS IN THE BALANCE.
!@#*$$!! IT!

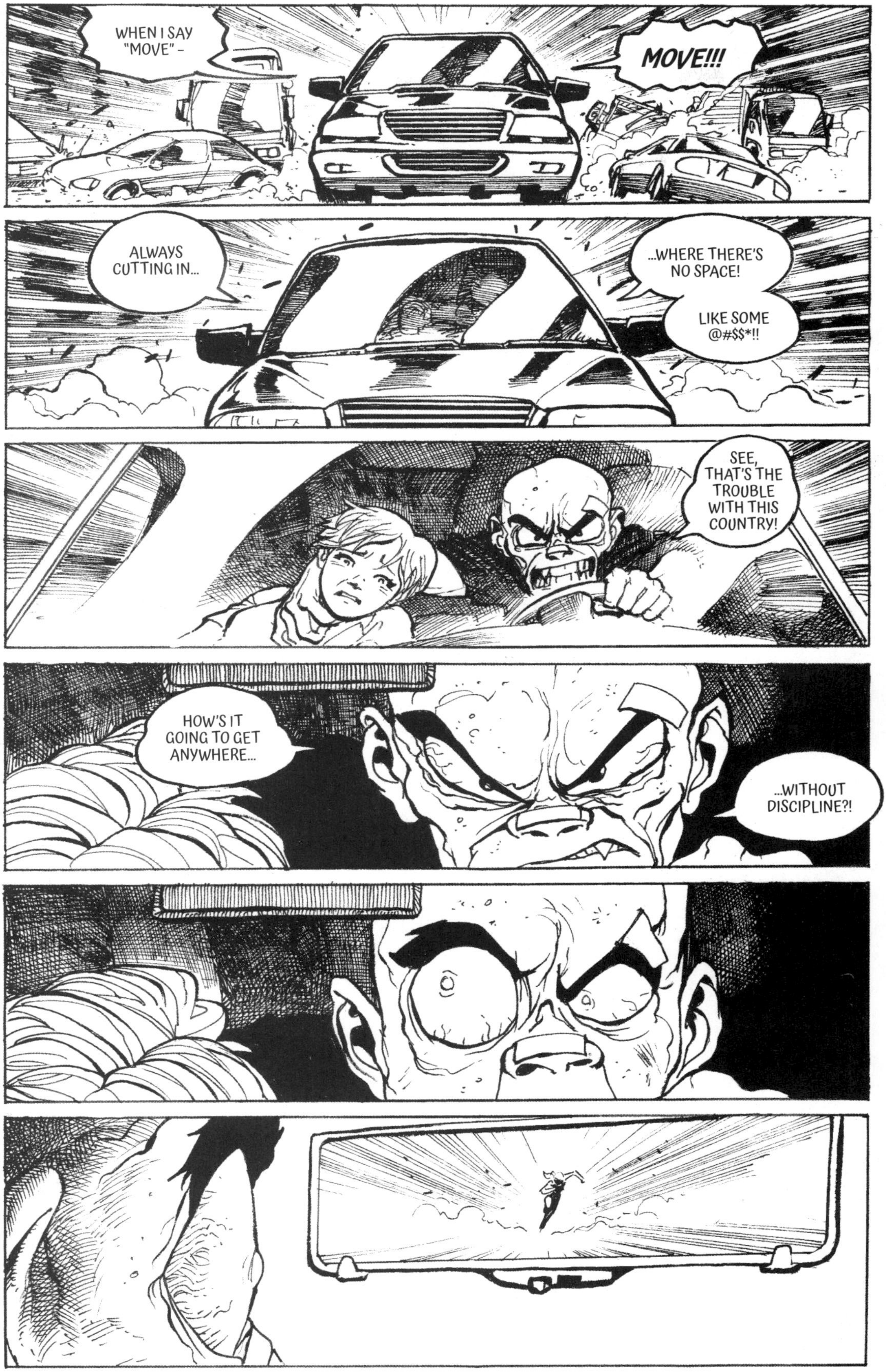
WHEN I SAY "MOVE" –
MOVE!!!
ALWAYS CUTTING IN...
...WHERE THERE'S NO SPACE!
LIKE SOME @#$$*!!
SEE, THAT'S THE TROUBLE WITH THIS COUNTRY!
HOW'S IT GOING TO GET ANYWHERE...
...WITHOUT DISCIPLINE?!

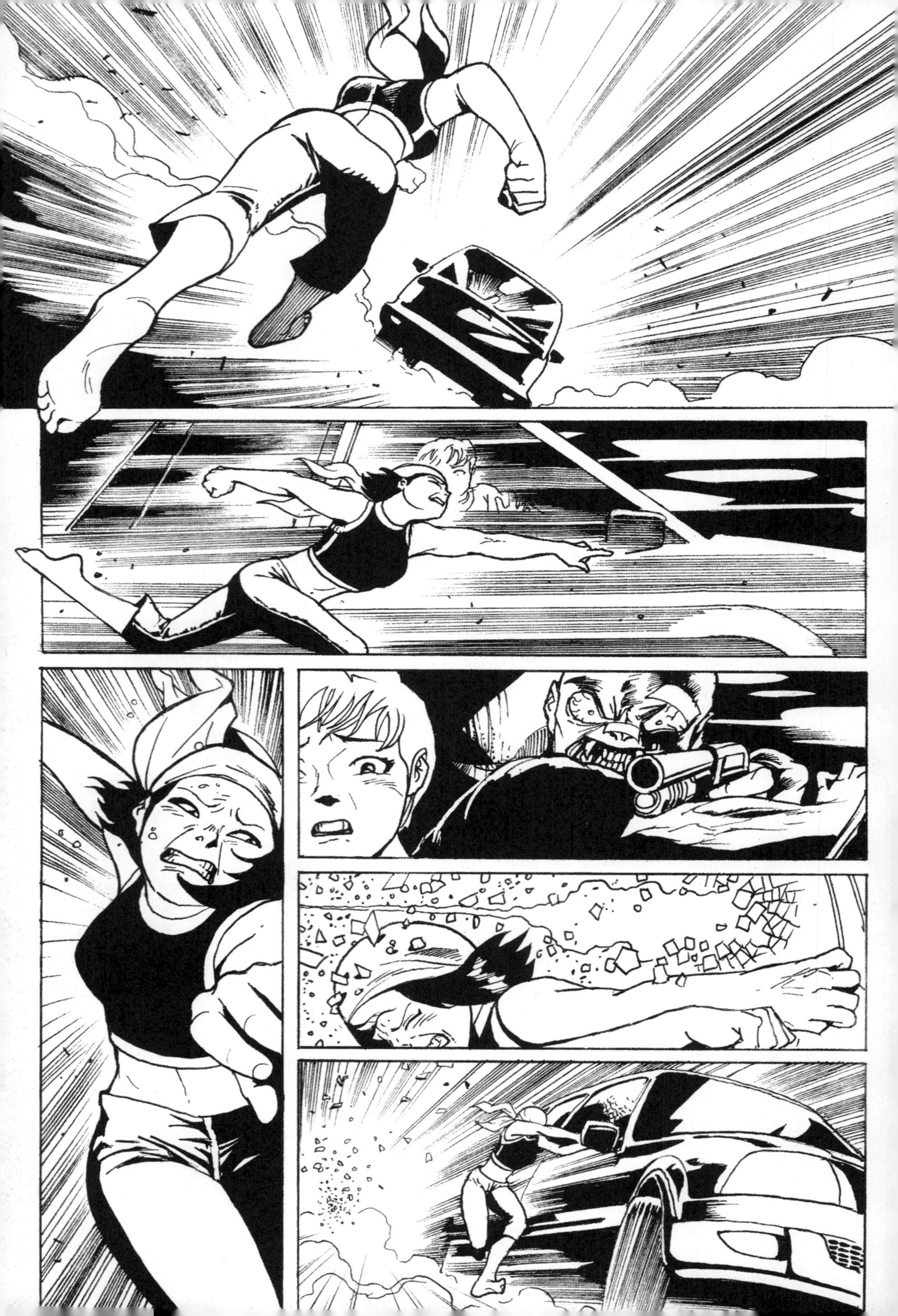

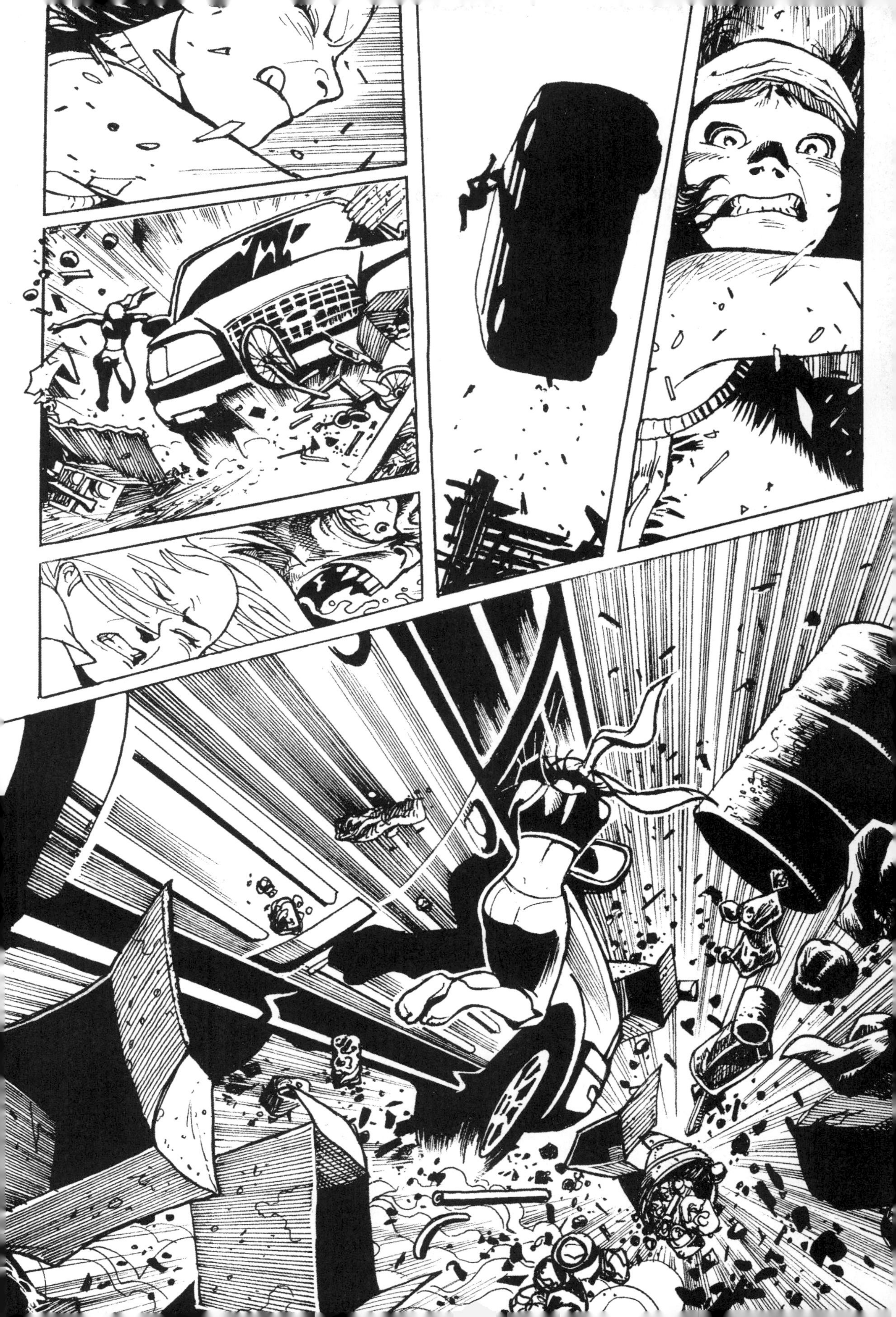

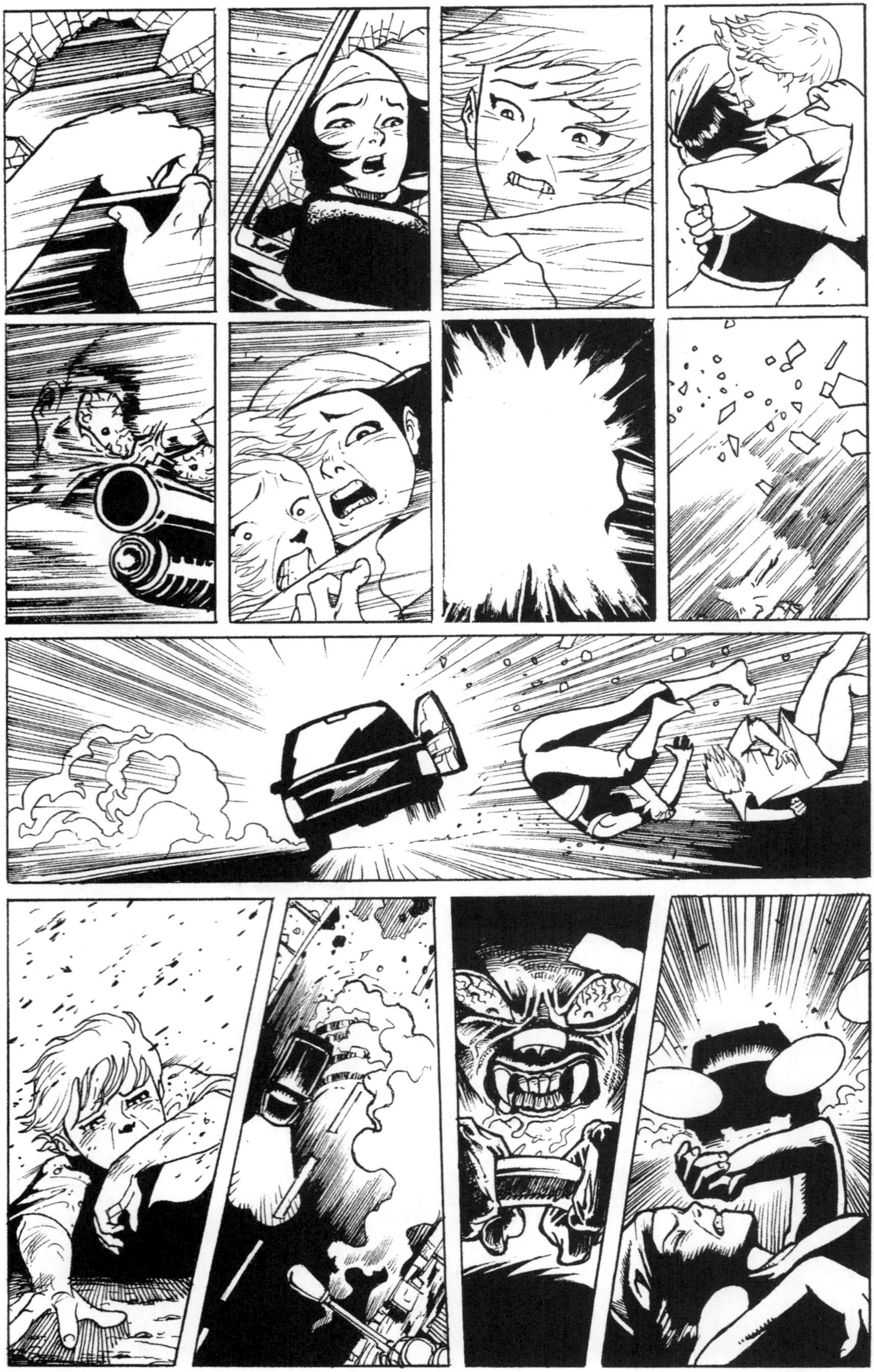

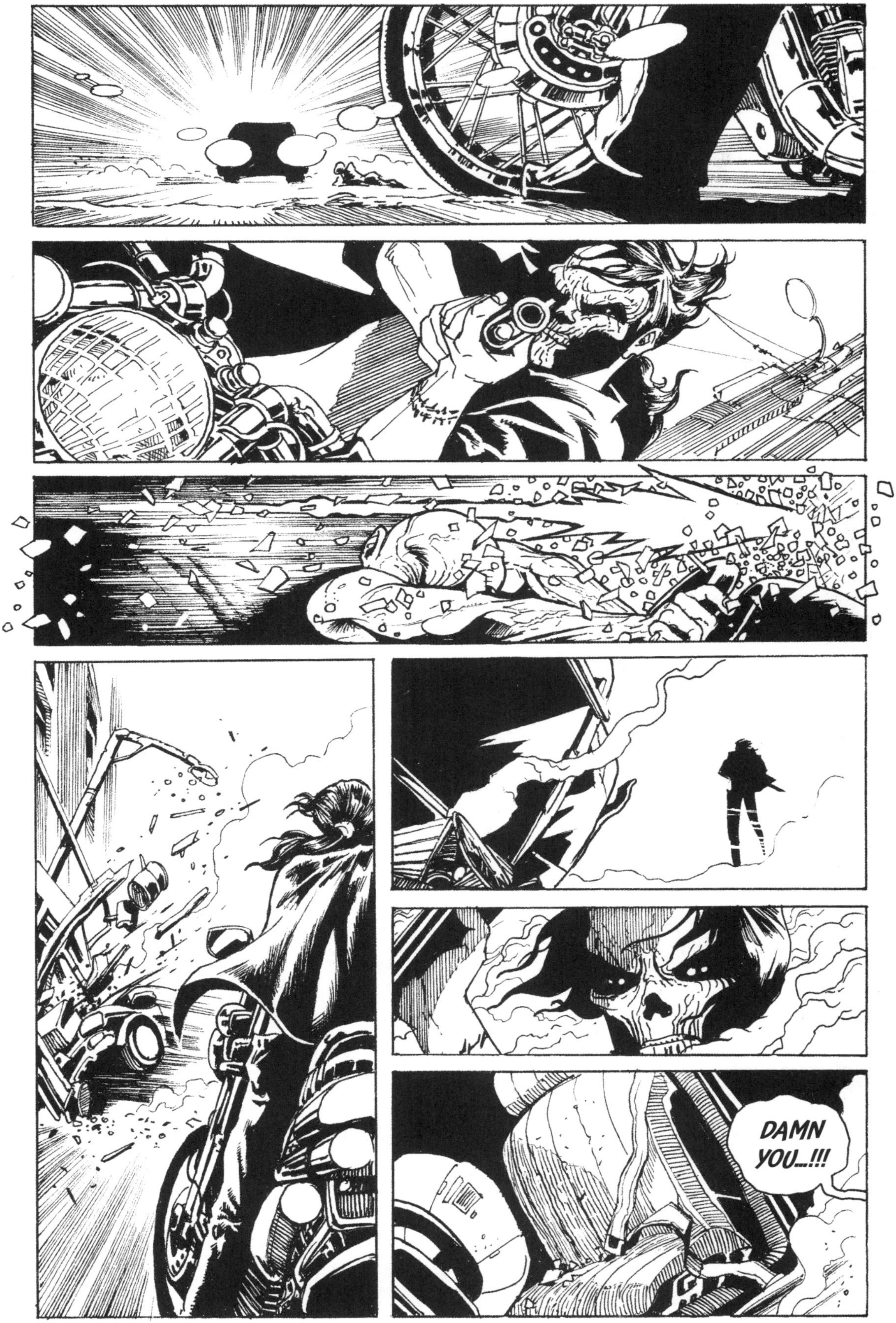
DAMN YOU...!!!

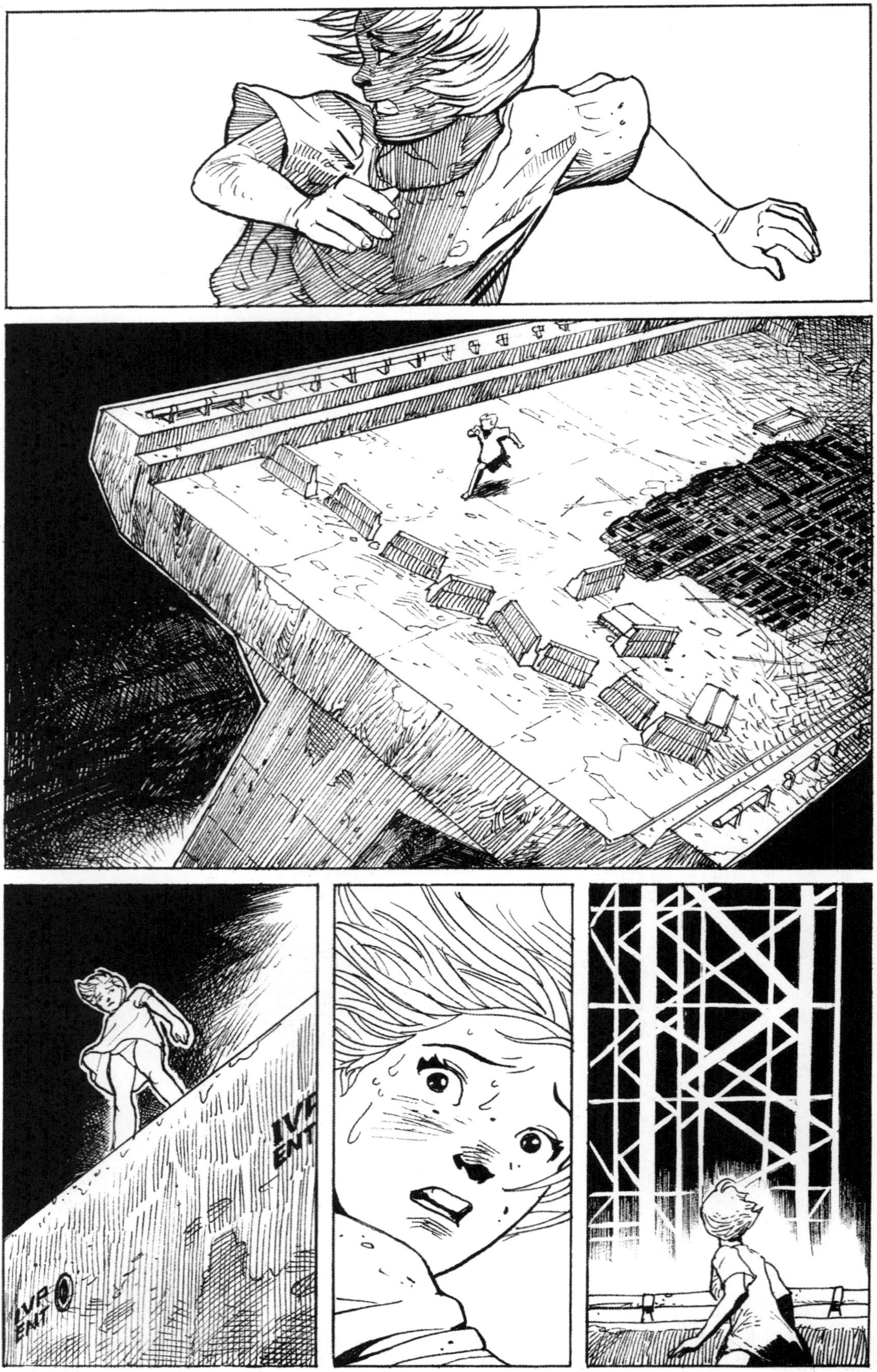

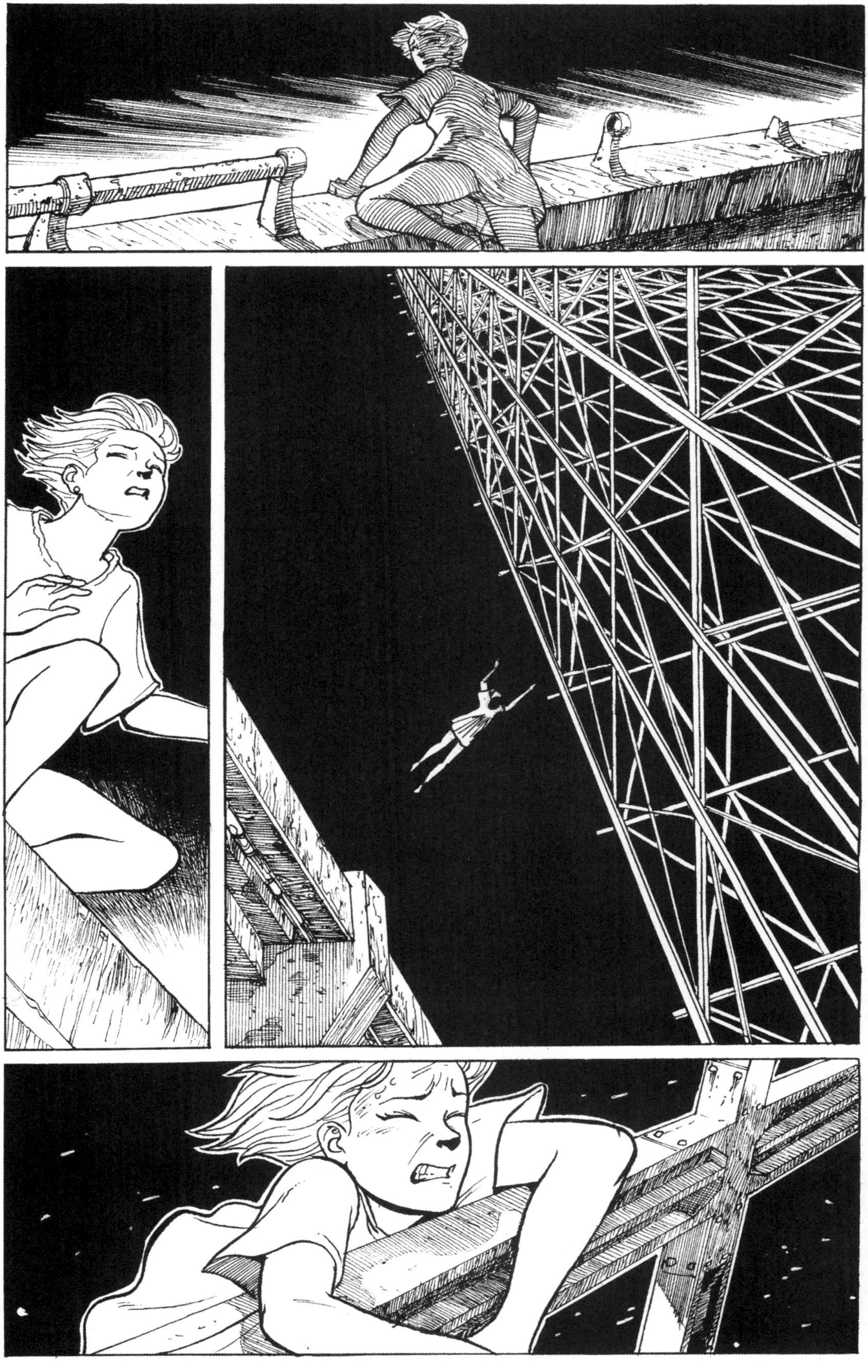

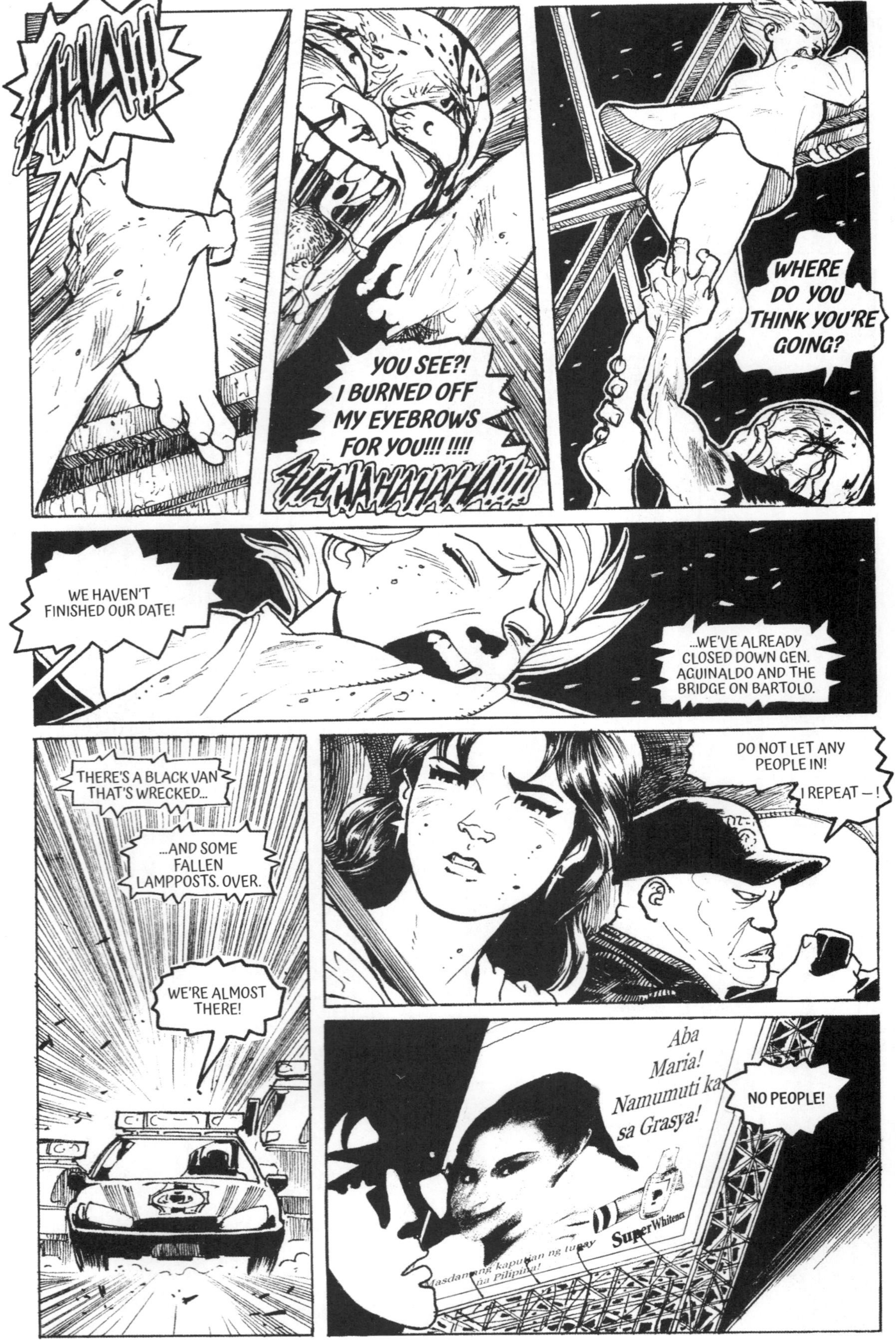
AHA!!!
YOU SEE?! I BURNED OFF MY EYEBROWS FOR YOU!!! !!!!
AHAHAHAHAHAHA!!!!
WHERE DO YOU THINK YOU'RE GOING?
WE HAVEN'T FINISHED OUR DATE!
...WE'VE ALREADY CLOSED DOWN GEN. AGUINALDO AND THE BRIDGE ON BARTOLO.
THERE'S A BLACK VAN THAT'S WRECKED...
...AND SOME FALLEN LAMPPOSTS. OVER.
DO NOT LET ANY PEOPLE IN!
I REPEAT —!
WE'RE ALMOST THERE!
Aba Maria! Namumuti ka sa Grasya!
NO PEOPLE!
SuperWhitener

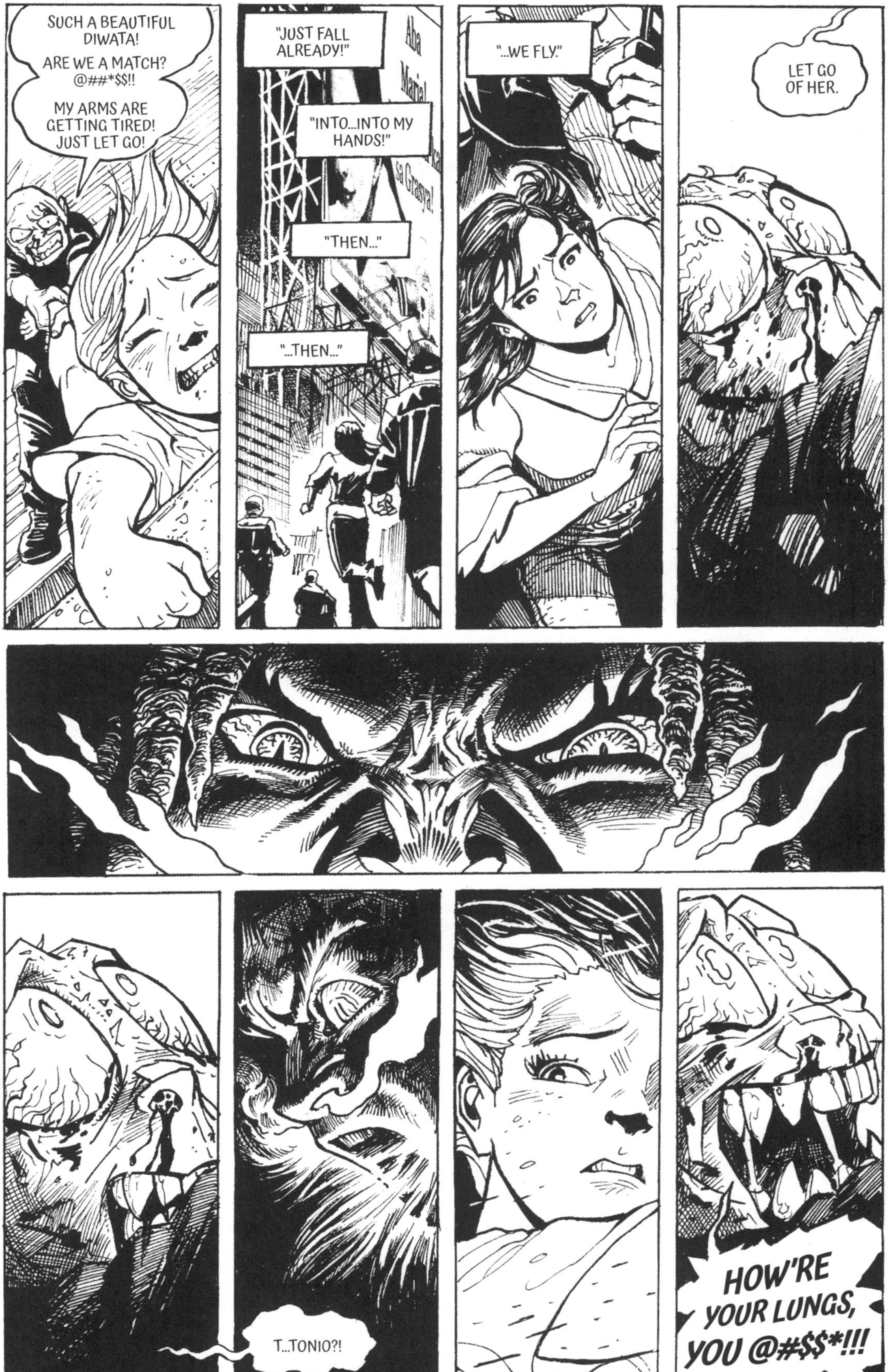
SUCH A BEAUTIFUL DIWATA!
ARE WE A MATCH? @##*$$!!
MY ARMS ARE GETTING TIRED! JUST LET GO!
"JUST FALL ALREADY!"
Aba
Maria!
sa Grasya!
"INTO...INTO MY HANDS!"
"THEN..."
"...THEN..."
"...WE FLY."
LET GO OF HER.
T...TONIO?!
HOW'RE YOUR LUNGS, YOU @#$$*!!!

FWOOOAAAAAAAAHHH

THE 216 IS HERE...

CALL IN THE FIRE DEPARTMENT TOO.

IT'S FINALLY OVER.

NOW YOU AND ANDO HAVE SOMETHING TO TALK ABOUT.

MMM...

AH... NEED SOME ASSISTANCE HERE AT... AT... AGUINALDO... SCOUT AROUND ALSO IF YOU CAN...

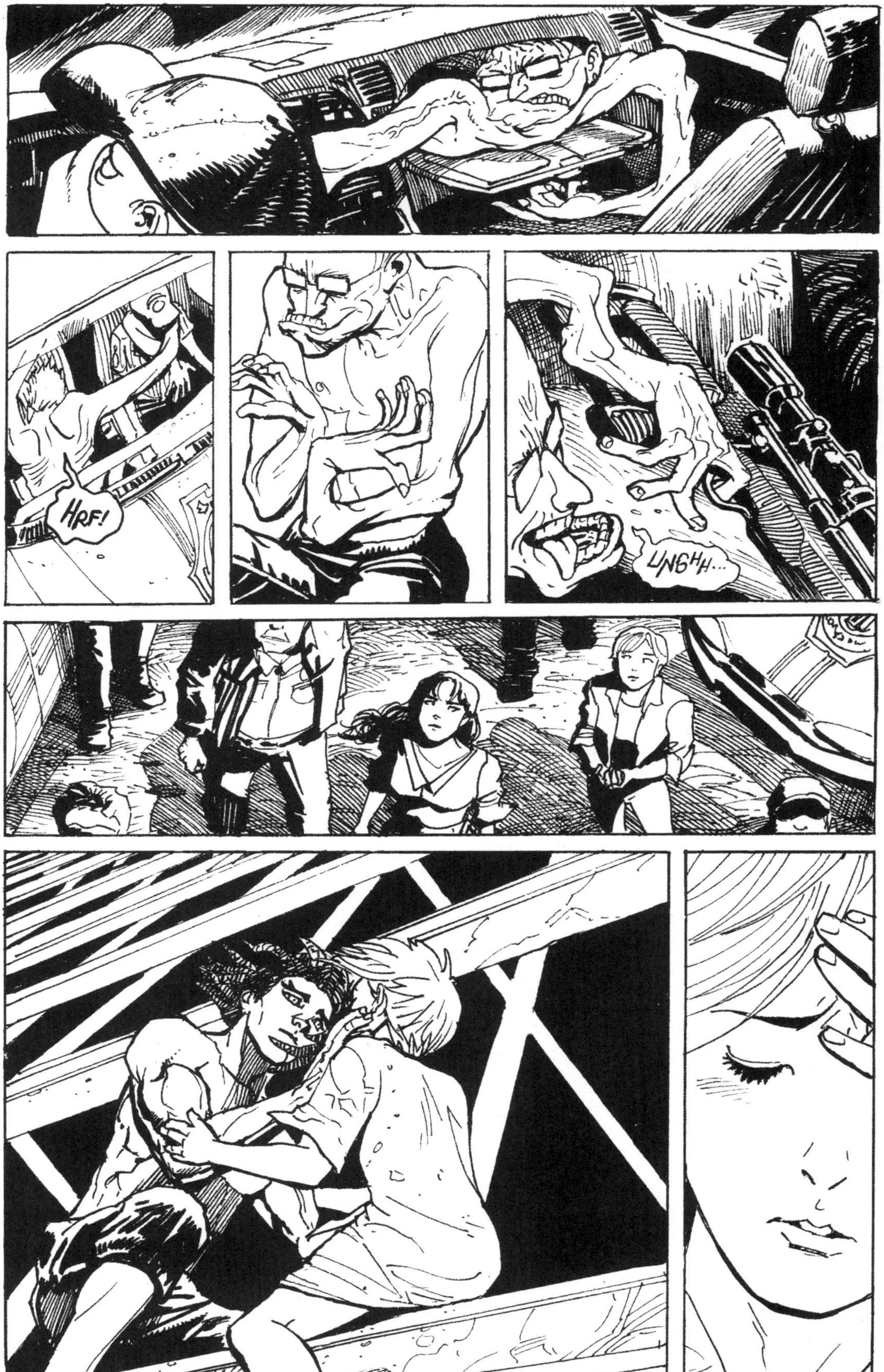
HRF!
UNGHH...

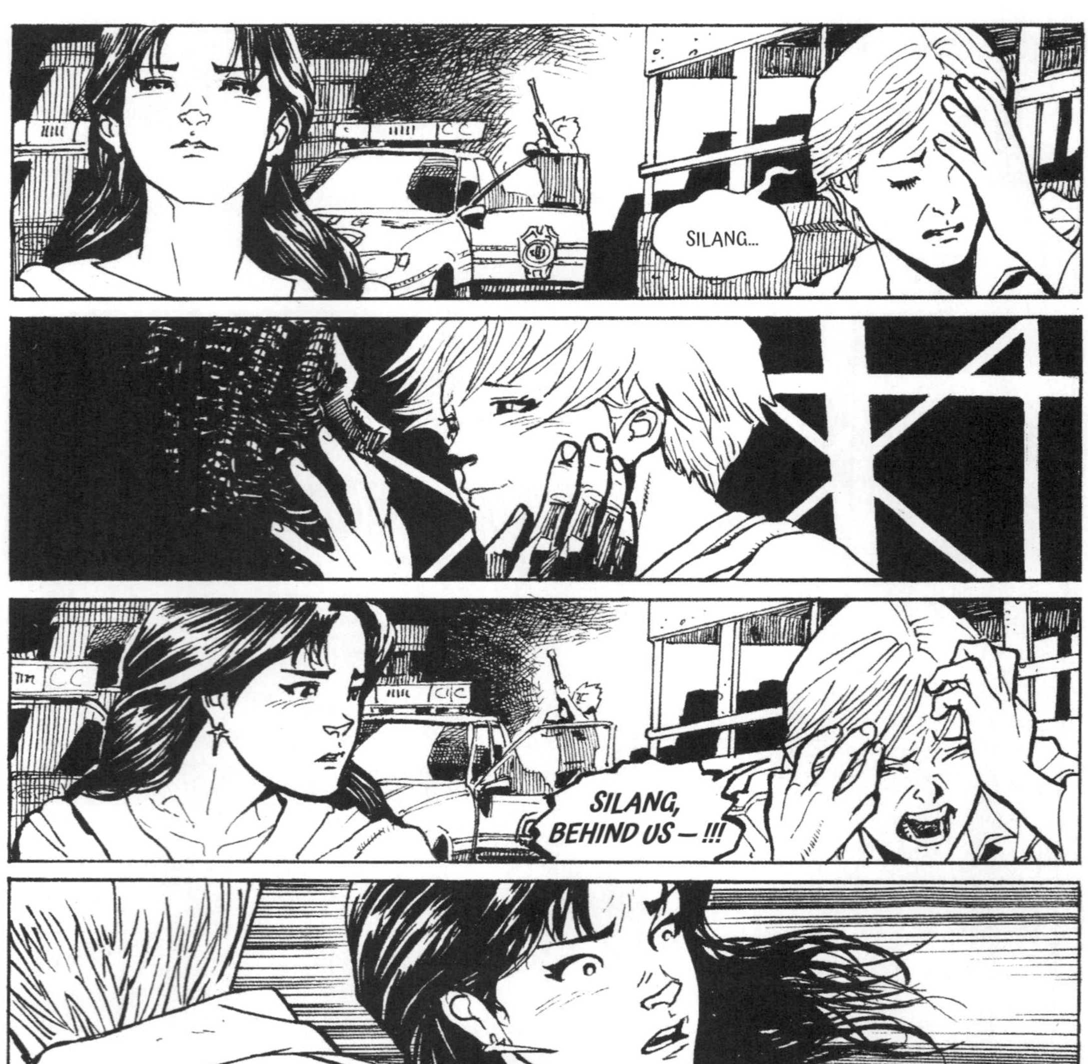
SILANG...
SILANG, BEHIND US — !!!

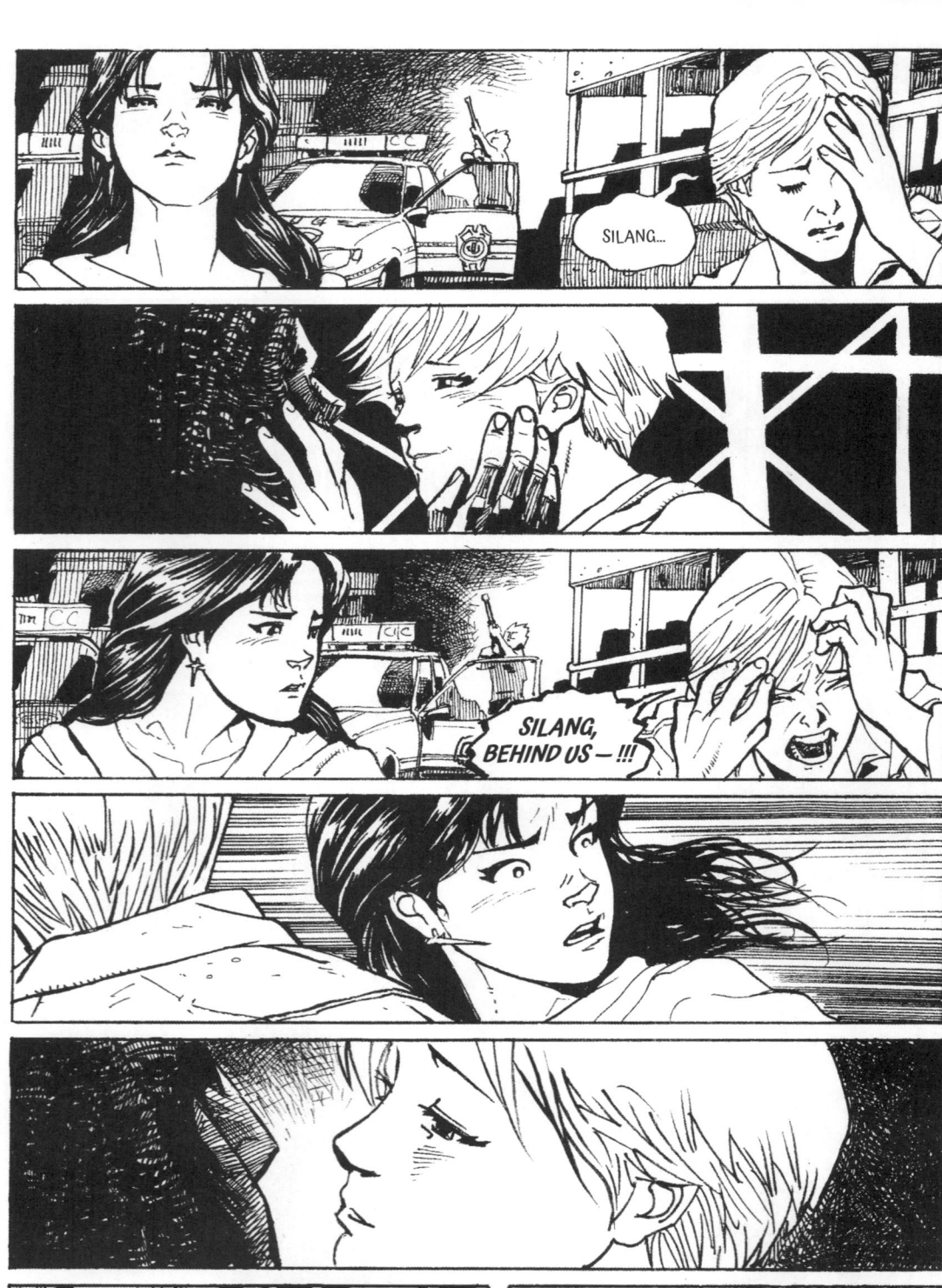

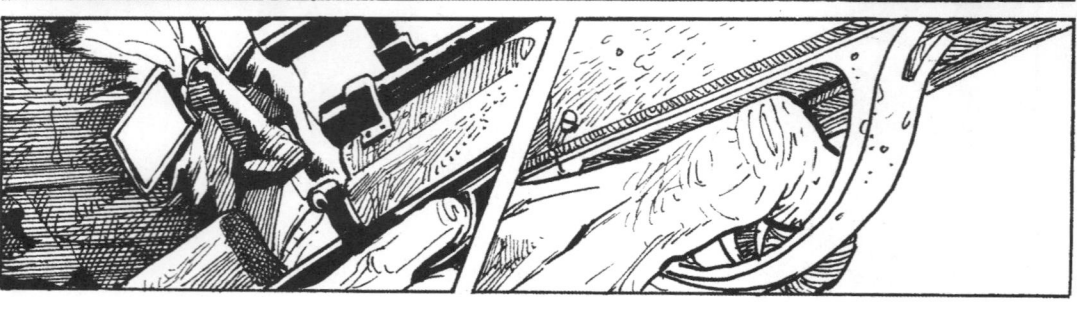

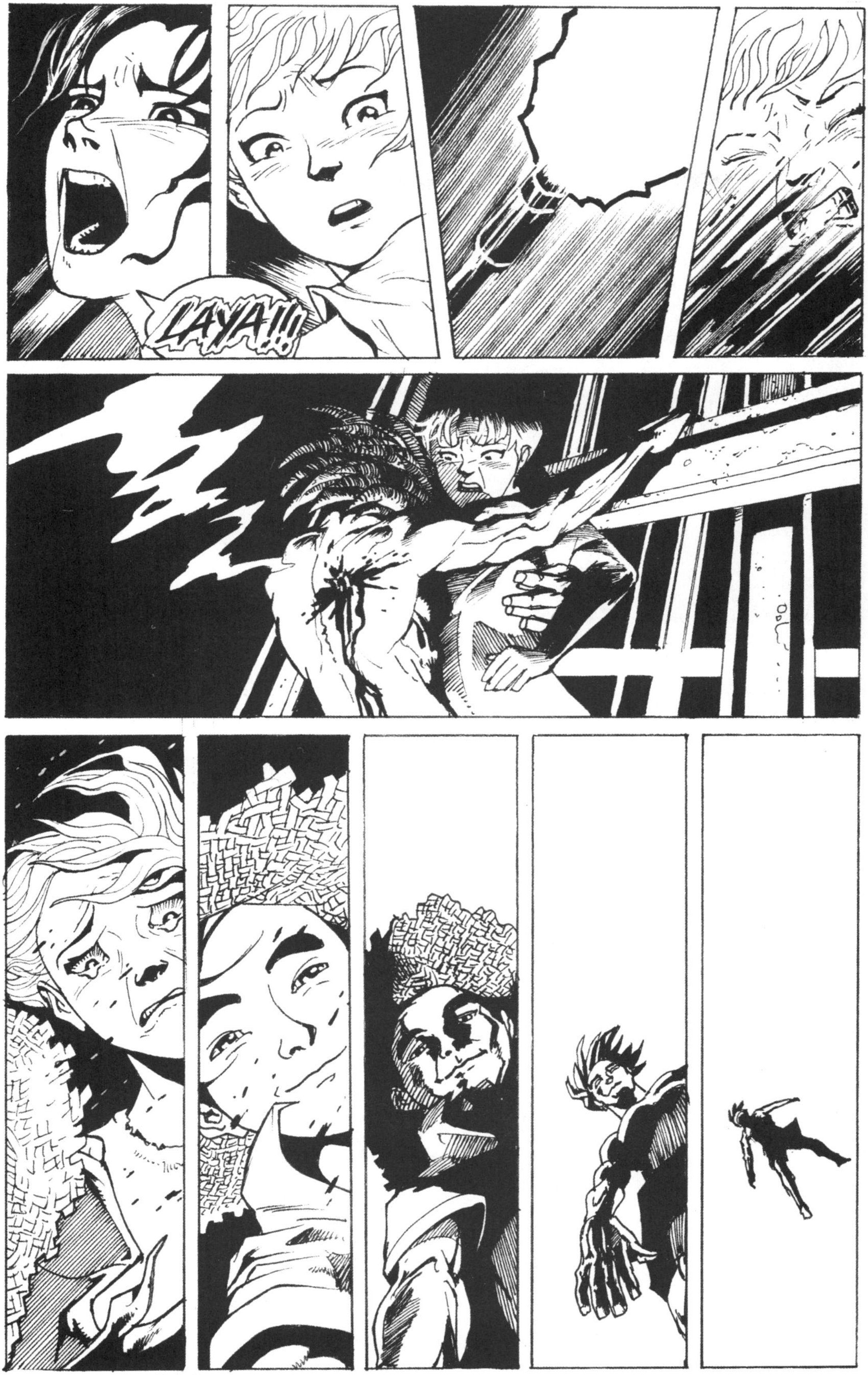
LAYA!!!

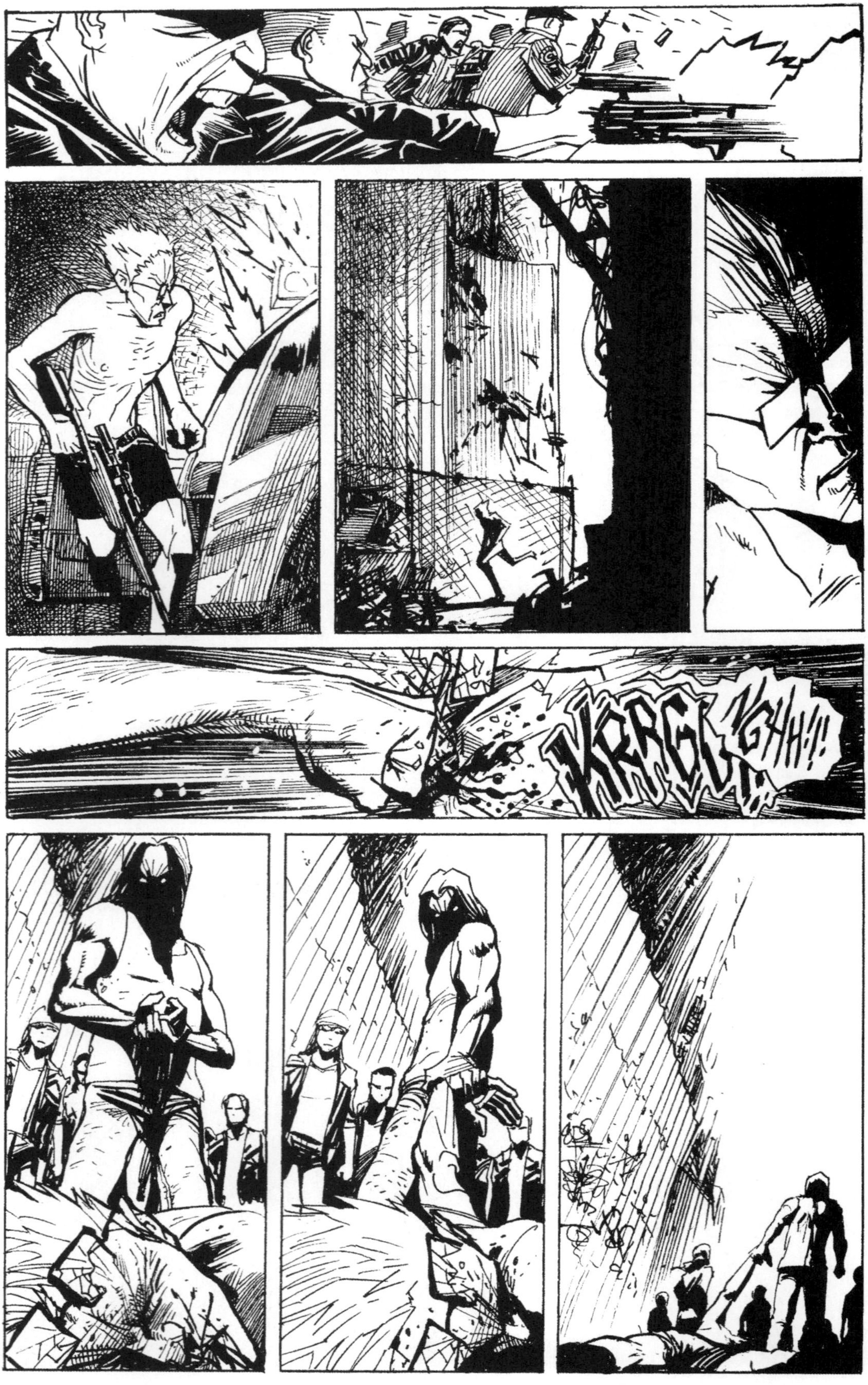
KRRGL!
NGHH!!

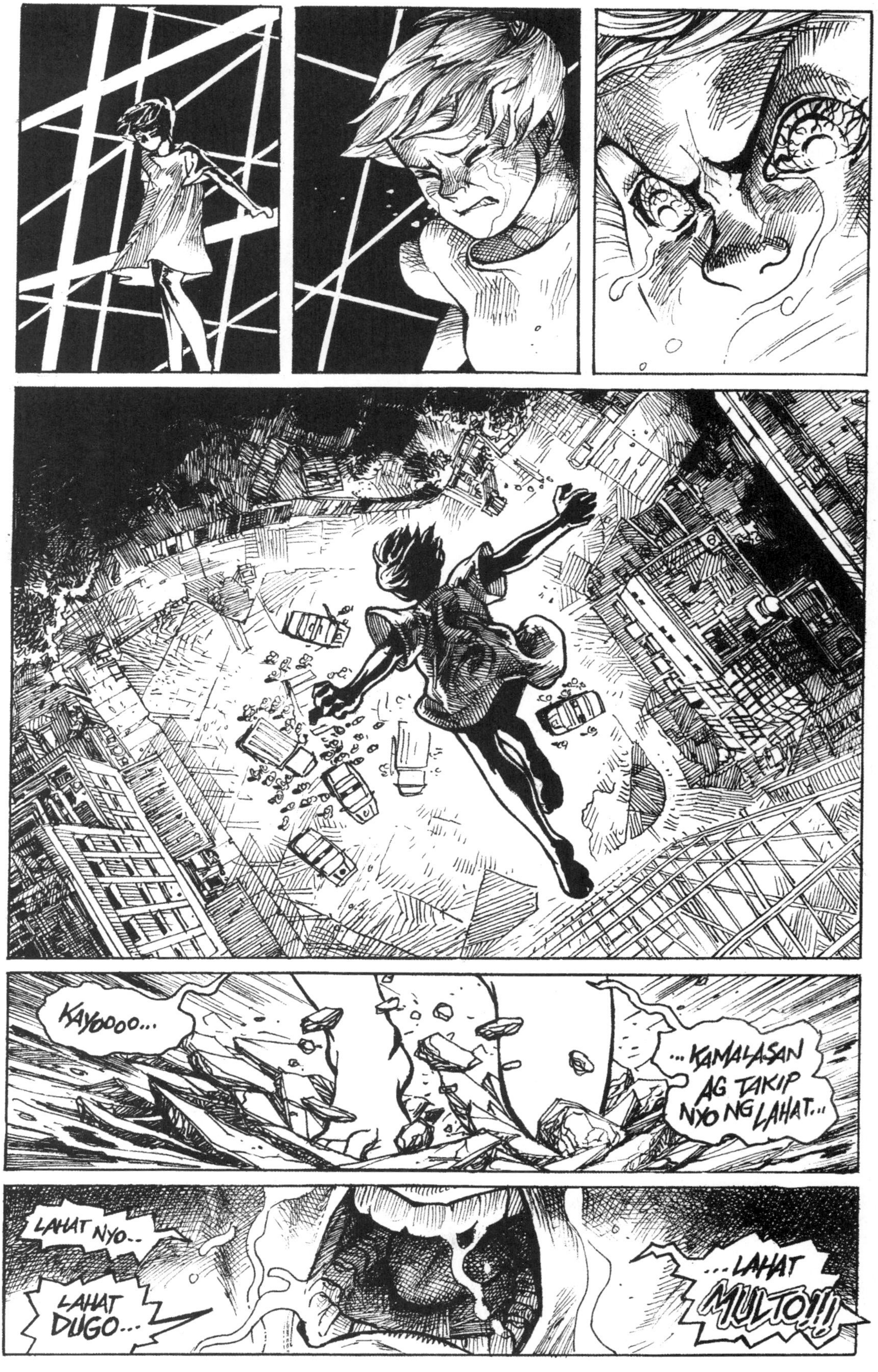
KAYOOOO...
...KAMALASAN
AG TAKIP
NYO NG LAHAT...
LAHAT NYO...
LAHAT
DUGO...
...LAHAT
MULTO!!!

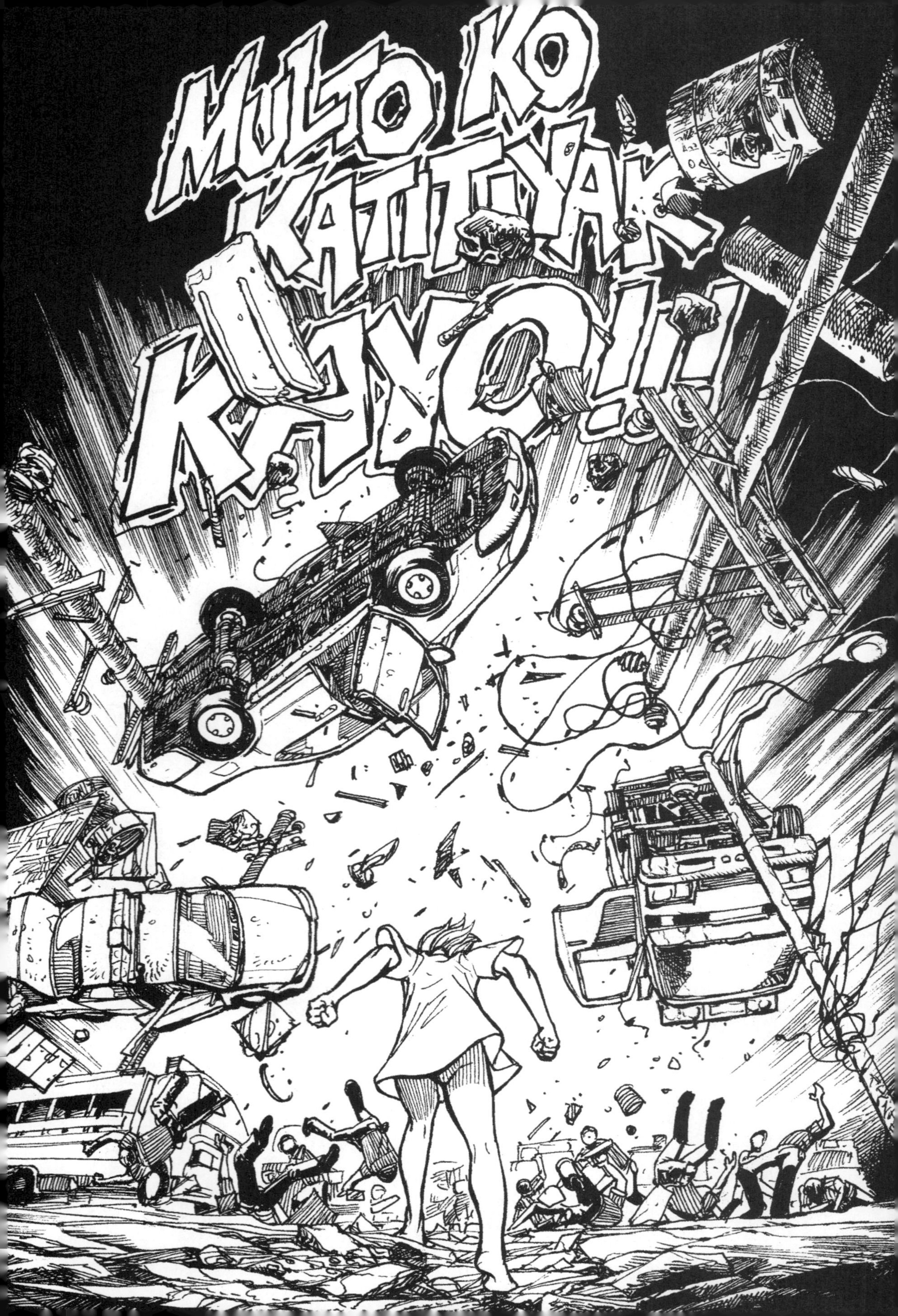
MULTO KO
KATITIYAK
KAYO!!

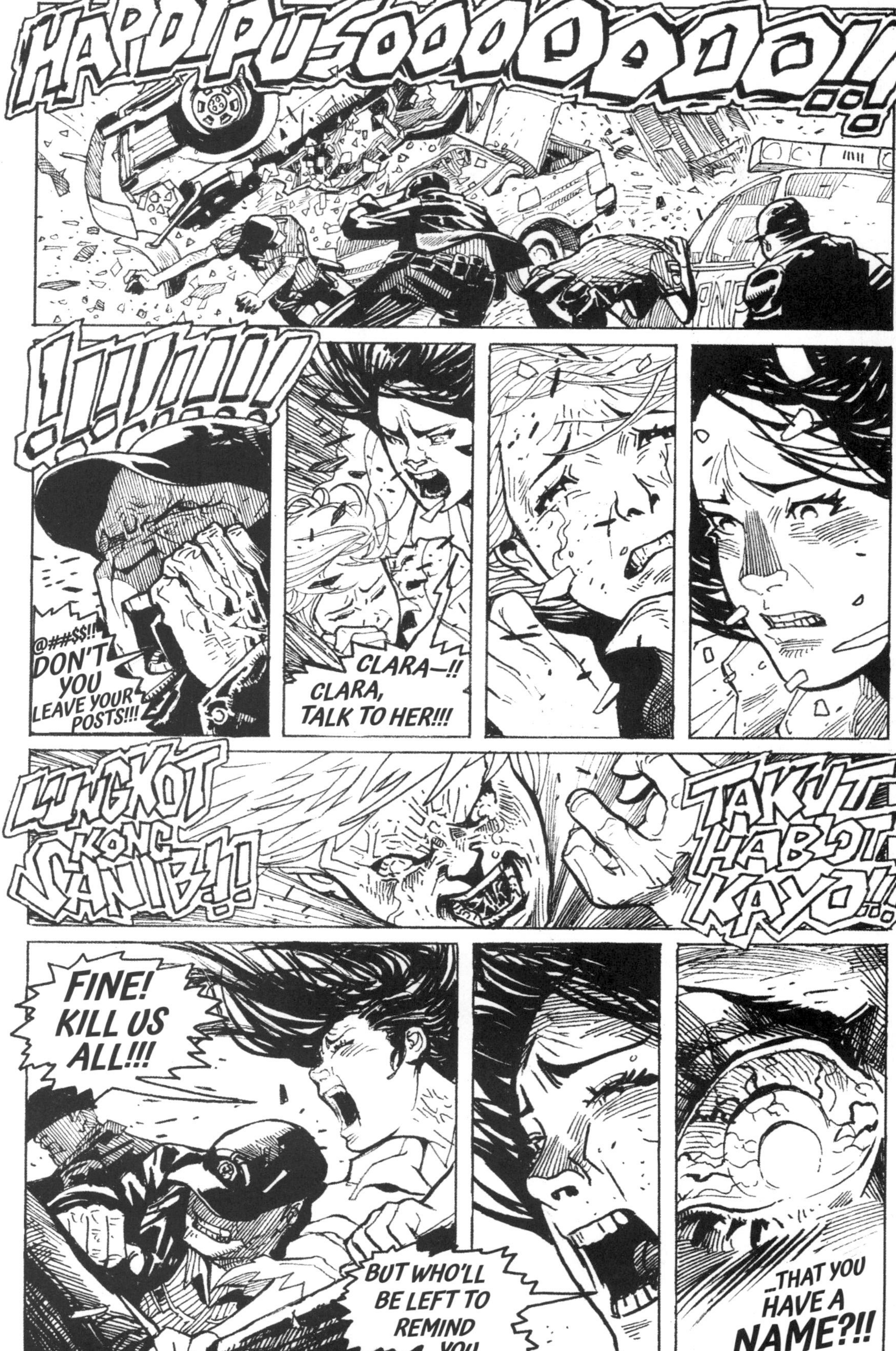
HAPDIPU-SOOOOOOOO!!
!!!!!!!
@##$$!! DON'T YOU LEAVE YOUR POSTS!!!
CLARA—!! CLARA, TALK TO HER!!!
LINGKOT KONG SANIB!!
TAKUT HABOT KAYO!!
FINE! KILL US ALL!!!
BUT WHO'LL BE LEFT TO REMIND YOU...
...THAT YOU HAVE A NAME?!!

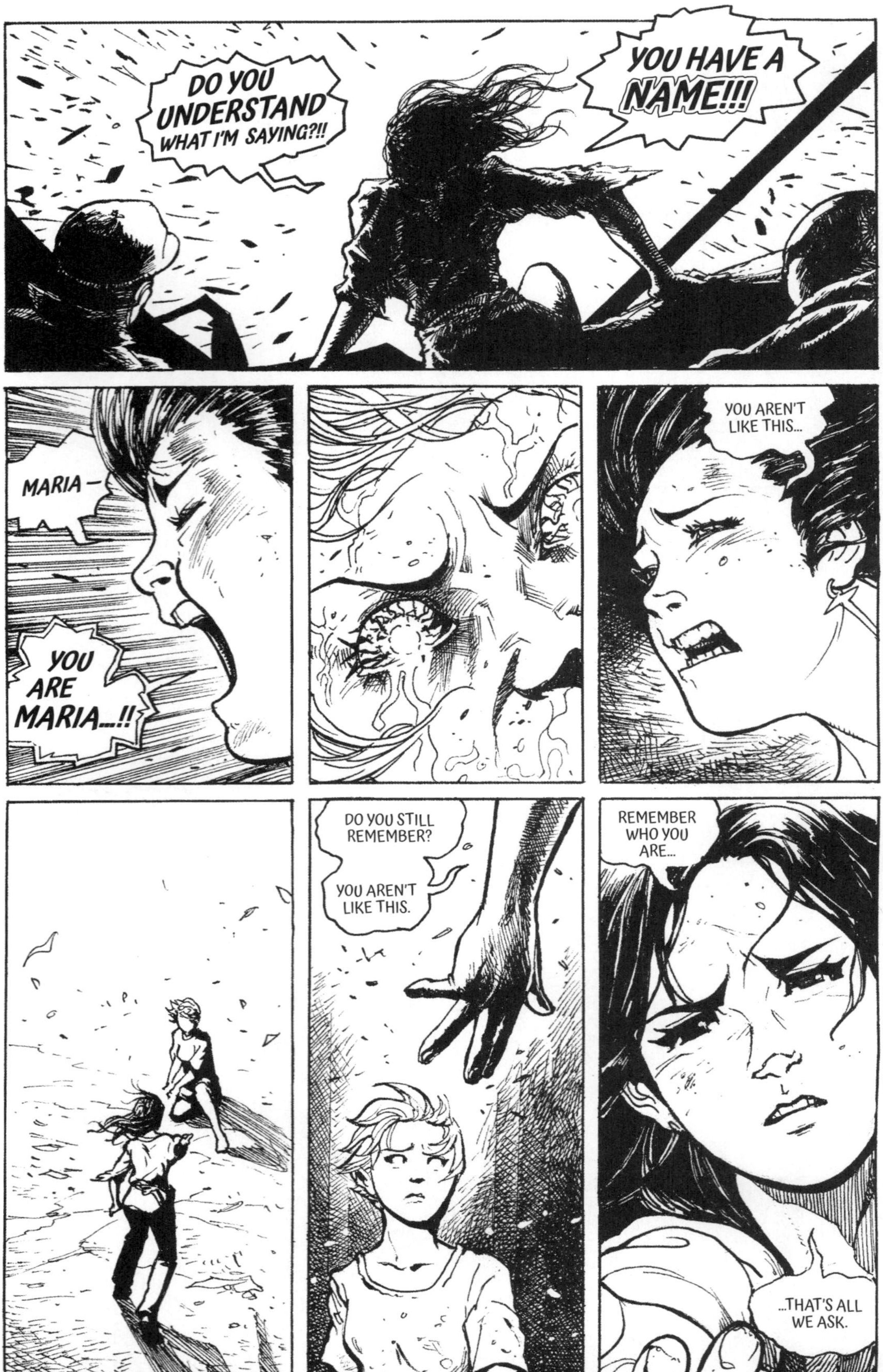
DO YOU UNDERSTAND WHAT I'M SAYING?!!
YOU HAVE A NAME!!!
MARIA —
YOU ARE MARIA...!!
YOU AREN'T LIKE THIS...
DO YOU STILL REMEMBER?
YOU AREN'T LIKE THIS.
REMEMBER WHO YOU ARE...
...THAT'S ALL WE ASK.

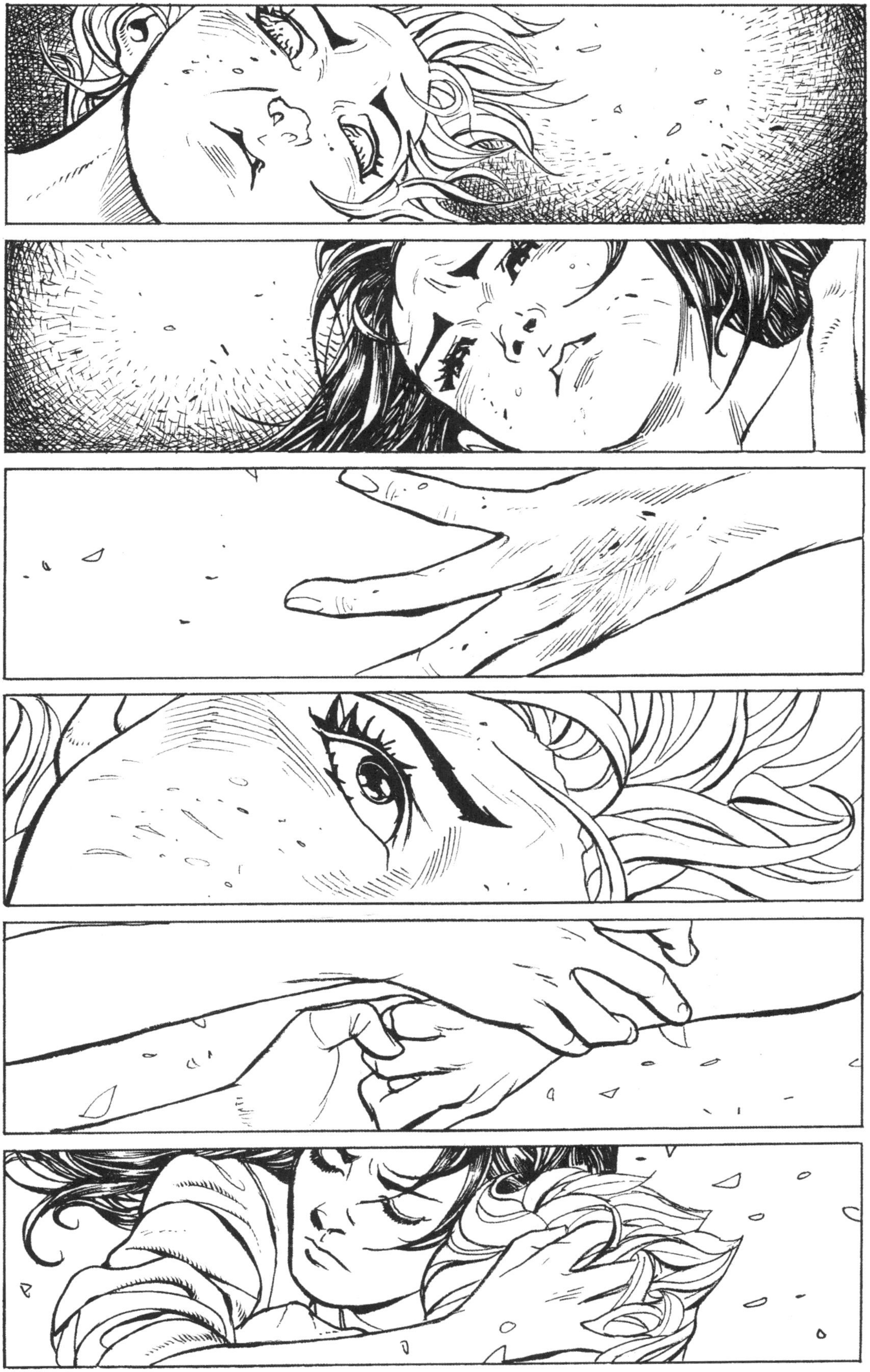

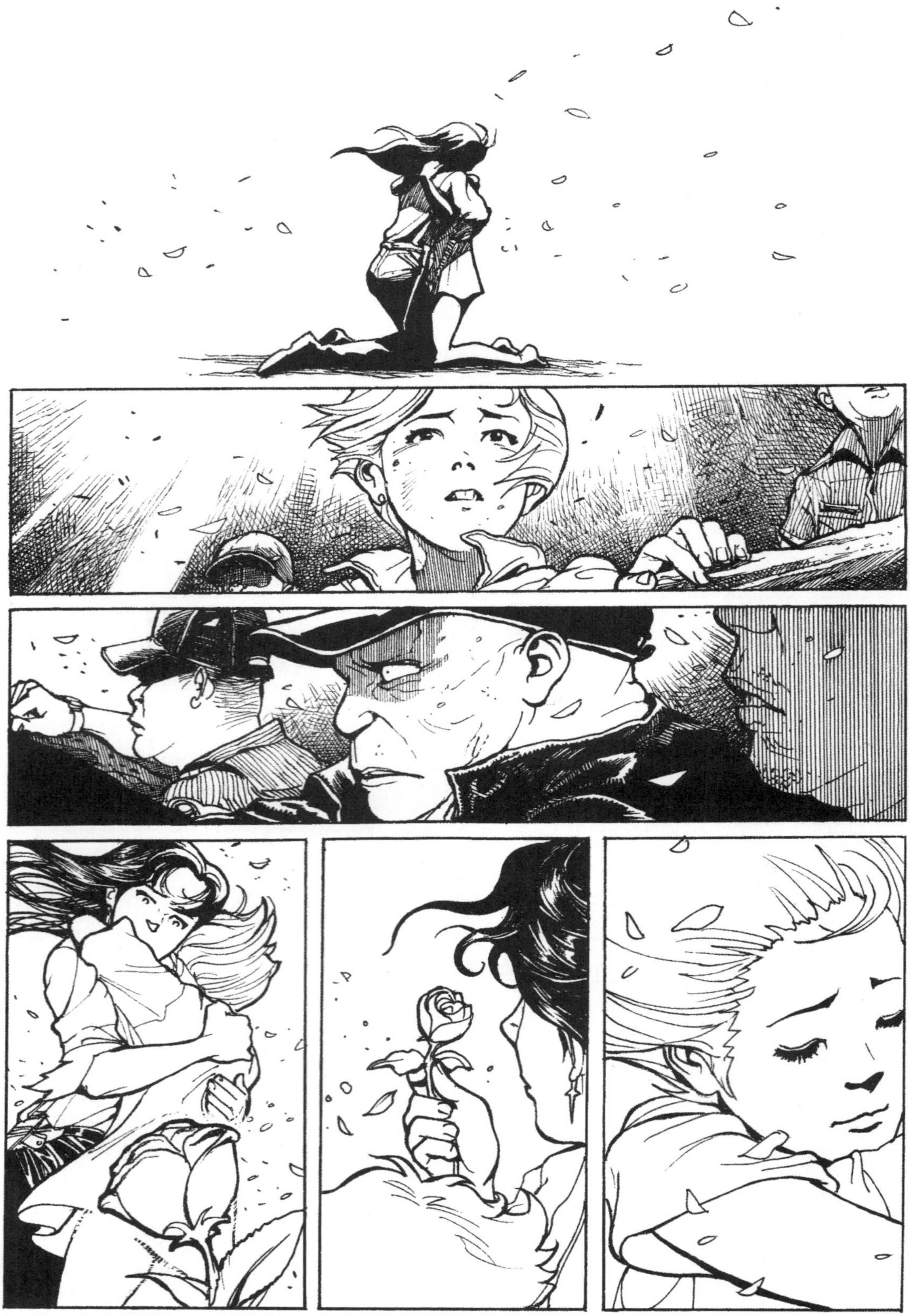

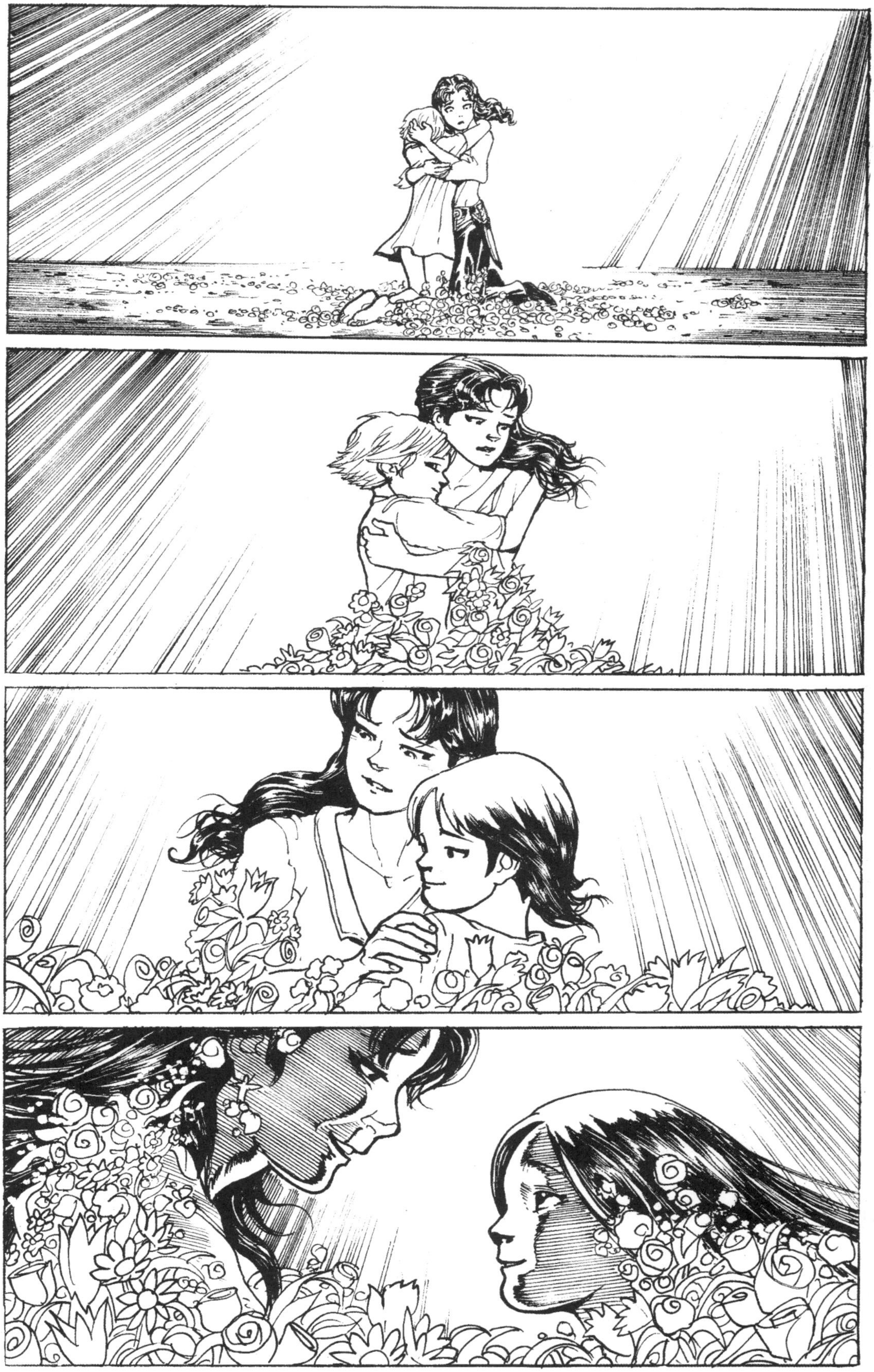

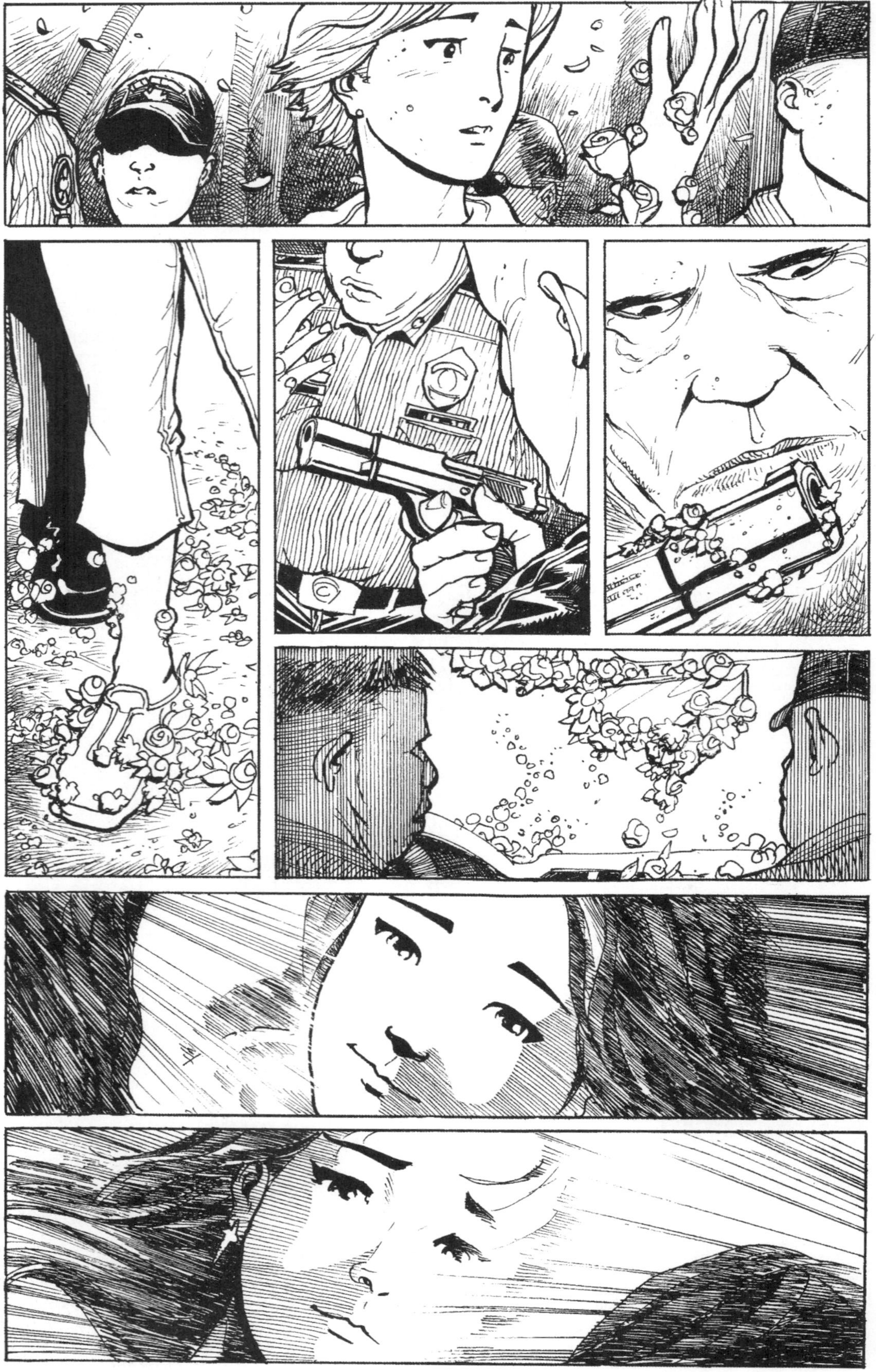

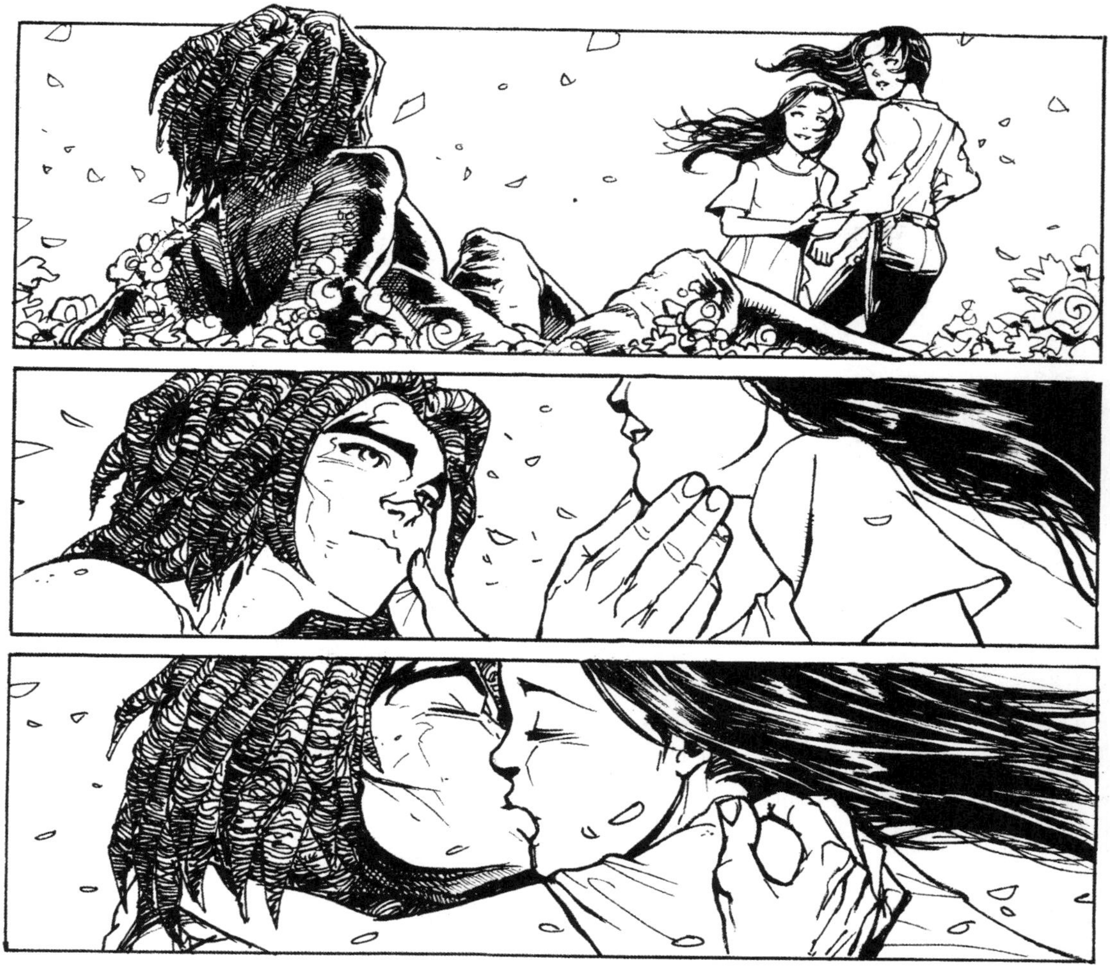

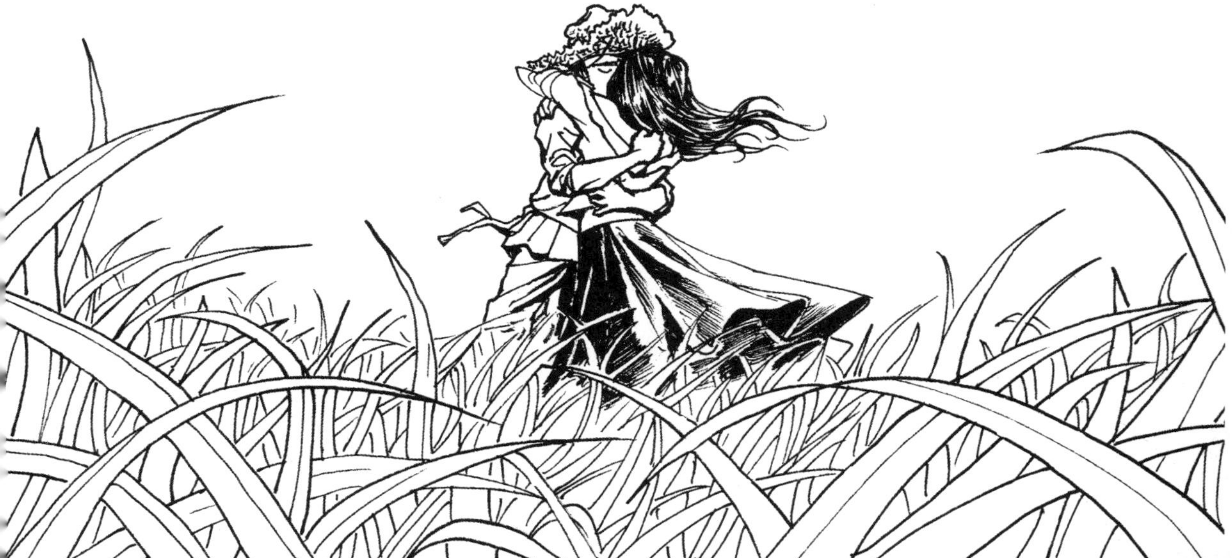

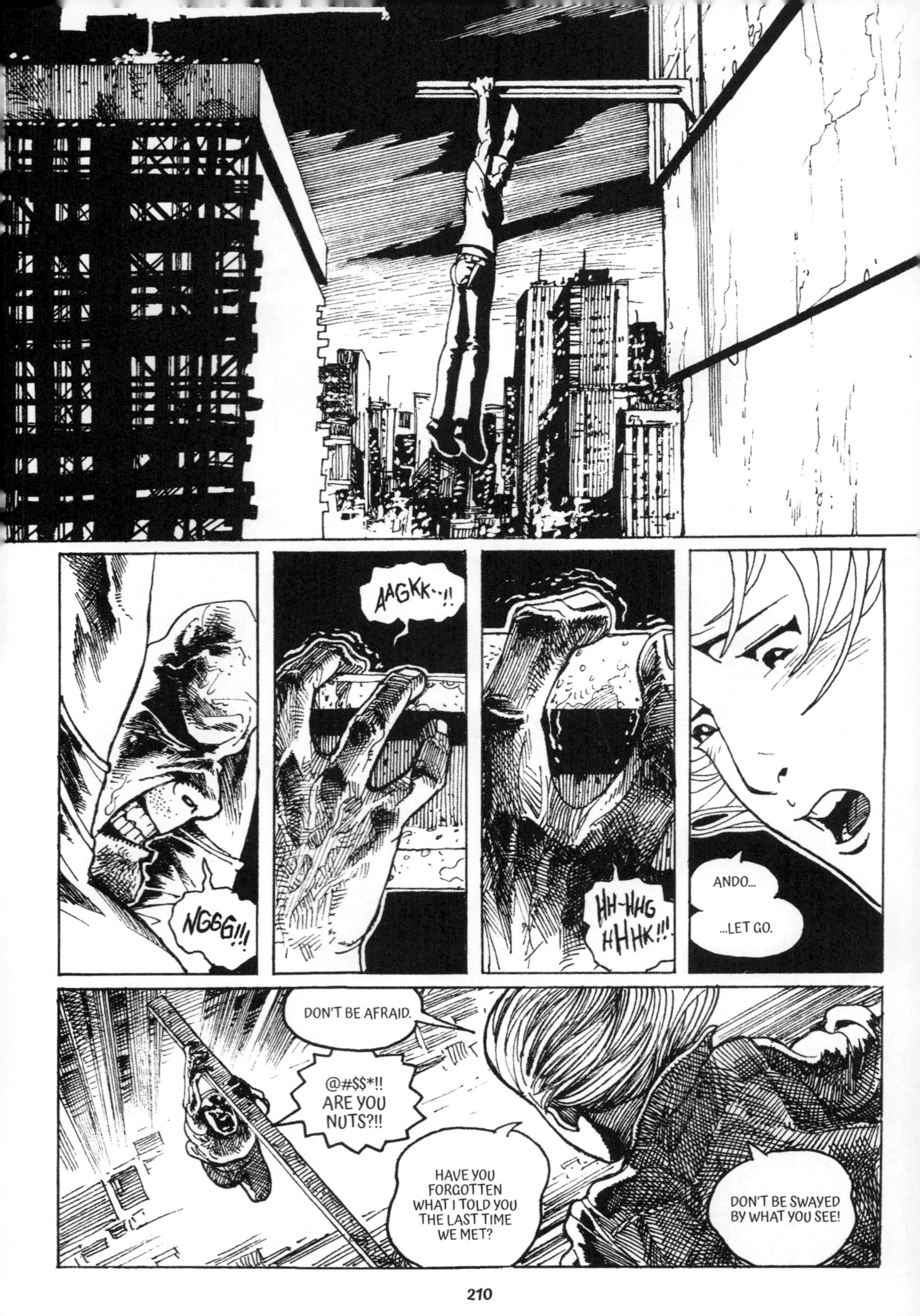

NGGG!!!
AAGKK..!!
HH-HHG HHHK!!!
ANDO...
...LET GO.
DON'T BE AFRAID.
@#$$*!! ARE YOU NUTS?!!
HAVE YOU FORGOTTEN WHAT I TOLD YOU THE LAST TIME WE MET?
DON'T BE SWAYED BY WHAT YOU SEE!

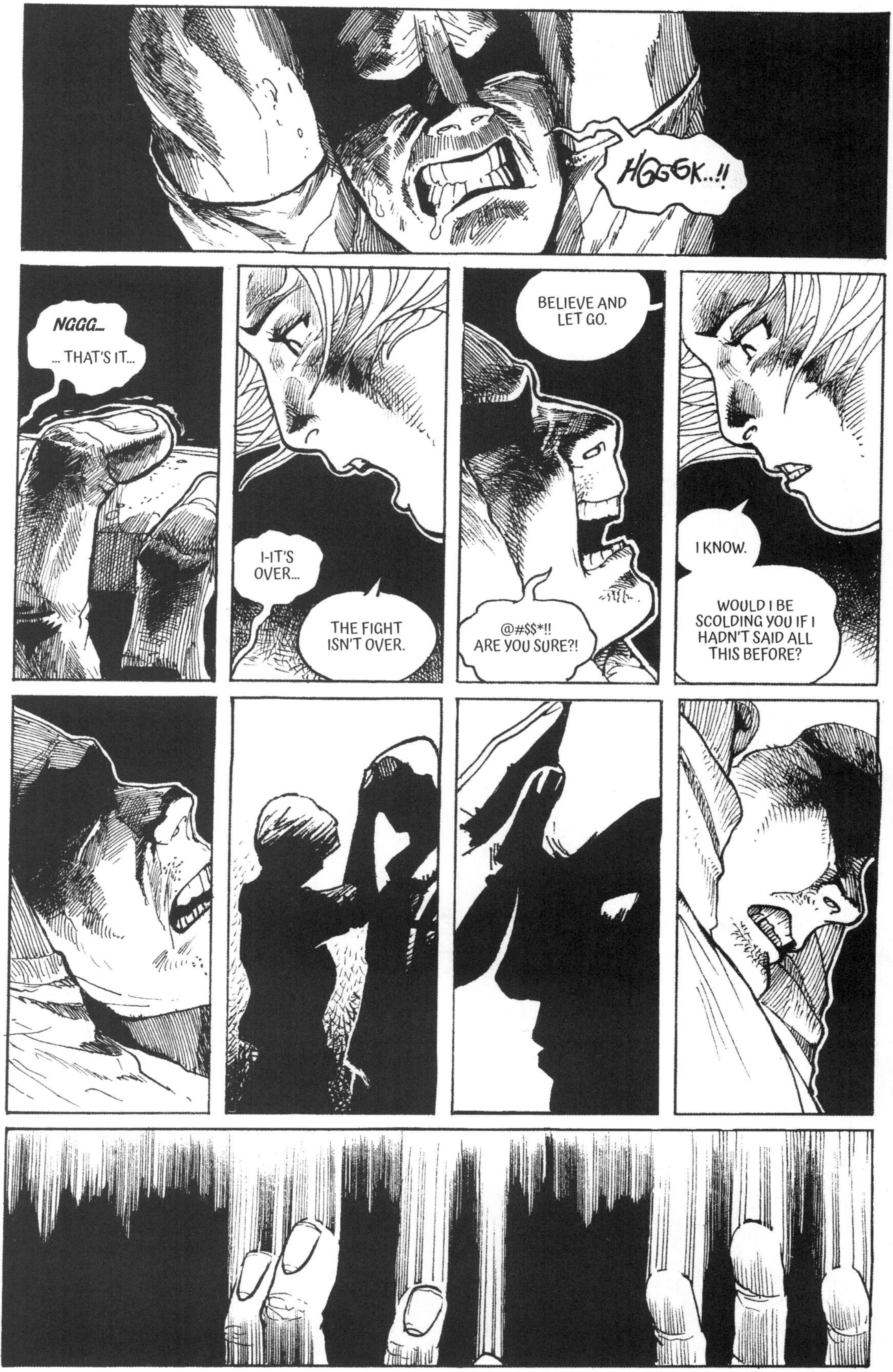
HGGGK..!!
NGGG...
... THAT'S IT...
I-IT'S OVER...
THE FIGHT ISN'T OVER.
BELIEVE AND LET GO.
@#$$*!! ARE YOU SURE?!
I KNOW.
WOULD I BE SCOLDING YOU IF I HADN'T SAID ALL THIS BEFORE?

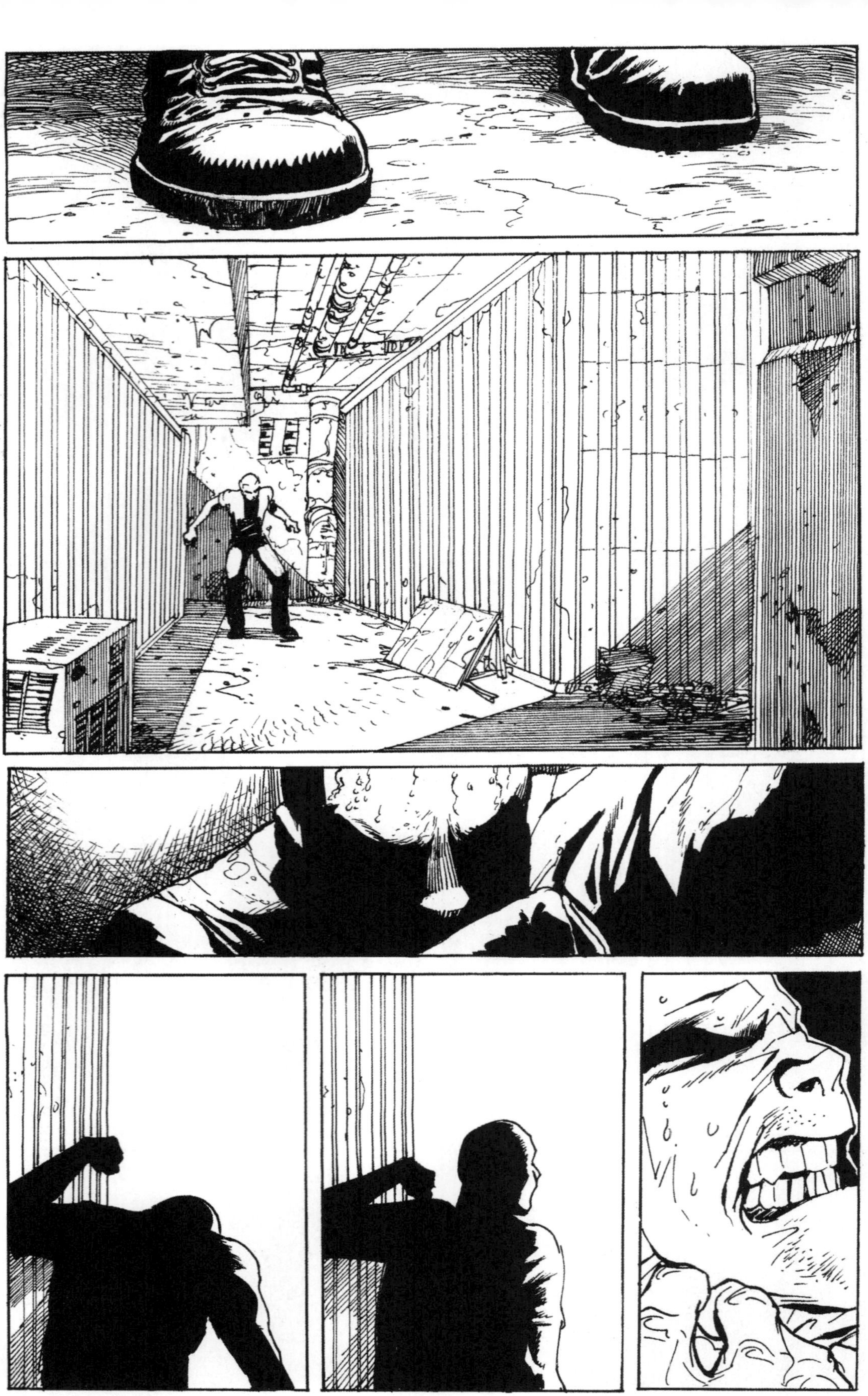

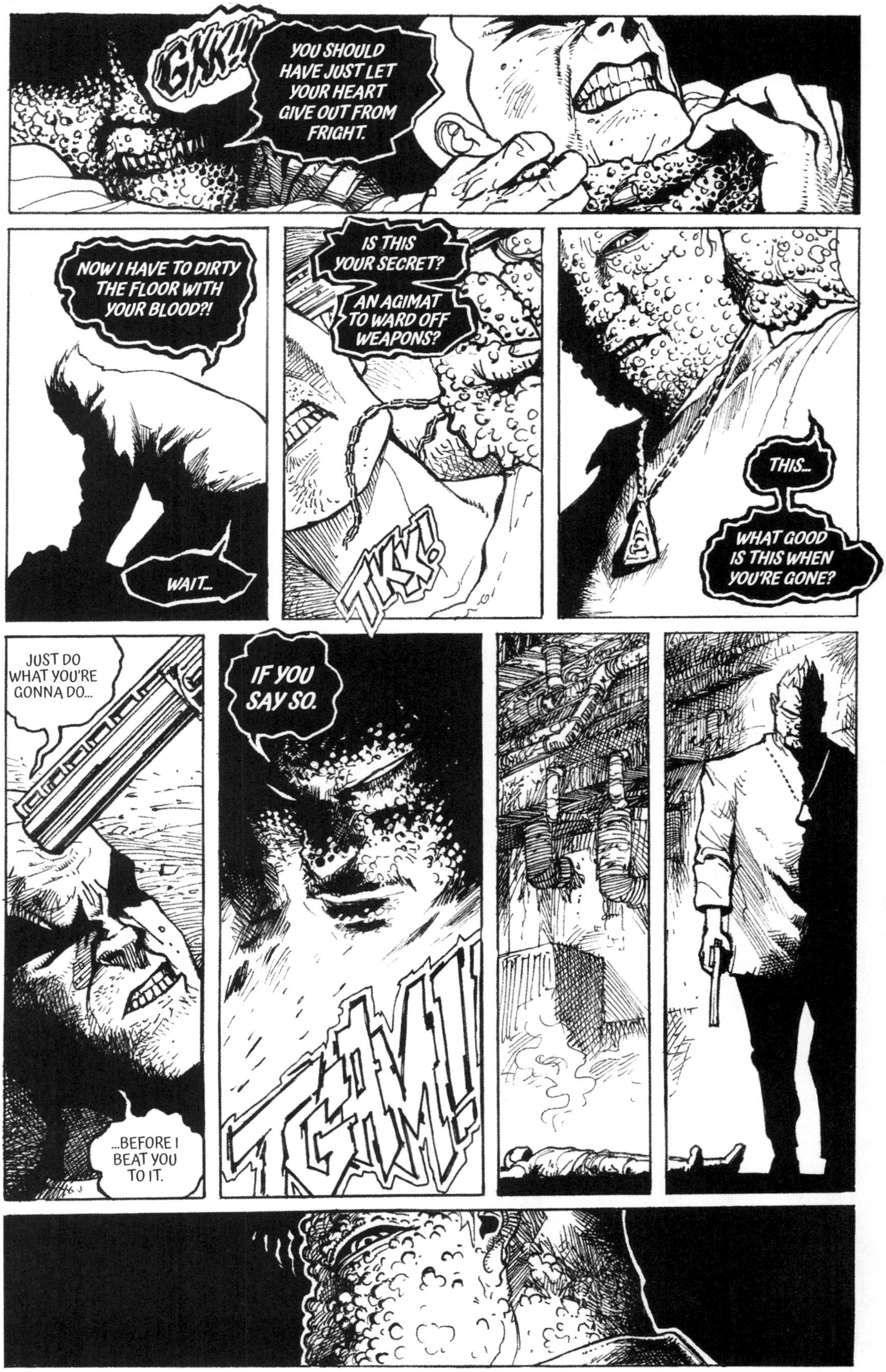
GKK!!
YOU SHOULD HAVE JUST LET YOUR HEART GIVE OUT FROM FRIGHT.
NOW I HAVE TO DIRTY THE FLOOR WITH YOUR BLOOD?!
WAIT...
IS THIS YOUR SECRET?
AN AGIMAT TO WARD OFF WEAPONS?
TKK!
THIS...
WHAT GOOD IS THIS WHEN YOU'RE GONE?
JUST DO WHAT YOU'RE GONNA DO...
...BEFORE I BEAT YOU TO IT.
IF YOU SAY SO.
TGM!

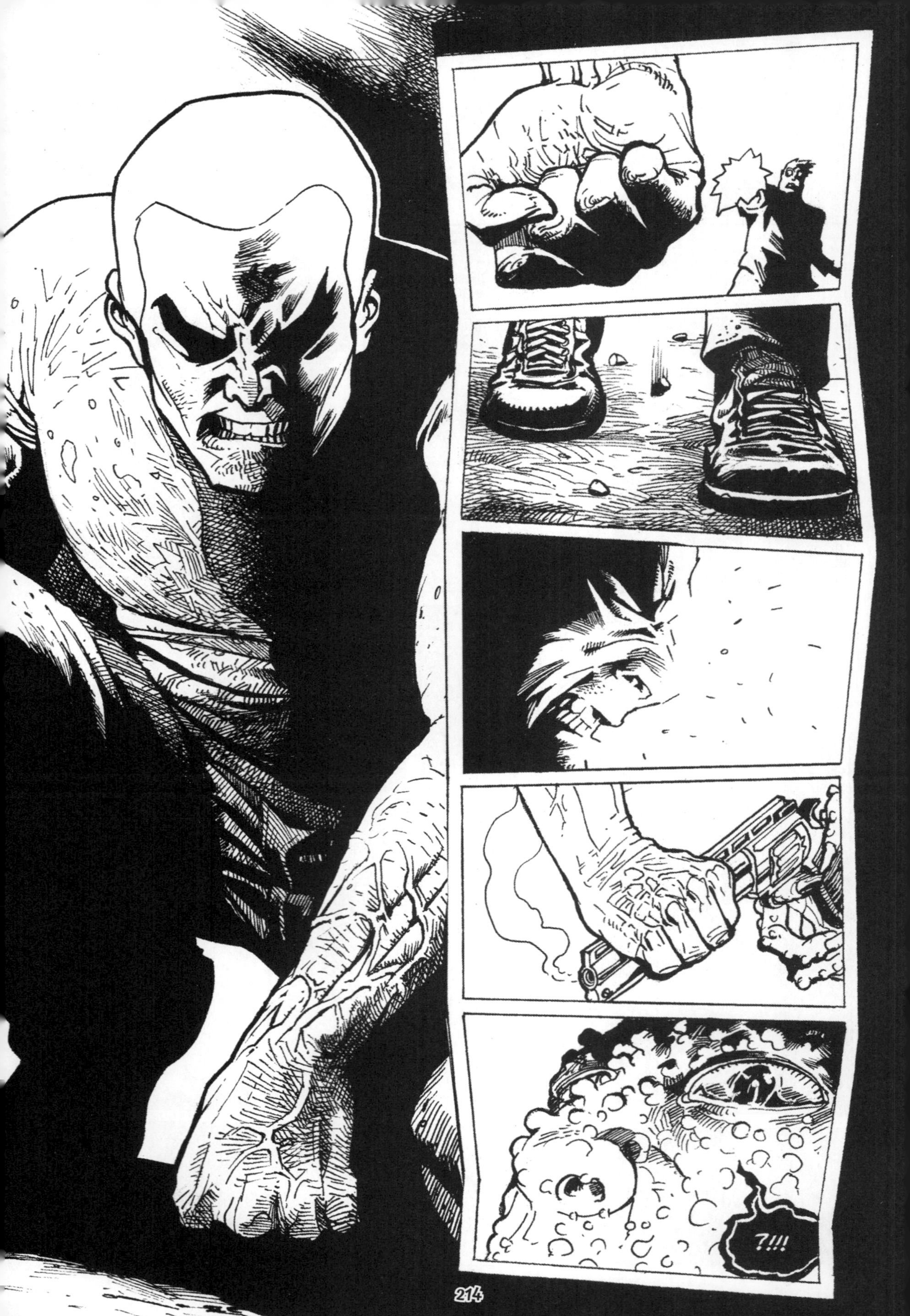
?!!!

A...A BOTTLECAP?

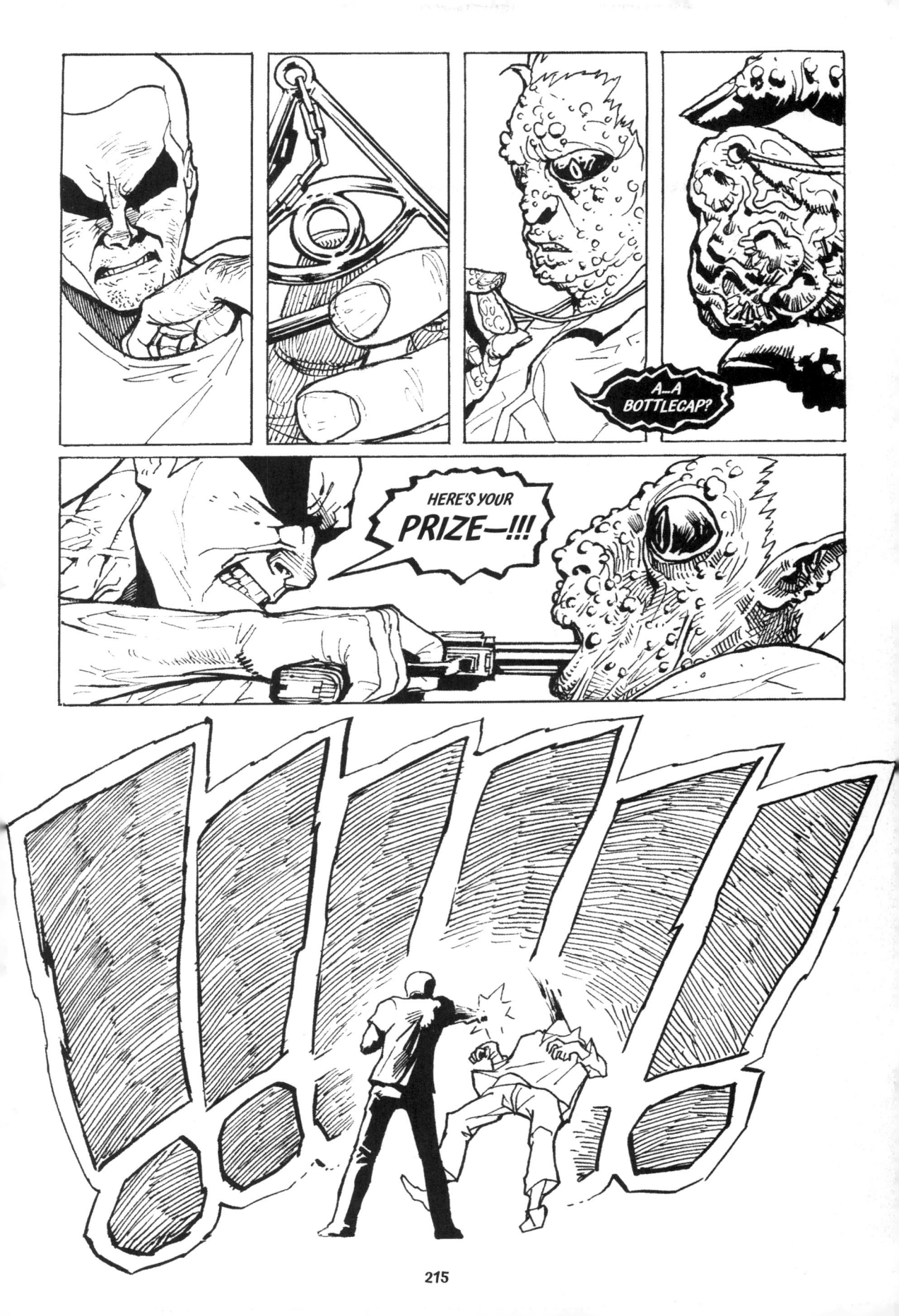

HERE'S YOUR PRIZE—!!!

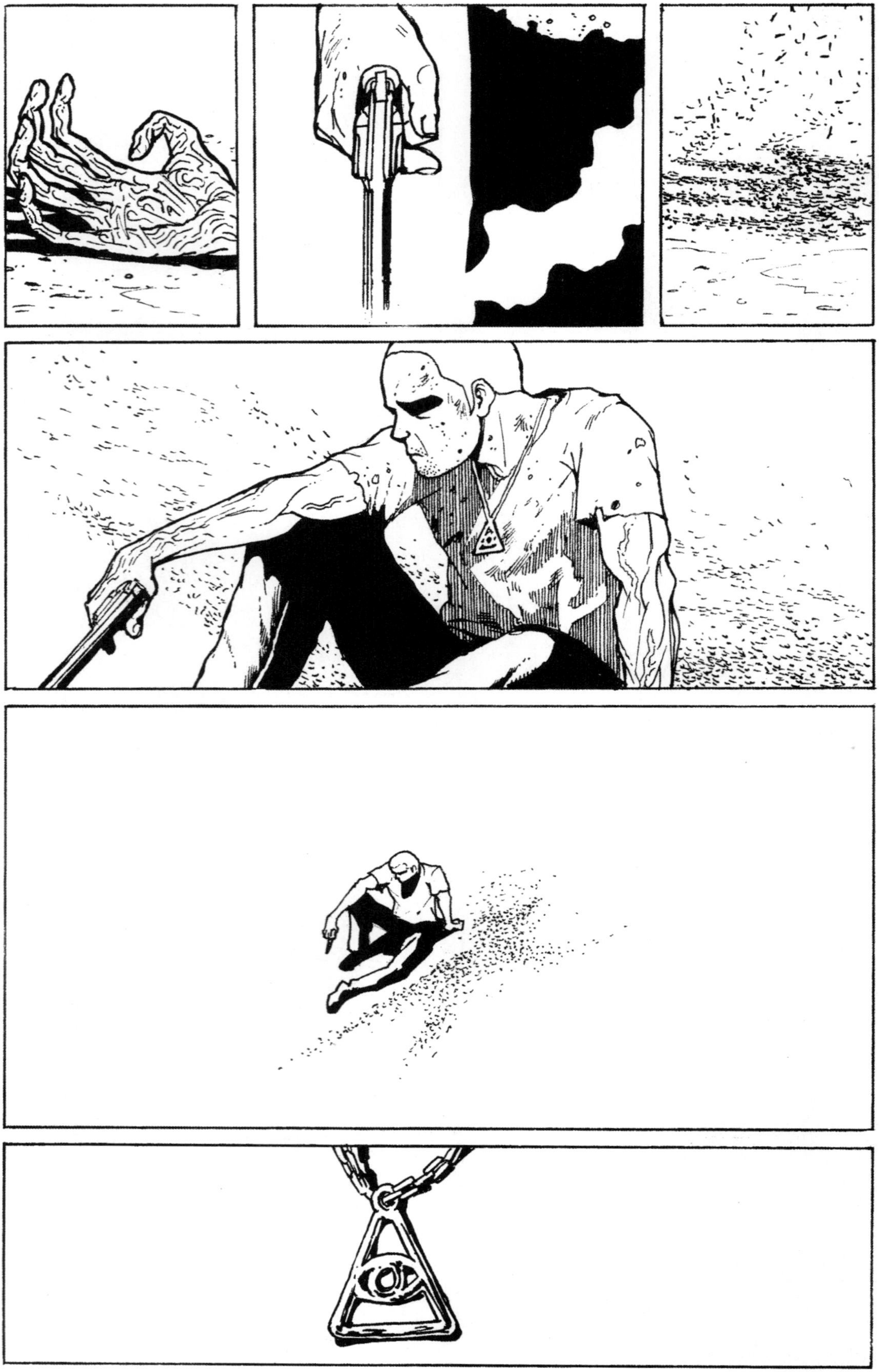

"...LET ME IN..."

"...KA ERNIE, WE'RE SPEAKING WITH A WITNESS..."

"WILL YOU TELL US WHAT HAPPENED LAST NIGHT?"

"ALL I KNOW IS THE WIND WAS REALLY STRONG, YEAH. COUPLE OF LAMPPOSTS FELL OVER. STUFF LIKE THAT."

"WE'LL NEVER BE APART..."

"FOR ETERNITY..."

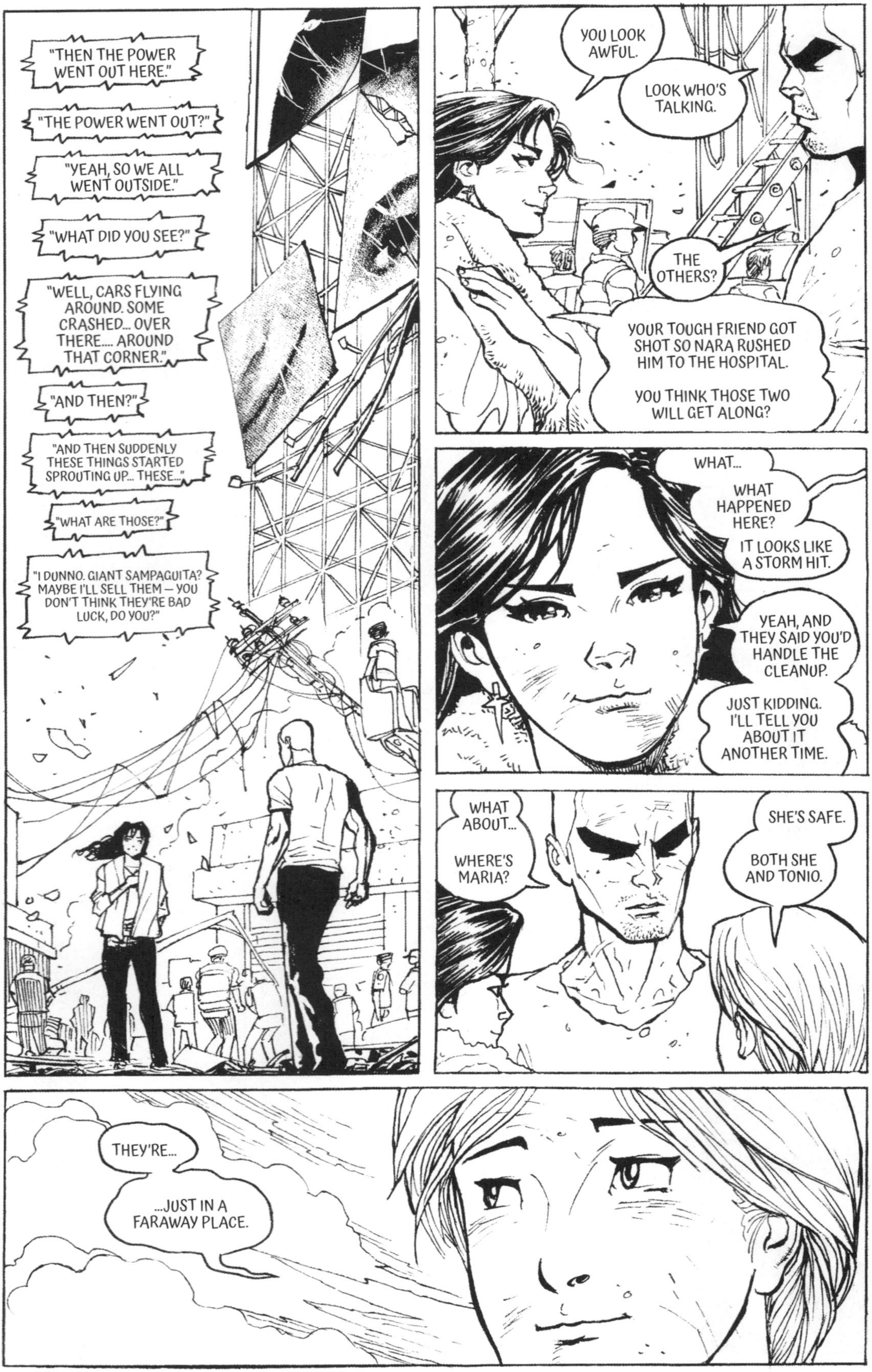
"THEN THE POWER WENT OUT HERE."
"THE POWER WENT OUT?"
"YEAH, SO WE ALL WENT OUTSIDE."
"WHAT DID YOU SEE?"
"WELL, CARS FLYING AROUND. SOME CRASHED... OVER THERE.... AROUND THAT CORNER."
"AND THEN?"
"AND THEN SUDDENLY THESE THINGS STARTED SPROUTING UP... THESE..."
"WHAT ARE THOSE?"
"I DUNNO. GIANT SAMPAGUITA? MAYBE I'LL SELL THEM — YOU DON'T THINK THEY'RE BAD LUCK, DO YOU?"
YOU LOOK AWFUL.
LOOK WHO'S TALKING.
THE OTHERS?
YOUR TOUGH FRIEND GOT SHOT SO NARA RUSHED HIM TO THE HOSPITAL.
YOU THINK THOSE TWO WILL GET ALONG?
WHAT...
WHAT HAPPENED HERE?
IT LOOKS LIKE A STORM HIT.
YEAH, AND THEY SAID YOU'D HANDLE THE CLEANUP.
JUST KIDDING. I'LL TELL YOU ABOUT IT ANOTHER TIME.
WHAT ABOUT...
WHERE'S MARIA?
SHE'S SAFE.
BOTH SHE AND TONIO.
THEY'RE...
...JUST IN A FARAWAY PLACE.

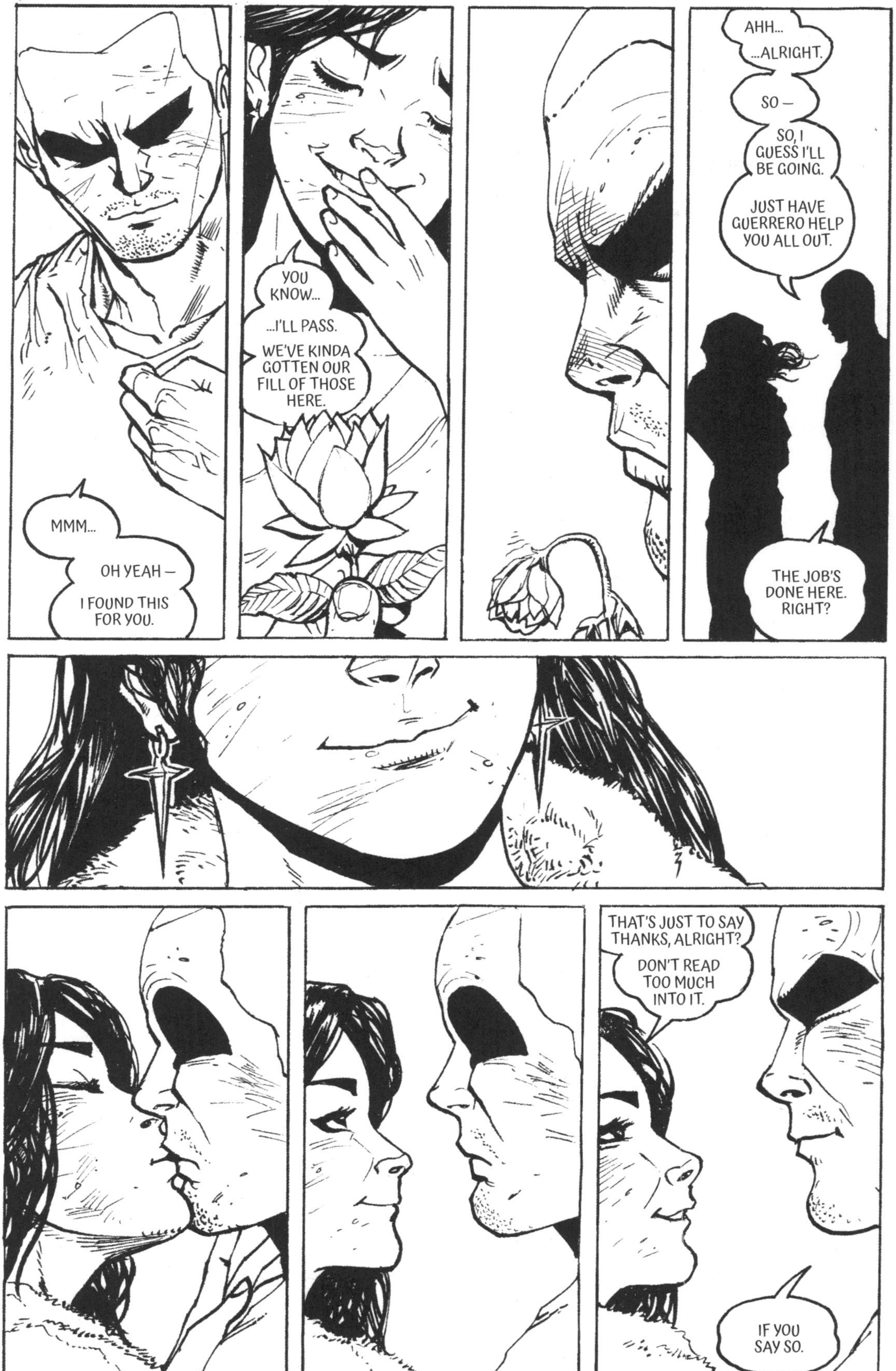
MMM...
OH YEAH —
I FOUND THIS FOR YOU.
YOU KNOW...
...I'LL PASS.
WE'VE KINDA GOTTEN OUR FILL OF THOSE HERE.
AHH...
...ALRIGHT.
SO —
SO, I GUESS I'LL BE GOING.
JUST HAVE GUERRERO HELP YOU ALL OUT.
THE JOB'S DONE HERE. RIGHT?
THAT'S JUST TO SAY THANKS, ALRIGHT?
DON'T READ TOO MUCH INTO IT.
IF YOU SAY SO.

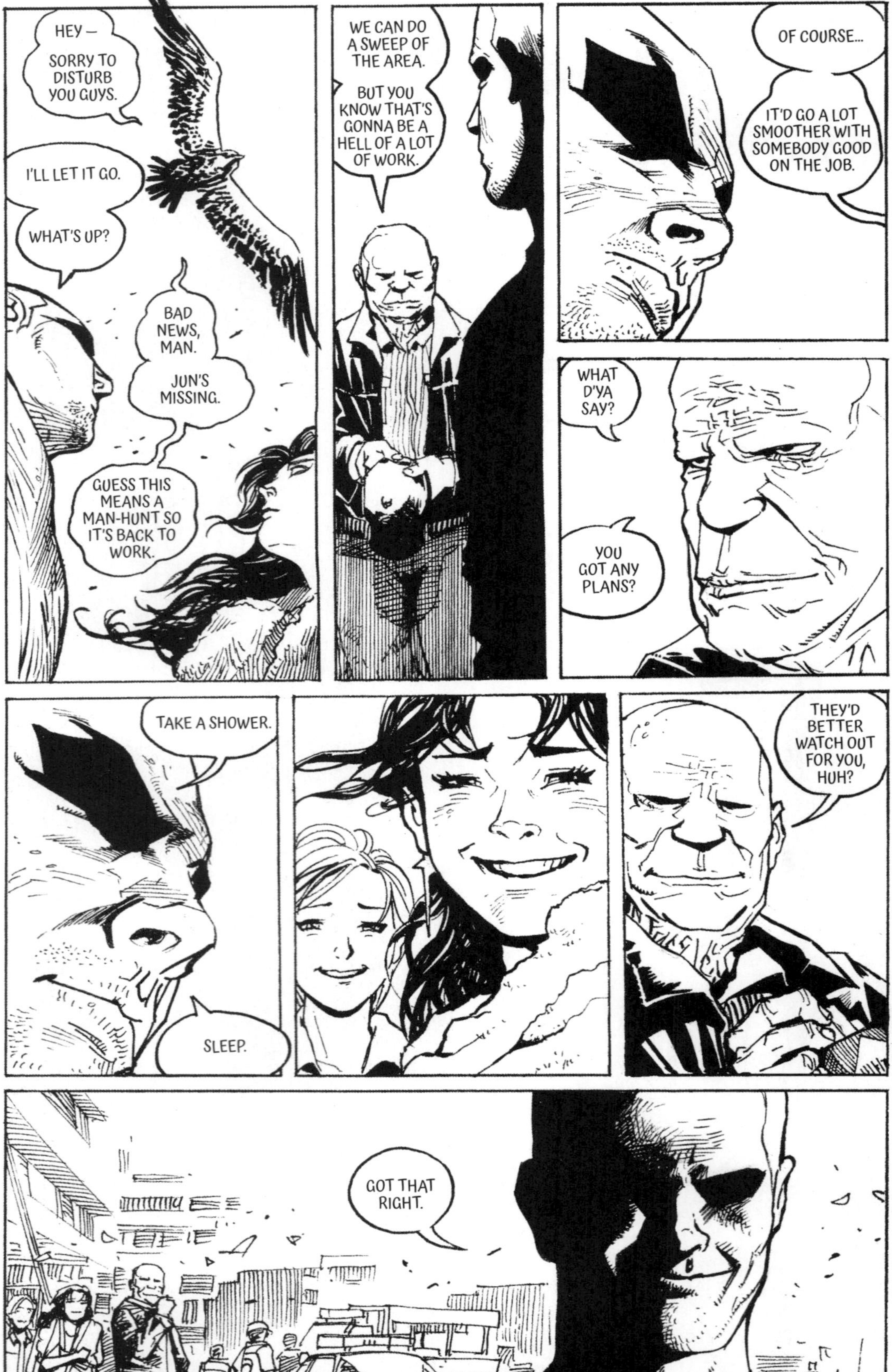
HEY —
SORRY TO DISTURB YOU GUYS.
I'LL LET IT GO.
WHAT'S UP?
BAD NEWS, MAN.
JUN'S MISSING.
GUESS THIS MEANS A MAN-HUNT SO IT'S BACK TO WORK.
WE CAN DO A SWEEP OF THE AREA.
BUT YOU KNOW THAT'S GONNA BE A HELL OF A LOT OF WORK.
OF COURSE...
IT'D GO A LOT SMOOTHER WITH SOMEBODY GOOD ON THE JOB.
WHAT D'YA SAY?
YOU GOT ANY PLANS?
TAKE A SHOWER.
SLEEP.
THEY'D BETTER WATCH OUT FOR YOU, HUH?
GOT THAT RIGHT.

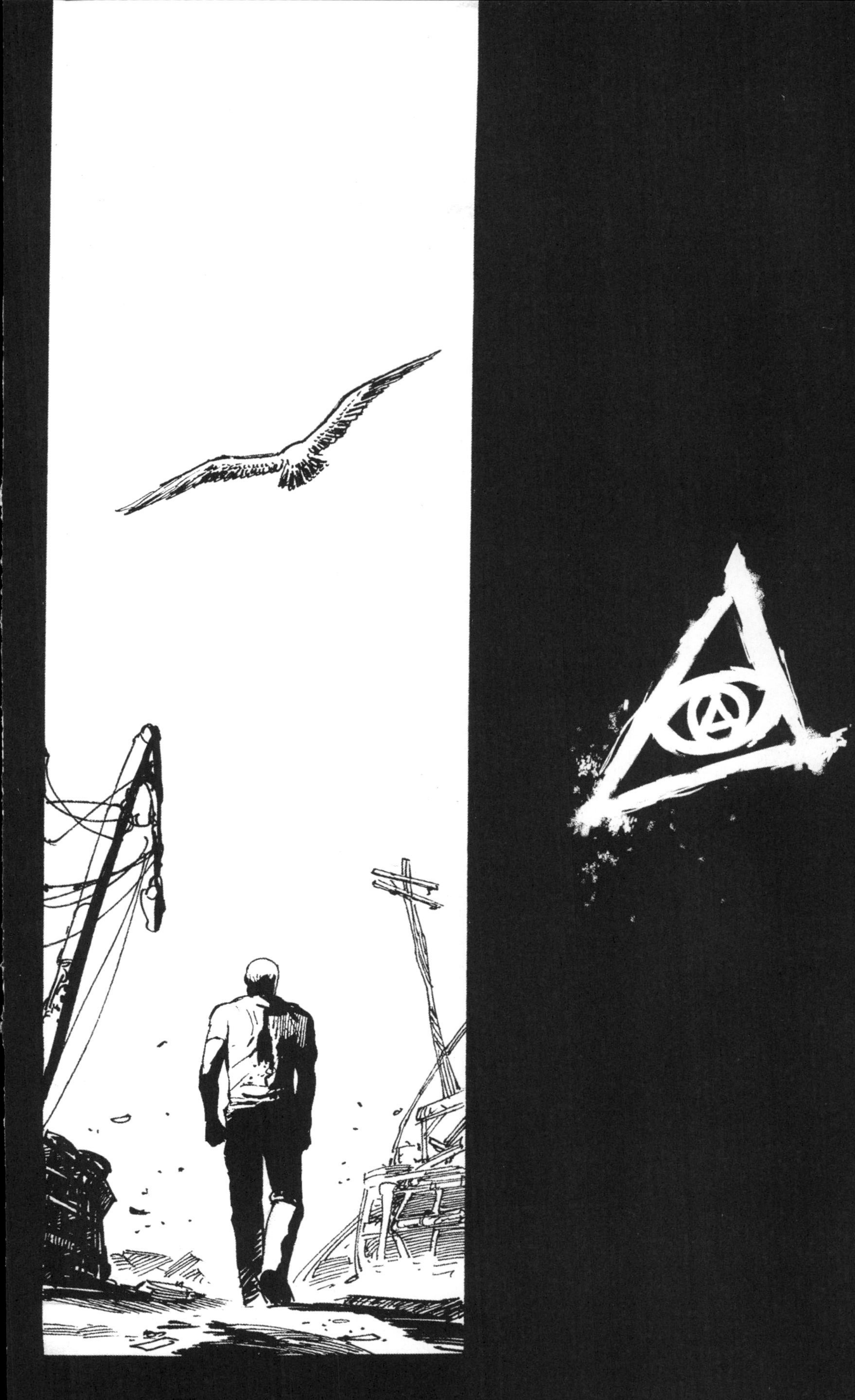

Thanks to my family Leonardo & Clemencia Arre,
Leslie & Aurora Bauzon, Lenn, Ate Ruby, & Gian,
Jing & Gladys, Calvin & Inches, and Abby & Bigsby;
Sheila dela Cuesta, Neva Kares Talladen,
Ramon de Veyra, Emil & Aimee Flores,
Robert & Shirley Magnuson, Marco Dimaano;
Jamie & Iyay Bautista and Nautilus Comics
for believing in me.

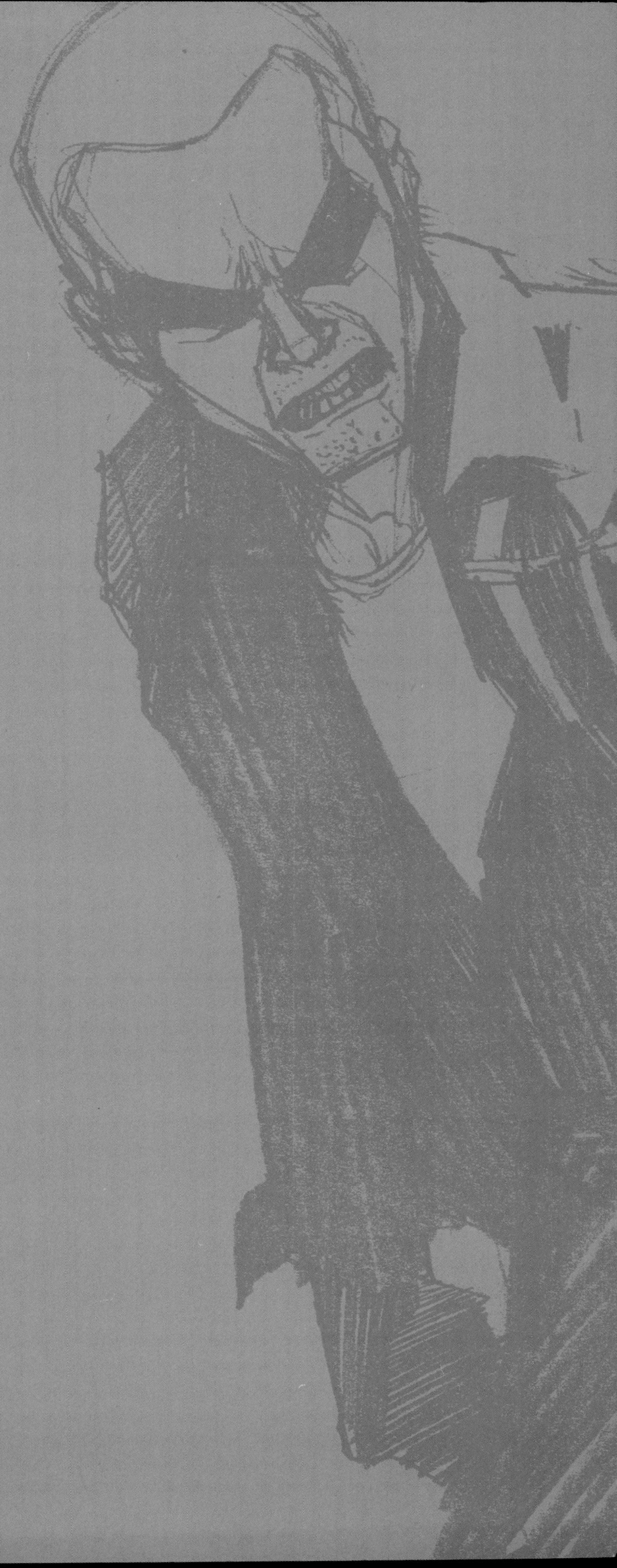

"Books to Span the East and West"

Tuttle Publishing was founded in 1832 in the small New England town of Rutland, Vermont [USA]. Our core values remain as strong today as they were then—to publish best-in-class books which bring people together one page at a time. In 1948, we established a publishing office in Japan—and Tuttle is now a leader in publishing English-language books about the arts, languages and cultures of Asia. The world has become a much smaller place today and Asia's economic and cultural influence has grown. Yet the need for meaningful dialogue and information about this diverse region has never been greater. Over the past seven decades, Tuttle has published thousands of books on subjects ranging from martial arts and paper crafts to language learning and literature—and our talented authors, illustrators, designers and photographers have won many prestigious awards. We welcome you to explore the wealth of information available on Asia at **www.tuttlepublishing.com**.

Published by Tuttle Publishing, an imprint of Periplus Editions (HK) Ltd.

www.tuttlepublishing.com

Copyright © 2022 Arnold Arre

All rights reserved. No part of this publication may be reproduced or utilized in any form or by any means, electronic or mechanical, including photocopying, recording, or by any information storage and retrieval system, without prior written permission from the publisher.

Library of Congress Cataloging-in-Publication Data is in process.

ISBN: 978-0-8048-5545-7

First edition
25 24 23 22

5 4 3 2 1

Printed in Singapore   2211TP

TUTTLE PUBLISHING® is a registered trademark of Tuttle Publishing, a division of Periplus Editions (HK) Ltd.

Distributed by
North America, Latin America & Europe
Tuttle Publishing
364 Innovation Drive,
North Clarendon,
VT 05759-9436, USA
Tel: 1 (802) 773-8930; Fax: 1 (802) 773-6993
info@tuttlepublishing.com
www.tuttlepublishing.com

Japan
Tuttle Publishing
Yaekari Building 3rd Floor
5-4-12 Osaki
Shinagawa-ku
Tokyo 141-0032
Tel: (81) 3 5437-0171; Fax: (81) 3 5437-0755
sales@tuttle.co.jp
www.tuttle.co.jp

Asia Pacific
Berkeley Books Pte. Ltd.
3 Kallang Sector #04-01
Singapore 349278
Tel: (65) 6741-2178; Fax: (65) 6741-2179
inquiries@periplus.com.sg
www.tuttlepublishing.com

This publication has been made possible with the financial support from the National Book Development Board (NBDB) Translation Subsidy Program.